BloodGifted

TIMA MARIA LACOBA

Published By
Tima Maria Lacoba

Bloodgifted

Book One of the Dantonville Legacy

By Tima Maria Lacoba

Revised 2016

"Bloodgifted is an intriguing, intricate and absorbing read. I'm already fascinated to know where the series will progress."

Lindsay J. Pryor, bestselling author of the Blackthorn Series.

Edited by Dionne Lister

Book Cover by JC Clarke thegraphicsshed@gmail.com

Formatting By Paradox Book Covers & Formatting

ISBN-10: 1477419209
ISBN-13: 978-1477419205

BOOKS BY TIMA MARIA LACOBA

Laura's Locket: A Dantonville Chronicle
BloodGifted: Book 1 of the Dantonville Legacy
BloodPledge: Book 2 of the Dantonville Legacy
BloodVault: Book 3 of the Dantonville Legacy
BloodWish: Book 4 of the Dantonville Legacy

Extras at the end of the book.

Read Chapter 1 of Bloodpledge.
Glossary – List of Names and Places
Connect with the Author

ACKNOWLEDGMENTS

To my wonderful family and friends, this is a big thank you for persevering with me when all I could talk about was my book. A big hug to Pam, Jackie and Pauline, and my dear sister-in-law Sue. You were there when I needed someone to listen to my ideas and proof read my latest pages. A special hug goes to Claudia, who also gave up endless weekends to help create the Bloodgifted trailers, redesign my website and who took all those fabulous pictures of The Abbey – the heritage listed house which serves as the Lebrettan mansion in the book.

And to the talented ladies in my writers group, who faithfully each week listened as I read the latest installment of my manuscript; patiently critiqued, edited and provided suggestions that transformed my embryonic scribblings into a living, breathing entity. This is to Decima, Siobhan, Lily, Jill, Connie, Jo, Colleen, Libby and Silda and Anne and Annie from Umina. You turned a fledging writer into an author. Also, to my friend and fellow writer, Lindsay – big hugs for your encouragement on this wonderful journey on which we've embarked.

Thank you to my long-time friend Dr Carolyn, who over a delicious morning tea provided me with her medical expertise.

And, of course, to my mum, my best friend, who kept me fed and watered on those days when nothing else existed beyond my laptop and Laura and Alec's world; who was there for me all the way, and kept me sane throughout the entire process.

You're the best!

Lastly, I'd like to thanks Lewis Carroll, whose wonderful book, *Alice In Wonderland,* inspired me to write in the first place.

This book is dedicated to all of you, and those who still believe in fairy tales.

CONTENTS

PROLOGUE

Villa of Antonius
Lugdunensis, Gaul
AD 263

I always believed I'd die in battle. It certainly would have been preferable to the way my life did end. One day I was a soldier in the service of Rome, the next a creature from my worst nightmares.

Demon. Bloodsucker. Vampire.

It was meant to have been just a routine patrol. A search, destroy and retrieve mission—search out the Pictish raiders who were attacking Roman settlements south of the Wall, destroy them and retrieve any captives.

Straightforward. Instead, it turned into the day from hell.

We were attacked and one of my men wounded. Nepos. I sent him back to the fort with another of my men, Melander, to make sure he got back safely. The rest of us got back on our horses and tracked the raiders to a small village deep in Pictish territory, north of the Wall.

We rode in, cornered and killed them—search and destroy accomplished. But as we searched for the Roman captives, native women emerged from their huts, dragging their bound prisoners after them—crying and pleading women and children—and slit their throats.

'They are sacrifices to our great goddess,' one of them screeched—a large, flame-haired woman with the beauty of a goddess.

I heard the quick indrawn breaths of my men. In other circumstances, I'd let them toss for her, but all I wanted was to slit her lily-white throat. Those captives had been Romans.

I dismounted, pulled out my sword and strode to her. 'I would have spared the lot of you. Not now.'

'Kill me, Roman, and you'll incur the wrath of the goddess, Melusine.'

As she spoke, people streamed out of the huts—mostly the old, moving slowly, their backs bent, and children. They stood behind her. Silent. Waiting.

'Don't make the mistake of thinking I fear your gods. I don't. You should fear me, woman, for sending your warriors into Roman territory and taking our people for your disgusting, savage rites.'

'Your people and mine aren't so different,' she said. 'We sacrifice to honour our gods, but you kill in your arenas for entertainment. Which one of us is the real savage?'

I was in no mood for a debate and raised my arm to give my men the signal. One good turn deserved another, I figured.

'Would you slaughter the innocent?' the woman cried.

'Innocent?' I pointed to the murdered Romans. 'They were innocent. Take a look! See the blood?'

'We sent them to the gods.'

'And you're about to follow.' I lowered my arm, and my men slowly started forward.

The children screamed and hid behind the women's skirts.

'Then hear me first, Romans.' She raised her arms and looked at each one of us in turn. 'You dishonoured our gods this day and took the blood due them, so their curse is now on you. Human blood will be your food. And as beasts that kill only in the night, so you too will walk in darkness. Sunlight will be your enemy. And you' —she pointed at me— 'will pass this on to your children and they to theirs for as long as the moon circles the earth.'

The bitch cursed us.

My men hesitated and looked to me. Even though I didn't believe her gods to be anywhere near as powerful as our Roman ones, we were in their territory, and her words made the hairs on my arms stand up. My wife, Gallia, was several months pregnant. What if…? I felt a sudden rush of fear.

I raised my sword and pressed it to her throat. 'Retract it, woman, and I'll spare your lives.'

'Only to sell us as slaves? It's better to die free! As I am Eithne of the Prythyn, servant of the great goddess, all I've said will surely come to pass.' She spat in my face.

I plunged my sword into her throat. My men finished off the rest. That's when the Curse began to take effect. Our skin started to blister, and our eyes—which had turned the colour of Phoenician purple—watered, even in that weak northern sun.

The horses shied and bolted. We had to make our way back to the fort at Vindobala on foot. Within two days, our incisors had lengthened. We couldn't keep food down. Instead, we developed an insatiable craving for blood.

As the days passed, or rather nights – since we couldn't travel by day anymore—we made our way back, drawn by the smell of human blood. It was strange how we could pick up the scent of humans from several miles away.

Then we made another discovery, this one almost as if in compensation for all our afflictions—we could run at incredible speed. We caught up with our horses, and blinded by our blood thirst, drank our beloved steeds dry. My Ferox's neck I crushed in my hands as if it were straw.

We had the strength of the gods—powerful—and ravenously hungry to the point of madness. I saw through a haze of red.

Finally we arrived back at the fort. The sentries on the walls didn't stand a chance. Nobody did. Trained men were no match for us. We attacked and sucked them dry, leaving their empty carcasses on the ground in our hunt for more.

That night we killed twenty-seven men.

As the sun came up, we ran and hid from its deadly rays in nearby woods. I hated what we had done and hated the witch who did this to us.

Yet, there was nothing we could do. The Thirst was uncontrollable, and the next night we returned to do more of the same. At this rate, we quickly decimated the fort of all soldiers, men who were our friends and brother-soldiers.

Worst of all, Nepos and Melander were among those we killed. We had become demons, like the evil *lamia*—the bloodsuckers of legend.

My men raged at the gods. Calixtus, Sempronius and Appius tried killing themselves, but no matter how deadly, the self-inflicted wounds simply healed again.

We weren't even allowed to die.

For the next few days we hid, doing our best to avoid human settlements. I was desperate to control this thing inside me. We decided to feed from the wild animals in the forest, rest in the daylight hours and rise at night to find a priest of Mithras, our god of the Legions, who could lift this wretched curse.

Eventually we found one who didn't run off in terror. The bag of gold we offered readily overcame any fear he may have felt at our approach.

He sprinkled us with holy water, sacrificed a bull and called on the god.

We waited but felt no change. Either Mithras wasn't listening, or—as Calixtus suggested—we'd offended him in some way.

In desperation we sought out a soothsayer. 'Only the one who uttered the curse can lift it,' he said. 'Smear her ashes onto your eyes, ears and lips then offer some of your blood and call upon her spirit. Speak nicely to her,' he added for good measure. 'A spirit will not respond to anger.'

Be nice?! I wanted to go down to Hades and kill her all over again.

But, since we had no choice, we did as he said.

We sped through the night, back to the Pictish village, found her body where she had fallen, rotting and putrid, along with the others we had slain.

My men gathered the bodies and burnt them, scattering their ashes to the wind, but *her* body we placed on a separate pyre, and as the flames rose, cut open our wrists and let our blood drip onto her corpse.

I spread my arms and called on her spirit.

She appeared. 'Why summon me, Roman?'

'To beg for mercy.' I clenched my jaw.

'As you had mercy on me and my people?'

'We don't deserve to be punished this way. Your people killed mine. Isn't that the truth?'

'My people did so to survive, as you Romans took more and more of our land, stole our cattle and sold our people into slavery or to fight in your arenas.'

'We brought you civilization!'

'At the cost of our freedom!'

'Then take your hatred out on me and not on my men.' I knelt before her and bowed my head, ready for whatever punishment she would mete out.

'Your men are not innocent. They knew what they were doing.'

'Then spare the children who will be born to me,' I cried as I thought of Gallia.

'As you spared mine?' Her spectre seemed to grow as she loomed over me.

'But they're innocent.'

'As was the child in my womb. For that alone I damn you!'

Until that moment, I still harboured a faint hope for a chance of reprieve. Now? Not a snowflake's chance in Hades.

Behind me, my men groaned.

Then she spoke again. 'What has been done cannot be undone. But this one thing I can grant. As one of my children escaped your sword, while hunting in the woods, so will I spare one of yours. Your wife will give birth to twins: Children of Light and Dark. The boy shall be as you, a drinker of blood, when he comes of age. But the girl will not. She will walk in the light.

'Unnatural length of life and youthfulness will be granted her and her descendants. They shall be known as Children of Light, and their blood shall sustain the Child of Darkness.

'And you, Roman, shall live through the long ages ahead till one born of your house—a Child of Light and Dark—willingly bears a child to one of Prythin blood, a descendant of my house. And the babe must be born on this spot.

'Only then the curse will be lifted, for the child shall carry the blood of both Roman and Prythin—one race, one blood. At that time you will be given a choice—to remain as you are or become human again. But know this: the longer you remain in this form, the faster will you age should you choose the latter. All your long years will come at once, and death will be your release. This is my mercy.'

From the Private Journals of Marcus Antonius Pulcher, Praefecus Equituum of the First Cohort of Frisians, Vindobala.

CHAPTER 1
MY BIRTHDAY

Present Day
LAURA

"Thou shalt not fear birthdays" has been my motto for the past few years. And I saw no reason to change it, regardless that this year I was turning that much-dreaded big Five-O.

For anyone else that may have been daunting enough, but for me, it was even more so, since my family's pedigree was unique, even weird. There was something in our genetic makeup that decreased our rate of ageing up to forty percent. With me, it was more like fifty. Lately, it had become even harder to convince people my unnatural youthful looks had nothing to do with any nip and tuck or a fabulous moisturising cream. And it was interesting the way women in particular scrutinised me with almost X-Ray vision trying to spot any evidence of cosmetic surgery. Good luck to them. For one thing, I was an absolute chicken when it came to sharp, pointy objects, and needles of any kind slipped into that category.

But I could understand. Who wouldn't mind looking twenty-something in their fifties?

I kept a photo from my twenty-fifth birthday in the top drawer of my dressing table, and when I turned thirty, I took it out and compared the face in the photo to the one staring out at me from the mirror. They were the same. I felt chuffed. Who wouldn't?

I put that photo away till my fortieth, when I again did my facial examination, and then again this morning, on my fiftieth. No change. But just to be absolutely sure, and prove to myself I wasn't on some delusional trip, I took my picture on my mobile phone and sent it, together with my twenty-fifth birthday photo, to my aunt Judy, my father's sister. She and I shared the same genetic anomaly – her biological age also lagged far behind her chronological.

Although approaching her centenary, my aunt appeared to be no older than her mid fifties, still slim, little grey, few lines and the picture of health.

It didn't take long for her to ring me. 'Happy Birthday Laura dear. Will I see you at your parents' tonight?'

'Of course. They're expecting me. I couldn't possibly disappoint. Besides, it's tradition.' I laughed. 'Now, I assume you received my text. Tell me I'm not delusional and the photos are the same.'

She laughed lightly. 'They are the same, so there's no need to question your state of mind.'

'That's a relief. So, how long am I going to look like this? Not that I'm complaining mind, but this is really getting strange and just a little … you know, inconvenient.'

I actually gave up travelling overseas as I could no longer handle the suspicious looks I received from hypersensitive customs officials, not to mention the interrogations and strip searches in little back rooms, all because my passport photo didn't match my chronological age. After the last experience, I decided it was best to holiday at home, or look for a disreputable solicitor who could provide me with a false passport.

'Exactly what I'd like to talk to you about,' my aunt replied.

'That sounds ominous.'

'No, no not at all. Everything's fine, dear, and we'll talk tonight. Now I have to go. Enjoy your day.' She rang off. Her voice had sounded cheery enough, yet beneath, I sensed a certain undercurrent.

The last time, our "little talk" had revolved around my delayed maturity. In high school, everyone else had hit puberty but me. I was the odd kid out – too self-conscious to tell even my closest friends I still hadn't gotten my periods. I was in Year Twelve. My mum had prepared me when I was younger, but neither of us expected it to be this late. She had no idea, but Aunt Judy did.

'That's normal for us, dear,' she had said. 'Physically, emotionally … you will mature far more slowly than everyone else. See it as a plus. When you reach your fifties, you'll still be young in so many ways. What woman wouldn't want that?'

At the time, I didn't appreciate the full meaning of her words.

She also explained the unusual gene we possessed gave us our rare blood type. So rare, in fact, it wasn't classified. She warned that I shouldn't donate blood.

After that wonderful revelation, I went on a research spree, trawling through every medical journal and science book I could find, looking for anything regarding strange blood types, delayed ageing, aliens, etcetera. Yes, I seriously considered whether my family were descended from aliens.

Thinking about my family, one member in each generation who inherited our weird gene lived well beyond their centenary. In fact, they enjoyed double the lifespan of the so-called four-score-and-ten most people were granted. Granddad Owen lived to be one hundred and thirty-two, and his father died aged one hundred and forty-seven. They didn't appear young though. Granddad looked to be at least in his eighties when he died.

Did that mean my physical appearance would eventually catch up? Surely I wasn't going to look this young a decade or so from now? Or would I? I would just have to wait and see.

Just as I began to wonder if I should be celebrating this birthday at all my best friend, Jenny, messaged me. 'Happy b/day u genetic freak u. C u @ lunch.'

Yep, Jen was my best friend—my bestie. She always knew how to make me smile the times I needed it. At sixteen years my junior, most strangers seeing us together assumed the reverse. So far, it hadn't affected our friendship, and I sincerely hoped it never would. Her dark hair was still bright and glossy, and the occasional grey that dared to appear was ripped out with gusto.

I hurried out of my unit to meet her.

The cicadas were humming; the scent of frangipanis filled the air and the sky blazed a sultry azure blue. It's what I've always called a South Pacific day. And in summer, there was no more glorious place on earth than Sydney, with the world's most beautiful beaches just a twenty-minute drive from my inner-city unit.

Jenny had booked a table at the Bar Oceania at the south end of Coogee. It was a popular spot, so I was lucky to find somewhere to park my car.

As I got out, I saw she'd managed to grab one of the sidewalk tables with a nifty umbrella on top. She sat sipping an iced tea, looking cool and relaxed in a floaty, pale-lilac dress, a smile on her face as she watched kids and adults jostle each other at the nearby gelato bar.

'They're doing a roaring trade today,' I said as I joined her.

'Reckon. We might get one later.' She rose from her seat to plant a kiss on my cheek. 'Anyway, Happy birthday, you. I've ordered us some peach-flavoured iced tea.'

'Thanks. When did you arrive?'

'Ten minutes ago. I wanted to get an outside table. Too nice a day to be indoors,' she said, pointing to the interior of the café which looked dark compared to the sharp brightness of our outdoor seating.

In the distance the waves crashed on the sand, and the aroma of garlic bread and sea salt tickled my nostrils. I took a deep, delicious breath.

The waitress appeared with our drinks just as Jenny slid a small pastel-coloured envelope in my direction. 'Go on, open it.' Her eyes shone.

'It's pointless to say you shouldn't have, right?'

'What do you think?'

I smiled and tore open the envelope. Inside was a ticket to the Sydney performance of the Edinburgh Military Tattoo. I may not have a drop of Scottish blood in me, but I always shivered with excitement at the sound of bagpipes, and a massed pipe band could reduce me to jelly.

I jumped out of my seat and gave her a big hug. 'Jen! I've been "uumming" and "aaahing" for the last couple of weeks, trying to decide whether or not to go to this. It's so expensive.' I loved my job as a teacher, but I certainly didn't go into the profession to get rich. The last I heard, the local garbage collector earned more.

'Yeah, but I know how much you love bagpipes and the whole military thing. And guess what?'

Before I could, she produced another ticket from her bag. 'I'm coming with you.' She waved it in my face.

'Since when are you a fan?'

'Since I saw the ad on telly. How could I possibly pass up seeing all those gorgeous men in skirts?'

I rolled my eyes. 'Kilts.'

'Whatever you say. And who knows, it could be a really windy night and we'll both find out what's beneath those things!' She wriggled her eyebrows at me.

I laughed. 'You're incredible and the best friend ever.'

She grinned. 'And don't you forget it. So, I can safely assume Matt hasn't got you these.'

'Ha! He hates bagpipes. Don't know what he has against them.'

I discreetly hid my Holiday In Scotland CDs after he said they reminded him of copulating cats.

Detective Inspector Matthew Sommers was the current man in my life. We met four months ago, and yes, I'd told him about my unusual bloodline. It didn't really bother him since I looked much younger, which suited him just fine. At around six feet tall, I barely reached his chin, and I loved the cute dimple, which formed in his left cheek whenever he smiled.

'Jen, there's no way I'd drag him to this. He'd come out of a sense of obligation and sit there with cotton wool stuffed in his ears.' I shook my head as I tried to picture it.

'You know, it would be almost worth it just to see him.' We both laughed, when out of the blue, Jenny said, 'You slept with him yet?'

'I was wondering when you'd get around to that.'

She grinned.

'Okay, yes, I finally did it.' My finger traced the pattern of the checks on the tablecloth, wondering why Italian restaurants seemed to favour red and white.

'C'mon, that's cause for celebration.' She raised and glass and we chinked. 'I was beginning to think you'd never get rid of it. Honestly, Laura, you were turning into the oldest virgin on the planet.'

'Shhh! Not so loud. The rest of the world doesn't have to know.' I noticed one or two heads turn toward us.

Matt and I had been together now for nearly four months, and it was only in last few weeks I'd finally succumbed.

'You did well to hold out so long.'

I lowered my glass. 'I didn't want to sleep with someone just for the sake of it. You know that. But it's different with Matt. It's getting serious.'

'Well, it must be if he went without sex all these months.' She laughed.

Matt and I had made love a few times. He was an attentive and considerate lover, yet I couldn't achieve fulfilment. Matt said it would take a while for my body to get used it—especially after that painful first time. I hoped it wouldn't be long, and before Jenny could grill me any further, I changed the subject. 'You remember my Aunt Judy, Dad's sister?'

'Yeah, yeah—massive gold bangles and chokers. What about her?'

'Spoke to her this morning. She asked if I'll be at Mum and Dad's tonight. Seems there's something important she needs to tell me.'

'Any idea?' Jen asked as she sipped on her iced tea.

I nodded. 'My ... little anomaly.'

'That could be interesting. Doesn't she carry the same anti-ageing thing as you?'

'It's not anti-ageing, just slower than everyone else. You know something, now that I think of it, she suddenly stopped taking part in any family events after her fiftieth, except for my birthday. She's never missed one of those. Oh, and when I was in school, she always turned up for Saturday sport.'

'Obviously you're her favourite, Laura.'

'I s'pose. She doesn't have any children of her own so it's nice to think she's kind of adopted me.'

'So, she's what—ninety now?'

'Late nineties, I think.' I tried to remember her exact age. Jenny twirled the ice at the bottom of glass with her straw, having just drained the last of her drink.

'Hundred,' I said.

'What?'

'She's going to be a hundred. Dad's planning a huge celebration.'

'How does she look?' Jenny angled her head to the side and regarded me with interest.

'Easily forty years younger, and still really attractive.'

She rolled her eyes and groaned. 'Huh! Why can't I be cursed like that?'

I was beginning to hate this growing difference between us. 'Jen, you're only thirty-four and beautiful. Men give themselves whiplash when you walk down the street.' It didn't work. I took a deep breath. 'Look, I know you can see the physical advantages, but…' and just as I was about to launch into my litany of disadvantages, Jenny put both index fingers into her ears and began to hum.

I sat back in my seat, folded my arms and waited for her to finish. 'I hate it when you do that.'

'I know,' she replied smugly. Then inching slightly forward to get closer to me, she quietly asked, 'If you had a choice, would you get rid of it?'

She continued to jiggle the ice in the bottom of her glass while waiting for my answer. I couldn't give her one. 'Thought so.' She sighed and leaned back.

It wasn't the first time this difference had cropped up between us, and I had a sense it was only going to grow as the years advanced. How would Jenny feel a decade from now if I still appeared no older than twenty-something and she'd be pushing her mid-forties? I really didn't want to think about it.

'Jen, I don't want this to ruin our friendship. I've got it; I'm stuck with it, and I'd be a liar if I said I didn't enjoy it.'

'I'm sure.'

'That's not fair.' Given the choice, what woman on this planet wouldn't give up her soul to have age-retarding DNA.

'You're telling me.' Jenny smiled, and the tension evaporated, yet I was glad when the waitress came to take our order.

***

Because I was an only child, my parents had always made my birthday a grand occasion, and Mum always created an incredible spread, with all my favourite foods. As I grew to adulthood, they saw no reason to change anything, so this evening, Matt and I were expected over at seven.

He arrived early, still in his work clothes—navy trousers and black, grey and white pinstriped shirt, sleeves rolled up to the elbows. The tie probably lay somewhere on the back seat of his car. Tonight he looked particularly drawn, and it made him appear older than his thirty-six years.

'Bad day?' I asked.

Matt didn't often share his cases with me, but sometimes he just needed to talk. 'We got a nasty one.' He rubbed tired eyes. 'Twelve-year-old kid. Some kind of puncture marks all over the body, entirely drained of blood.' I grimaced as he continued. 'Third one this week. We've got half the department on this case. Got to catch him—or whatever we're dealing with—before there's a fourth killing.'

'It's been on the news, but not about the missing blood.'

'No, we kept that from the media.'

'Guess I can understand why. They'd have a field day.' I ran my arms around his strong, athletic frame and hugged him. 'But I have faith in you, Detective Inspector Matthew Sommers. You'll get them.'

Matt's arms encircled me. 'I wish the Commissioner had as much faith in me as you do. He's been screaming at us to catch this bastard before there's another killing. The oldest vic was fifteen, and they're getting younger. I had to inform the parents.'

I reached up and brushed away a lock of wavy light-brown hair from his forehead. He was always more affected by crimes involving children or young people. The hardest part was informing the parents and loved ones of a death, especially that of a child. To him, it was almost personal.

'Look, if you don't want to go tonight to Mum and Dad's....' I bit my lip. I'd been looking forward to this evening.

Matt gazed at me. 'If it was up to me, I'd take you out to dinner—just the two of us—then go back to my place and spend the night together.' He leaned in and kissed my neck, then trailed his lips along my jaw before finding my mouth.

Oh, it felt good, and if I weren't expected at my parent's place, I'd take him up on the offer.

'Pity your family's expecting you,' he murmured against my lips.

'There's always after dinner,' I suggested.

His eyes crinkled into a smile. 'All right, then. Oh, I nearly forgot … Happy Birthday.' He held out a small rectangular, beautifully wrapped package that had been sticking out of his trouser pocket.

I had pretended not to notice when he walked in.

'It's why I'm early. I'd rather you unwrap it here than at your parents.'

I looked up at him with a surprised smile, took the package and hurriedly ripped off the pretty wrapping in my excitement. Beneath lay a dark green velvet box. I opened it, and my breath left me. Nestled in the dark velvet lining was a teardrop milky opal pendant with matching earrings framed in a delicate filigree gold setting. They were absolutely stunning. All I could do was stare. 'Oh, Matt! They're beautiful!'

'I remember you once mentioned how much you liked opals. So, I thought—' Matt began.

Before he could finish, I threw an arm around his neck and kissed him. I could feel his mouth turning up into a smile beneath my lips.

'Mmmm, I guess that means you like them,' he murmured softly before returning my kiss.

'Yes thanks,' I managed to breathe a little while later.

'For the present or the kiss?' he teased.

'Both.'

'I should give you presents more often then.' He cupped my face in his hands and kissed me, his tongue sliding into my mouth enticing mine to play.

For the moment, I forgot we were expected elsewhere and reached up on tiptoes to press myself closer to him, inhale his scent—earthy, like newly turned soil, cotton … sweat. 'You need to take a shower, Detective.'

'Only if you join me.' The dimple in his cheek danced.

The photo of my parents on the wall behind him reminded me we didn't have much time. I pulled back reluctantly. 'Later,' I teased.

Matt stroked my throat. 'Put the opals on. Let's see how they look.'

He took the velvet box, and placed it on the hall table. As he lifted the pendant from its silken bed, I turned and gathered my long hair to one side to let him slip the lovely jewel around my neck. He joined the clasp, then bent his head and trailed his warm lips along the length of my throat as his hands slid to caress my shoulders. 'Would you like the earrings now?' he said softly as his lips nibbled my left earlobe.

'Uh huh. But I need my ears back.'

He chuckled and released me long enough for me to take the precious little gems from their box and place them in my ears. Then he turned me around to face him. 'Beautiful. The opals are perfect with your complexion.' His eyes roamed over me. 'New dress?'

'My birthday present to me. What do you think?'

I took a step back and did a little twirl, feeling the soft fabric billow out from my ankles. It wasn't every day I shopped for a new dress, but the occasion called for one. And this sapphire-and-cream chiffon, ankle-length creation with delicate butterfly sleeves had beckoned to me as I passed the store window.

I'd applied a little makeup, just a touch of bronze to highlight my eyes. I'd also splurged on a new plum-toned lipstick. Instead of my customary ponytail, I let my waist-length hair hang loosely down my back.

'Very nice.' His eyes lingered on me then he pulled me close again for another kiss. 'We'll leave early. I want you all to myself tonight—all night!'

I smiled as Matt tucked my arm into his and led me to his car.

CHAPTER 2
SURPRISE

LAURA

My parents had always wanted a large family. Sadly, it never eventuated. After having me, the doctors informed Mum she couldn't have any more children. So, I grew up in the biggest house on the street. The timber-framed, two-storey building boasted six bedrooms, two bathrooms and a large living area spacious enough to accommodate a floor-to-ceiling Christmas tree. Here we were and my devoted mother had created an amazing spread for the occasion. She would have made a successful chef had she wanted to.

She always shone at these family get-togethers, basking in the praise heaped on her latest offerings. Yet, tonight, she seemed strangely quiet, and every so often I'd catch her casting furtive glances in Aunt Judy's direction. I wondered whether to follow her into the kitchen and ask if everything was all right when Aunt Judy caught my attention.

She was still a striking woman, beautiful even, roughly my height with clear and alert lavender eyes—a by-product of our shared biological inheritance for, apart from her and Granddad, no other member of my family sported our particular colour.

'New dress, dear? It looks lovely on you,' she said, in her delightful husky voice.

I smiled.

'How about we go for a stroll in the garden later, after dinner. There's an important matter I need to speak to you about.'

'So you said this morning.'

She looked at the opals around my neck. 'From Matt?'

'Uh huh. Aren't they gorgeous?' I smiled at him across the table.

'Yes, they are.' Her smile didn't reach her eyes. If anything, she appeared concerned.

'So, how was your day, Baby Girl?' Dad asked. It was his pet name for me.

'It was excellent! Jen and I lunched at Coogee and … look.' I fished the coveted tickets out of my bag and waved them around. 'It's to the Edinburgh Military Tattoo. They're actually here in Sydney in February.' I cast a mock accusing glance at my bagpipe-hating boyfriend and added, 'Don't worry; you're safe. Jen bought two. She and I are going.'

Matt gave me a sheepish but relieved smile. 'Tell her thanks for me.'

I was glad to see that he'd been able to switch off from the day's events. His deep grey eyes were animated as he swirled the glass of sparkling white he held. The lights from the candles on the table illuminated the touch of gold in his brown hair, and for a moment I had the impulse to lean across the table and curl some of it round my finger. He'd already hinted at us making our relationship permanent, although he never actually came out and said it. I tried to imagine myself as his wife and played around with calling myself Mrs Sommers—Mrs Laura Sommers—and yet, as I did so, something within me niggled; a tiny voice of doubt. I was still musing on it when Matt waved his hand in front of my face.

'Hey, where are you?' he asked softly, giving me a dimpled smile.

'Somewhere nice.'

Just then, Dad announced that the One Day Cricket was on — Australia versus Pakistan. Ah, the magic word—cricket. My father suddenly had Matt's attention, as well as Clancy, our border collie. After giving me an apologetic look, Matt and my dad retired into the living room. It was male bonding time. My birthday dinner was officially over. So much for leaving early and going back to his place!

'Ready for that stroll now?' Aunt Judy linked her arm in mine and led me through the now vacated dining area while my mum cleared away the dishes. I felt a twinge of guilt as I passed her in the kitchen and mouthed a silent apology.

'It's fine, Laura. You go.' She abruptly turned away and began stacking the dishwasher.

'Come on, dear.'

Aunt Judy and I walked out the back entrance and down the narrow brick-paved pathway that led to a low stone wall separating the house from a council-owned park. Opening the wooden back gate, she led me onto the quiet path that ran alongside the gently coursing Cook's River. A gentle breeze sighed through the upper branches of the weeping willows that lined the sloping bank, bringing the sweet scent of a summer evening to lazily drift around us.

She stopped, released my arm and turned to face me. 'Laura dear ...' she looked at me pensively, '... I knew this time would come, but still it's hard to know where to begin, especially as—' she paused, her face flushed, and her hands, which lightly gripped my elbows, shook slightly, '—you'll have difficulty believing it. But nevertheless, all I'm about to tell you is the truth. Never doubt it.'

Well, "curiouser and curiouser," as *Alice in Wonderland* remarked. As a child, it had always been my favourite story – that of an ordinary girl who suddenly finds herself in a strange and perplexing world.

'What do you know about vampires?' she said, her clear voice nudging me out of my reverie.

'Excuse me?' For a moment I wasn't sure if I heard her correctly.

'Vampires dear. What do you know of them?'

I looked at her dumbfounded. 'From movies, books, popular folklore?'

'Wherever.'

'Well, as far as I know they're mythological bloodsucking creatures, like overgrown mosquitoes, who ravish hormone-riddled teenage girls and go "poof" in the sunlight.'

I laughed.

Aunt Judy merely smiled. 'Some of what you've said is correct,' she replied.

'Which part?' Surely, she wasn't serious!

'Not the teenage girls, dear. They actually prefer slightly older, more experienced individuals—of either sex. Nor do they, as you so succinctly put it, "go poof" in the sunlight!'

Then it hit me—the reason for my aunt's sudden withdrawal from many of our family functions after her fiftieth birthday and her apparent belief in vampires. She'd hit menopause with a bang and went nuts! So, this was the payoff for enjoying delayed ageing and longevity. I should have known something this good would have a serious drawback. Was this what my aunt was trying to prepare me for? My run of sanity had come to an end? Somehow I doubted I'd be sharing this particular piece of information with Matt.

'Laura, I haven't lost my mind, contrary to what you're evidently thinking right now.' She looked at me sympathetically. 'The look on your face says it all, dear. I did tell you you'd find this hard to believe, let alone accept.'

'Well, what did you expect? It's not something a sane adult seriously discusses. And what does it have to do with me anyway?'

'Everything dear,' she said with quiet conviction. 'Let's walk, and I'll try to tell you as much as I can. The rest will come from someone else.'

'You're really serious!'

'Yes dear, I am.'

We looked at each other for a moment. She appeared completely sane. 'All right, I'll go along with this for a while and only because you're my favourite aunt. Who is this someone else?'

'A vampire by the name of Alec Munro. A meeting between you two has been arranged for tonight.'

She had to be kidding! I looked at her incredulously, still willing to admit to the insanity theory.

'Alec has been my Guardian since my fiftieth birthday. All those among the Dantonvilles who carry our rare gene have always had a vampire protector.'

She stopped for a moment to gauge my reaction.

I stood there, open-mouthed. 'Guarded by a vampire,' I eventually managed to say. There was now no doubt; my dear aunt was completely nuts! Should I be humouring her or having a serious talk with Dad about referring her to a psychologist?

The expression on my face must have said it all, for Aunt Judy laughed and shook her head. 'Laura, dear, when I was first told, I had the same difficulty accepting it as you. Now, I think nothing of it.'

I couldn't help asking—sceptically—'How long has this been going on?'

'Over one thousand-eight-hundred years.'

My eyes widened. No nutter could possibly be that precise. 'Anyone else in the family know about this?'

'Only your … parents.'

This time my jaw hung open. My parents? I then recalled the way mum had kept glancing at Aunt Judy during dinner. The anxious look on her face, almost … fearful.

An awful sense of apprehension stole over me. If all this was true, then why hadn't *they* prepared me? Neither had dropped a single hint. 'Why haven't they told me all this? Why you?'

'It could only come from me, dear—the person who has firsthand experience of these things. There's a lot they don't know.' Her tone was sympathetic.

I shook my head. 'I'm sorry, Aunt Judy. I just can't accept this. It's ridiculous.' As I turned to walk back to the house, she grabbed hold of my arm.

'Laura, please! I'm not crazy. John and Eilene know all about this, and they also know why we're out here tonight.'

I stopped and stared at her.

'Please, hear me out. Give me that at least before dismissing me outright.'

'It's not you I'm dismissing, but this … vampire rubbish.' I didn't want to listen any more than I wanted to believe my aunt was going senile.

'Let me show you something, and then tell me if you still think I'm out of my mind.'

The night crickets chirped as she waited for my answer. I exhaled loudly. 'All right.'

She carefully removed the magnificent gold bangle that covered most of her right wrist and held it out for me to examine. In the dim light of a streetlamp, one of several along this walk, I could make out two distinct puncture marks larger than any mosquito could inflict. Satisfied she had shown me enough, the bangle was slipped back into place. Yet, I continued to stare at the spot as if my eyes could see straight through the metal to those distinctive marks.

'That's impossible!' I struggled to find a rational explanation.

'There's no such thing. The world's full of impossibilities.'

I shook my head.

'Don't be afraid to say it, Laura. They're bite marks, and they weren't made by an animal.' She then did the same with the pearl choker around her throat. 'Have a good look. Go on: touch them. I don't mind.'

I swallowed hard and gingerly let my fingers rest on the two slightly raised dark bumps on her neck. They seemed so real, felt real. Why on earth would she go to such lengths to convince me to believe in something so absurd? Either that, or—and my skin crawled at the thought—she was mixed up with some weird Goth cult. Heaven knows there were plenty around. But I was surprised an intelligent woman like my aunt would get herself caught up in such nonsense. And at her age!

I really needed to talk to Dad; perhaps he could get her some psychiatric help.

'Aunt Judy, let's go back to the house.'

She sighed. 'I see you need more proof. Give me your hand, dear.'

'Why?' Oh, what now?

She held out her own hand. I obliged and placed my right hand in hers. I watched my aunt entwine our fingers and the gold snake ring she always wore came to life before my eyes. It unwound itself from her finger, slithered toward my hand and wound itself three times around my middle finger.

I yelped and snatched my hand away but it was too late. No matter how hard I tugged, it wouldn't budge. The thing seemed glued in place.

'Take it off! Take it off!'

'It won't hurt you, Laura. You're its owner now. Stop trying to remove it.' She placed both hands on my wrists.

'What is it, and why can't I take it off?'

'It's called the Serpent Ring—for obvious reasons. It was mine for fifty years, and now it's yours.'

I gazed at it in horrified fascination as its two blood-red eyes stared back. Whether they were either garnets or rubies, I had no idea, but they looked alive, almost as if they knew me. It was the oddest sensation.

'It's the symbol of the Ingenii or Bloodgifted.'

'What on earth is going on?'

'Exactly as I've been trying to tell you. That,' she said, pointing to the ring, 'was no trick. I'd never deceive you, Laura. This is just too important, and you mean too much to me.'

'No, no… I can't…' *There's no such thing as vampires and magic rings*, my poor brain was telling me. Pity, the rest of my senses weren't listening.

She grasped my shoulders. 'My dear, dear girl, there are things in this world that are beyond explanation, and we—you and I—are a part of that. This isn't something you can ignore or run away from. If you don't accept what I'm preparing you for, your life will be in danger, and not even Matt will be able to protect you.'

I pulled out of her grasp. 'What do you mean, danger?'

'Unless you have a protector, every vampire will try to claim you. Our blood contains a substance that enhances their already considerable strength and power, but above all, it gives them the ability to daywalk. For creatures of the night, this is a coveted gift.'

I was shocked into silence as my rational mind struggled to accept my aunt's words. Yet, there was no denying what I had just witnessed. The ring felt warm on my finger. Its unnatural eyes gave off a slight glow in the darkening sky. There was no place to fit batteries, if it was trick. I examined the ring from all directions. And my aunt would never play such a sick joke on me.

'It's all true, Laura. I would never do that to you.'

'You read minds, too?'

'Your face, dear, and if it's any consolation, I reacted exactly the same way when I was told.'

'When was that?' My throat constricted.

'Well … actually, I was a lot younger than you are now, but that's another story.' She waved her hand. 'Normally, the Bloodgifted are told when they turn fifty. It's known as our coming of age. I've rehearsed this scene a thousand times in my head; exactly what I would say to you when the time came. You think this is easy for me, Laura? It's not very flattering when my favourite girl looks at me like I'm an idiot or bordering on dementia!'

I bit my lip. 'It's just that … this whole thing….'

'I know, I know. This doesn't happen in the real world, but Laura dear, for the Dantonvilles down through the ages, this has been *our* reality.'

She paused momentarily, then, as if speaking to a child, said slowly, 'Because we are descended from a vampire—one man who was cursed into that form. His altered genetic structure has been passed down to us. That's why our blood is unique. In the human world it's not even classified—as you well know—and the reason we don't age as everyone else.'

Now I understood the term, "being struck dumb". I had no answer to this latest revelation.

'Our guardian,' she continued, 'is also descended from our ancestor, but in a different way—a parallel family line. But you'll learn more of that when the time comes. For now, all you need to know is that our blood makes him stronger, and see and hear farther than others of his kind … rogue groups who would use us to kill their enemies and turn humanity into vampire fodder. I guess you'd liken the guardianship to a type of police force.' She pursed her lips and glanced up at the stars. 'This is the price of our youth and longevity, Laura dear. It's the only reason we have this inheritance. Did you never question why you were different?'

It took a while to find my voice. Eventually I croaked, 'Yes.' I cleared my throat. 'Of course I did, but … well, nothing like this.'

'Everything has a cost.'

'Yes, but … does that mean I'm– we're– part … vampire?' That last word came out in a whisper. I simply couldn't say the word out loud as my rational mind rebelled against it.

'No, we're the human side of the family. The only thing we have in common with them is our eye colour.'

I felt like pinching myself to prove this bizarre conversation was actually taking place, that I hadn't somehow stumbled into the twilight zone.

'I know how difficult this is for you, dear, and I do understand, believe me, but I still have so much to tell you, and there's not much time.' She glanced around.

'What do you mean?'

'Tonight is very important—learning what you are and your meeting with Alec. Please, bear with me and hear everything I have to say.' She looked imploringly at me.

'Tell me, then.' I folded my arms and closed my eyes.

I heard her sigh. 'As I said earlier, it's not just your fiftieth birthday. In vampire reckoning it's your coming of age. That means it's time for you to know everything—your heritage. For the last fifty years, Alec has been feeding from me. That ends this night. According to vampire tradition, *you* must now replace me – for the next fifty years.'

I sucked in a breath. 'Okay, that's it! I've had enough. Not listening to any more.' I sprinted for the house.

'Laura! Please?'

The catch in my aunt's voice stopped me. I turned to see her running after me. 'I'm not lying to you, and I'm not mad.'

I stood there, my heart pounding, wishing to be anywhere but here. Wishing I were with Matt watching the cricket, no matter how boring I always found it.

'Look at me, Laura,' she said, as she reached me. 'Do I look terrified or hurt or damaged in any way?'

I shook my head.

'You've known me your entire life. At any time did I appear to you afraid or unhappy?'

'No.'

'Then trust me in this.'

I loved my aunt almost as my own mother, and if all this was true, then I had to do just that. 'What do you want from me?'

My aunt took hold of my right hand. 'I hoped the serpent ring would convince you if I couldn't.' She turned it to the light. 'It's your destiny, dear, as it was once mine, and for the record, being bitten isn't as bad as it sounds. Actually, the experience can be quite pleasant.' She smiled.

Before I had a chance to come to terms with that incredible statement, she added, 'There's no one else but you, Laura. I can't continue. It's forbidden. My blood is losing its potency. Yours, on the other hand, is just reaching its full strength.'

A small period of silence ensued as she let me digest that last shocker.

'I have no choice then?'

'No, dear. You don't.' She squeezed my hand. 'Just like I didn't, nor your grandfather, nor the countless number of Dantonvilles before us. When we come of age, a hormone is released into our bloodstream that only vampires can smell. They home in on it, like hounds on a scent. If you don't have a guardian, they'll swarm here and fight amongst themselves to claim you. So whether you like it or not, you need a guardian.'

'And in return, you allow him to bite you? Is that how it works?' Talk about a bargain from hell. 'Then why aren't you a vampire?'

'It doesn't work that way. Don't believe what you see in the movies. Blood has to be shared between donor and recipient. A vampire has to practically empty a person of all their blood then let their own be taken in return. A few bites here and there won't transform anyone, otherwise half the population would be vampire.'

'Oh, right. Okay.' I really had no idea what to say.

'And one other thing.' Her gaze drifted to the serpent ring on my hand, tapping it with her finger. '*This* has the ability to shield your presence from other vampires.'

'Shield? As in, invisible?' I stared at the beautiful magical serpent, its golden scales appearing to shimmer as if it knew it was the subject of our conversation.

'Not exactly. Vampires have a type of sixth sense where they can detect the presence of others long before they see them. The ring blocks that. I'd love to tell you more, but unfortunately, we need to get back before it gets fully dark.'

'Why?'

'From tonight, your blood is like a pheromone to any vampire within a ten-mile radius. And I don't want to be out here when they rise.'

'Please tell me I'm dreaming.' Or was it a nightmare?

'I know this has come as a shock, but it's going to be your life from now on.'

'Understatement.'

'Oh, Laura, I know it's frightening, but believe me when I say Alec will help you.' Her eyes warmed when she spoke his name, making me wonder what sort of relationship they shared. 'As I said earlier, a meeting has been arranged for tonight. It's best you and he get to know each other before the changeover. There are some practical details you both need to discuss.'

'Are you *sure* he's not just some sicko who *believes* himself to be a vampire?' Somehow I knew I was clutching at straws. The golden serpent coiled around my finger, proof of that.

'No dear, he hasn't aged a day in the half century I've known him. And before you ask, no, it has nothing to do with botox or plastic surgery.' She shook her head.

I closed my eyes and shook my head. How on earth was I going to explain this to Matt? 'Aunt Judy, did you ever share this with anyone else?'

'Good heavens, no. I could never tell anyone. Who'd believe me?' Her eyes widened and she had the look of someone speaking to an idiot.

'Yet you're expecting me to.'

'It's the world we belong to,' she answered emphatically.

'I've got to tell Matt.' I turned and looked toward the house. Matt was in there right now, watching the cricket, blissfully unaware that the world held creatures outside his sphere of reckoning. And up until tonight, so had I. Yet how could I keep this from him?

'Why?'

'We've been dating for a few months. You think he won't notice bite marks on my wrists? I won't be able to fob it off on large mosquitoes forever.'

'How serious is your relationship?' Again I saw that concerned look in her eyes.

'I think it's very serious.' I smiled when I thought of him.

'I see.' She linked our arms and we headed home. 'Understand one thing, Laura. If you share this with him, he'll either think you're a lunatic or, he might attempt something stupid.'

'Stupid as in he might go and plant a stake in the vampire's heart or something?' I asked hopefully. Wasn't that the traditional method used to kill a vampire? Now, there was a way to end this so-called legacy.

Aunt Judy gave me a very disapproving look. 'Laura, don't even think of such a thing. Vampires are secretive creatures. They don't like their existence to be known, for obvious reasons. If Alec believes Matt to be a danger he won't hesitate to act. If you're … fond of Matt, you can't tell him.'

The old adage "between a rock and a hard place" came to mind.

'So, where do I meet this Alec Munro?' I sighed.

'St Andrews Cathedral.'

'In the city?' I didn't know what I expected, but not somewhere teeming with people.

'It's a convenient halfway meeting point for the two of you.'

'Mmpphhh!' I snorted. 'Isn't that rather ironic? Meeting in a church?' Weren't vampires meant to be anti-Christian and allergic to holy water and crucifixes?

'He's not the Prince of Darkness, dear. A church is just another building. Walk in, he will find you.'

'Swapping the old for the new is he?' I couldn't help but be a little bitchy with the whole situation.

My aunt looked at me soberly, but said nothing. We reached my parent's house and I was about to turn into the gate, when she softly laid her hand on my arm. 'One last thing, a delicate matter.'

What new surprise was she going to spring on me this time?

'Sex.'

I raised my eyebrows. 'Go on,' I said, when she paused, searching for the appropriate words it seemed.

'Part of your coming of age means your libido will substantially increase. You already know that we don't normally have children until after fifty, that we simply can't conceive before then. But that same hormone that kicks in now enables you to conceive. It's part of being one of the Bloodgifted.'

I nodded.

'Laura dear, perhaps it's time to consider … if you and Matt are in a sexual relationship—'

'Aunt Judy!'

'I'm just saying, that now, with your coming of age, nothing will stop you conceiving. The Pill doesn't work on us, and condoms aren't always reliable.'

Oh crap!

'Now you've been made aware of your situation, think carefully. Would you want any child of yours in this position?'

'Is that why you never had children?'

She looked long and thoughtfully at me, and for just a moment, it appeared as if she were on the verge of tears. But then she smiled, almost wistfully, and cupping my cheek with her hand said, 'You're like a daughter to me, Laura. I didn't really miss out.'

I was touched and again reminded why I loved her almost as much as my own mum.

'Clever little mutation though; it skipped you and came via Dad.' Our unusual gene usually passed from first-born to first-born, but it appeared my aunt wasn't the carrier even though she was Dad's older sister. Somehow, he inherited it instead and passed it onto me. Weird.

She didn't say any more as we re-entered the house.

Mum waited for us on the back porch. Her hands gripped the wooden railing as if for support, and it was impossible to miss the pained expression on her face. Her eyes darted from me to Aunt Judy then to the serpent ring on my hand.

'Oh, Laura! You know.' My mother's lip trembled. 'I'm so, so sorry. Having to keep the truth from you all these years.'

'It's all true, then—the vampires …'

'Yes, my love. All of it.'

'So, monsters really do exist.' A tiny part of me still hoped it was nonsense. With my mother's words, that hope dissipated like mist on a hot summer's day and I hugged her till the tears stopped. My mind reeled with tonight's revelations, and it wasn't over yet.

Now I had to persuade my detective boyfriend to stay behind while I went to keep a date with a vampire. And he's not going to like it, I thought. Oh, this was going to be interesting.

'Happy Birthday, Laura,' I muttered to myself.

CHAPTER 3
SERVITUDE

ALEC

Luc had asked me to come over at seven. I assumed it had to do with the coming ceremony, since Judith's time as Ingenii had finally ended. So, after parking my car near the front porch of his Vaucluse mansion, I went up to his study on the first landing.

'Come in, Alec,' he said, as he sensed my presence. Our hearing was such we could communicate in whispers, even up to several miles away.

At his desk, laptop open, eyes glued to the screen as he perused the various figures of his many investments, sat Lucien Lebrettan, Arch Elder of the Brethren, husband to the outgoing Ingenii, Judith Dantonville, and my sire. His skill with the real-estate market made him a millionaire many times over, especially as he owned some of the city's most prestigious buildings. He was also a generous benefactor to various charities, including the hospital and medical research lab I had established.

'How much are you worth now?' I asked as I stretched out on his dark green Chesterfield. It had been made to accommodate his six-foot-two frame. My legs just squeezed in as I had an extra inch on him.

'Several billion, I think. I could give you the exact figure.' His fingers tapped on the keyboard.

'Don't worry about it. I know you've got more than enough to buy yourself a decent place to live instead of this draughty, old mausoleum?' I would have torn it down long ago to build something modern and less forbidding in appearance. Luc's house was an old Victorian gothic mansion. It virtually screamed, "vampire".

'It's big enough to house everyone.'

'Luc, you have enough money to build whatever you want. Find a good architect to design one for you.'

'I know,' he chuckled, 'but this place reminds me of home.'

I rolled my eyes. It had the features he needed—at least a dozen bedrooms with ensuites, a large eat-in kitchen for the human staff and visitors, a well-stocked wine cellar beneath the house, a library, a reception room, and a newly refurbished gymnasium, which his men used on a daily basis. There was also a grand ballroom on the top floor, which as far as I knew, had been used on only one occasion. I was sure most of the household forgot it was there. But, overall, the place was a cliché.

Luc's men occupied four of those bedrooms—the former soldiers who had made up Marcus Antonius's third-century military command. Of the original ten, only four remained. Sextus Terentius, who went by the name Terens—he dropped Sextus when some of the men jokingly started calling him "Sexy Terry" for short. Then there was Calixtus, who went by the name, Cal; Sempronius, or Sam; and Justinus, who preferred to be called Jake.

Luc lowered the lid of his laptop and reclined in his leather chair. 'Now, when was the last time you saw my little girl?'

Almost every time I walk into this room. Luc had framed photos of her plastered all over the walls. 'Is that what you asked me here for? I thought it was to arrange things for the Ritual?' It was only three days away and although it would follow the same pattern as the previous one, fifty years ago, this occasion was going to be special as the incoming Ingenii was Luc's daughter.

'I'll get to that. What I want to know is, have you seen her lately?'

I waved my hand to indicate is walls. 'All the time.'

He chuckled. 'I meant physically.'

I turned my head to look at him. 'No. Why should I?'

He pursed his lips. 'That's what I thought.'

My scalp prickled. Luc had something brewing and I had the distinct feeling I wasn't going to like it. Nothing was ever straightforward when he was involved. 'If it's about Laura becoming the next Ingenii, we've already planned for that.'

'Yes, yes, all that's fine.' He rubbed his chin. I knew that sign. 'I have a proposition for you.'

'I knew it! Whatever it is, I'm not interested.'

'Hear me out. It's to your advantage.'

'Last time you said that, I ended up princeps.' Which essentially made me guardian to an Ingenii—Judith, daughter of Owen Dantonville. The man I hated.

He rose from behind the desk and stood in front of it. 'Laura has a boyfriend; he's human, a policeman. I'd like you to draw her away from him.'

I raised my eyebrows. 'Why should I do that?'

'He's unsuitable.'

'Luc, this isn't the middle ages in case you're forgetting what century we're in. She can date whomever she wants.' As long as it wasn't me.

'She's just come of age. You know what that means. She mustn't bear the human's child.'

'So, what can I do about it?'

'Seduce her, and make sure any child she bears is yours.'

It took a second or so before I burst out laughing. Even knowing Luc as well as I did, his request took me by surprise. 'You're not serious!'

From the deadpan look in his eyes, he was. 'You needn't marry her—'

I sat up and faced him. 'You bet I won't marry her! I've done the wife and child thing, and … I'm not repeating that experience again.' *It took me to hell and back.* 'Not for you, not for anyone.'

'I'm not asking you for that. Only father her child.'

What the hell? 'Forget it.' I lay back down and linked my arms behind my head. 'If you need If you need someone to seduce your daughter, ask Terens. They don't call him "Sexy Terry" for nothing.'

Sextus Terentius, or Terens, had been a junior officer, or Tribune, in Marcus Antonius's Roman patrol. On most nights, when not on guardian duty or in bed with a woman—or two—he could be found in the gym working out alone or sparring with Sam. Terens was a deadly swordsman, and his skill with the blade was only surpassed by his prowess with the opposite sex.

'If Terens had any Pictish blood in him, believe me, I would have,' Luc replied.

For a moment, I was lost for words. But it was just too much and I laughed again. 'Even were I to agree, which I won't, 'I shook my finger at him. 'You think she'd go along with something like that?'

'She doesn't need to know.'

Holy mother of…. Luc had done a lot of questionable things in the past, but, even for him, this was low. 'You're that desperate to end the curse, you'd do this to your own daughter? You're unbelievable.'

'I'm doing it for her.'

'Or for yourself?' I turned and looked into his eyes trying to see beyond his hard exterior. I had no doubt he loved Laura, but this was a cold-blooded way to protect her and end the damned legacy.

'They're the same.'

'No, Luc. This is going too far.'

His expression hardened, his gaze spearing mine. 'Do this for me, and I'll cancel what's left of your servitude time.'

My gut dropped. It was the first time he'd brought it up in many years. 'I've only got five years to go. I can wait.'

'Unless I decide to increase the time,' he said slowly. 'Maybe even permanently.'

Son of a bitch! He could do it, too. I stood up and faced him, my fists held in check by my side. 'You know, you can be a real bastard.'

I may be princeps, but Luc was the power behind the throne. Newly made blood drinkers stayed in servitude to their maker for a century. It ensured they were fully trained and inducted into the Brethren community before being given their independence, for sires and dammes were responsible for the actions of their juveniles. If deemed necessary, servitude time could be increased. Sometimes, sires stuck to the maximum time as it provided them with free service. It was the closest thing to slavery in the Brethren world.

Strictly, juveniles couldn't be part of the eldership, let alone princeps, but Luc had somehow arranged it for me.

The man knew how to bend the rules when it suited him. How it affected others, I doubted he even cared.

We glared at each other for what seemed like an age, until he pushed away from his desk, came toward me and planted a hand on my shoulder. 'Alec, I wouldn't ask this of you if there was any other way.'

'You're not *asking* me; you're blackmailing me!'

'Semantics.' He waved his hand.

'Call it whatever you want; it amounts to the same thing. You get your way, even if it means alienating those closest to you.' Our friendship had grown over the years, and sometimes it was easy to forget he was my sire, except the times he took advantage of his position.

'It's a risk I'm willing to take.'

I went to the window behind his desk and stared blindly out, trying to control my anger. 'You know what I went through after my wife and child died, and yet you're asking me to go through it again?'

'Ingenii don't die in childbirth, Alec. They're much stronger than humans. You have nothing to fear. Besides,' —he joined me at the window— 'you won't be marrying her so there'll be no emotional ties. Just get her pregnant. That's all I ask. And I'll grant you you're freedom.'

Indecision warred within me, my stomach churning as if I'd swallowed boiling rocks. Could I do this? If Laura bore my child and the curse were lifted, there'd be a chance—just a mere chance—her blood could become normal and she'd have no need of a guardian either. I'd be free of that responsibility.

'Alec, you and Laura can end this curse.' He joined me and placed his hand on my shoulder again. 'She's my only child. Do you think I like the idea of her being food for one of our kind? If it must be, then at least let it be you. And it must end here. I want my grandchildren to be free. You can ensure that.'

Wasn't I the lucky one! 'I tolerated Judith for your sake, even though I hated her father. And now you're asking me to help produce another generation of them?'

'It has to be you, Alec. You know the prophecy as well as I. *Only one born to the House of Antonius, born of Light and Darkness,*' he quoted, *'who willingly fathers a child to one born of Prythin blood, of the House of Eithne, will end the curse.'*

'And you're convinced she and I are the Destined Ones?'

You,' he squeezed my shoulder, 'are of Pictish blood, direct descendant of the witch Eithne who uttered the curse. Laura is the child of Light and Darkness—Ingenii and vampire—direct descendant of Marcus Antonius Pulcher. What more can I say?' He folded his arms and looked at me as if that settled everything.

As far as I was concerned, it didn't. I had no intention of being a pawn in Luc's chess game with destiny and being manoeuvred around a board like a helpless piece of ivory. And from where I stood, it appeared as if I was being skilfully played. Yet there was no denying the truth of my ancestry. Luc revealed it to me roughly the same time he explained his connection to the Dantonvilles, not long after he transformed me in 1918.

One evening he took me to the library and showed me Marcus's sword. It hung prominently in the centre of the wall, surrounded by various pieces of military equipment—chain mail, leg greaves and helmet from which the horsehair plumes had long ago rotted away. They were physical reminders of his Roman past and subsequent damnation. The long cavalry sword was still smeared with the witch's blood, appearing as a dark stain against the rusting metal.

'I smelled the witch's blood in you the day you arrived at the military hospital,' Luc had told me. It had been a stunning revelation, and at the time, I remember wondering whether he had changed me in order to end his family's curse.

'No,' he'd replied. 'You're the first human I've done that to. I never wanted to condemn anyone to this type of existence. I decided to keep an eye on you and keep you safe. I had no idea what else to do. Then when you were shot, it appeared fate had stepped in and made it for me.'

Since then, it had been a closed subject between us. Until now. Although every cell in my body revolted against it, somewhere deep in my DNA I knew it was the truth. My mouth dried. I needed time to think this through, yet time was exactly what I didn't have. It was only three days till the Bloodgifted Ritual, when the changeover was to officially take place.

'I know you want to have the choice, Alec, but very few of us ever have that luxury. I didn't. Please do this for me. Otherwise, my

Laura will be with that human, who is not of the witch's blood. She'll bear his children, and the curse will continue into the next generation. I don't care about myself—I've been this way for too long, but I want my descendants free.'

I tried to see it from Luc's perspective. He was a father, and I, too, had been one for a short time—long ago. I rubbed my chest. Even after all this time, that wound hadn't completely healed. Had my son lived, would I have done anything less? I really didn't know.

I released a shaky breath. Decision made. 'This is the last time, Luc. After this, I'm under no obligation to you, the girl, or to this entire family.'

He slapped me on the back. 'Done!'

This was absurd. If any other vampire but Luc had changed me, I'd be sterile like the rest of the Brethren. But, like his father, Marcus Antonius, Luc carried the same cursed, fertile gene, which he then passed down to me through blood exchange.

Lucky me!

'Now, when was the last time you fed? You look hungry.'

Once again, Luc got his own way, and the matter was now closed.

'Been a few days,' I said resignedly. 'You know Judith's blood is waning, and I normally top up at the hospital, but blood supplies are getting low and I don't want to use up what there is.'

'Mmmm, people aren't donating blood as they used to. Never mind.' He bent and took a bottle of blood from the mini bar beneath his desk and handed it to me. 'Drink it. It's not Ingenii, but it'll help stave off the worst of the hunger till Laura replaces Judith.' He sat at his desk again. 'I've arranged for the two of you to meet at St Andrews Cathedral tonight at nine.' He glanced at the clock on the wall. 'Judy should be telling Laura all about it now and driving her there afterwards.'

I nodded and drank. It was normal for an Ingenii to learn of their dark heritage on the night of their fiftieth birthday. 'Then I'd better get going. Lot more traffic on the road this time of the year.'

'Yes, yes, I know. So we'd better get to the Ritual. We don't want a challenger. You must remain princeps. I've consulted with the other Elders, and we've decided to change the order of events. The Ritual will be first to secure her bond with you followed by the usual festivities. I want my daughter safe.'

It made sense. There was always the possibility someone could try to kidnap her before the public affirmation and cause another war. Until last night, only a handful of trusted people had known of her existence. Now, with her coming of age, her very blood proclaimed her alive and well. Her scent was strong enough to draw blood drinkers within a ten-mile radius. And word would spread from there.

'When are you going to tell her who her real parents are? She should know—now especially,' I said.

'After the ceremony. Judy and I thought, perhaps, you could persuade her to stay the night—here—and we would tell her everything. It's time. But till then, we still have to be careful. She's Ingenii with vampire blood. Who knows how powerful such a combination can be. So far, she's shown no signs of anything out of the ordinary.' He shrugged, rose and walked to the photographs hanging on the wall between the bookcases. Each one showed a picture of Laura, from her infancy till the present. He doted on her, even though she had no knowledge of him. 'I don't want to think what could happen at the Ritual if the Brethren were to find out. We could face several challenges.'

'You won't be able to hide it for long. If those photographs are anything to go by, she's the spitting image of you.'

'I know.' He sighed. 'Bring her here around seven-thirty on Monday, will you? I'll be waiting.'

'What about John and Eilene?' Judith's brother and sister-in-law had looked after Laura since she'd been a baby, and, in many ways they were her parents, also.

'They'll be there. Laura and John have become quite close.' There was a dark note in his voice.

'What did you expect? She knows him as her father, and he's been there when she needed a father. Don't hold it against him. After all, it was you who begged him to take her when she was a baby.' Maybe I spoke too sharply. I saw him stiffen. 'Forgive me Luc. You and Judith faced a dreadful situation, and you had no other choice.'

'No, you're right. John and Eilene are her parents as well. They were there for her. I owe them much.'

It was time for me to leave. I emptied the bottle and left it sitting on Luc's desk then made my way to my car. Within thirty minutes I was driving down the ramp that led to the secure parking area of the

Pitt Street apartments where I lived. It was easier to leave the car there and walk, than try to find a parking spot in the city.

It didn't take long for me to get to the imposing sandstone structure of St Andrews. I walked at the supernatural speed of my kind and to passers by I was simply a blur, a light breeze that wafted past them. I stepped through the glass doors into the cool confines of the cathedral. To my right was a semi-hidden alcove stacked high with extra seating. It gave a perfect vantage point from which I could observe all who entered. And there I waited for Laura Dantonville.

CHAPTER 4
MEETING A VAMPIRE

LAURA

Christmas was only two weeks away, and the streets thronged with eager shoppers. My aunt dropped me off in the large open court in front of St Andrews Cathedral, a popular meeting point in the city.

'Aren't you coming in with me?'

'No dear.' She hesitated. 'I can't. This is now between you and Alec. It might be awkward my sitting there and listening.'

'For you or for him?'

'For you, dear. There are some personal details the two of you will be discussing. You wouldn't want me there.' Aunt Judy patted my hand. 'Go in, dear. He's waiting.'

I took a deep breath and opened the car door.

'Laura dear,' she said just before I stepped out. 'You have absolutely nothing to fear. Alec is here to protect you.'

A vampire was going to protect me from other vampires. Great!

I made my way through the crowds to the main entrance of the cathedral. Before leaving, I'd asked Matt if he could pick me up after the cricket. I'd told him Aunt Judy wanted me to meet an old friend, saying she was happy to brave the traffic.

It was the least she could do.

I pushed open the heavy glass doors and stepped into the cool, dark recess. The scent of old polished wood rose from the lengths of pews stretching the length of the nave. To my left, a well-worn, stone-paved path led past them and through the length of the interior, while a shallow ramp on my right disappeared into a semi-concealed alcove ringed with high-backed wooden chairs. Which way? If in doubt, follow the yellow-brick road. Turning left, I followed the stone-path down the aisle. I shook my head. What was I doing here? Meeting a vampire, the voice in my head replied.

'He will find you,' my aunt had said. Right now, I didn't know if I wanted to be found. It was unnerving—surrealistic even—searching for an unnatural creature in a gothic building.

How appropriate. All I needed was for the cathedral organ to start playing creepy music!

At least I wasn't totally alone. Here and there, a few people milled around, even though most were outside grabbing that last minute Christmas bargain as shopping hours had been extended. In the balcony at the end of the nave, a choir rehearsed *The Messiah*. I'm sure they'd hear me scream if this Alec Munro proved less benign than my aunt had suggested. Why didn't I bring Matt? I should have simply ignored her warning and dragged him along anyway.

I followed the stone-path to the back entrance, around the massive sandstone baptismal font and up the other side. Every now and then, the Choir Master stopped the singers mid-note for a correction before continuing their rehearsal. Three Christmas trees, bedecked with massive gold bows, had been positioned on either side of the communion table, while an impressive green wreath hung from the edge of the elevated pulpit.

I realized that the stone path led to the small chair-lined alcove I'd originally noticed on entering. It was separated from the aisle by an ornately carved wooden partition, and there, leaning nonchalantly against the narrow opening, stood the man I'd been sent to meet. If not for his dark lavender eyes—almost mesmerizing in their intensity—confirming my aunt's words, I could have believed an angel had stepped out from one of the stained-glass windows and materialized before me, such was his otherworldly beauty.

I sucked in a breath as everything but him faded from view.

How did I not see him earlier?

As I drank in this vision my mind reminded me that this being was no angel. Quite the opposite, even if he didn't fit my image of a vampire.

But then I really didn't know what to expect – black cape, nasty protruding fangs, glowing red eyes and as pale as death, perhaps? This man belied those preconceptions, and no vampire I saw in the movies ever looked that good in cream silk business shirt and slate-grey trousers, which hung seductively low on his lean hips. His sleeves were rolled up at the elbows and the top button of his shirt left undone allowing his tie to hang loose.

I swallowed. Was this the blood-sucking creature whose bite left those marks on my aunt's wrist? No wonder she'd said I wouldn't mind!

His full, sensual lips curved upwards in a smile and he softly called my name. 'Laura.'

Hmmm, nice voice. Deep and rich. It flowed over me like hot caramel, and somehow I knew it would be just as addictive. But this man wasn't human, I reminded myself. I took a deep breath and stepped forward, determined not to allow any of the reticence I felt to show.

He reached out, took my hand in his, raised it to his lips and gently kissed my fingers. His eyes only left my face for a fleeting moment when he glanced towards the serpent ring on my finger. His old-world courteous gesture surprised me.

'Alec Munro, I presume?'

His smile widened, showing immaculate white teeth. No fangs? Where were they? He held my hand and escorted me into the alcove. 'It's not ideal, but it will provide us with some privacy.'

He led me to one of the smaller wooden chairs then sat opposite me in one of the large high-backed "thrones" normally reserved for the bishop.

'Laura,' he began, and his smile faded. 'I understand if you feel a certain amount of resentment right now. You should be home celebrating your birthday with loved ones instead of sitting here with me.'

Oh, how right you are there! I felt like saying aloud. Instead, what came out was, 'I wish I'd been told sooner.'

I tried to keep my voice calm. A combination of anger, fear and being in the presence of such a potentially dangerous, yet stunningly attractive individual warred within me.

'Would it have helped?'

'Of course, it would! To tell me such a thing and expect me to believe it is … well, I'm still dealing with it.'

'Fair enough,' he said, 'but it's traditional for the Bloodgifted to be told at their coming of age. I'm sure Judith explained that to you. Children or even young adults are not very good at keeping secrets. And this is a very big secret.' He smiled at me like an indulgent parent. My fear fled.

'Don't patronise me! And I'm certainly not a *young* adult.'

'In my world you are. Fifty is no more than an infant, and as Ingenii—I assume she explained the term?' I nodded. 'You've just come of age, meaning you're no older than a twenty-one-year old, with the same maturity level.'

Of all the condescending…. 'Well, since I'm so "immature", it's a wonder you want me as your personal blood bank. Perhaps we should call it quits right now?' I rose and turned toward the entrance.

In less time than it took to blink, Alec Munro stood in front of me and blocked the way. His eyes crinkled at the corners. Was he laughing at me? 'My, my, what a temper. You remind me of someone I know.'

'How fortunate. Please, move out of my way.'

'No!'

I turned on my heel intending to leave through the other exit I'd noticed. Immediately, he was there, arms crossed over his chest. 'We could do this all night, and I really don't have the time, Laura.'

'How did you do that?'

'It's normal for my kind to move quickly. Now, may I suggest we start again, as we have a lot to discuss?'

I thought about it for a while as my curiosity wrestled with the desire to walk out of here, and leave the so-called vampire to find another blood donor. 'And if I don't want to do this?'

'Laura, please understand, you don't have a choice in this – as I don't. You're far safer with me than any others of my kind. They wouldn't bother even discussing it.'

His eyes held mine, and I couldn't pull away. Was that a vampire thing?

'I know this is overwhelming. Please believe me when I say I would prefer you accept me willingly, and in return, I promise to protect you.'

Aunt Judy had said something similar. No, I didn't have a choice, and since it looked like Alec Munro wasn't going to let me leave anyway, I thought it best to stay and learn everything I needed to know about this otherworld I'd been dragged into. Perhaps he sensed my change of mind, for he stretched out his hand and indicated the chair I'd recently vacated.

I reluctantly sat back down. He did the same.

'All right, so are you *really* what my aunt says you are?'

He leaned forward. 'Surely Judith—'

'Yes,' I interrupted, nodding my head '… but I want to hear it from you.'

He cocked his head to one side and regarded me, a slight crease marring the perfect smoothness of his brow. 'Are you afraid of the word, *vampire*?'

'No.' Actually yes, but there was no way I was telling him that.

'Really? Then you're very brave.' The smile returned. 'That's exactly what I am—a real-life vampire, and I need to feed on human blood to survive. Although we prefer to call ourselves Brethren. Vampire is the human term.'

I blinked. Well, at least he called a spade a spade. Then his words reminded me of something Matt had said—bodies emptied of blood. Was this the killer Matt was hunting? The question hung in my mind. 'How much blood do you need?' I asked and shifted further back into my seat.

His eyes narrowed. 'Are you afraid of me?'

'No, I'm not!' I said, rather too quickly.

'Then why are you creating a distance between us? You're nervous, I can smell it.'

'Sure it's just not my deodorant? I've had a busy day.' It was out of my mouth before I could stop it, but the way he could read my emotions rankled me. *Calm down, he's not going to hurt you*, I told myself.

Alec lifted one eyebrow, and a broad smile lit his face. My breath nearly left me. It was dazzling. 'Maybe I was wrong,' he said and sat back in his chair. 'Several swallows are all I need to keep me alive.' His gaze slowly—and deliberately, it seemed to me—slid to my throat.

Well, if he thought he was going to get any blood out of me tonight, he had another thing coming! 'So, you would never need to – um, drain a person of all their blood?'

'Not necessary. Only the juveniles do that—newly turned vampires who haven't yet learnt to control their appetite. They feed till they make themselves sick. The blood lust is very powerful when a human is newly transformed. It takes time and training to bring it under control.'

'I see. Like a kid gorging themselves on chocolate until they throw up and never do it again.'

'Exactly. For a mature one to do that … totally irresponsible. We're trying to live among humans inconspicuously, not draw attention to ourselves.'

It made sense. As an experienced primary school teacher, I'd learnt how to spot the lie. There was none in Alec Munro's eyes – once they moved off my throat. 'How many vamp– Brethren are there in the city?'

'Not that many. Couple of hundred.'

Another eye-opener. Matt had quite a job on his hands if Alec Munro wasn't the only vampire in town. 'Then why don't we—humans—know about it?'

'Precisely what we try to avoid. We abide by certain rules too and one of them forbids the deliberate killing of humans, although every now and then, the blood lust can lead to … how can I put it? Accidents. We make allowances. But generally, we feed from willing donors. There are enough people in this city who know about us and are quite willing to share their blood. They believe they're doing a service to the local vampire community. I guess it's their way of giving to the blood bank.' A wry smile lit his face.

I blinked. The things I'd been ignorant of. 'I'm glad you don't kill.'

'I didn't say that.' Alec sat back in his seat and watched me. He'd been my aunt's guardian and he was now mine. I had nothing to fear from him. He needed me just as much as I needed him.

I leaned forward in my seat. 'That's because you don't need to as long as you've got me. My aunt said our blood is more powerful than any human's. Why would you bother going somewhere else?'

'Humans aren't the only ones who like a change in diet.'

Okay, I didn't think of that. 'Seriously?'

He steepled his fingers and pressed them against his mouth, as his eyes remained resolutely on mine. I'd swear they were laughing.

Well, two could play at that game. 'Does that include feeding from animals?'

'No.'

'Pity. You could have kept the rat population down.'

His mouth crinkled up into a definite smile. 'Are you baiting me, Miss Dantonville?'

'I wouldn't dream of it!' Although that was exactly what I was doing. I didn't know this man—this creature—and who knew what he would do if I angered him, yet here I was allowing my temper to control my tongue. It was stupid, but I couldn't help myself.

'Oh, I believe you are.' His head angled to one side as he regarded me. 'That's a dangerous game to play.'

'I'm only returning the compliment, Mr Munro,' I replied, and a nervous tingle ran the length of my spine. I hoped that with that last remark, I hadn't gone too far. But it was too late to take it back.

'Doctor Munro.'

'You have a profession?' I couldn't hide my surprise.

'Even the evil undead have a mortgage these days,' came the dry reply.

'Is that how you see yourself?'

He was silent for a moment before he said, 'Evil, undead, or a member of the legions of the debt ridden?'

I suppressed my laugh, as a string of images of vampires rising from their coffins to see their bank manager for a loan flitted through my mind. But that wasn't what I wanted to know. This man was supposedly a vampire, yet so far I'd seen no tangible evidence of that, only sensed it.

'Evil,' I answered.

'Everyone carries the potential for evil inside them, and my kind has a greater propensity for it. The temptation to kill is stronger because human blood is our food. Your kind doesn't hesitate to kill their food source, and it's not regarded as evil.'

Tell that to the vegans. 'But humans are not animals. We have a soul. It's immoral to murder.'

'You'll find that my kind live under a different set of moral rules.'

'All of you were human at one time. Surely being transformed hasn't destroyed your souls?' I couldn't possibly believe the man sitting before me was soulless. He wasn't some sort of walking corpse.

'Some believe so.'

'Do you?'

He lifted his hand to his chest and fingered something lying beneath his shirt. 'No. I believe in a God of mercy and retribution, and, one day, I don't want to find myself on the wrong side.'

'I thought vampires were immortal.' So much for that myth.

'No, no one is. Yet I can understand how it arose. We age very slowly, around one year in every five hundred. Our blood is thicker and flows sluggishly, like mud almost. It considerably slows the metabolism.'

'What about the myths? How accurate are they?'

'Which particular ones?'

'You know, sunlight, garlic, crucifixes, holy water—the usual,' I replied, trying to sound casual about it.

He looked down onto his breast, pulled out a delicate gold crucifix with its chain and dangled it in front of me. 'My mother's. I keep it for sentimental reasons.' He dropped it back into place beneath his shirt, held up his fingers, palms forward in the surrender position and said light-heartedly, 'Look, no burns.'

He had a sense of humour. Great! At least he wasn't laughing at me. I think. 'That's one,' I indicated with my index finger. 'What about the others?'

'My kind can't tolerate direct sunlight. It kills. Vampirism creates a kind of allergy to sunshine so understandably most of my kind prefer the evenings. And before you ask, no, SPF 30 does *not* help.' He gave me another broad smile. 'Being your family's guardian sets me apart from the others. My feeding from a Bloodgifted Dantonville provides me with a certain tolerance to daylight. I can come out during the day and even sit in the sun for an extended period, though not for too long. It dangerously weakens me.'

'No 'poof' and a pile of dust then?' I asked.

'Not me, no. Sorry to disappoint you.'

I couldn't tell if he meant that last remark to be taken seriously or not. His mouth did twitch a bit, but he could have had a muscle spasm for all I knew.

'What is it in our blood gives you this ability anyway?' Perhaps he could provide the answers my aunt hadn't.

He gazed at me a while as if unsure whether to answer or not. 'How much has Judith told you?'

'She mentioned some distant ancestor who was cursed and became what you are. His DNA was altered.'

'Yes, that's true. He was a Roman—Marcus Antonius Pulcher. But enough of his humanity remained and passed down to his descendants. It's *that* which lives on in your veins and gives me immunity to daylight, plus a few added extras.'

'Like strength, supersonic hearing.' I deliberately whispered those last two words.

He chuckled. 'I wouldn't call it supersonic, but it's very good. Judith managed to tell you quite a bit.'

'As much as she could, I suppose. What did he do to earn such terrible retribution?'

'Nothing any other soldier in his position wouldn't have done.' He paused a while, his brow crinkled. 'I'm not the one to reveal his story though, Laura. That'll come from another.'

The tightness of his mouth indicated I'd be getting no further information out of him on that subject. I made a mental note to ask my aunt when I next had the opportunity, and then went back to my interrogation. 'Okay, what about the garlic and holy water?'

'Well, if you eat it, I'll certainly taste it.'

'Like a baby at its mother's breast?'

He placed both hands on the carved wooden arms and contemplated me for a while before letting out a little chuckle. 'Touché.'

Blast. I was beginning to like him, when he wasn't being patronising. He gazed at me, possibly trying to gauge my mettle as much as I was trying to gauge his. To a certain extent, we were both in foreign waters. It was then I glimpsed the ring. He wore an identical one to mine so there had to be some significance. He saw my eyes widen in recognition.

'Yes,' he answered my silent question. 'It's the twin of the one Judith passed on to you. It's known as the Serpent Ring, for obvious reasons.'

'She never mentioned there were two, nor that you'd be wearing the other one.'

'What exactly did she say?'

I repeated what Aunt Judy had told me, including the strange word she'd used.

He nodded in affirmation and twirled it around his finger as he listened. Then he added: 'The rings were created from the same source by your ancestor. One always passes to the current Ingenii and the other to their Guardian. I was Judith's, and now I'm ... all yours.'

A mischievous smile lit his face as he leaned forward and interlaced the fingers of his right hand with mine. For the briefest moment the red stones in the serpents' eyes flashed as they met and our hands were illuminated in a warm, rosy glow.

'Is it supposed to do that?'

'Yes, but I've never seen such an immediate and strong reaction.' He sounded just as surprised.

We both raised our eyes and gazed at each other. My mouth went dry, and, self-consciously, I tried to take my hand back, but he simply held on. 'The eyes light up whenever one of us is near. They also signal danger by turning black, although that hasn't happened during my guardianship,' he said.

'Has it ever?'

'I think once, during my predecessor's time, several hundred years ago.'

It rolled off his tongue so easily that I wondered whether I would ever get used to the concept of the world being inhabited by beings who were centuries, or even millennia old.

'How old are you?'

'One hundred and twenty-three.'

'Humph, so you're a veritable youngster,' I replied glibly.

Alec's eyes narrowed, he released my hand and shifted back in his seat. For some reason, my comment hit a nerve. 'Among my kind, yes, although I was twenty-nine at my transformation,' he said.

I was tempted to make some kind of patronising remark, but the forbidding expression on his face made me rethink it. Instead I asked, 'How did it happen?

'My predecessor transformed me. His name is Lucien Lebrettan, and he was your grandfather's guardian.'

'Then why didn't he stay on for my aunt? Or is there a time limit for guardians as well?'

He looked at me as if deciding something. 'No, we can stay on indefinitely, as long as the Ingenii accepts us. Luc had another reason for stepping down. But that's another story and not for me to tell. When you meet him, you can ask him.'

'Luc?' He pronounced it, Luke.

'He prefers that to Lucien.' He reached down to touch the ring on my hand, outlining its shape before lightly stroking the length of my finger.

It was such a simple action, yet the impact it had on me was astounding. Delicious warmth spread from my belly to my legs. He smiled, and I had a dreadful feeling he knew. If he could smell fear, then … heat suffused my cheeks at the implication. I moved my hand out of his reach.

'The rings,' he said, 'enable the wearers to communicate telepathically. Comes in handy if one of us is in trouble and there's no mobile phone at hand.'

I blinked and refocused. 'Hear each other's thoughts?' That was spooky. 'Like, right now?'

'No, it usually happens only in extreme circumstances.'

By that I guessed he meant danger, and it didn't exactly thrill me. Maybe it was the fact that I came from a fairly sheltered environment and my experience of anything remotely resembling danger only came at the post-Christmas sales when I was liable to be trampled to death by some maniacal bargain hunters.

'It never happened while Judith was Ingenii, and I see no reason why it should be any different with you,' he said.

Either my face was an open book, or he lied about the not-being-able-to-hear-each-other's-thoughts-till-we-were-in-danger   bit. Most likely it was the former. Alec Munro didn't seem the lying type, and under the current circumstances it would have been pointless, especially as we were going to be together, so to speak, for the next fifty years. And, there was something about him that made me want to believe him, as well as a certain predatory charm that drew me like a magnet. Yet at the same time, the sense that I was in the presence of something powerful and dangerous lurked at the edge of my consciousness. But rather than be afraid, I found it strangely exhilarating.

I needed time to take it all in. 'Can you give me a few minutes?'

'Of course.'

I took a deep breath, rose from my chair and walked to the alcove entrance. There were people about. Some sat in the pews in quiet contemplation, while in the background, the choir still rehearsed. Behind me Alec waited. My earlier fantasy—seeing him with a stake through his heart—now repulsed me. I took another deep breath and came to a decision. My aunt trusted me to accept my scary family legacy, and, even though I wanted nothing to do with it, I felt I couldn't let her down.

A faint pulsing light filled the room.

'The rings,' Alec murmured. I jumped for his voice came from directly behind me. How hadn't I heard him move? 'Look at your ring.'

The serpent's eyes were pulsing, and as I watched they gradually died down until once again they looked no more alive than any other piece of jewellery.

'Okay, so, what does that mean?' I asked.

'We're bonded.'

'Excuse me?' I angled my head to look up at him as he loomed over me. Why did he have to be so tall? He had at least a couple of inches on Matt. At this rate, I would need some serious physiotherapy on my neck.

'It only happens when an Ingenii has accepted her guardian.'

'But I never said….'

'There's no other explanation.' I must have had a shocked look on my face for he added, 'Don't worry; it's not like a marriage, but as long as you're under my protection, where you go, I go, and vice versa.'

'You're not serious!'

'Indeed I am. I can't protect you if we're in separate states or cities, and since you'll be sharing your blood with me, it's imperative we live close by.'

Well, I guess that made sense. As long as he didn't decide to move into my apartment. That'd be fun to explain to Matt.

'All right then,' I sighed. 'What happens now?'

He lifted his hand and traced a trail down the length of my cheek ending at the hollow of my throat. It was so unexpected and sensual my body responded with a deep and delicious fluttering in my stomach, while the pulse in my throat throbbed, almost painfully. His eyes lightened for a fraction of a second, and when I saw his head dip and lean in, I took a compulsive step backward. His gaze was on my throat as if deciding which side was the tastier. I had a feeling he was not admiring my lovely new opal pendant.

'Oh no, you don't, Alec Munro,' I said, and placed my hand on his chest.

He straightened, and a smile lit his eyes. 'It's your choice. My place or yours?'

'Um, yours.' I didn't want to risk any of my friends, especially Matt, seeing a strange man entering and leaving my unit.

'Which days do you prefer?'

'How often do you need to see me?' An image of myself, reclining on an old-fashioned chaise lounge, with Alec leaning over me, fangs deep in my throat, sent a shiver through me. The trouble was, I couldn't tell whether the shiver came from fear or something else I wasn't willing to admit to.

'Every third day is sufficient,' he replied.

'Don't you need to—um, eat or feed every day?'

'No, your blood is very rich.'

Oh lovely. 'Mondays and Thursdays I suppose. Weekends I'm with my boyfriend, Matt.'

'I see.' He pulled out a business card from his trouser pocket and handed it to me. 'My apartment is walking distance from here. I'll send a car for you.'

'No, thanks. I've got my own car,' I said.

'Not a good idea. The first few times I feed from you, you'll experience some weakness till your body begins to compensate for the blood loss. You could pass out at the wheel. Either I drive you, or you stay the night.' A wicked glint lit his eyes.

Was he serious? As far as I was concerned, this was going to be a strictly platonic relationship. 'I doubt my boyfriend will like that.'

His smile was enigmatic. It was infuriating, as if he knew something I didn't.

'You know what? For all I know this could be a con. How do I know you are what you really say you are?' Yet as I said it, I knew it to be wrong. My aunt hadn't been fooled these last fifty years, and the bite marks on her wrist were real. All my instincts told me that what he'd said tonight was the truth. But there, I'd challenged him anyway.

A crease appeared between his brows. 'You do like to live dangerously, don't you?' Something about his eyes changed, just for a split second.

I blinked. 'Your eyes changed.'

'Did it frighten you?'

'Not really.'

'That's interesting.' He cocked his head to one side.

'So, what does a vampire look like?' I ventured to ask. By now my curiosity was at the point of no return.

'Terrifying.' His voice deepened slightly, and there was a cold edge to it, which made me all the more curious.

'Can I see it?'

'Why?'

'Are you afraid I'll run screaming out of here?'

His eyes narrowed and pierced me with such a stare, I wondered if I'd said the wrong thing. 'Fear is a vampire's greatest weapon, Laura. We smell it on a human, and it acts like a magnet, drawing us to the prey. We love to hunt, and the adrenaline rushing through a human's body intensifies the blood making it thicker, richer and, thereby, tastier. If you were to try to run, you'd only be doing me a favour.'

My throat constricted as I pictured a scene straight from a horror movie.

He rose from his chair and circled me where I sat. It was such a graceful, fluid movement, so like a predator, that for a moment I understood what a gazelle must feel like when stalked by a panther. A second later, his hands were on the arms of my chair, and he was leaning toward me, his eyes pale as near-luminescent orbs, the pupils narrowed into the vertical slits of a serpent.

I gasped and froze.

'This is what I am and have been for nearly a century. Satisfied that I've been telling you the truth?' His voice was like honey over ice, both seductive and cruel.

After the initial shock I gathered together my courage. Strangely enough, there was something about his close proximity that excited me. 'If that's all it is,' I said, trying to keep the tremor, which had little to do with fear, out of my voice. 'Then it's not that scary.'

His eyes widened, even in that form. 'You want to see more?' He straightened up, ran his hand through his hair and went to lean against the wall behind me.

'It gets worse?' I swivelled around in my chair to face him.

'Oh yes.'

Ever since I was a child I was incredibly curious – wanting to know how everything worked, where things came from, how, why? I drove my parents crazy. I should have outgrown it, but hadn't.

'Show me,' I said, and hopped out of my chair to stand in front of him.

Alec appeared to be fighting some inner battle, for his eyes changed back into human form then narrowed again as I watched. 'If I do, you must not show fear. Do you understand, Laura?'

Before I could answer, a low growl escaped his lips and I found myself pinned against the wall, my hands held securely above my head. Long pointed fangs slid down from his upper jaw. I didn't have to touch them to know they'd be razor sharp as well.

'Scary enough for you?' His voice hissed down at me. 'Never bait a vampire, darling. It could prove fatal.'

If only I'd bitten my tongue, earlier. My body trembled, and I wanted nothing more than to break free from his powerful grip. The pressure of his hands on my wrists was starting to hurt. His alien eyes bored into mine, while his cool breath fanned my face. The fear he'd warned me about, took hold. His nostrils flared, and he leaned down toward my throat where I felt the merest brush of his fangs against my skin.

I screamed.

'Laura!' Matt's voice echoed from the nave. Other voices and loud footsteps rang through the building.

Alec growled, glanced in the direction of Matt's voice then abruptly released me and in less than a heartbeat had disappeared down the ramp into the shadows. I remained against the wall, just as he had left me. The realization of what had occurred hit. My knees turned to jelly and I slid slowly down onto the cool stone floor.

That's how Matt found me.

CHAPTER 5
PRESENT AND PAST

ALEC

From the darkness of the side-entrance ramp I watched as Laura sank
to the floor. The room filled with humans and the young man who
broke through them to sprint to her side. He lifted her into his arms
and cradled her.

I left the scene and walked through the darkened city streets
behind the cathedral, where the homeless huddled in the doorways of
the closed office buildings. I tried not to smell their fear. It didn't
help that I was still hungry, even after that small bottle I downed at
Luc's. The days between Ingenii changeovers were the most
dangerous, for I was at my weakest, and being so close to Laura
tonight, inhaling her scent, hearing the power of her blood rushing
beneath her skin was almost overwhelming. I could look but not
touch, nor taste. It was forbidden until the Coming-of-Age Ritual this
Monday night. I was meant to have told her all that, but instead ... I
shook my head.

Idiot! Why had I given in to her curiosity? Damn the girl! She
had a curious streak, which overrode her sense. And in my present

weakness, I had made a near-fatal error of judgement, risking exposure of our world to human eyes. The blame was all mine.

I knew it was Laura the moment she entered through the glass-front doors; the photos in Luc's office didn't do her justice. Her resemblance to her father, was even more pronounced. Only her hair differed, as she had Judith's rich, golden-copper locks, rather than Luc's pale blonde. The dappled light from the cathedral's stained glass windows illuminated its fiery depths. Would it feel as silky as it looked?

Smooth fair skin, body draped by a long dress, which revealed enticing curves, and with her long flame-coloured hair swaying seductively as it lapped at the edges of her waist, she was indeed a beauty. Combined with her Ingenii scent, I came close to losing control.

The last time I'd physically seen her, Laura Dantonville had been a baby, barely three months old. John, Judith's brother, and his wife Eilene, had been expecting their first child at the exact same time as Judith was expecting hers. Both women gave birth on the same day, in the same hospital. Sadly, Eilene's baby died of SIDS three months later. Fearing for Laura's safety, should the Brethren community learn of her unique bloodline, Luc had used the unhappy circumstance to swap their living baby for the dead one. If our world believed Judith's child dead, there was a chance Laura could secretly grow up in the relative safety of John's family.

Coveted for its powerful properties, Ingenii blood was like catnip to any Brethren. But Laura's, even more so as Luc's blood flowed through her veins. The combination of the two would make it doubly potent. Anyone who sought to overthrow the rule of law established by the Principate and instigate their own murderous regime only needed to gain possession of the current Bloodgifted. No one would be able to withstand them. As an infant, her blood would have had none of the strength of a mature Ingenii, but simply having her in their control would've ensured Luc's—and the other Elders—co-operation. They could then feed on humans indiscriminately.

It was one hell of a bad scenario.

I hadn't known what to expect when I met her, but she had surprised me—smart with a sharp tongue that expressed precisely what she thought. What's more, she wasn't intimidated, and that impressed me. It had been a long time since any woman had roused my curiosity, and I had a suspicion Laura was going to test my resolve to maintain an emotional detachment during my time as her guardian.

It wasn't far to my Pitt St apartment. Within fifteen minutes I was pressing my outstretched hands against the glass of the wall-to-wall tinted windows of my penthouse suite, blindly staring out at the city panorama spread out before me. The spectacle of the myriad office lights playing in the still harbour waters usually had me enthralled, but not tonight.

Instead, I saw another Dantonville—Doctor Owen Clarke Dantonville—Laura's grandfather and the man responsible for my being in this position.

***

The year was 1916. I'd enlisted following the death in childbirth of my wife and newborn son. The army sent me to northern France to serve at the 3rd Australian Field hospital at Abbeville. That's where I met Owen, the leading physician and Ingenii, although I didn't know it then. What I did notice about him were the unusual colour of his eyes—a striking shade of lavender.

Owen had signed up in 1914. As he'd enthusiastically told me, he had to be in it, worried it would all be over by Christmas and he would've missed the adventure of his life. It little mattered to him that he had a wife and child—a six-year old daughter, Judith—at home. He later confided to me that he had fallen in love with a local girl, Marie Deschesne.

'I'm not going back when this is all over,' Owen declared, late in 1918. 'I'm staying to help rebuild. They need doctors and hospitals.'

'You sure this has nothing to do with Marie?'

He'd licked his lips and looked around. 'She's pregnant.'

'Well, that complicates things.'

'Henrietta's family is wealthy. She doesn't need me. Marie does.'

'What about your child?'

'I'll have a child here as well, and little Judy won't remember me,' he'd said.

'Owen, all I'm asking is that you think carefully before committing yourself to this decision.'

He'd laughed and shook his head. 'I'm already committed, Alec. I love her more than I ever loved my wife. And what do you have to return to Sydney for? Your wife and child are dead.' I'd learnt quickly he'd lacked even an iota of the sensitivity needed in a medic. 'Stay here, with us. You're one of the finest doctors I've ever worked with.'

Owen had known my sudden enlistment in the Medical Corps had nothing to do with national pride or adventure; it had been simply an emotional escape. But, he'd been right; what did I have to go home to? An empty house loaded with painful memories? I could certainly do without those.

'Stop blaming yourself, Alec. From what you've told me, you did everything possible to save them. There was nothing more you could have done.' He'd placed his hand on my shoulder. 'Let them go.'

'The way you're letting go of your wife and child?'

'I'll let that pass. You're still grieving.' And then he'd left to do the rounds.

The next evening I'd decided to check some of the medical stores in the supply depot, a short walk from the main building. I'd opened the door to discover Owen and Lucien Lebrettan sitting together. Both jumped up, embarrassed at what I believed I had interrupted. I'd turned to leave when Owen called me back. Lucien had politely excused himself and left.

That's how Lucien—or Luc as he preferred to be called—and I had met. Owen had introduced me to him not long after my arrival. What struck me about him were his eyes—identical in colour to Owen's. Were they brothers? But they looked nothing alike. And unlike Owen's slightly bombastic nature, Luc was amicable, although somewhat aloof, and rarely spoke to anyone except Owen. He never joined the rest of the hospital staff at meals.

'Alec, it's not what you think,' Owen had said.

'Look, it's really none of my business.' I'd gone to a shelf to check the bottles of ether.

'Luc and I are family. There was something we had to discuss—privately.'

That had explained the similarity in their eyes. But he'd been rolling his shirtsleeve down over his right wrist. I'd scanned the morphine levels, but nothing had seemed amiss. It wasn't uncommon for doctors to become addicted to drugs in the course of their work.

'You don't need to explain to me.'

'I don't want you, of all people, to be under the wrong impression.'

Luc had left the door open after his hasty exit, and we heard one of the nurses urgently calling us.

'Doctor Munro! Doctor Dantonville!'

'Stores Depot, Marsden. What's wrong?' Owen had called out.

Nurse Alice Marsden's teary face appeared in the doorway. 'Stan's been killed.'

Stanley Blake had been our ambulance driver and a conscientious objector. It had been another pointless death.

'Now what do we do?' Owen had turned in the direction of the hospital, an expression on his face, at that time, I hadn't liked.

'Forget about using any of the wounded. They're not fit.' I wouldn't't've put it past him. Even if one or two had been close to resuming active duty, those men understood horses, not automobiles.

'I can drive.' Alice's voice had taken me by surprise and we had both looked at her in astonishment.

'No, Alice. Out of the question,' I had said and before I could add anything further, Owen had rushed past me and out the door.

'Looks like it's me.'

'Owen!' I'd grabbed his arm. 'What the hell do you think you're doing? We can't spare you.'

'Stay here. You're a much better surgeon than me anyway. Someone's got to bring the wounded back.' He'd brushed off my arm and strode toward the ambulance, when the distant rumble of cannon fire had reached us. 'I ... uh ... can't ask you to come with me, can I?'

Crazy man. 'What? Committing suicide is not my idea of grieving.'

Then Luc had appeared, as if from nowhere.

'Talk some sense into him,' I'd said. 'The madman wants to drive to the Front and collect the wounded—under sniper fire.'

Luc's eyes had narrowed as his gaze had darted from me to Owen. 'Owen, you *cannot* do this. You know why. I forbid you from taking this course of action.' His deep voice held such unmistakable menace the hairs on my arms had stood up.

Owen had retreated till his back was against the wall of the Stores Depot, his lips pulled back in a grimace.

Nurse Alice had followed us out. I'd pulled her aside and murmured, 'Go tell the Communications Officer to contact the other field hospitals. Perhaps they have a driver to spare.' After a fearful glance at Luc, she'd hurried off. From the corner of my eye, I'd glimpsed Owen snatch his pistol from its holder and aim it at Luc. 'Owen, put it down,' I'd said, knowing his skills with a pistol were as bad as his use of the scalpel.

'No. Don't tell me what to do!' He'd swung around and pointed the gun at me.

I'd stiffened. Luc had snarled, and, quicker than a heartbeat had snatched the pistol from Owen, but not before it had discharged with a loud crack. I'd felt a thump to my chest, but no pain, even as my blood had spread out over my surgical coat. I'd staggered backwards and fell to the ground as a great weakness had came over me. The bullet had entered my heart. I'd barely registered Owen's, 'Oh shit!'

'Owen, you fool. What have you done?' Luc had cried.

'I didn't … didn't mean to shoot him. Oh God! Oh God!'

'Then why did you take the gun?'

'I, I …shit! Just don't let him die, Luc. Please. Oh, God, it's my fault. You can't let him die.' Owen had ripped open my surgical coat and hissed through his teeth. He'd taken my wrist to check my pulse. 'Hurry up!'

'You have any idea what you're asking me to do?'

'Of course I bloody well do, and we don't have much time.'

'I can't simply transform a person because you want me to.'

'They'll hang me, Luc. If he dies, they'll hang me. Then where'll you be without your Ingenii? You need me more than I need you.'

'There's always your daughter, Judith.'

'She's still a babe, and her blood won't be at full strength till she comes of age. You know that. And what'll you do till then? Especially as the daylight tolerance begins to wane? You won't be able to hide *that* for long.'

I thought I'd heard a snarl.

'If you weren't Ingenii, I'd—'

'Do what? Drain me? Then it's just as well I am. Now hurry up, his pulse is weakening.'

By that time, I'd closed my eyes barely aware of my surroundings.

'All right then, but think carefully,' Luc had said slowly in a calm, deep voice. 'Do you really want me to change him?'

'Yes.' Desperation had strangled Owen's voice.

'Without asking his consent? Are you willing to risk that?'

'Yes! Now, now!'

'Help me remove his coat.'

Owen had ripped off my surgical coat and shirt, and held out my wrist.

'No, too late. It must be closer to the heart,' Luc had told him.

Next thing I knew, Luc's warm breath was fanning my neck, before he bit down and sucked the blood from my throat. I had lost the strength to fight. Weakness had spread through my body followed by numbing cold. Death beckoned.

'Will it work?'

'Undo my shirt buttons; he's nearly drained.' Luc's voice had come from next to my ear. 'Do you have your surgical knife?'

'Yes ….'

'Slice just below my left nipple. I'll do the rest.'

It was later I learned, that Owen had turned my head and pressed my face into Luc's chest.

'Drink, Doctor Munro or you will die,' Luc had said.

Hot, sticky liquid had entered my mouth. Lacking the strength to resist, I had gulped and partly choked.

'Alec, please. Drink,' Owen had pleaded with me.

The liquid had tasted warm and sweet, and as I gulped more greedily my strength had returned and slowly, so had my awareness.

'What about the bullet?' Owen had asked Luc.

'The enzyme will dissolve it.'

Seconds later, their voices had become clearer. I'd felt Luc shudder. 'Ah, nearly done. But the complete transformation is only just beginning. He cannot stay here. I hope you realize that.'

'Alec, can you hear me?' Owen's voice had been close to my ear.

I'd angled my mouth away from the source of the liquid and tried to raise myself. 'Owen,' I'd managed to croak. 'What's happening?'

'Um, I accidentally shot you. But you're all right now.'

Luc had snorted, and I'd turned towards the sound. He'd been holding my head while Owen had supported my body. Seeing I was able to sit up on my own, he'd stood and began re-buttoning his shirt. I'd looked at my chest for the bloody hole that should have been there and saw … nothing. The skin was as smooth and unmarked as a baby's.

Shock had rippled through me, as what I was seeing was unnatural.

I stood and took a tentative step. Then came the auditory overload. A cacophony of sounds assaulted my brain, making me clap my hands over my ears. Voices reached me—men and women—one discussing a patient's medication, another reading a letter aloud and someone moaning. But we were in the supply depot, at least four-hundred yards from the main hospital building. How could I have possibly heard individual voices from that distance?

I'd panicked and spun around to see Luc and Owen watching me —one wary, the other fearful. On one of the shelves behind Luc's head, I had easily made out the tiny letters on a jar of ointment, yet the light in the storeroom had been dim. It wasn't possible, yet there I was seeing as clearly in the dark as if it was day.

'What's happened to me?' Even my voice sounded different—deeper, stronger, more resonant.

'Alec, you would have died. I asked Luc to change you.'

'Change me? What do you mean?'

Luc had come toward me. We stood almost eye-to-eye. 'Listen to me, Doctor Munro.' His strange eyes had bored into mine. 'Your body has undergone a physiological transformation. Over the next couple of days, your eyes will grow sensitive to light, and your skin will burn much more easily in the daylight. You will find your strength ten times greater than that of an ordinary man, and your sight and hearing far sharper and keener. Nothing will escape you, and nothing will be able to outrun you. You will also lose the taste for food as your body develops a thirst for blood only—human blood.'

My breath had caught in my throat. This wasn't possible. None of it was! My mind had grappled with the implications.

'I can help you through the change,' he'd offered. 'But it will take time.'

Luc helped me transition into a new life after Owen had managed to concoct a believable story about my disappearance from the hospital. I'd been officially listed as Missing In Action, presumed dead. Thankfully there had been no one alive back home in Australia who would've missed me. I had been an only child and both my parents were dead. No, I wasn't missed.

After moving in with Luc, I had avoided human contact, and tried to satisfy my craving for human blood by feeding from animals, particularly from nearby farms. I had drained several of them and unintentionally deprived local farmers of some of their livestock. But it never satisfied, and I had grown weak.

Luc had disapproved. 'Alec, you can't go on like this.'

'I won't take from humans.'

'Your stubbornness angers me. You know there are many here who willingly share their blood with us. Let them, and stop doing this to yourself, and to the farmers.'

I gave in.

Luc owned a large three-story house in the suburb of Le Vesinet in Paris. With its many bedrooms and beautiful landscaped gardens screening it from the street, it was a home as well as a gathering place for most of the blood drinkers in that city. It was also frequented by humans who knew our secret and who allowed us to feed from them whenever necessary. They were known as *Donneur de Sang* or Donsang—blood givers.

Eventually my cravings were brought under control, and I learnt to feed from several individuals—preferably women—every few days. Luc became my mentor and master for the next one-hundred years.

My new sense of hearing picked up everything within a six-and-a-half-mile radius. Silence became a luxury, as did sunlight. Unlike Luc, I wasn't able to walk around during the day. My skin burned and my retinas felt like they were being scalded.

Luc later revealed the reason for his ability to walk unhindered during the day. That's how I learned about the Bloodgifted or Ingenii. All the things I once believed impossible—vampires and the power of ancient curses—were now part of my existence.

That memory brought me back to the present.

I stared at the city lights and wondered whether Owen's granddaughter, Laura Dantonville, would ever want to set eyes on me again. Yet, I needed—wanted—to see her again, to prepare her for the most frightening experience of her life.

A bunch of flowers and invitation to coffee perhaps?

CHAPTER 6
A SECRET SHARED

LAURA

'Laura?' Matt poked his head into the small alcove along with several other people. My scream must have brought everyone in the cathedral running. He barged his way through and wrapped his arms around me. 'What happened?' His voice sounded curt, concerned.

For a moment, I simply couldn't speak. Part shock, part guilt tied my tongue. I'd persuaded Alec to prove to me he was a vampire, and now I'd have to explain it to Matt. I was working out just how much to tell him when he lifted me up off the stone floor and held me close till I stopped shaking.

'Did someone hurt you?' His voice softened.

I shook my head, wrapped my arms around his neck and clung to him.

'Give— me a— minute,' I managed to say between hiccups. It didn't happen very often, but when I become upset, or if I attempted to lie, I hiccupped.

Matt wiped the tears from my cheeks with a handkerchief then offered it to me. 'Laura, look at me, babe. Tell me what happened.'

I glanced at him and at the sea of curious faces behind him. 'Shall we call the police?' Someone suggested.

'I am the police,' Matt said over his shoulder.

'I'll bring the young lady a glass of water,' another voice said.

'I'm all right– really– just shock. Please– tell them to– go away,' I hiccupped and looked imploringly at Matt.

Matt turned his head toward the onlookers. 'Thank you for coming, but the young lady will be all right now.' He waited for them to disperse.

Only one elderly gent came back with a glass of water and handed it to Matt who passed it to me. 'Drink, babe.' He nodded his thanks to the man.

As I drank, Matt reached for a nearby chair and placed it opposite me so our knees touched. He took my now empty glass and placed it on the seat of another chair. Holding my hands, he turned them so my palms faced upwards and stared down at them. When his gaze returned to mine, his eyes were glacial. They were normally the colour of an overcast sky, a light grey-blue, but when angry, they turned icy-blue. I looked down. Red blotches covered my wrists. By tomorrow they'd be blue.

'Okay to talk now?'

'Yeah.' The hiccups had stopped and I felt more composed.

'I want to know what frightened you and how you got these red marks on your wrists, Laura.'

'Is this Matt my boyfriend or D.I. Sommers asking?'

'Both.'

I was silent for a while. Unless I gave him an answer we would be here all night. No pressure.

'Laura.'

'Okay. Let me ask you something first.'

His eyes narrowed. 'Go ahead.'

'In the time you've known me, have I ever lied to you?'

He raised one eyebrow. 'No, because you're a lousy liar. You hiccup.'

Well, for once it was going to work to my advantage. 'So, if I tell you what happened, you'll know whether I'm lying or not?'

'For sure,' he answered confidently.

'Good.'

I took a deep breath. Matt's thumbs stroked the inside of my wrists. This was going to be interesting. 'I was sent here to meet a man named Alec Munro. He's a … vampire.' I winced. 'And closely connected to my family. Aunt Judy knows all about it—she told me when we went for our walk. Like her and Grandpa Owen, I carry something in my blood that keeps me young and gives long life. It's what makes these creatures stronger and able to walk around in daylight. But only one of them is allowed to feed from us and he's the Guardian. Aunt Judy is getting old, so now it's my turn to take over. She gave me her ring.'

I turned my right hand over in his so the serpent was visible. 'It … um, kind of … slithered off her hand onto mine, like it was alive. Alec Munro has one exactly the same. It's only worn by the Bloodgifted and their vampire guardian and passed on every fifty years to the next in line. And that's me.'

I stopped and waited for the reaction.

Matt hadn't said a word. Except for a slight lift of both eyebrows when I explained how I got the ring, and then at the mention of the word "vampire," his expression had remained neutral. I noticed his thumbs no longer stroked my wrists.

'The red marks?' he quietly insisted.

I recounted my meeting with Alec till the moment he transformed so dramatically in front of me when he grabbed my wrists and pinned me against the wall. 'That was my fault. I asked him to show me. He was reluctant, but I needed to see the truth for myself … and I did.'

Matt released my hands and sat back in his chair. I had no idea if he really believed me, or whether he was thinking of having me committed. 'Laura, there's no way you could have made up a story like that without hiccupping all the way through it, so you obviously believe it. But vampires don't exist, babe. Someone's playing you for the fool.'

'I'm no fool, Matthew Sommers! And this was definitely no trick. I know what I saw. Have you ever seen me overreact? This was not natural. His fangs slid out, like a snake, and no contacts I know of change your eyes like that. It was real. And why would my aunt lie to me? What reason could she possibly have? Besides, Mum backed her up. She said it's all true.'

'Your mum as well?' He frowned. Matt had met my mum and knew her to be level-headed. 'Look, Laura,' he said gently. 'This guy terrified you and hurt you, and that makes me angry enough to bring him in.' He shook his head. 'I should never have let you come here alone. You said he fled after hearing my voice?'

'I'm a grown woman, Matt. I can go wherever and whenever I please!'

'I know, babe. Normally I'd agree with you, but this incident kind of changes things. What if I'd been late?' He didn't need to add more as the implication hung there. 'Tell me which way he fled.'

I pointed to the ramp that led to George Street.

'Laura, if this Munro thinks he's some kind of vampire, it explains those kids' bodies we're finding, drained of all their blood and covered with puncture marks. He could be our killer and using some kind of syringe to suck out their blood.'

I felt the blood drain from my face. Alec Munro was a doctor, so he'd have syringes galore. That still didn't explain what I saw. 'No, Matt, I can't believe it's him. It just doesn't make sense.'

'Why's that?'

'He's been living here for decades. According to my aunt, my grandfather knew him, and she knows him, and surely she would have noticed something after all this time. She'd never have sent me to meet a killer. And why now, after all this time should he suddenly start to kill?'

'For all we know, this guy could be conning her. After all, she's a rich woman. She's got her own house in Milsons Point.'

'That's insulting!'

'Babe, after everything's that's happened, my instincts are screaming at me to examine all possibilities and check this out.'

'Always the cop, huh?'

'Do I have to apologise for that?' He looked at me with tender eyes.

I shook my head. 'No.'

He kissed the inside of my palm. 'Now I'm going to make a suggestion. Either I can take you home and I'll go to your aunt's from there or you can come with me. Think about it.'

I took a deep breath and considered it from Matt's perspective. He got a shock seeing me in a heap on the floor and probably thought I'd been raped. Could I blame him for playing the knight in shining armour, wanting to go after the dragon? And there was no way I'd let him go to Aunt Judy's without me. How could I face her afterwards?

'I'll come with you.'

'Okay then.' He got up and pulled me to my feet.

'You're really convinced he's the killer, aren't you?'

He rubbed his forehead. 'I don't know. That's why I need to chase this up. Laura, for all I know, you may have met a serial killer. What if you'd ended up his next victim and I had to identify your body on the autopsy slab?' He shivered and drew me into his arms. Then he swore. 'To think you were alone with him while I was watching the bloody cricket. If I'd lost you....' He spoke into my hair, his voice thick with emotion. 'Damn! If we'd only gone back to my place as we'd originally planned.'

'Matt, I'm all right, and I honestly don't believe Alec Munro is the one you're looking for. I can't explain it, but I just know it's not him. Logically, if he were the killer, wouldn't he try to hide that fact? Why reveal it to me tonight?' I moved my hands from his chest to circle his broad back and pressed myself closer to him.

Matt looked anxiously down at me with a doubtful air.

'I remembered what you said tonight about those kids, and I asked him.' I quickly placed a finger over his lips, as I could see he was about to protest. 'Wait. I didn't mention anything about your investigation, or the bodies. I simply asked him about … feeding, and if he needs to empty a person of all their blood.'

I waited for his breathing to slow before removing my finger.

'And?'

'They don't. It's forbidden.'

I hesitated, wondering how much more I should tell him. What was the point, when, by the sceptical expression on his face, he refused to believe in the possibility of the supernatural? And till this evening, so had I. The slithering serpent ring was partially responsible, and the fact that the two most important women in my life—Aunt Judy and my mum—were neither liars nor loopy.

'He could be part of some sort of Goth organisation. They believe in this vampire stuff, even put luminescent contacts into their eyes to simulate a vampire glow and have their teeth sharpened.'

'How do you know?'

'You wouldn't believe some of the case files that come across my desk. There's a place in Surry Hills, a nightclub they frequent. We've been making enquiries there, but so far nothing connects them to the murders.'

'I don't want to believe Alec Munro killed those kids, Matt.' Could he be that good a liar that I was taken in? And has he been lying to my aunt all these years?

'Well, he's not going to get another chance. The name sounds familiar.'

I was sure Matt was going through the police Wanted File in his head. Then I remembered the card Alec handed me. I pulled out of his embrace, fished it out of my bag and passed it to him.

Matt took a long hard look. 'Munro Research Labs. So what are they using the blood for? Some sort of illegal experiments or something?' He removed a notebook from his pocket and copied the card's details, before handing it back to me. He then looked earnestly into my eyes. 'Still okay to go to your aunt's?'

'No, not really, but there's no way I'm letting you go there without me.'

He leaned down and kissed me then took my hand as we walked to his parked car in the Restricted-for-Cathedral-Staff-Only area. At this time of night his was the only vehicle there.

We drove down George Street and turning down Kent joined the Bradfield Highway leading to the Harbour Bridge. My aunt lived at Milsons Point, in a quiet tree-lined street that sloped down to the harbour. Like the majority of properties in this area, hers was an old Federation house that, somehow, had escaped the modernisation trend of the seventies. She'd been lovingly restoring it.

As we drove up, I noticed a champagne-coloured BMW parked in her driveway. Visitors?

'I don't recognise that car,' I said. 'This could be awkward if she has visitors.'

'Point. But we've come this far. Want to play it by ear?' He turned to me.

'You do the talking.'

He smiled. 'That I can do.'

We walked hand-in-hand to her front door where Matt pressed the brass doorbell. I angled myself slightly behind him on hearing the light pad of her footsteps on the hallway rug. 'You're doing the talking, remember?' I whispered.

Matt squeezed my hand.

'Laura, Matthew, what brings you here this late?' She slowly opened the door, her green silk wrap-around slightly fanning in the breeze.

'We need to speak to you about Laura's meeting tonight. Something happened which distressed her.' Matt knew how to come straight to the point.

'I'm so sorry, Aunt Judy. Matt knows everything.'

Her face betrayed both shock and disappointment. 'You had better come in then.' She moved away from the door so we could enter and make our way into the living room. 'Please, be seated.' She pointed to a cream linen sofa. 'You know everything?'

Before Matt had a chance to answer, I told her what had happened, including the way he found me. Aunt Judy sat tensed on the edge of a recliner.

'I see.' She paused for a moment and appeared to be thinking.

'I thought you wanted me to do the talking,' Matt whispered.

'Couldn't help it.' I shrugged.

'And he changed in front of you?' Aunt Judy asked.

'At my urging, so it's not his fault. I didn't realise it would affect me like that. It was probably silly of me to ask, but I wanted proof.'

'There's no need to defend the guy, babe.' Matt pressed my knee then turned to my aunt. 'How long have you known this Alec Munro?'

'Over fifty years.'

'And in all that time, have you ever known him to be part of any organisation involving vampires? He ever talk about taking blood or killing, for instance?'

I guessed there was no way to be subtle about that, and for the first time, I saw Matt the policeman, in action.

She turned narrowed eyes onto him. 'He's a doctor, Matthew. He often takes blood from patients. And he's a member of many organisations, all medical and reputable.'

I didn't like the sudden chill in her voice, but Matt seemed to ignore it. 'Unfortunately, some of the most respectable people have been known to be killers.' He briefly glanced at me. 'We've had a string of murders lately. Bodies covered in puncture marks entirely drained of blood. So far we've managed to keep it from the media.'

She paled, and her eyes widened even further. 'I heard about those horrible murders. But nothing about them being drained of blood. Is that why you've come here? To interrogate me?'

'I'm sorry, Judith, but after finding Laura distressed and bearing the signs of being manhandled by someone who claims to be a vampire, you can understand why.'

'That's perfectly natural,' a voice said.

I turned to see a tall blonde-haired man enter the room. My jaw dropped. Not only was he extremely attractive, he looked young enough to be her son. Early-to-mid-thirties perhaps? Carrying two steaming cups in his hands, he walked over to my aunt, handed her one then seated himself on the soft arm of her recliner. It was a casual yet very intimate gesture.

So, this was the man Aunt Judy had been hiding all these years! My parents knew she had someone in her life, but nobody had ever met him. He was one of those open secrets, the one everyone knew about but didn't mention. Why? Was she worried about their obvious age difference? In this day and age? If I could have a younger boyfriend, why shouldn't she? Good for you, Aunt Judy, I felt like saying.

He turned his head and smiled warmly at me, his lavender eyes sparkling. My chest constricted. Should I tell Matt or let him make this wonderful discovery all on his own? I glanced at my aunt to see her looking poignantly at me, as though begging me to say nothing.

'Ah, I'm forgetting my manners,' the man said, and in one fluid motion, he rose, took two steps toward Matt and extended his hand. 'My name is Lucien Lebrettan. My friends call me Luc. I'm a close friend of both Judith and Alec. We've known each other for many years.'

I stared up at him, open-mouthed. This was the man who had transformed Alec Munro, and he was my aunt's boyfriend. How old must he be, if he was my grandfather's guardian? I took a good long look at him as Matt rose and leaned forward to return the shake. 'Detective Inspector Matthew Sommers.'

Odd, but there was something strangely familiar about Lucien Lebrettan, yet I knew I'd never met him before, and I had a pretty good memory for faces.

Next to me, Matt tensed. The colour leached from his face and a bead of sweat appeared on his upper lip. His voice shook slightly as his eyes flicked between the three of us. Matt had just worked it out. 'Your eyes! They're the same colour. What is this?'

'I tried to tell you, Matt.'

He shook his head. 'There's no such thing!'

'No such thing as what, Detective?' Luc asked as he resumed his seat next to my aunt.

'Vampires. It's a delusion.'

'Interesting,' Luc replied. 'You'd never contemplate the possibility of their existence?'

Aunt Judy and I exchanged looks. She was probably wondering where Luc was headed with this as much as I was.

'No. From my experience, everything has a logical explanation, and there are enough monsters in human form out there without having to blame it on the supernatural.'

'Very true. On the other hand, it's not good to have a closed mind.'

Matt's eyes turned icy-blue. 'I don't think I have a problem there.'

'Oh, but I think you do, and it's clouding your judgement, so much so that you're questioning Laura's intelligence and accusing my wife of either being a liar or delusional.'

Wife!?

Matt's lips thinned. 'I'm not questioning Laura's intelligence nor her aunt's belief in vampires. Clever charlatans can fool even those with the highest IQs. And unless someone can show me to the contrary, that's exactly what I'll go on believing.'

'Is that so?' Luc's eyes lightened and turned reptilian. Two pointy, white incisors slid down from his upper jaw. 'Time you believed, Detective.'

'What the hell?' Matt jumped up, and his hand went automatically to his hip—where his gun would be. He had to leave it at work when off duty.

'You're in no danger, Detective,' Luc said. 'Unless you threaten my family. So please sit back down.'

Matt's chest heaved, his wide eyes as he stared into Luc's before he dropped back into the chair.

In a blur of movement, Luc appeared at the long glass cabinet where my aunt kept her knick-knacks, assortment of souvenirs, drinking glasses and brandy. Pouring a glassful, he returned and held it out to Matt. 'Here, drink this. It'll help.' The fangs and reptilian eyes were gone.

Matt hesitated then took it, downing it in one go. 'What the hell are you?'

'What you refuse to believe in.' Luc resumed his seat on the arm of the recliner he shared with Aunt Judy. I clasped Matt's shaking hand.

'It's not possible!' His other hand clutched the wine glass so strongly I worried he'd break it and cut himself.

How would Luc—a vampire—react to the sight of blood?

'There's no such thing,' Luc retorted.

'It's ... it's a trick! It's got to be.' Matt shook his head.

'Would you like me to show you again? Hang upside down from the ceiling, perhaps?'

'Luc, that won't be necessary.' Judy placed her hand on his arm.

He could do that?

'I know how difficult this is for you, Detective,' Luc said, 'but, "there are more things in heaven and earth", as Shakespeare so wisely put it.' He smiled.

'Knew him personally, did you?' Matt sarcastically asked. His colour returned, and, although his hand shook slightly in mine, I could see him recovering his temper.

'Actually—'

Matt held up his hand. 'I don't want to know.'

Luc shrugged. 'Suit yourself. Now, regarding these murders. They have nothing to do with my kind. For one thing, there are enough people in this city who give their blood voluntarily, so we don't need to kill. This city is our home, and I would like to keep it that way. We don't need publicity, as I'm sure you understand.'

'Right now, I'm having trouble understanding what the hell you are. And I'm still not sure it isn't all just a clever trick; some sort of illusion.'

'In your line of work, you rely on evidence as well as your gut feelings. What do they tell you?'

Matt stared at Luc for several minutes before lowering his head. 'I don't know.'

'Yes, you do, but fear is holding you back.'

Matt's head shot up.

'You're having difficulty accepting what you don't understand and can't control,' Luc said.

Aunt Judy placed her hand on Luc's arm. 'I'm sorry you had to learn of this, Matthew, truly sorry.' She gave me that disappointed look once more. If I could have crawled under a rock there and then, I would have. 'This has been a secret among the Dantonvilles for generations, Laura. How could you have divulged it to someone who is not a member of the family? Wasn't my warning enough?'

Again I cringed. What could I say?

'It's not Laura's fault,' Matt stated. 'I insisted she tell me everything and she was in shock.' He looked accusingly at Aunt Judy.

'Understandable,' Luc said.

'Matthew, you simply showed up at the cathedral at the wrong time. In another few minutes Alec would have explained everything, I'm sure,' Aunt Judy said.

'Yeah well, he didn't,' Matt retorted.

My aunt had no reply.

'You know the truth now, Detective,' Luc said. 'How are you going to use it?'

Matt sat in thought. I squeezed his hand and he turned his head toward me. 'I wouldn't hurt you for the world. Guess I'm caught between that proverbial rock and a hard place.'

'I'm sorry,' I whispered.

Matt squeezed my hand in return and looked up at Luc. 'You know I can't tell anyone. It would ruin my reputation.'

And my life, I felt like adding.

Luc nodded.

'Laura, dear, I think it's time you went home. Matthew has a lot to think about.'

That was an understatement, but she was right. It had been a long day, and now it was developing into a long night as well. We'd had enough shocks to last a lifetime, and the impact was only beginning to settle in.

'C'mon Matt, let's go.'

He looked down at me. 'Yeah, we need to talk.'

We rose from the settee. 'I may need to question both of you further, in an official capacity. Please don't leave the city,' he said, his eyes on Lucien Lebrettan.

Aunt Judy remained seated with Luc's arm still around her. She hadn't touched her drink. Neither of them moved as we made our way to the front door.

'Matt, I can't just leave like this. Hold on a minute.'

I went back to the living room. Aunt Judy and Luc looked up as I entered. 'Aunt Judy, please don't be angry with me.'

She rushed to me with open arms, remorse etched on her face. 'Oh, Laura dear, I could never be angry with you.' She hugged me. 'You got a fright, and of course Matthew would want to chase that up.'

'If only I hadn't insisted Alec show me. I've always been my own worst enemy sometimes.'

'You were ever the curious one.' There was no hint of accusation. 'Never mind that now, dear. It'll be all right.' She glanced behind me. 'Matthew's waiting. I don't envy you the drive home.'

I let out a deep breath and closed my eyes. Neither did I.

It was quiet in the car. Matt's hands clenched the steering wheel so tightly his knuckles gleamed white in the eerie dashboard lights.

'Laura?'

'Yes?'

'Sorry I didn't believe you, babe. I just....'

'I know. You can't help it. You're a cop and you work from physical evidence. Anything as weird as this comes along and you need to find a logical explanation.'

We were driving through the centre of the city when Matt stopped in a loading zone.

'Why are you stopping? You'll get a ticket.'

He slapped the steering wheel so hard that I jumped. 'My judgement has never been affected before. But this ... this isn't a normal situation.' He reached out and placed his hand over mine. 'I'll never question you again.'

'I'll remind you of that.'

'I wanted to kill him, Laura. Shit! I was scared, and that's just not me.'

'For Pete's sake, Matt, you're only human. Who wouldn't be affected when faced with—well, the unnatural.'

He banged the steering wheel again. 'They're real. They're fuckin' real!' He rubbed his face with both hands. 'And responsible for these murders.'

'Not my aunt! Not her.' Nor Luc or Alec. I thought it best not to voice that opinion.

'Yeah, I agree. She was genuinely shocked, but … I can't believe what I saw tonight. That guy, Lebrettan, changed right in front of me, and the way he moved… Hell. No human being can move that fast. Every part of me is screaming that this isn't real. My experience … everything I believe about life is … phhhfffftttt.' He flicked his hand. 'Don't know what to believe anymore.'

'Matt, look at me.'

He slowly turned to face me, let his hands drop from the steering wheel to land limply in his lap.

'Nothing's really changed. We're the same. The world's still the same. Only there's more in it than we thought.'

'No babe, everything's different.' His eyes looked bleak.

'Even us?'

'What do you mean?'

'After everything's that's happened this evening, you sure you still want to be involved with my strange family? I'm vampire food, Matt.'

That brought the spark back into his eyes, and he placed both hands on my shoulders. 'Unless I can stop it.'

'Really? How are you going to do that?'

'We'll think of something.' He was about to start the engine when his mobile phone rang. 'Oh no, no, no. Not now.' He closed his eyes and leaned his head against the back of the seat.

'Can't you ignore it?'

He shook his head, retrieved it from his front pocket and answered it. 'Sommers. Where? Okay, on my way.' As he put it back in his pocket, Matt turned to me. 'Another murder. Sorry, babe, but I gotta go.'

'Of all the lousy timing.'

'I know, and I hate to leave you like this, but … you be okay if I drop you home? I'll try and get back soon as I can.'

'Don't have much choice, do I? I don't seem to have any choices anymore.' His face looked crestfallen, so I ran my hand down his stubble. 'Go, do your job. I'll be okay.'

Matt dropped me off at my flat and walked me to the door. After kissing me goodbye, he raced to his car and sped down the street.

It was then I felt as if I was being watched. Goosebumps rose on my arms. Yet, it could just have been the result of being scared out of my wits tonight. My nerves were probably on edge. Not waiting to find out which, I opened the door, hurried in and locked it firmly behind me. But, try as I might, I couldn't dislodge the vampire's face from my mind.

CHAPTER 7
JUST COFFEE

LAURA

It felt good to sleep in. If not for the sharp light finding chinks in my bedroom curtains, I would probably have slept longer. After all, I was on holidays, and there was no need to get up before lunchtime. I made a mental note to get some block out for these curtains—the sun rose much too early in summer.

I stretched like a lazy cat and thought back to last night. Was it a dream or was Alec Munro a delicious—but scary—figment of my imagination? Light glinted on the antique gold ring on my right hand. I sat bolt upright.

It had been no dream.

I turned my head and focused on Matt, who lay stretched out next to me, asleep. Who knew what time he got back that he hadn't woken me. It must have been very late. So much for a sexy night together.

Careful not to wake him, I peeled back the light summer cover, climbed out of bed and tiptoed into the living area. On the way to the kitchen, I glanced at the clock. It was nine-fifteen—time for coffee, but a sudden loud knocking on the front door had me racing to open it before it woke Matt.

A teenager stood there grinning, his face nearly obscured by a glorious bunch of yellow roses. 'You Miss Dantonville?' He looked me up and down.

'None other.'

'These are for you, then. Someone must like you.' He thrust them at me. 'You got a boyfriend?' His grin was cheeky.

He looked no older than sixteen, and I felt like clipping him across the ear. 'Yeah, I do, and he's a cop.' I grinned back. The kid couldn't leave the building quickly enough. I closed the door quietly, carried the flowers into the kitchen and opened the accompanying card.

Laura,

Please accept my apology for the distress I caused you last night and for my hasty exit. Grant me a chance to explain.

Have coffee with me,

10.00am 'Orlando's,'

Darling St.

Alec

I could think of a dozen reasons to throw out the card, but not the flowers—they were too pretty—and never see him again. Yet, what would happen if I didn't see him? Would the ugly scenario Aunt Judy described last night really take place? The thought I could be taken by force chilled me. No matter how much I hated the idea, I needed Alec Munro. Monster or not, he was my supposed protector. If I didn't show up at the café this morning, I could be putting myself in an even more dangerous position.

What about Matt? I could guess what he would say—if he were awake. But he wasn't, and I had to make a decision. I closed my eyes and weighed up the pros and cons, but really, the decision had been made for me. As of last night, my life was no longer my own.

I jumped into the shower, after which I donned a white cotton blouse and floral knee-length silk skirt, and since it felt like it was going to be another hot December day, I pulled my long hair back into a ponytail and slipped on a pair of sandals. And, just in case Matt woke before I returned, I left him a brief note explaining my reason for meeting the man he believed responsible for the latest spate of killings in the city.

The café Alec indicated in his note was only a short stroll from my flat in Rozelle. It was located in Darling Street, right in the middle of the main shopping strip, surrounded by expensive boutiques and trendy delicatessen-style eateries. The craft market, in the grounds of the local primary school, was already teeming with eager shoppers while jugglers and buskers entertained passers-by.

Alec sat at one of the outside tables, wearing a black T-shirt, which emphasised every taut muscle, stonewashed jeans and designer sunglasses. One leg casually bent over the other, he was seemingly immersed in a newspaper, ignoring the attention of two women at a nearby table. He looked so human, I almost wondered if what I'd seen last night was real.

He looked up as I approached, smiled and removed his sunglasses. In the daylight, his lavender-coloured eyes looked even more stunning. 'Laura. Thank you for coming.' He stood and pulled out a chair for me. 'Can I order you something?'

'Skim cappuccino, thanks. Oh, and thank you for the flowers. They're lovely.'

'You're welcome.' He waved the waitress over and gave our orders then settled back in his chair.

'I didn't know vamp … your kind could drink coffee.' Worried someone may have overheard, I dropped my voice and quickly glanced around.

His eyes turned a deep, and even more attractive, shade of violet. 'It's one of the few drinks I can enjoy.'

'Any others?'

'Some liquors, red wine, brandy.'

As the waitress returned with our coffee—Alec's was a short black – he took a sip. I looked on, fascinated. 'Convinced?' he asked.

I smiled and sipped my own.

'Last night, I took the risk of revealing' —he lowered his voice— 'what I am.'

'At my urging,' I reminded him.

'It's dangerous to tempt evil, Laura, and I don't recommend you do it often.'

I swallowed. Even in that bright morning sun, he exuded a tightly controlled power that I felt could break loose any moment.

'You warned me, but I wanted to see for myself.' And it got me into trouble.

'The beast you saw is powerful, and sometimes I forget my own speed and strength.'

'Why did you run off?'

He looked away. 'I didn't think we'd be interrupted. As it was....'

'I screamed, and half the cathedral staff came running, including my boyfriend, Matt. I'd asked him to pick me up within an hour. I honestly thought that would be enough time.'

He turned back to me. 'And of course, on finding you distressed—'

'With red marks around my wrists....' I held them out for him to see.

'He wanted to know what happened.' He said this more to himself than to me.

I nodded.

Alec inhaled sharply and stroked the marks with his thumbs. Overnight, the initial redness had become pale purplish blotches.

I pulled my hands free and wrapped them around my coffee cup. 'So he knows about you, now. And, something else.' I paused wondering how I was going to tell him about Matt. 'He's a detective, and there's been a series of murders involving young people.' I looked up at him tentatively. 'Their bodies were ... exsanguinated.'

'Does he love you?'

I couldn't see the connection, and was that any of his business? I replied anyway. 'Yes.'

'Then he has every right to know and be afraid for you. After all, you were alone with me last night.' He looked at me in a way that left no doubt he could have taken my blood whether I offered it or not.

'But he sees you as a suspect. Aren't you worried he'll expose you?'

'Do you want him to?'

'No!' And the truth of that surprised me. Was it for Alec's sake I didn't want his kind exposed, or more for my aunt's? I really didn't know.

'Then I'm in no danger. Think about it. Who'd believe that a real blood drinker is committing these crimes?'

Good point. Mention the word "vampire" and Matt could kiss his career goodbye.

Alec looked at me quizzically. 'So you thought you'd ask some questions of your own.' He leaned toward me over the table and placed his folded hands much too close to mine. I inched back and didn't reply.

'How do you know I didn't do it?'

Could he have done it? Would a real killer have thrown suspicion on himself, even as a joke? I had a feeling Alec Munro was playing with me. 'Didn't you say it's forbidden for your kind to kill? You'd be breaking your own laws.'

'True, but, regrettably, accidents do happen.'

'As you mentioned last night. So they may not be murders, but accidents?' I couldn't disguise the horror in my voice.

'Possibly. I can't be certain till I get more details.'

'Have you had any "accidents"?' After seeing him change last night, I believed he could kill. He even said so.

'No.' His eyes looked candidly into mine, and I felt the need to believe him. But was that "no" a "no, I don't have accidents", or "if I kill, it's no accident"?

I thought it best not to press the issue.

As we spoke, I noticed the way he shifted his chair further into the shade as the morning sun slowly encroached on our table. It seemed so normal sitting here having coffee with him, that I'd temporarily forgotten his sensitivity to sunlight.

'How much longer can you stay out?'

'Another hour, not much more.'

'Then I'd better go and let you get under cover.' I stood to leave.

'Not yet.' Alec reached out, caught my hand, and my body gave a jolt. 'There's something I need to tell you; that's the other reason I asked you here.'

I snatched my hand back and sat.

'This coming Monday, first full moon after the coming of age of a Bloodgifted, we'll be holding a special ceremony where you'll be introduced to the rest of our community. It's a Coming-of-Age rite that'll publicly endorse you, the incoming Bloodgifted, and chosen guardian. We simply refer to it as the Ritual.'

I didn't like the sound of this, but it was important for me to know exactly what to expect. 'What kind of ceremony?'

Alec lowered his voice further. I shifted my chair closer to his, into the shade. The café was quickly filling up with a Saturday crowd, and, understandably, he didn't want to be overheard. I noticed two women at the next table stopped talking. They seemed to be eavesdropping on our conversation.

Good luck to them. Who'd believe it?

With his face barely inches from mine, I became conscious of his scent—musky with a hint of pine. It reminded me of a walk in the woods after rain, fresh and exhilarating. My body tingled, but I didn't dare move my seat back, as I didn't want him to think I was afraid. In some respect I was, but not in a physical sense. Alec Munro had me thinking about my relationship with Matt and why I'd never experienced such a thrill in his company. I was beginning to fear what it meant and was unsure what to do about it.

'This ritual is one of the most important ceremonies for our kind,' he said, breaking into my thoughts. 'It's a public affirmation of the Bloodgifted and Guardian. You'll be presented to the Brethren and their *donsang*—'

'Their what?'

He smiled. 'Sorry, I'm so used to these terms; I forget you're not familiar with them. *Donsang* is our word for blood givers. And I am the current princeps.'

'Princeps?'

'The guardian responsible for the Bloodgifted. It's a position of power—I'm counted among the Elders, and together with them, make judgements of life and death. In some cases, mine is the final decision. I'm also responsible for upholding Brethren Law in this city, keeping both sides safe, and one blissfully unaware of the other.'

'Quite a job! Something like a prince, then?'

'Something like that. '

'So I'm in the presence of royalty am I?'

He stopped speaking, as if stuck for words, then lowered his head and chuckled. 'Yes, I suppose I am, but only,' —he raised his head— 'because you are a princess.

'Excuse me?'

'Laura, your bloodline makes you royalty among my kind, and it's only my association with you that makes me princeps.'

'Oh.' Now I was the one stuck for words, but before I had a chance to ask him to elaborate on that, Alec continued.

'As I was saying, you will be publicly asked to choose your guardian. You must name me, after which we will raise our rings to all assembled and wait for the serpents' affirmation.'

I looked down at my ring. 'You mean the glowing eyes, like they did last night?'

'Exactly like that.'

'And if they don't?'

'I might be challenged, and another blood drinker will be given the opportunity to claim my position and you. If the serpents eyes flash while on his or her hand, it's they who become your guardian.'

'What happens to the loser?'

'They die.'

I must have looked alarmed, for he quickly added, 'That hasn't happened in a very long time.'

'How long?'

'About four-hundred years.'

I recalled him mentioning the rings turning black during times of danger. It must have happened then.

'Right now I need you to understand what's going to happen.'

'Okay, back to this challenge. If I get this right, it's a risk for you too?'

'Yes. If I step down before the Ritual commences, I'll be allowed to live. But if I step up and am rejected, I'll be executed.'

I nearly choked on my coffee. 'Why?'

'To avoid a civil war. In the past, the princeps had been challenged, and because the challenger was allowed to live, a faction built up around him. It led to civil war. Some of the Elders were killed along with hundreds of humans. Entire villages were sucked dry before the survivors took up arms and burned down every house they thought belonged to a Brethren. The rebels even managed to capture the Ingenii and drain him.' My eyes widened. 'Both sides suffered. Eventually, the rebellion was put down, the rebels beheaded and their bodies exposed to the sun. But the princeps had to wait several years for the next Ingenii to come of age. It was a tense time. Nobody who remembers those days wants them to return.'

I understood what he meant. History was filled with wars begun by rivals for the same throne, so why should the vampire world be any different?

'Listen to me, Laura. You and I both saw the way the rings reacted when they met. You have already chosen me, so a challenger won't succeed.'

'Well, I hope you're right.' I sighed. 'Is there more? Alec?'

'One... minor thing. I must feed from you before the entire assembly for our bonding to be recognized.'

Was he serious? 'Wrist?'

Alec shook his head. 'Neck,' he mouthed.

'That's a minor thing?' My voice rose and I glanced around to see if anyone had noticed, but people were absorbed in their own conversations, even those two women who seemed to be eavesdropping earlier.

'Laura, you need to know there's an element of risk involved. Unlike ordinary humans, your blood has a quality that makes it intoxicating, and I need to exercise extreme control so I don't kill you.' I stared at him. 'It's one of the reasons the Elders are there—in case I lose control, they'll pull me off you in time.'

I temporarily lost the power of speech and had to fight the urge to run back home to Matt. 'Has it ever happened?' I cleared my throat to hide the tremble in my voice.

'Nearly. It takes time getting used to a young Ingenii's powerful blood. First Taste is always fraught with danger. Yours' —he inhaled deeply— 'is fresh and potent.' His eyes slightly lightened.

I breathed hard while Alec signalled the waitress to bring another cup of strong coffee—for me. 'Pity they don't serve alcohol here. I'd prefer brandy right now.'

'The Elders will be there Laura, to make sure we don't lose you.'

'Well, there's a comforting thought.' I wondered if my aunt deliberately chose not to mention this to me. Smart woman.

He smiled. When my second cup of coffee arrived, I gulped most it down and started coughing—damn that was hot.

'Um, one other thing.'

I stared at him over the rim of my coffee cup.

'The Elders will examine your neck ... to be sure I've taken your blood before approving us before the assembly.'

This was unreal, like a dream, yet everything around me seemed solid—people chatting, cups clinking against saucers, the delicious aroma of brewed coffee and fresh rolls, someone laughing—all real.

And this strange, beautiful man sitting so close to me was real too, but he inhabited a very different reality.

The idea suddenly came to me. If Matt and I were to have a future together, then he needed to be there with me. 'Can I bring Matt?'

'No.'

He said it without hesitation. I blinked. 'Why?'

'Apart from parents of the Ingenii and donsangs, all other humans are forbidden.'

'My parents will be there?'

He gave a curt nod.

'But Matt's my partner—'

'As in blood givers, Laura. Each of the Brethren are required to bring their donsangs—their food source. It's not possible to provide enough *refreshment* to cater for my kind at these large gatherings. And for this occasion, I'm your partner. Your boyfriend would be seen as unattached and could possibly end up as someone's … snack.'

'No!'

He nodded.

'And if he was my husband?'

'But, he's not.'

'Yet.'

Alec said nothing but looked at me unblinking and twirled the serpent ring on his finger until the silence stretched uncomfortably between us. I broke first. 'Anything else I should know?'

'Yes. We've got company.'

Alec's gaze moved over my shoulder. I turned to look, but it was difficult to make out anyone specific from the groups of people milling around the various shops and cafes on our side of the street. I glanced back at him and frowned, but he simply indicated the direction with a nod. There at the far end, on the other side of the road, barely distinguishable from those around him, was Matt. Only his height and familiar gait gave him away as he made his very determined way to our table.

I groaned inwardly and checked my watch. How long had we been sitting here? And what was Matt doing awake? It then occurred to me—how could Alec have spotted him at such a distance? His vision had to be phenomenal. Also, how did Alec know Matt? They'd never met.

'How did you know?'

'Last night, I watched him come to you.'

'You what?'

'To make sure you were safe before I left.'

He wanted to make sure I was okay? He'd scared me half to death, yet he was concerned enough to hang around and risk being seen when Matt arrived. I honestly didn't know what to think of him.

Looking behind me again, I could see Matt practically running down the street only to get stopped by traffic lights. His lower shirt button was undone, and as the breeze caught the end, I saw the gun strapped to his belt. He was supposed to leave it at work when off duty.

My hands shook.

'Are you afraid of him?' There was a dangerous edge to Alec's voice.

'Of Matt? No. It's just that ...' I took a deep breath and wondered how to answer him. No way I could mention Matt was packing a gun. Instead I said, 'I left him sleeping. We had a late night.' He raised his eyebrows, and I knew what ran through his mind. But really, it was none of his business. 'I thought I could meet you and be back before he got up. I ... left a note and your card sitting on the table ... next to your flowers.'

A look of understanding crossed his face. 'Ah!'

'He would have prevented me coming otherwise.' Or he would've come with me.

'I see.'

Matt wasn't smiling when he arrived, his lips in a tight line, his eyes stormy as they darted from me to Alec and back again. 'We'll talk about this later,' he said icily and leaned down to give me a quick kiss.

My stomach clenched. 'Matt, I'm sorry, but I thought I'd be back before you woke up so you wouldn't worry.' I seemed to be doing a lot of apologising lately, but I didn't regret my decision to meet Alec this morning. Oddly, I enjoyed his company, and time seemed to stand still while we talked.

'Laura kindly came at my request.' Alec voice was low, dangerous, as he slowly looked Matt up and down.

I swallowed. 'Matt, this is—'

'Dr Alec Munro,' Matt finished for me.

Alec rose and extended his hand without a welcoming smile. 'Detective Sommers.'

Matt gripped it and returned the shake. 'Laura's mentioned me. Good. In that case, let's not pretend we don't know why I'm here.'

My stomach churned. Seating himself next to me and directly opposite Alec, Matt reached for my hand and interlaced our fingers while his eyes never left Alec's face. Awkward was not a strong enough word to describe this situation.

Tension plus.

'Let me hazard a guess,' Alec replied coolly. 'Protecting your interest?'

I slid my other hand under the table onto my knee to stop it bouncing, which it always did when I was nervous.

'Protecting my girl,' Matt corrected him.

Alec's gaze returned to me. 'She's worth it.'

I shifted uncomfortably. This was not good. Matt tensed, so it was just as well I was holding his gun hand. 'Matt, let's go. I have things to do.' I stood.

He didn't budge. 'Not yet, babe. I need to ask Doctor Munro a few questions.'

'You're off duty,' I reminded him.

'It's okay. This is the perfect opportunity.'

'Matt, please, not here,' I hissed.

'Don't worry, babe, it won't take long.'

I wondered whether it was concern for my safety or his pursuit of a perceived murderer that made him rush down here. And since I didn't have the answer, I sighed and sat miserably back down.

Alec seemed to enjoy watching our exchange—a slight smile played about his lips. Well, actually, it was more of a smirk. He lounged back in his chair, folded his arms across his chest and said, 'Ask away.'

I signalled the waitress for my third cup of coffee. At this rate I was going to be awake for the next three days.

'Since when has your lot been able to come out during the day?' Matt asked.

'They can't, normally.'

'You're the exception?'

'Obviously.'

'Laura's bloodline, huh?'

Alec gave a simple nod, and his eyes strayed to the gun at Matt's belt. 'Since when are *your* lot allowed to carry a weapon when off duty?'

'When my girl leaves a note telling me she's meeting a person of interest. I'd be a fool to leave it behind.'

He said it calmly, but I felt him tense, and his hand in mine began to sweat. I'm sure it had little to do with the day's heat.

'Or a fool to think you could intimidate me with it.' Alec indicated Matt's gun with a nod of his head. '*That* poses no danger to my kind, but it does to everyone in this café. Perhaps you should have thought of that before bringing it.'

Matt smiled. 'I did a little research last night and discovered a certain substance that's quite nasty to your kind. Wood. How do you know I'm not packing that?'

Alec's smirk grew. 'If you did, Detective, it wouldn't be in your holster right now. All I can smell is lead, but nice try. Maybe next time the bluff'll pay off.'

They stared at each other, neither willing to back down. It was like watching two roosters face off, yet Matt's comment about the wood prompted me to intervene. 'What does wood do to you?'

'Not all wood, just certain types. As snake venom is to you, so wood is to us.' The furniture in this café was metal. Was that why he'd chosen to meet here? 'You didn't mention this last night.'

'You didn't ask.' His eyes softened and a smile replaced the smirk.

I stared back, unable to break away.

'You like to drink?' The sharp edge in Matt's voice made me blink, breaking eye contact from Alec.

'Depends what type of beverage we're discussing.' Alec's gaze shifted slowly from me to Matt.

It was going on midday, and the sun had crept further toward Alec's side of the table but this time he didn't shift his chair and I knew he couldn't be out for much longer. He'd only told Matt half the truth, and I wasn't about to say otherwise since Matt appeared to position his chair to prevent Alec from inching into the shade. The sunlight had reached Alec's left shoulder and he tried to angle his body away. I watched as Matt extended his leg and let it rest on the crossbar of Alec's chair, effectively preventing him from moving.

I couldn't believe he'd do such a thing. It was a side to him I'd never seen before. Was this how he behaved at work everyday? I didn't know Matt well at all. For a moment, I disliked him—that shocked me.

'Adolescent blood. Twelve to thirteen year olds?' Matt suggestively asked.

I glared at him and kicked the side of his leg.

'This isn't the most appropriate place to ask me that,' Alec answered in a quiet voice. 'But since we're on the subject, I prefer mine a little older and more mature.' His gaze slid to me.

A muscle ticked in Matt's jaw. Alec seemed to be pushing all his buttons. Matt's hands balled into fists, forgetting one of them held mine. I winced and tried to pull free.

'You're hurting her,' Alec warned.

'And you didn't?' Matt spat out. He unwound our fingers and turned my wrist up to expose the discolouration. I'd never seen him so angry.

Alec blanched at Matt's comment. 'Let her go, Sommers,' he said quietly, dangerously. His eyes paled.

Conversation in the café stilled. Heads turned in our direction. My heart stopped. On top of everything I'd had to cope with since my life had been turned upside down, we were now the centre of attention of a trendy café crowd. Could things get any worse? I had to leave—and quickly—before it all became too much.

I snatched my hand from Matt's grasp, picked up my handbag and stood.

'Where are you going?' Matt asked and grabbed my arm.

'Let go, Matt. If you want to cause a scene, you're on your own 'cause I refuse to be part of it.' I leaned down till our faces were barely a breath apart. 'I didn't mean any harm by coming here and meeting Alec in a public place, so please have the decency to respect my judgement.' I straightened. 'I'm going shopping.'

'I'll be in touch, Laura.' Alec stood and inclined his head toward me.

It was unusual to see such old-world manners. It was nice.

'The hell, you will!' Matt rose to face him, his chair scraping across the floor.

I briefly closed my eyes, ignoring my desire to scream, turned my back on Matt and walked away just as my coffee arrived.

CHAPTER 8
THE BOYFRIEND

ALEC

Laura walked off and left me alone with Sommers, which was not exactly the scenario I had envisaged for the day. Yet, on the other hand, maybe Sommers was right and this was a good opportunity to find out about those exsanguinated bodies and determine whether he would be a future threat.

I could see why Laura was attracted to him—he was confident and intelligent. But, he'd demonstrated a tendency to order her about. Unless tempered, that could develop into something hard and brutal. I didn't like the idea of Laura ending up with such a man. She was bright and independent, and he would only stifle her.

I shunted the thought aside. The woman was haunting my thoughts, and I had no intention of becoming emotionally involved, yet I couldn't rid my mind of the endearing way she bit the side of her lower lip when she appeared to be thinking something through. And when she smiled, the two small freckles above her upper lip dimpled slightly.

Enough! I grabbed my chair and pulled it into the shade. At the scrape of my chair legs, Sommers turned. I was once again seated with my arms folded on the table.

'Please, sit down, Detective. We need to clear some things up.'

'Is that so? If you think–'

I raised my hand palm outward and pointed to the chair.

He dropped into Laura's vacated seat, keeping a safe distance. Wise move. I hadn't fed in days and his blood smelled good. In fact, everyone did. If only they knew about the predator in their midst. I clenched my teeth and kept a tight reign on my hunger.

'Let me explain something to you. Regardless of your objections, Laura needs my protection and in return for it, she will allow me to feed. I'm sure she explained this to you.'

'She did.'

'To keep her safe, I will need your co-operation, not belligerence.'

His lips thinned, but at least he stopped objecting. 'All right, you have it – for now.'

'That'll do. Now, tell me about those bodies.'

'Three juveniles entirely emptied of blood.'

'When was this?' I couldn't let him know Laura had already mentioned it to me.

'The last five days.'

A lot of Brethren had arrived in Sydney for the Coming-of-Age ceremony. Among them, some of the oldest vampires on the planet – Zhao from China, Kwome from Nigeria, and Maris Quesnel, from France—who together with Luc, Marcus Antonius Pulcher and myself, made up the eldership. They would be conducting the ceremony. Each had arrived with an entourage in privately chartered flights. Normally they would have been welcome to stay in Luc's extensive mansion in Vaucluse, but fearing for Laura's safety, the house had been cleared of all but our immediate circle.

Sommers watched me closely. If I were indeed a suspect, he'd be waiting for any clue, any word or expression that would confirm his suspicions.

'Any marks on them?'

'Plenty. Coroner found punctures on the pulse points—neck, ankles, wrists, back of the knees, inner arm and groin. Whoever did it took their time and drained them slowly.' He grimaced.

'Ages?'

'The oldest was no more than fifteen and the youngest only twelve. I thought we were dealing with a psychopath who thought himself a vamp but never imagined it might be the real thing.'

'It doesn't mean one of my kind did it. It could still be a human.'

'Lebrettan said roughly the same when I questioned him last night.'

He watched me closely. I knew he was hoping the mention of Luc's name would get a reaction out of me, but I had no intention of giving him the satisfaction. Yet the description he gave... suspicion entered my mind.

His brows knitted together as he stared at me. 'You know who it is.'

'Give me a day or so.' I needed evidence. 'Can you get me a read out of the saliva in the victims' wounds?'

'It's one of your lot after all, isn't it?' He looked at me accusingly.

'I'm not sure.'

'They're in the case file. Why, can you get me a match?'

I sat back. 'Possibly.'

'This happened on my turf, Munro and I want him.' He leaned across the table, and his eyes narrowed.

'And what will you do then? How are you going to hold one of my kind? We're many times stronger than humans—no jail can hold us. Iron bars are like paper, and bullets are useless. A cornered blood drinker is a very dangerous creature. You'll lose a lot of men.'

He swore under his breath, but I hadn't finished. 'What happens when daylight comes? You know the old myths: one touch of sunbeam and you've got a pile of ash without a suspect. Hard to explain that one away.' I watched as Sommers's expression changed from frustration to exasperation. 'Even if you somehow manage to convince them these murders are being committed by a real vampire,' I continued, 'do you honestly think they'll release that information to the public? Imagine the panic, the media circus. You know very well that won't happen.'

The city authorities would do anything to hush this up and expect those involved to keep their mouths shut as well. Sommers could wave his career, let alone his promotion, goodbye.

'Shit!'

'Couldn't have put it better myself.'

He threw me a filthy look, so I knew I had him in a corner with limited choices.

'I'm going to ask you to let me handle this. *If* it's one of my kind, I'll find the one responsible and deal with them.'

From the look on his face, Sommers hated the idea, and I didn't need to sense the subtle chemical changes in his body to know that. This was not how things were done in his world—not an accepted investigative procedure, and he was not in control.

'Why should I trust you?'

'You want to do this another way?'

He looked to be weighing up his options. 'Okay, we'll try your way first.'

'I'll find the one responsible, because I'm the only one who can.'

He removed a notebook from his pocket and wrote down a number. 'You can reach me on this.' He ripped the page out and slid it across the table to me. 'But if we find another blood-drained body, I'm coming after you.'

'Don't threaten me, Sommers.' I leaned closer to him. 'Or you might just find yourself suffering from pernicious anaemia.'

He paled. 'You son of a bitch!' He slid his chair back and walked out.

I left the café and made my way to the nearest florist, where I picked a single long-stemmed crimson rose with a matching silken ribbon tied around the stem. I added a card, wrote a brief message to Laura and tied it to the stem. Now all that was left was to drive to her flat and leave it at her door.

I parked in front of her block of units and walked through the main corridor, stopping at the first door on the right. I didn't sense her presence inside, but her perfume permeated the corridor—a delicious fruity scent with a hint of jasmine. It was the same one she had worn last night. I inhaled deeply as her face appeared in my mind. There was no denying I was looking forward to seeing her again.

Within fifteen minutes of leaving the rose at her door—and acknowledging Jake and Cal, who were on guard duty at her flat tonight—I'd driven to my city apartment. Weakness had spread further, and my body was shaking. Bright light, which streamed in through the harbour-facing windows, and which I had enjoyed these last fifty years, now hurt my eyes.

After lowering the outside shutters and downing a bag of Judith's blood from the fridge, I finally dragged my body up the stairs to the loft. Without bothering to undress, I dropped into my bed and let the regenerating sleep take me.

CHAPTER 9
MY GIRL

LAURA

After turning my back on Matt and Alec, I went in search of a suitable dress for the Ritual on Monday night. The walk, together with the banal business of shopping, gave me much-needed time to think and adjust to my new role, as a walking blood bank to creatures I once believed existed only in fiction. Every now and then, as I scoured the boutiques and tried on countless gowns, my eyes focused on my neck as I imagined two puncture marks there.

Each time, it made me shiver, but what I found more disturbing was the image of Alec Munro's mouth on my neck. It didn't so much fill me with fear as with a growing excitement.

What was wrong with me?

I shook my head, checked myself in the mirror, and walked out with a lovely pale, silver-blue silk dress with delicate shoulder straps and a pair of peep-toe silver shoes. Since I didn't have a matching evening bag, I went looking for one of those, too. By the time I got back to my flat, it was around six in the evening and Matt hadn't rung or messaged. That worried me. Unless he popped around, I'd be spending Saturday evening on my own. I couldn't begin to imagine what had happened between him and Alec after I'd left.

As I walked down the corridor to my front door, my eyes caught something on the ground—a single red rose with a note attached. I picked it up.

Dear Laura,
Looking forward to Monday night.
Will come for you at 9pm. SEP
Alec

'Well, I'm committed now,' I said aloud, hoping no one was within earshot. I raised the flower and inhaled its sweet scent, wishing Matt would give me flowers occasionally.

As I unlocked my door, I heard a movement from the living area. My first thought was burglars. But what did I have worth stealing? I dropped my bags and removed one of my shoes. It had a pointy heel and hopefully could cause some damage. I peered into the room.

'What are you thinking of doing with that shoe, Laura?' a cool male voice asked.

It had come so unexpectedly from the direction of the sofa that I squealed. 'Matt! What are you doing here?'

'We swapped keys, remember? And for your information, I've been here most of the afternoon, waiting for you to come home. Where've you been?'

The temptation to throw the shoe at him was overwhelming, but I controlled the urge, lowered my arm and switched on the light instead. Matt was comfortably settled on the sofa, feet up on my coffee table looking annoyed.

Well, that wasn't my fault. 'I do have a mobile you know. Why didn't you call?'

'I prefer to see you.'

'I told you I was going shopping.' I pointed to the bags on the floor.

Matt got up from the sofa and made his way toward me. My stomach did a little flip. He must have gone home to shower and change, for he wore a clean, tight-fitting, light-grey T-shirt that showed every muscle. Without a word, he took the shoe from my hand and dropped it, drew me tightly to him and lifted my chin to meet his mouth. For the next few minutes I forgot what day it was, with his lips firm on mine, caressing, teasing, demanding.

'My girl,' he murmured, caressing the back of my neck before gently removing the band around my ponytail to let my hair fall freely over my shoulders and down my back. Interweaving his fingers in its thickness, he pressed my mouth more forcibly to his.

I stood on tiptoes, reached up and slipped my arms around his neck. His hair felt damp as I twirled some of it around my fingers.

'In a better mood now than you were this morning?' I asked.

'Yeah. I wasn't happy finding the bed empty when I woke up.'

'I thought that might've been it.'

After kissing me again, he said, 'By the way, were you thinking of doing something violent with that shoe?'

'Uh huh.'

He shook with laughter before lowering his head to kiss me again. 'Laura, what if I really was a burglar?'

'I'd hope my scream would have scared you off.'

'I'm going to install a burglar alarm in here.'

'To keep you away?'

He laughed, and went back to nibbling my lower lip.

I enjoyed his kisses, although it seemed as if he were trying too hard. Ensuring I was his? Just then my stomach rumbled, reminding me I hadn't eaten anything today, and I had a feeling Matt hadn't either.

'You eaten yet?'

'No, and by the sounds of things, neither have you.'

'You like stroganoff? Got some in the freezer. Cooked up a whole batch the other day.'

'Love some.'

While I reheated our meal, Matt set the table. 'I've got tickets for the footy Monday night. Starts at seven thirty. I can pick you up after work.'

Oh crap! 'Matt, I can't go. I've got to attend a special ceremony that introduces me to … them.' I couldn't say the word "vampire." 'It's always held on the first full moon after the Bloodgifted comes of age.'

Matt looked like thunder. 'The same night?'

'If I don't show, they'll come after me and Alec won't be able to protect me from them all.'

'Oh, hell!' He slammed the dishes down and one cracked.

'Hey, that's my only dinner set, Matthew Sommers!'

He swore.

I put the stroganoff on the table and circled my arms around his waist. 'It's only one night. The next takes place fifty years from now. You can survive without me for one night.'

'How you getting there?'

I hesitated. 'Alec's picking me up.'

Matt's face darkened further. I placed my finger on his lips to stop any protest. 'Alec Munro's my chauffer and my guardian. That's all. Trust me?'

'It's him I don't trust.'

I reached up and kissed him.

'Okay, I'll go with Jonno.' Jonathan Besser was Matt's partner. 'But, if Munro makes a pass at you, I'll personally rip his teeth out.'

I laughed and reached up to kiss him again. While we ate, I related what Alec had told me about the Ritual, omitting the if-he-loses-control-while-feeding-I-die bit. It was best Matt didn't know about that. He'd go ballistic.

'What?' Matt's eyes frosted over when I explained my prearranged "feeding sessions" with Alec that were to be a few times a week.

I sighed. 'Matt, he needs me, so he's not going to do anything stupid. It'll only be an hour at the most, and he's driving me there and back.'

Matt huffed and shook his head. 'I hate this. I hate this whole damn thing.'

I sat on his lap. 'I know, but there's nothing either of us can do about it. Look at it as the price for my protection.'

'I can think of another way.' His eyes narrowed. 'Eliminate the lot of them.'

My blood chilled. 'Matt, you can't! There's too many—over two hundred in this city alone.' The thought of him turning vampire hunter and going after Alec and Luc horrified me. He could be killed, but what struck me more was that I cared for Alec's safety. I cupped Matt's face in my hands. 'Promise me you won't do anything rash.

Let me handle it. My family's been doing this for over a thousand years, and as you can see, we're still here. Please don't interfere.'

He looked at me long and hard before finally letting out a resigned breath, although the stormy look in his eyes didn't disappear. 'I won't make any promises.'

'I'll take that as a "yes".'

'You can wrap me around your little finger, you know that?' He slapped me lightly on the bottom.

'Liar! You always do whatever you want and somehow get me to go along.'

He laughed, rose with me in his arms and headed for the bedroom.

'Matt … I can't!'

'Why? Is it that time of the month?'

'No, it's not that. But if we make love, I'll conceive for sure. Aunt Judy told me last night.'

'I've got protection.'

'You want to risk it? If I fall pregnant now, our child will carry my gene, and … well, you know what that means.'

Matt put me down. 'So, when can we have sex?'

'I don't know.' I leaned back against the wall and hoped he wouldn't press me.

'This is ridiculous! First the game and now this. When will it end, Laura?'

'Let me check with Aunt Judy. She might know a way around.' There has to be a way. Surely my aunt and Luc didn't abstain all these years?

'And if not?'

'I don't have the answers. This is new to me, too.'

He let out an exasperated breath. 'Okay, fine. I take it oral isn't off limits?'

'Not at all. You may touch and taste all you want, Detective Sommers.'

A slow smile spread across his face, highlighting his dimple. 'You do taste delicious, Miss Dantonville.'

I laughed as he picked me up—caveman style, over his shoulder—and carried me into the bedroom.

CHAPTER 10
THE RITUAL

LAURA

On Monday night Alec arrived promptly at nine. When I opened my door, there he stood, looking absolutely gorgeous in a black tuxedo – what, no long, black cloak?—dazzling smile and a bouquet of flowers. His lavender eyes widened as he handed me the bouquet.

'You're a vision, Laura.'

'Thank you.'

He took hold of my hand and brought it to his lips; his eyes never left my face.

'Let me put the flowers in water before we go.' Alec followed me to the kitchen. Well, there went another vampire myth—vampires didn't need to be specifically invited in.

'Nice apartment. How long have you lived here?'

'About eleven years.'

I'd bought the unit after finally persuading my parents I needed some independence—a place of my own. The problem was, most people believed I was in my late teens and too young to live on my own. Even the Real-Estate agent hadn't taken me seriously till I produced my driver's license, which had shown my age as thirty-nine.

I arranged Alec's flowers in a crystal vase and placed them in the centre of my dining-room table. The mix of daisies, baby's breath and pink roses, interspersed with greenery, were lovely. I inhaled the delicious scent of the roses and heard a snap. Alec had broken off a rose bud and slid it into the comb that secured a section of my hair. His hand slid down the loose strands while his eyes travelled slowly over my face, down the length of my body and back again. It was so sensual; I wasn't sure whether he was trying to seduce me or whether this was normal vampire behaviour. Either way, it made my toes curl.

'You treat all Ingenii like this?'

He chuckled. 'Only showing my appreciation.'

'I'm flattered.'

His gaze held mine, and it took some effort to break away. I collected my purse from the sofa. 'Where are we going?'

'Vaucluse. The Ritual is being held there.'

Rich part of town, big houses. 'Will there be a lot of people?'

'Several hundred.'

My breath caught in my throat. He turned me around to face him, his hands firm yet gentle on my shoulders. 'I won't let anyone touch you, and I'll do my best to make my bite as painless as possible.'

I shuddered. 'I was bitten by a dog once, and it hurt like hell.'

Something flickered in his eyes. 'If that dog were still alive, I'd kill it.'

I gasped. Was he serious? 'There's no need … really. It was a long time ago.' I was horrified and made a mental note not to buy a pet for the next fifty years—just in case. 'What about your bite?'

'Vampire saliva contains a type of anaesthetic which deadens the pain – when we choose to use it. I will tonight.'

He'd better. 'And you won't lose control?' I tried to keep the tremor from my voice.

'I won't. Promise.' He smiled, offered me his arm and led me to his car—a blue Mercedes Sports.

'Do all vampires drive pretentious sports cars?' I waved my hand at the vehicle. I needed to focus on something other than the coming ceremony.

'You want to take the bus?'

'You got something against my proletariat sensibilities?'

He chuckled and opened the door for me. 'Laura, your family lives in Earlwood, not exactly working class.'

'True, but I can sympathise.'

'The Mercedes has more fuel economy than most small cars, and it's better mechanically.'

I laughed. 'Trying to justify yourself, huh? Any excuse to drive a hot sports car,' I teased as I buckled my seatbelt.

Alec lowered his head, shook it, but when he looked back at me, his eyes were smiling. 'Okay. I surrender. Can I drive now?'

I flashed him a smile as he started the engine, and it really purred. I'd never been in a sports car. This was a new experience and I was going to make the most of it.

'How fast does it go?' I started to play with the shiny buttons on the dashboard.

'Not so fast that your boyfriend will arrest me.'

'He'd enjoy doing that.' I stared out at the city lights as Alec wove through the Monday-night traffic.

'I'm sure he would. How long have you known each other?'

'About four months.' Really, we were still getting to know each other.

'Enough time to form an attachment,' he said quietly.

It was hard to tell whether he meant that rhetorically or not. When I didn't answer straight away he raised his eyebrows.

'Yes, I suppose it is.'

'Do you love him?'

I didn't know what to say. Our relationship was still relatively new and I wasn't sure how I felt. Nor did I particularly wish to discuss it with Alec Munro. 'Why do you ask?'

'You didn't answer my question.'

'And I'm not going to. It's private.' I turned my head to look at him, but he kept his gaze on the road.

Neither of us spoke. I would have loved to know what he was thinking. Then he said something I didn't expect. 'You know how to dance, Laura? As in someone's arms, not standing in front of your partner and jiggling.'

'Jiggling?'

He smiled. 'You know what I mean.'

I really had to concentrate, as his smile had a way of leaving me breathless. 'Oh, I think I can manage.'

Part of my training as a primary school teacher was in physical education, with dancing part of the curriculum. I could do a mean waltz.

'There's dancing and entertainment after the ceremony.'

'Vampires dance?'

He laughed. 'Wait till you see the band leader.'

Curiouser and Curiouser.

His face grew serious. 'Laura, when we arrive, please don't go wandering anywhere on your own. Many among my kind can't be trusted. They're envious and … dangerous. They'd love to possess you. I wouldn't put it past some to try to abduct you … stop the ceremony from taking place.'

'You didn't tell me this before.' And I wish he hadn't told me now.

'I didn't want to frighten you.'

More like, he didn't want to scare me off from attending tonight. Good move. 'But once the Ritual's over, I'm safe?'

'Yes.'

I took a deep breath and willed my heartbeat to slow to its normal pace.

'I have friends here as well, one in particular who'll protect you at all costs. My sire, Luc. The ceremony is being held at his house.'

'I met him at my aunt's place last night.' And he terrified Matt so much he would have gone for his gun if he'd been wearing it.

Alec glanced at me again. 'He's one of the five officiates.'

'Oh, okay. You mentioned the other night that he was my grandfather, Owen's guardian.'

'That's right.'

My family had kept such a secret all these generations. Granddad knew I'd inherit one day, yet he had barely ever spoken to me. He'd been a busy doctor with his own practice and family never figured high in his priorities, but still, you'd think on his deathbed—a few years ago—he could have mentioned something.

My mind reeled with questions. One was whether Alec had ever known my grandfather, but that would have to wait. We turned into a private lane. Massive iron gates loomed ahead. Security guards in grey uniform scrutinised the car as we entered.

Did he say house? The sandstone building at the end of the driveway was a magnificent neo-Gothic mansion of a style popular sometime in the late nineteenth century. A copper-clad tower dominated one side. I gaped at turrets, arches with stained-glass windows and ornate gables, while stone gargoyles stared impassively down at all who entered.

Perfect place for a vampire gathering.

As Alec drove in, I rolled down the windows and inhaled the heady scent of eucalypt from the trees that lined the expansive driveway. Crushed gum nuts and leaves crunched under the tyres as he turned the car into a large clearing capable of accommodating up to a hundred vehicles. An area had been cordoned off for parking and was filled almost to capacity with limousines and luxury cars, including one or two Ferraris, a Porsche, even a sleek red Corvette.

'Sports cars!' I turned to him with an I-rest-my-case look.

He smiled and eased into a spot marked: Reserved for Princeps. Coming around to my side, he opened the door and linked my arm through his as we made our way to the front entrance. 'Laura, stay close to me the whole night. Promise me.' A deep crease marred the smoothness of his brow.

'Promise.'

The impressive, heavily lacquered front door had eucalyptus leaves carved into it along the outside edge, and two multi-coloured glass window panels greeted the visitor at eye level. I did a quick scan for cobwebs and scuttling spiders, but there were none. Then I wondered if we'd be greeted by the obligatory creepy butler, like Lurch from the *Addams Family*. I held my breath as the door opened. Golden light flooded the porch, and soft music filtered through as a tall, blonde-haired man stepped out. It was Luc Lebrettan.

I think I gave an audible sigh of relief.

He smiled warmly and lifted my hand to his lips. 'Laura, it's a pleasure to see you once more.'

Again, I experienced a sense of familiarity and felt the same prickling as on the previous night.

'I believe you and Luc have already met?' Alec asked.

'Yes, at my aunt's.' Alec had said he was one of the five officiates, which meant he had to be one of the oldest vampires here.

'There has been a change in the order of events. The Ritual will be performed first, followed by the usual festivities,' Luc said and glanced briefly at Alec. 'I'm sure Alec has explained to you the situation we would like to avoid. Ensuring your safety is our first priority.' There was the same hint of a French accent I'd noticed at our first meeting.

'I understand,' I said.

'Let's go in.' He tucked my arm into his so I was sandwiched between him and Alec.

Luc led us through the house, but there was no time to stop and admire the amazing interior. A marble staircase led to an upper floor divided into two separate wings. Above us loomed stone arches balanced on pedestals in the shape of sculpted angels. Stencilled images of griffins, dragons and other medieval mythological creatures decorated the walls. Our footsteps echoed on the white marble floor, which was here and there interspersed with boldly coloured Victorian tiles featuring scrolls, fleur-de-lis and acanthus leaves.

I leaned over to Alec and nudged him in the ribs. 'Why does Luc own such a castle?' I whispered.

'It reminds him of home,' Alec replied in a low voice.

'France, Laura. I'm originally from the Rhone valley. My family has a Chateau there. I'll tell you about it sometime.'

I'd forgotten about vampire hearing.

We reached a set of double doors. Waiting for us were eight figures who inclined their heads as we approached. Among them, in a floor-length white silk cloak, was Aunt Judy. The fabric swished as she came to my side to hug me.

'Don't be nervous, dear. I'm sure Alec explained everything. I've been through this myself. It's going to be fine.' She smiled reassuringly.

The other figures—seven men and one woman—regarded me curiously. They were a mix of ages and impossibly attractive. Did being transformed into a vampire make one stunning, or did they simply pick on the young and beautiful? Three were wrapped in gold cloaks, while the other four were covered in scarlet. I could just make out sword tips protruding from beneath the cloaks of the four in red.

'Laura.' Alec drew my attention to the gold-cloaked figures. 'I would like to introduce the Elders—Maris, Kwame and Zhao.' I inclined my head, assuming that was the correct form of greeting.

The woman, Maris, was a tall, stunning blonde. I may as well have been invisible, for she barely acknowledged me as she locked her lavender gaze on Alec. Her eyes narrowed at seeing our linked hands. Was there some history between them?

Kwame, the most striking of the group, was a well-built black man who stood at least six feet five. He had a regal air about him, but his smile was welcoming. It was difficult to place his age, but he could have been anywhere in his late thirties. The gold cloak made a perfect contrast to his dark skin.

Beside him stood Zhao, the shortest of the five. He stood about five feet ten. His bald head gleamed in the light and even though he didn't smile, his eyes showed a depth of understanding that only came through great age. I wondered how old he was.

'Laura, I'd like you to meet my friends, Terens, Jake, Cal and Sam.' He introduced the four scarlet-cloaked figures.

They were all so tall, like Alec, that I was glad I wore a pair of high-heeled shoes. It made looking up at them a little easier.

Terens smiled and winked at me. His straight deep-auburn hair fell into his eyes when he dipped his head in greeting, and a diamond stud blinked in one ear. Next to Alec, he was the sexiest man I'd ever seen. But that wasn't the reason I took an instant liking to him. For one strange moment, I felt as if I'd known him, somewhere, long ago. Just as quickly, I dismissed the idea.

Jake stepped forward, and he too gave a low bow and broad smile. His long, wavy brown hair, close-cropped beard and aquiline nose gave him an aristocratic appearance. 'Welcome to the family, Laura,' he said.

I liked him too.

Of the three, Cal had the stockiest build. With hair the colour of wet sand, and dimples in both cheeks when his lips curled up into a closed-mouthed smile, he looked decidedly roguish. I had the feeling it wouldn't take much to make him laugh.

But, I could be wrong, for his right hand lovingly stroked the hilt of the sword at his side.

Lastly, there was Sam, who, with his light-brown hair and gentle lavender eyes would make any male model envious. He gave me a smile that faded as his eyes turned to the woman, Maris, and speared her with a … warning? His hand, too, rested on the hilt of his sword. Just as I was determining whether I should be worried, Zhao came forward, slipped a white silk cloak over Alec's shoulders and tied the smooth fabric in place with ribbons.

Alec searched for my hand, grasped it and squeezed reassuringly. I felt a sudden surge of electricity. It was not the first time this had happened, and I really wanted to attribute it to the rings, yet something deep within told me otherwise. Did he feel it too? His eyes appeared to turn a darker shade.

He lifted my hand to his lips. That's when I noticed the glow. His ring shone brightly and bathed his face—and mine—in a ruby-like aura. In my own ring, the eyes of the serpents blazed.

Now I knew its significance. No one seeing that would be crazy enough to challenge. My aunt looked overjoyed as she and the officiates in white cloaks took up their positions in front of us. The four in red took up the rear.

'Ready?' Luc asked, as he threw a gold cloak over his shoulders.

I briefly closed my eyes and took a deep breath. 'Ready.'

He pushed open the doors, which folded back on themselves, to reveal an expansive lawn that fell away to the water's edge. In front of us, a roped-off pathway led to a white wisteria-covered pavilion, standing on three sandstone platforms, elevating it above the level of the surrounding garden. I gasped as hundreds of pale faces turned towards us. The crowd silently rose from their seats. Music played in the distance.

Too aware of their eyes on me, my first instinct was to turn and run. There was such a mix of people and many looked no older than their twenties. It was impossible to tell who was vampire and who was donsang until I came close enough to make out their eyes. There wasn't a fang or reptile eye in sight.

Luc must have sensed my hesitation for, like Alec, he grasped my other hand just as the Elders started the procession and we stepped onto the grassy path. I was determined not to let my fear of being the centre of attention—especially among this particular company—paralyse me.

Taking slow, deep breaths, I lifted my chin and looked defiantly around.

Alec squeezed my hand. 'Good girl,' he whispered.

The assembled guests were in formal wear, black tie for men, evening gowns for women. There wasn't a black cape, swishy cloak or "Morticia" dress in sight. I hadn't expected stunning designer creations. Vampires clearly had taste.

As we progressed towards the pavilion, a few murmured "Princeps" and "Ingenii" came from the crowd. All inclined their heads slightly as we passed. Waiting under the arch stood another tall, gold-cloaked figure—a strikingly handsome man with olive skin and dark hair. It was difficult to gauge his age. In his right hand gleamed the longest, most menacing sword I had ever seen.

'Who is that?' I whispered to Alec.

'Marcus Antonius Pulcher, the Cardinal Elder and your ancestor. He's leading the ceremony.'

I looked on, stunned, until out of the corner of my eye I glimpsed a familiar face in the crowd. My Dad. Alec told me my parents would be here, but the seat next to him was empty. It didn't surprise me. Mum simply wouldn't have had the strength to cope with something like this.

Dad smiled sadly at me as we passed.

We reached the pavilion steps, and I desperately hoped no one would suddenly jump out and challenge Alec. Sometime during our procession, the music had stopped. The absolute silence was eerie. It was as if everyone waited for something to happen. My nervousness increased.

Light glinted on the silken cloaks of the Elders in front of us as they ascended the sandstone steps. All bowed their heads towards Marcus's imposing figure. Alec and Luc—with me between— followed behind.

'Marcus.' Luc dipped his head and placed my hand in the man's large outstretched palm. He bowed to me and kissed my fingertips. I looked into the saddest pair of eyes I'd ever encountered.

'Welcome, Laura,' he said in a rich baritone voice before directing me to face the assembled crowd.

Alec released my other hand and moved slightly to my right as the Elders arranged themselves in a crescent behind us. Aunt Judy stepped to my side, faced the crowd with me and took my hand.

Everyone waited.

Marcus Antonius bowed deeply to the gathering and his voice boomed in the silence. 'I, Marcus Antonius Pulcher, welcome you all, Brethren. We gather to recognise the new Ingenii. Child of the House of the Antonii, descendant of Antonia Pulchra, my daughter and her son, Paulus....'

I listened, rapt, as he recited a long list of names. The first were all Latin, followed by French, until the last few. They were English and culminated in me. I realised he was individually naming each Ingenii, from the very beginning till the present—an oral history.

After he completed the recitation, my Aunt Judy spoke. 'I, Judith Mary Dantonville, of the House of the Antonii, do this night, in the presence of the Brethren, willingly relinquish my position as Ingenii and pass it to Laura Anne Dantonville, of the House of the Antonii.'

While she spoke, Maris came up behind her, removed the cloak from around her shoulders, and placed it over mine. She let the silken ties hang down the front of my gown. My aunt gave me a smile and squeezed my hand before stepping off the dais to take her seat beside my dad.

Marcus Antonius leaned over and whispered, 'Laura, just repeat what I say.'

I nodded. Alec's presence close behind me made my body tingle.

'I, Laura Anne Dantonville, of the House of the Antonii,' I repeated nervously after Marcus, 'this night willingly accept, in the presence of the Brethren, my position by blood as Ingenii to him, whom I choose as my guardian.'

'Well done,' Marcus whispered in my ear. He raised my hand to expose the serpent ring and addressed the crowd. 'The Ritual will now commence. *Sanguis ingenii, Laura, est deligere.* The *Ingenii*, Laura is to choose.'

I was surprised to hear him speaking Latin. Just how old was this ceremony? And how many here could understand it? Maybe that's why he repeated everything in English.

'I choose Alec Munro,' I said.

'*Quid audient provocare?* Who dares challenge?'

A flash of red caught my eye as four scarlet-clad figures strode to the front of the dais, positioned themselves on either side of Alec and me and simultaneously threw back their cloaks to reveal their broad swords.

I held my breath.

No one moved. No one uttered a word, although a few glances through narrowed eyes were aimed at us. Marcus Antonius waited. Alec's face was taut and his mouth pressed into a tight line. Though not reptilian, his eyes were fierce.

Once again, Marcus Antonius's voice cut through the stillness. '*Nullus.* No one', he declared triumphantly. '*Sino serpens dicere!* Allow the serpents to speak!'

Alec moved to stand next to me, and Marcus Antonius placed my hand in his, intertwined our fingers and raised them in the air with our rings facing the crowd. A ripple of sound grew into an acclamation. I caught my breath as brilliant scarlet light flared from our linked hands and illuminated the assembled crowd, making them appear as if bathed in blood.

Alec turned his face to me. His eyes were a deep jacaranda-blue, and the dazzling smile he wore took my breath away.

Gasps and murmurs came from the crowd, but there was no time to ponder its significance as Marcus Antonius held up his hand for silence.

'*Consummato*. Consummate,' he announced.

Alec released my hand and took a step away. From the corner of my eye, I saw the movement of gold as Maris and Zhao came forward, removed our white cloaks and let them drop to the floor. As Zhao resumed his position in the crescent, Maris leaned over me, her breath cool on my neck as she slowly lowered the chiffon strap of my dress. Her proximity and the cold touch of her fingers made me shiver. Then, as she swept my hair to one side exposing my throat, her hand seemed to linger, and I dared a quick glance. For the briefest of moments, naked hunger flashed from her eyes. Just as suddenly it was gone, but the image remained, a reminder that I was surrounded by creatures who lived in darkness and thrived on human blood. How many here would kill Alec to possess me if they got the chance?

My stomach tightened. But it was too late to turn and run, and showing fear among these creatures would be risky.

After exposing my left shoulder and neck, Maris resumed her place in the crescent, but the foul impression she left behind wrapped itself around me like a shroud.

'Alec,' I barely breathed.

'Don't show fear,' he whispered. 'Remember what I told you.'

His voice had an instant comforting effect. He moved to stand behind me. One hand encircled my waist, drawing me close to him while his other hand gently lifted my chin and angled my head back onto his shoulder.

Okay, here it comes. I shut my eyes tight.

I heard his quick intake of breath and felt his heart beat strongly against my back. Mine beat just as hard. I whispered so low I may have been simply mouthing the words, but I knew he would hear. 'Will it hurt?'

'Just a sting.' His voice was thick. 'I'll make it as quick and painless as possible. Think of something to distract you,' he whispered back.

Close my eyes and think of chocolate cake, perhaps? I gritted my teeth and hoped it would be over soon.

I felt his cool lips on my naked shoulder as he made his slow, sensual way along my collarbone towards my neck. Was this part of the Ritual or was he deliberately trying to distract me? If it was the latter, then it was certainly working.

Then it came—the sharp sting as his fangs penetrated my skin. I let out a faint, brief scream. My back arched, which threw my head more deeply into the hard muscle of his shoulder. I clutched at his arm. Alec's grip tightened, and his hand cupping my chin and jaw, held me like a vice.

Locked in his powerful embrace, an odd sense of reality settled over me. He was feeding from my body—my blood was being drawn out as he sucked and swallowed. Once or twice he shuddered. Then strangely, a sense of contentment flooded through me, and my breathing evened.

He kept drinking, taking larger and larger gulps. My sense of peace increased until I floated in nothingness. Then dizziness hit— and panic. He was taking too much.

'Alec, stop.' I whispered. 'Please!'

My dizziness increased, and I tugged at his arm, my fingers gripping so hard that my nails dug into his flesh.

His body tensed, his fangs withdrew, and his tongue gently licked the wound.

It was over.

Then, unexpectedly, he turned my head toward him, placed his mouth hard on mine and deftly parted my lips. I tasted my blood on his tongue, and as his kiss deepened, a new sensation flooded through me erasing all others. Excitement.

Unbidden, my tongue rose to meet his, and I feverishly returned his kiss. I forgot the watching guests, my father and my aunt, even Matt. There was only Alec. He filled my senses, and that moment was the only thing that mattered. I didn't want the kiss to end, and then, to my embarrassment, my body began to tremble. My eyes opened as his mouth lifted from mine. I looked straight into a dark purple whorl as Alec stared down at me, his breathing as ragged as my own. It was Marcus Antonius's voice that jolted us both into awareness.

'*Magni Investigo*. Great Ones, investigate,' he commanded.

Alec still held me, supporting me as my weak legs threatened to give way. I was vaguely aware of the glint of light on golden silk as the Elders surrounded us and one by one placed their fingers on the puncture wound on my neck.

Each nodded to Marcus in confirmation.

'*Vidistis*. You have seen. First Blood has been taken,' he declared. '*Approbo Princeps Alexandrius Monrovius*. Acclaim Alexander Munro as princeps.'

The seated crowd rose and clapped.

'Are you all right?' Alec whispered anxiously into my ear.

'Y-e-s.'

'You're trembling.'

'Mmmm.' I couldn't speak as my body shook from a combination of blood loss and shock.

'Here, drink this.' Luc had come to my side with a glass of brandy as Marcus Antonius and the Elders went to greet the gathering crowd at the foot of the stairs. Alec scooped me up and carried me to a seat in a quiet corner of the pavilion. I tried to sip the brandy, but my body shook so much he had to place his hands over mine to guide it to my lips.

The fiery liquid flowed down my throat and warmed me. But another sort of fire shot through me at the touch of Alec's hands on mine.

'Another one,' Alec ordered.

For once I didn't mind being told what to do, and I took a larger gulp this time. The heat of the alcohol mingled with the other new sensation within me.

Alec removed his jacket and placed it around my shoulders while I sipped the rest of the brandy.

'Laura!' I heard my dad's voice at the same time as I saw him push his way past the Elders and bound up the stairs towards me. The next instant he enveloped me in a bear hug.

Alec stepped back.

'Let's see what he's done to you.' My dad's face looked stricken as he stared at the puncture marks on my neck.

'Dad, please don't.' I gathered my hair and used it to cover that side of my neck from his and other prying eyes. I'd been prodded like a piece of meat enough.

'Baby, you're shaking.' He pulled Alec's jacket closer around my shoulders.

'I'll be okay, Dad. The brandy's helping.'

'My baby girl.' The emotion in his voice was raw and for the first time in my life, I saw tears well in his eyes.

I heard a low growl from Luc. Dad angled his head to look up at him. For a brief moment, their gazes locked. Dad's body trembled, not from fear but anger. I could see it on his face when he turned back to me.

Luc watched us, his own expression threatening. I didn't have time to think about it as Dad spoke to me.

'Those animals!' He choked. 'When you screamed, Judith had to restrain me from running up there and ripping him off you.'

'Oh, Dad.' I hugged him. 'Why didn't you tell me about this?'

He pulled back and shook his head. 'How, Laura? I've been dreading this day since you were a baby, hoping, somehow, it would never come.' Sorrow punctuated his every word. 'How could I tell you … prepare you for something like … this?' A combination of anger, disgust and pain crossed his face, and I began to understand a little of the burden he had carried all these years.

'How's Mum?'

He couldn't answer and his face crumbled. I hugged him again as a thick lump welled in my throat. My parents had kept this a secret all these years, and the fact that she wasn't here tonight spoke volumes. She simply wouldn't have had the mental strength to deal with it. My dad was always the strong one, like his sister.

Over his shoulder I glanced up at my aunt. She'd followed my father up the steps and stood hand in hand with Luc. They looked concerned and … something else I couldn't quite put my finger on.

'Laura, you're our little girl,' my dad quietly said in my ear. 'No matter what happens, you'll always be our little girl.'

I pulled back and looked at him. It was such an odd thing to say.

'I know.' I patted his shoulder. 'But I'm a big girl now – I've just come of age.' I tried to make it sound trivial. 'I'll be okay. Aunt Judy was, and so will I.' I kissed his wrinkled cheek and whispered, 'Please don't worry about me.'

'Now, *that's* not possible,' he said.

Music began to play and caterers, balancing trays of food in their hands, mingled through the crowd.

Food for the humans.

Chairs were being cleared to create space for dancing. At the far end of the roped-off area, tabled seating had been prepared, and some groups were already converging to claim a spot. Others had taken to the dance floor and were moving to the strains of *Moonlight Serenade*.

On impulse, I glanced at the bandleader. Alec had mentioned him in the car during the drive here. No, it couldn't be! Yet he bore a striking resemblance to the 1940s bandleader, Glenn Miller. But then, who knows? It would certainly explain his sudden disappearance before the end of the war.

Alec approached and I smiled up at him. My trembling had ceased, and I was hungry. 'Feeling better?' he asked.

'Much.'

He looked at my dad. 'Do you mind if I take Laura and give her something to eat, John?'

My dad's expression wasn't exactly friendly, but I knew Alec understood.

'I'm okay, Dad.' I squeezed his arm.

'All right,' he said with a sigh and rose, leaving us.

I felt warmer and started to remove Alec's jacket from around my shoulders.

'No. Leave it on for now, Laura. I want to be sure you're over the shock.'

'Is this Dr Munro speaking?' I teased.

It was good to see his dazzling smile again. 'Absolutely.' He placed his arm around my waist, helped me up and led me to one of the food-laden tables. 'Eat,' he ordered.

'Stop being so bossy,' I said, while biting into a delicious salmon canapé.

He took a plate and chose a bit of everything on offer. Finding two available chairs, he sat me down in one and placed the laden dish in front of me.

'Are you expecting me to eat all that?'

'I intend to enjoy dancing with you the rest of the evening.'

He loosened his bow tie and undid the top buttons of his shirt. When we first met, he'd done the same thing, and I realised then, he was not a man for formal wear. Straddling the other chair, he rested his arms on the back and gazed at me.

'And you're just going to watch?' I said.

'That's right. To make sure you eat.'

There was no arguing with him and besides, he was right. The food helped, and soon my strength returned. As for my response to his unexpected kiss, I simply dismissed it as a natural reaction to being bitten by a vampire. After all, Aunt Judy said my libido would be affected.

It must be normal—I think.

CHAPTER 11
FRIENDS AND OTHER CREATURES

ALEC

It was done. The worst part of the evening was over. Now she could relax and enjoy the rest of the night and, hopefully, forget about her attachment to that human. And just for tonight, I wanted to forget what Luc wanted me to do.

Her courage impressed me. She'd been through a traumatic experience, yet here she was smiling up at me and enjoying the evening as if this was just another formal event. She could have refused to come, taken the first plane out of here, even though they could have found her and dragged her through the Ritual against her will.

The colour returned to her cheeks as she ate. I'd nearly taken too much. The blood lust hit the moment I experienced that first incredible taste. It was more potent than anything I could have imagined. My body felt on fire after the first sip—burning, strength growing and filling me with unquenchable energy. I wanted to roar with the sheer magnitude of it. Only her voice prevented me losing control.

If I'd kept going, would the Elders have been able to stop me in time? Laura could have been the shortest-lived Ingenii in Brethren history. No more Ingenii, no more curse; the end of the Dantonville Legacy. So simple. So why didn't I do it? Was it because she was Luc's little girl, and in spite of his dubious dealings, I liked him? Possibly, but that wasn't all. It had something to do with Laura herself – she intrigued, even fascinated me, and I wanted to find out why.

'Alec.' Jake waved me over to join him and the other men.

He'd recently arrived back in the country after a few months' absence checking out a growing threat to the Principate in Eastern Europe. Like Terens, Jake—Justinus as he was originally known – had been one of the Roman legionaries in Marcus Antonius's patrol. He'd also been a physician and so understood the struggle I experienced as I underwent the change from human to vampire.

Over the centuries, he'd shown himself to be a skilled diplomat, and Luc often sent him to quell serious disputes among the Brethren in other parts of the world. When not employed in that capacity, he—like Sam, Terens and Cal—were part of the Ingenii's security. For the last fifty years, they'd been an unseen nocturnal guard around Judith and Laura.

I waved back and said I'd join them later. They were my brothers, more so than any I could have had in reality. They all regarded Laura as their surrogate niece. And tonight, just like every other night since she was born, they were her protectors.

And not one of them had any idea what Luc had ordered me to do.

CHAPTER 12
VAMPIRE BALL

LAURA

The summer sunset melted into a clear, starry night. Fairy lights, draped around the pavilion and woven through the branches of the trees near the water's edge, glittered and danced in unison with the twinkling lights of the city on the gently undulating harbour waters. It was magical.

The band struck up the *Charleston,* and one of the Brethren came and asked me to dance. I wondered if he had lived through the nineteen twenties, as he danced particularly well. His name was Russell, a good-looking man with a jovial smile. Luckily, the *Charleston* was one of my favourite dances.

Russell knew how to tell a joke, and I found myself laughing at his silly punch lines. I wanted to ask him how he became a blood drinker, but—unsure of vampire etiquette—I said nothing. When the music finished, he held onto me for the next one, but I wasn't ready for a body-hugging tango.

Over his shoulder my eyes connected with Alec's, and I sent him a silent plea. He answered with an understanding grin, courteously cut in, and escorted me back to our table.

'Is he always like that?' I asked.

'Oh yes, he loves parties and beautiful women.' He looked down at me with a wide smile. 'Owns a movie studio and is always on the lookout for fresh talent.' He suggestively lifted one eyebrow.

'Uh huh, okaaay. Well, regardless, he's a lot of fun. You know he tells some dirty jokes, but they're actually very funny.' I'd surprised myself, as I generally avoided humour of that sort.

'Laura, I didn't know you liked dirty jokes!' He looked shocked.

'I do not!' I said in my most indignant voice. 'Alec Munro don't you dare think...'

His eyes sparkled with amusement—he was thoroughly enjoying himself at my expense. 'Laura.' He tickled me under the chin. 'It was too good to resist.'

I sighed and smiled. With the stress and anxiety of the Ritual past, the tension had visibly lifted from his shoulders. His eyes, a definite dark purple tonight, shone down at me. He looked even more heart-stoppingly gorgeous, if such a thing were possible.

'You like him, don't you?' I asked, trying to keep my thoughts on a safer track.

'Yes, he's a friend. Flew over from the USA just to see you—and me of course!'

'As in, on a plane, not... you know, on his own?' I remembered reading somewhere that some vampires could fly.

Alec laughed. 'Yes, Laura, a regular commercial flight, although a privately chartered one. Actually' —he glanced around— 'there's the pilot.'

I followed the direction of his gaze to a young woman dressed in black satin pants and sable bustier with white lace collar and sleeves. Her curly collar-length hair bounced as she laughed, presumably at something the man beside her had just said. Something about her face seemed vaguely familiar, yet I couldn't place it. I'd never met her before, of that I was sure.

'Amelia runs her own chartered flight company. Flies us wherever we need to go,' Alec said.

Then it clicked. I'd seen her picture in a recent documentary on TV. 'Amelia? As in Amelia Earhart, the American pilot who disappeared in the nineteen thirties? You mean she's ... um, one of you?'

'Yes, that's right. She had arranged her own disappearance to cover it up.' He spoke so nonchalantly. I was still processing it when he pointed again. 'Over there. Know who that is?'

A tall, blonde man with flecks of silver in his hair was in an intense finger-wagging discussion with another man.

I gasped. His was a face known to all Australians, for it had been plastered on every newspaper when he disappeared while spearfishing at a local beach. Most believed a shark had taken him since his body was never found. It was not every day a country lost its leader to a ravenous fish.

My jaw dropped—yet again—as I stared at Harold Holt, Prime Minister of Australia in the nineteen-sixties.

This was getting ridiculous. How many other famous people were actually vampires? I began to scan the faces around me in my own version of Spot-the-Celebrity, and as I did so, my eyes returned to Maris's group. Russell stood among them and gazed back at me. My curiosity vanished as a nervous tingle ran the length of my spine.

'Alec?'

'Yes?'

'I'm … sorry. Nothing.' I dismissed the feeling. Russell had been amusing. Maybe it was just my imagination.

Alec looked at me, and his smile faded. 'What is it? Something's worrying you.'

'I'm just not used to being surrounded by vampires, I guess.' I dropped my voice as well as my eyes.

'Laura, my friends and I are watching out for you, and nothing can happen here.' He gently stroked the side of my face with his thumb. The nervous feeling passed, and I smiled up at him. 'Dance with me,' he suggested and wrapped one arm tight around my waist as we moved to the strains of *Stranger in the Night*.

How appropriate.

We talked while we danced. Once or twice his eyes drifted over my head and scanned the crowd before coming back to me. He'd smile and lead me into another dance. Occasionally someone would cut in and Alec graciously bowed out. It appeared many wanted to meet me. When we eventually sat down, he excused himself to speak with his friends, who were lounging at the bar. It gave me the opportunity to slip my shoes off and place my feet on his vacated chair. I always hated new shoes. As far as I was concerned, they were modern torture devices.

Terens—one of the red-cloaked guards at the Ritual—laughed. He had joined our table after Maris left. Zhao had also excused himself once the music started.

'Laura, you're a delight,' Terens said. 'I could never see Judith doing that.'

I wriggled my toes. That made him laugh even more. It struck me that he had officiated at my aunt's Coming-of-Age ceremony as well. It was easy to forget that most of the guests were vampires who could be hundreds of years old, making Alec a veritable youngster in comparison.

Meanwhile, Alec was deep in conversation with Luc and Jake and the other two guards, Sam and Cal. They had draped their red cloaks over one end of the bar and were leaning back against the counter, each with a drink in his hand. Their swords, interestingly, were still strapped to their sides. I noticed there was one man I hadn't been introduced to.

'Terens, who's that with the blonde ponytail, standing next to Luc?'

'That's Jean, a distant relative of Luc's. Knew Napoleon, fought in his wars.'

Wow, I was in the presence of individuals who had lived through some of history's most momentous events. How I would have loved to have them address my Sixth Grade class. If only. I sighed.

As Terens spoke I noticed that Jean—who gazed at me far more than the others—bore a striking resemblance to someone I'd met a long time ago; when I was eighteen, on holiday in Italy and ready for romance. His name was Philippe. He was handsome, and he had kissed me. Over the years though, the memory had faded, and it was hard to recall every detail of his face. But it couldn't be him, as he'd be in his late fifties by now, probably with a large family, receding hairline and a thickening waist. I smiled inwardly at the image and turned back to Terens.

'He's the quiet one out of all of us. Hard to know what he's thinking sometimes,' he said, almost to himself.

'So, how long have you known Alec?'

'Not that long, really. Since just after the Great War.'

I tried to keep my jaw firmly locked. Obviously a vampire's perception of time was different from my own. Perhaps a near century was only a blip on their radar.

'We met in Paris just after his transformation.' Terens looked thoughtful. 'He was finding it hard.'

The way he pronounced Paris betrayed his French origins. He had the barest hint of an accent, although unlike Luc he didn't drop the occasional French expression. I enjoyed listening to him for not only was he was a wealth of information about Alec, but his voice—like the rest of his kind, I was beginning to learn—was melodic, almost hypnotic.

'Being a vampire?' I asked.

'Yes. It's not easy at first. One day he might tell you all about it.'

I looked at Alec's group. Every now and then they glanced in my direction, their expressions serious. Was there something wrong?

'Terens, is there anything I should be concerned about?'

He scanned the sea of faces. 'Some here would love to see the Principate abolished. They hate the boundaries imposed by Luc and Alec. I don't know whether he told you our kind are forbidden to kill humans.'

I nodded. 'He has. You don't need much to stay alive.'

'Exactly. Besides, it's more fun to enjoy a little nip here' —his finger brushed a section of my throat— 'and there' —his finger moved to the other side— 'from several different ladies.' His touch was almost erotic and the smile he gave me would melt the heart of any female.

Were all male vampires so sensual? I removed his hand from my neck and placed it firmly on the table. 'You mentioned boundaries?'

His expression sobered. 'Not all of our kind see humans as a protected species. They've been blood drinkers too long, and it's too easy to forget we were all human once. For now, we and humans get along just fine' —a grin spread across his face— 'because they don't know about us. Safer all round.' He took a sip of his drink. 'Besides, among our kind, the penalty for murder is severe. As long as Alec's princeps and your guardian, it'll stay that way. He's too strong for them to take him on, but imagine if they had you? Not only would they slaughter him, but this city would become a killing field.'

I gasped at the horrifying images his words evoked.

'Look around, pet.' His hand swept the air. 'Not every eye here is friendly.'

'I have noticed.' I glanced in Maris's direction.

She stood huddled in a little group who silently watched Alec. She'd flicked back her gold cloak displaying a dress any porn star would have been proud of—siren red with a plunging V neckline that barely covered her ample breasts and ended somewhere in the vicinity of her navel. A deep slit slashed open the front of the skirt, stopping just below her panties. I wouldn't have been surprised if she hadn't worn any knickers.

Her lavender eyes would have been stunning in contrast to her flowing platinum locks but for their coldness. Dead eyes.

Several in her group turned and stared at me. Cold hostility emanated from their fierce expressions. A shudder rippled through me.

'Yup.' Terens lowered his voice. 'Maris. Watch out for her— nasty piece of work. She and Alec were lovers once, and everyone knows she wants him back.'

I was right; there was history between them, and no doubt that dress was for his benefit. Was there a possibility Alec still harboured feelings for her? 'Is Alec ... still interested?'

'Not as far as I know.'

I suddenly felt guilty for being relieved. What was wrong with me?

Alec returned to our table, and his eyebrows shot up on seeing my naked feet, which I hurriedly removed from his chair. The band began to play *Serenade in Blue*. A slow smile spread across his face. There was no time to slip back into my shoes. He pulled me to my feet and into his arms, and we swayed to the haunting melody, Maris temporarily forgotten. Everyone seemed to disappear as he held me close. When he interlaced our fingers, a thrill rushed through me.

I'd never experienced such a sensation, and in my mind, I kept reliving his kiss. Had it been merely part of the ceremony or something more? I would ask him tomorrow ... maybe.

Twice he examined his bite marks and stroked my neck. I had to fight down the delicious tingle I felt at his touch.

'Remarkable,' he said.

'What is?'

'They've healed so quickly.'

'I've always been a fast healer. Nothing new.'

'This fast, Laura? The wound's almost closed over—it looks like nothing more than a couple of freckles. I want to keep an eye on you, so rather than taking you home, would you mind if we stayed here tonight? Luc has far more rooms in this mausoleum than he needs, and I know he'd like us to stay.'

His fingers lingered on my neck, and I wondered if it really was the medico in him that prompted the suggestion. Guiltily, I hoped it wasn't. My mind was still coming to terms with the fact that this man was a vampire, an honest-to-goodness bloodsucker, who less than a few hours ago, had drunk my blood. His mouth had been on my throat to feed, not to caress as a lover would. Yet, in spite of it, I couldn't deny my growing attraction to him.

I thought about his question. 'What about change of clothes?'

'Don't worry. You'll find whatever you need. Guest rooms are all well stocked.'

'Well, okay then.' I didn't really mind, as I'd get a chance to explore the house in the morning.

When I was in school, I became a member of the National Trust just so I could wander through old Georgian and Victorian mansions on their Open Days. I imagined myself dressed in a tight corset and muslin dress, walking through those period-decorated rooms in the hope of meeting Mr Darcy.

A young woman approached our table. Her straight, shoulder-length brown hair framed blue eyes. Blue eyes! What a pleasant surprise – someone who wasn't a vampire.

'Sorry to interrupt,' she said, enthusiastically, 'but I was so curious to meet you. My name is Lora as well, though mine is spelled L-O-R-A.'

'Nice to meet you, Lora, spelt L-O-R-A. Mine's just the old-fashioned kind.'

'While you two ladies are discussing variations in spelling,' Alec said, 'I'll go speak to Luc, spelt L-U-C. Please excuse me.' And he was gone.

Smart-arse. 'Come, sit down.' I patted Alec's empty chair.

She had a dainty upturned, freckled nose. Her wide-eyes followed Alec as he walked to another table.

'He is *so* hot! You are *so* lucky!'

I eventually got her to sit and look at me rather than Alec.

'So, Lora, who are you with?' I asked, to keep her attention.

'Over there.' She pointed to a young man lounging against the bar with the same brown-coloured, shoulder-length hair. He looked no older than her and I could only guess at what colour his eyes would have been before his transformation.

'Wayne. Isn't he cute? We met at a rave party.'

'Vampires go to those things?' I asked, fascinated.

'Oh yeah, all the time.' She sounded surprised that I didn't know. 'I think you're *so* brave, going up there.' She pointed to the pavilion. 'And letting him, you know—bite you publicly like that. I mean, when Wayne and I go for it, it's like, you know, just the two of us.' She sing-songed her way through all that in one breath.

'I didn't have much choice, and Alec helped me through it.'

She sighed deeply and looked at Alec again. I bit my lip to stop myself from laughing. Lora had the biggest crush I'd ever seen. I wondered how her boyfriend felt about it.

'How often do you, um, let him feed from you?' I wanted to know how other vampire-human couples behaved, compared to Alec and myself. Not that he and I were actually a couple....

'Oh, almost every day. He has to eat just like we do.' Her voice was matter-of-fact, which pulled me from my mental wrestling.

I looked closely, but couldn't see any fang marks on her. 'So, where does he bite you?'

She smiled coyly and placed her hand high up on her inner thigh.

My eyes must have widened to the size of dinner plates.

'I don't like people to see any, you know, like fang marks, so he takes a little drink when … you know.' She smiled at me with a knowing look.

I guessed that some of the couples here tonight had more than just a blood-sharing relationship as occasionally some disappeared into the house and didn't come out again.

'What about you and Alec?' she asked, all wide-eyed curiosity.

'We only met on Friday night, and I have a boyfriend.' Whom I pictured ripping out Alec's teeth for kissing me tonight.

'Bummer!' She looked sorry for me. 'Never mind; you might get lucky.'

I didn't want to consider that.

Lora turned her head sideways to glance at her boyfriend, who waved for her to come over. 'Oops, gotta go. It was *so* nice meeting you, Laura. See ya.' And she breezed away.

Seeing Lora leave, Alec sauntered back to his seat, laughter in his eyes.

'Were you listening?' I asked.

'Of course. Fascinating conversation.' His lips twitched.

If Alexander Munro had any thoughts of going anywhere near that part of my anatomy, he had Buckley's! But I couldn't prevent the image of his dark head bent over my thigh from surfacing. Heat suffused my cheeks.

I could hear Terens chuckling.

Men!

'My Lord Princeps, may I dance with Lady Laura?' A voice asked.

I looked up to see a young man, no more than seventeen or eighteen, who bowed slightly and extended his hand toward me. I smiled at him then glanced at Alec. The look I saw on his and Terens's face filled me with alarm. I'd already danced with several blood drinkers tonight, so what was it about this one that made them so tense?

Alec looked at me questioningly. 'Laura?'

'I don't mind,' I answered.

With a tight smile, he laid my hand in that of the young man.

'My name is Douglas, Lady,' the young man said politely.

'Please call me Laura.'

He curled his arm around my waist and led me into a slow dance. Douglas had beach-blonde hair and could have passed for a surfer kid. He wasn't all that tall either, maybe two or three inches more than me.

'Do you mind if I ask how long you've been a vampire?' I attempted some small talk.

'Since nineteen sixty-five. I went for a walk along the beach one night with this really cute girl, and, well ...' Temporarily releasing my hand, he curled two fingers and dug them into his neck.

'Okay.' What could I say to that? 'Surely it needs more than one bite to change you, doesn't it?'

'Oh yeah. She took a lot of bites and then I drank her blood ....' His eyes danced.

'Why?'

'I wanted to be with her forever.'

'How old were you?'

'Seventeen.'

Seventeen! I'd guessed right, but what would a kid of that age know about lifetime commitments? I wondered if he'd regretted his decision, but I wasn't about to ask. He seemed nice, like a regular kid, but he held me too close. That's when I noticed the hint of something "other" in his eyes. They'd turned a lighter shade of lavender—almost opalescent—and I couldn't suppress a shiver.

'What if you wanted to choose someone else?' he asked.

'What?'

'You didn't really get a chance to choose did you?' His hand tightened over mine.

'The ring glowed, Douglas, and it chose Alec.'

'But you're the Bloodgifted. You could have anyone.'

I could see where he was headed. 'Like you, perhaps?'

'Why not?' he answered, and a sly grin spread across his face.

Huh, so beach boy wanted to be head boy! 'Forget it, Douglas. This dance is over.'

He dropped the friendly expression, and his pupils narrowed to snake-like slits. 'Not till I say so.'

My stomach plummeted. As I tried to manoeuvre out of his embrace, his grip tightened, painfully squeezing my fingers. His smile broadened to reveal fangs.

'And I say it's over. Now.' Alec's voice was quiet, menacing. He had appeared from nowhere.

Douglas's face paled as he released his grip, but there was no disguising the expression of pure hate etched on his face. With a final, leering glance in my direction, he slunk into the shadows. Alec's gaze followed him before coming back to me.

I flexed my fingers to restore circulation, hoping nobody noticed our little exchange. Couples continued dancing as if nothing had happened.

'Are you all right?' he asked.

'Yes, yes, I'm fine. He seemed so nice at first—just a kid.'

Alec took hold of my sore fingers and gently massaged them. 'Mmmm, just a kid!' He snorted. 'Don't forget, Laura, our kind look young, but many are decades, even centuries old.'

Douglas mentioned he was changed in nineteen sixty-five when he was only seventeen, which meant he had to be in his early sixties. Definitely, not a kid.

'I think he wants your job.'

'Well, he's not getting it.'

Alec looked dangerous; his eyes were cold and near-reptilian. I knew he could have killed Douglas, had he so chosen. I tried to swing the mood around since I'd been enjoying this part of the evening and didn't want to be reminded that the finely attired creatures with whom I'd been dancing and conversing weren't human.

'Shall we dance—*My Lord Princeps*?' I mocked.

His expression softened. He drew me close and twirled me into the crowd. I glanced over his shoulder to where Maris stood with her little group. Her eyes never left Alec, but he never glanced in her direction. Only once did she look at me, and when I attempted a smile, her cold eyes narrowed.

I'd made an enemy without trying.

CHAPTER 13
TRIALS OF A PRINCEPS

ALEC

Since Laura was happy to rest her feet, I left her in Terens's care and made my way to Jake's table. Cal was with him, as well as Jean and Sam. Luc joined us while Judith escorted her brother, John, back up to the house.

'Nice ceremony. I like the little addition—the kissing bit.' Cal's face broke into a wide grin.

'It was just the First Blood lust, nothing more.' I swiped a glass of red from the tray as a waiter strolled past.

'Well, you certainly didn't seem to suffer from that condition with the previous Ingenii.' He chuckled while downing his favourite non-blood drink—Armagnac. He owned a distillery in France, which sent him several crates of the stuff. Recently, he'd been mixing it with Luc's best Scotch whisky and chilled blood, and calling it a Bloody Cally.

'Judith's blood wasn't as potent,' I said.

He lifted an eyebrow and grinned.

'It's nothing.' I reiterated.

'I would have loved to see Luc kiss Owen like that.' Jake said, and the others laughed.

Owen Dantonville, Laura's grandfather and Judith's father, was a self-centred man. If he hadn't been Ingenii, I believe Luc would have killed him—and enjoyed doing it.

To my relief, Luc brought our conversation back to the present. 'As long as Laura's here, she's safe. When this is over, I want a double guard around her flat.'

'You suspect trouble?' Cal asked.

With a tilt of his head, Luc indicated Maris and the closely huddled group around her.

'Why her?' Sam asked.

'Alec, tell them,' Luc replied.

'Drained bodies lying in the streets. Young kids. It only started with her arrival.'

Cal shook his head in disgust. 'How the hell did she become an Elder?'

'Lack of older female Brethren after we executed three in the First Rebellion and one in the Second,' Luc said.

'Damn! Forgot.'

The repercussions were serious. She had to be stopped, but the last thing we wanted was an enemy in the eldership. She couldn't sway the other Elders, but by virtue of her position, she could gather a sizeable following of like-minded Brethren and cause trouble. Civil War couldn't be ruled out.

'You believe they'd actually try something against the Principate?' Jake's expression darkened.

'We all know what she's capable of,' I said.

Sam nodded. 'She'd go after Laura.' He knew her best, for they had once been lovers, before he became her sire. They had met on the eve of the French Revolution, and he'd kept her hidden during the worst excesses of that murderous regime. The rest of her family hadn't been that lucky.

They were together the entire period of her servitude, and when she began to display the cruellest aspects of her nature, Sam's affections grew cold. He forbade her to kill anyone bar the criminals who roamed the streets at night in search of victims of their own. As her creator, he had the power to order her extermination. But once out of servitude, she indulged her perverse tastes.

'I told Laura she'd be safe after the Ritual.'

No one spoke for a while, and I had the feeling they were remembering the past, when two previous Ingenii had been attacked. One had been killed, and the next in line had been a juvenile. His blood hadn't yet matured. Luc and his men had hidden the boy till he came of age. In the meantime, they'd hunted down the rebel ringleaders and brought them before the Elders who executed fifteen of them and forced the rest to take the Pledge.

Those events had occurred long before my time, but Luc had told me some of the history, and I'd read the rest in Marcus Antonius's Chronicle, which sat on a lectern—accessible to everyone—in the library at Luc's house.

The Pledge had been invoked on two occasions, each time after a rebellion. The first took place over a thousand years ago after the abduction and murder of the fifteenth Ingenii, Clement D'Antonville. The Second Rebellion was only four-hundred-years ago when the twenty-sixth Ingenii, Robert D'Antonville, fought off several of the Brethren who tried to take him. Fortunately, as an accomplished swordsman, he'd fought them off till Luc and the others had arrived.

According to Marcus's Chronicle, The Pledge was created to safeguard the Principate from future attack. The prefects—leaders of the Brethren in their respective nations—had to swear an oath of allegiance on the Serpent Rings, to protect the Ingenii and Guardian at the cost of their own life. Those who defied the oath were destroyed. The rings flashed fire and incinerated them.

'Can we invoke the Pledge?' I asked.

'We could,' Luc said. 'Problem is, it costs energy. The fire from the serpents' eyes comes from a combination of the ring and you. The more you use it, the weaker you'll become.'

'Is that common knowledge?' I asked.

'No, and I'd like to keep it that way. After the First Rebellion, I only needed to use it twice, and after that the rest of the rebels backed away. They never got a chance to see how exhausted I was.'

'And the Second Rebellion?'

'Those who had taken the oath stayed well away, although one or two incited the juveniles to rebel. So we made the young ones take the oath and executed the leaders,' Luc said.

'Now we have a new batch of juveniles.' With a subtle jerk of his head, Sam indicated Maris's group.

At that, we turned to look. Their hushed whispers stopped abruptly. Maris gave me a slow, seductive smile and ushered them to the other side of the garden.

'Couldn't catch everything. They're deliberately blocking me. What about you?' Cal asked.

'No, same with me.' I turned a questioning eye on Luc, but he shook his head.

'They're planning something. I can sense it.' Jake cracked his knuckles.

Cal nodded and rested his hand on the hilt of his sword. The other held a goblet of wine.

'But that's not enough to force the Pledge.' Luc's voice was grim.

'So, there's nothing we can do?' Sam slammed his hand down on the counter and dug his nails into the laminate surface.

'Just keep watch. For now.' Luc's gaze shifted to his daughter, and the tense lines around his mouth relaxed.

'You know something, Alec?' Cal said. 'I think you may have placed Laura in danger without meaning to.'

'What?'

'Kissing her during the Ritual would piss off any woman.'

'Especially her,' Sam pointed out.

'We broke up decades ago. I made it very plain. She can't possibly think…?'

'Not as far as she's concerned,' Jake said. 'Damn it, Alec! Her eyes haven't left you all night. I've been watching. And we all saw that sex-laden smile she shot you. Smelt her arousal from here.'

I ran my hand through my hair and let out a frustrated breath, then cursed my foolishness in allowing myself to become infatuated with the woman in my early vampire years. 'It's over. Has been since nineteen-twenty-three, and she knows it.'

'Women can be clingy,' Cal said and drained the last of the Armagnac in his goblet.

Jean had been silent the whole evening, yet his glances continually strayed towards Laura. 'If Maris comes near Laura I'll kill her.' He bared his teeth and the glass he held shattered in his grip.

His heated reaction was unusual. He'd never expressed an interest in any woman, which gave Cal endless opportunities for teasing. Jean always took it with good humour, but from the scent that clung to him, I knew he satisfied his physical needs in female company, although where and with whom, he never revealed.

I looked at him closely—really closely—and what I saw made me uneasy, for Jean did not look at Laura like a benevolent uncle. I sensed something deeper and darker.

'That's why we're here, Jean. To protect her,' Luc said. 'I know you care for Laura, as do we all, but Alec is her guardian.' It sounded like a warning.

I remember my surprise at Jean's decision to move here in the late seventies. We all knew how much he loved Paris. He must have had a very good reason to leave.

Jean turned to me, and he smiled, but there was no mistaking the flash of anger that preceded it. And that could stem from only one thing—Jean was in love with Laura. My fists clenched. Why hadn't he challenged me during the Ritual? Was it out of respect for our friendship, or was there another reason? I had to find out, although I didn't believe Jean posed any danger.

I glanced at Laura then scanned the room to see how many other eyes were on her. There were a lot—mostly male. Was it her looks or her blood that drew them? Possibly both.

Luc watched Maris's group in silence. His pupils began to slit, the pale irises narrow.

I placed my hand on his arm. 'Not here. We don't have definite proof. Once we do, it's my responsibility as princeps to order her execution.'

Sommers had sent through the DNA results I'd requested. There were two distinct types, so there had to be more than one new killer. Unfortunately neither had appeared in their database. Until I could match them with a living sample, I could only guess. Yet I was convinced they were here tonight, and one of them was Maris. The trick was to obtain that sample.

'Do we have it yet?' I asked Luc.

He had instructed one of the drinks waiters to discreetly put Maris's used glass into a plastic bag, taking care to avoid contaminating the rim. We couldn't afford to have her DNA compromised. It would go straight to the lab for analysis, and if the result confirmed my suspicions, we could act.

I sent Cal to fetch the glass and watched him weave his way through the crowd.

'All yours,' he said, when he came back and handed me the coveted parcel with the remains of her drink visible through the plastic. *Bloody Russian*, her favourite—Tia Maria, vodka and blood.

'Thank you,' I replied. 'I'll keep it till I can get it to the lab.'

'I don't think she suspects a thing,' he said.

'Couldn't care less if she did,' Luc replied gruffly.

I headed back to our table and Laura smiled at my approach. I dropped the plastic bag into my jacket pocket, which hung across the back of my chair and swung her into my arms for another dance. The more contact we had, the more strongly my scent would cling to her, and even those Brethren unable to attend the Ritual would know she belonged to me. Later I asked if I could examine her neck. It had healed very quickly—more so than normal. I wondered if it was because she was part-vampire. After all, none of us had any idea what to expect. All we could do was watch and wait.

One of Maris's group asked Laura to dance. I didn't sense any immediate danger, so with Laura's permission, I placed her hand in his.

Terens came to my side. 'I don't like it.'

I looked over to the bar, where the others stood, alert—and watching. Luc turned his head in my direction, his brow creased in a frown. I shook my head.

'Jean, Jake,' I heard him say, and he indicated the dance floor with his head. Obeying, they both moved and followed Laura and Douglas at a discreet distance.

Douglas appeared innocuous, but I kept an ear to every word that came out of his mouth. His scent changed, and the nice-surfer-boy image slipped. Laura stood up to him, but when his fangs appeared and she struggled to escape his hold, I moved.

Even as I did so, Jean and Jake bore down on them while Sam attempted to restrain Luc. I was at her side first, and quietly took hold of the situation. I let slip a glimpse of my own beast. Douglas drew back when he saw his peril. He disappeared into the crowd, but not back to Maris's group. Jean and Jake, with a nod to me, followed him out.

Laura flexed her fingers. He'd hurt her, and the urge to kill him overwhelmed me and threatened to destroy a perfectly pleasant evening. I concentrated on massaging her hand; I needed a distraction. There was an unwritten code that personal grievances among the Brethren had to be set aside for the period of the Ritual. No killings, and not even I could violate it.

The rest of the night was, thankfully, uneventful. By four a.m. Laura could barely keep her eyes open, and when she slowly lowered her head onto her arms over the back of her seat, it was time to go. I picked her up and carried her into the house. Judith and Luc came as well and directed me to her bedroom. It was one of the largest and most beautifully furnished in the house; originally her room before they made the heart-wrenching decision to place her with John's family.

I laid her on the bed and kissed her soft cheek as Judith removed her shoes and pulled the covers over her. I was about to leave when she stirred and opened her eyes.

'Alec?' she murmured.

'Yes. Go back to sleep.'

I waited until her eyes closed and her breathing evened before I left.

***

Most of the guests drifted off. Terens and Sam were meant to be on guard duty tonight, but with Laura here, they had the night off. Still, Sam mentioned they might swing past her flat and check things out before going hunting. Both were unattached, and the occasional hunt kept their skills honed.

I wandered up to the games room, where the men had congregated. Jake, Cal and Jean were at the billiards table and had just started to play. Each held a goblet of O positive.

'How's Laura,' Jake asked, sinking a yellow ball. 'It's never easy for the Ingenii—finding out what they are and then having to go through the Ritual. Takes courage.'

'Yes, it does,' I agreed.

'Does she know?' Jean asked as he chalked his graphite cue.

He was referring to Laura's true parentage. 'Not yet. That's up to Luc.' I made myself comfortable in one of the leather armchairs. 'Jake, you and Jean followed that kid, Douglas. He didn't return to Maris's group. Where did he go?'

'They had a boat moored at the jetty, and he scurried down there like a rat. That area's not secure. What's the use of having guards at the entrance gate when they can slip in harbour-side? Sam needs to get onto it.'

He was right. I hadn't thought of that. On the other hand, not even Maris would risk doing something to one of the Bloodgifted here. The penalty for violating the sanctity of an Elder's house was death.

I extended my senses and heard the rhythm of Laura's heart. Slow and steady, she was asleep and safe. 'They won't try anything here.'

'No, not here, but Laura lives alone,' he pointed out. 'Even though she's supposed to be untouchable, Maris won't respect that.'

I sighed. Laura was independent, but could I persuade her to stay here? Of course, I could always move in with her. That would go down well with Sommers. For a moment I enjoyed that mental picture. I had to think of something, and it looked more and more like that would be arranged—once I made him aware of the danger Laura faced. As a police detective, I was sure he'd be more than willing to provide her with some human protection. With him inside and us outside, I doubted even Maris would be that bold.

Although the Games Room was completely sealed from sunlight, we could all sense the dawn. Cal was the first to get drowsy. He laid down his cue, moved to the drinks cabinet and located a full bottle of Armagnac. Waving goodbye with it, he headed out the door.

'You actually going to drink all that?' Jake called after him.

'Why not?'

Jake shook his head, raised his eyes and laughed. 'What you need is a woman!'

'Had one.' His voice trailed from the corridor.

'Recently? Listen, there's this really great place…' Jake sunk his last red ball, dropped his cue on the felt tabletop and hurried after him.

Jean lingered. 'What if something were to happen to you? Who would be Laura's guardian then?'

'Why ask?'

'Just curious. Has it ever happened?'

'No.'

He stared at me, a rather curious expression on his face, before walking past me and out the door. As I watched his retreating back, there was no doubt in my mind that he resented me. But, was he a danger? I shook my head and dismissed the idea as far-fetched. After all, Jean was part of our intimate circle, our family. Yet rivalries did exist, even in the closest of families. My scalp began to prickle as I thought back over the last few months. I'd noticed him getting more withdrawn, keeping to himself and disappearing for days without letting anyone know of his whereabouts. Lately, he'd taken to blocking his emotions when around us. But earlier this evening, he had slipped. Anger emanated from him in waves when Luc reminded him I was Laura's guardian.

The more I thought about it, the greater my unease. Jean would have to be confronted. As I considered when would be the best time, I realised Sam and Terens hadn't returned. It was daylight. I temporarily shunted my concerns aside and extended my senses to try and pick up any hint of them.

Most Brethren could pick out voices within a three-mile radius. Mine extended to double that, yet I couldn't hear anything from them. Perhaps they were in the city, beyond my range, and had decided to sleep at one of the safe houses run by the Brethren. Many were staffed by human females who enjoyed servicing our kind. They would probably turn up this evening.

The rest of the house was quiet, apart from the sound of three distinct human heartbeats—John's, Judith's and Laura's. Luc's heart, like mine, beat once every ten minutes, and he had just joined me in the Games Room.

'What are we going to do about Laura?' I asked.

'We can't force her to stay here. She's stubborn.' He picked up the black ball and tossed it around in his hands.

'Like her father.'

He chuckled. 'Perhaps you can move in with her.'

'Have you developed mind reading skills? I thought about it, but Sommers might object.' I'd enjoy that.

'Well then, perhaps it's time to talk to him. He needs to know.'

'You or me?'

'I think it'd be best from me. I'll speak to him when he comes for her tonight.'

'Fine.'

Since it was only about six a.m., and I didn't expect anyone to wake till at least eleven, I took Maris's DNA sample—still in my jacket pocket—to the lab to see if it matched the read-out Sommers had given me.

Sunshine greeted me as I left the house, but not the drowsiness of the day-sleep, nor the burning pain or blistered skin that every blood drinker fears. I drove to Rozelle, to the Munro Research Laboratories and the small private hospital attached to the facility, just off Victoria Road. Several gum trees lined the entrance partially obscuring the sign. I made a mental note to get their branches trimmed as I drove around the block and entered the "Staff Only" parking area.

Phil, the lead technician arrived at the same time. A tall, gangly man in his mid-forties, he'd given up trying to maintain the few stray hairs that clung to his scalp and had shaved it all off. His bald pate shone in the morning sun as he greeted me at the entrance.

'Morning boss. Good evening, was it?' He smiled.

I'd forgotten I was still in my tux—minus the jacket and bow tie. 'Very good evening. Glad it's over, though.'

'Yeah. I don't like those dress-up things. Gimme jeans and T-shirt any day.'

I couldn't help but agree. 'Phil, I've got an extra job for you,' I said as we entered the building.

I rarely made such requests and he gave me a quizzical look. 'Sure. What is it?'

I lifted the plastic bag containing the cocktail glass from my jacket pocket and handed it to him. 'I need the DNA on this glass analysed. Fax the results to me ASAP.' I dug my wallet out, scribbled down Luc's fax number on my notepad and tore off the sheet. 'At this number.'

He took it and nodded. 'It'll take at least seventy-two hours, assuming this is a good sample.' He held it up.

'It is.'

'Skin, saliva … the whole works?'

'Whatever you can get. And while you're at it, text me the results of the LD#5 sample will you?'

'On it,' he said and disappeared through the sliding steel doors into the main lab.

I returned to my car and drove back to Luc's. Along the way, I stopped at a newsagent and bought the morning papers. For the next few hours, I scoured every page and hoped I wouldn't find any news about murdered children. I expected Luc's warning to be taken seriously.

On top of that I wondered how to protect Laura from rogue vampires, and, most importantly, how to seduce her before the day was out. If I didn't there was a good chance Sommers would persuade her to marry him, and the curse would continue—and with it my servitude.

CHAPTER 14
BREAKFAST

LAURA

The persistent buzzing of my mobile phone woke me. I reached out, grabbed it from the bedside table and switched it off. What time was it? I opened one eye and checked my watch—eleven a.m. I had no idea what time I got to bed last night—or was it early this morning? —and I didn't feel like getting up. Images from the Ritual mingled with my dreams, and Alec dominated each one.

I struggled to bring Matt's face to mind and decided to ring him, only to find he'd left me a message.

Hi Babe, tried to ring, your phone was off. Pick u up t/nite @8. Loved Sat nite & LOVE YOU. There was a smiley attached.

I smiled at the memory of Saturday night, put the phone down then sat wondering what to do first—shower, go exploring or have breakfast? If the house was anything like my room it was going to be a major expedition. It was then I realised I still wore my evening gown.

Whoever had placed me in this room hadn't bothered to remove my dress. Maybe just as well; an image—or was it a dream?—of Alec laying me on the bed popped into my head. I wasn't sure whether I should be excited or discomforted. But whichever, that man had a disturbing effect on me.

Well, I wasn't going to think of that now. On the bedside table lay a note:

Look in the closet.

Attached was a map of the house with directions to the kitchen. I recognised Alec's handwriting.

I shook my head and smiled. He was considerate as well as charming, and I wanted to see him again.

The room was enormous. I'd slept very comfortably in an amazing four-poster canopied bed that could have accommodated at least three people. It was covered in drapery printed with rosebuds and flowery garlands. Dark-stained floors and beams gave the bedroom an old-world, even Tudor, look. A solid chest sat at the foot of the bed while cotton rugs, in the same rosebud print as the drapes, covered the floors.

I decided to look for the closet mentioned in the note. Slipping out of bed, I wandered to one of two closed doors—the one nearest my bed. It opened to reveal the biggest walk-in wardrobe I'd ever seen, with more clothes, shoes, handbags and assorted accessories than any woman could ever use.

I felt like Alice in Wonderland.

I selected a pair of loose-fitting, cream-coloured silk shorts, and a simple cotton blouse. There was even a matching pair of cream-coloured, ankle-laced wedge-heeled sandals. I tried them on, and they fit me perfectly.

I lay my new clothes on the bed and went to the other closed door, adjacent to the windows. Peering in, I found my bathroom.

At least the same size as the room I'd slept in, the bathroom had an Edwardian look. Pale salmon flowery-print wallpaper covered the walls, and matching cotton curtains hung over the large box window at the far end. In the centre of the room, like a regal queen, sat a luxurious two-stepped marble bath with its own shelf displaying a set of Vogue magazines, a little china bowl of pot-pourri and a wicker basket brimming with various goodies—bath bombs, coloured glass jars filled with bubble-bath and deliciously scented miniature soaps, shampoo and conditioner. There were even gold-plated tap fittings. The vanity boasted a marble washbasin. Two thick white towels and a bathrobe hung next to the door.

I gasped at the opulence but couldn't resist a long, decadent soak.

After lying there for nearly half an hour, my stomach rumbled, reminding me it was way past the time for breakfast.

With Alec's map in hand, I stepped into the corridor.

Portraits lined the walls. Most were of men, painted in various styles. As I checked the plaques beneath each, and the dates at which they were painted, I realised these were my ancestors – Ingenii all.

It was a gallery of Dantonvilles.

The closer I got to the stairs, the more recent the portraits, until I stood before one I recognised—my grandfather, Owen Dantonville. Next to him hung a youthful picture of my aunt Judy. She'd been beautiful, and in many ways still was. Her rich dark copper hair, like mine, contrasted vividly with her lavender eyes.

The space next to her was empty. I guessed that was where my portrait would go—one day.

I headed down the stairs, following the directions on the map, and found the kitchen. It could have swallowed up my entire unit – it was the size of an industrial lab. I wondered why a vampire would need such a huge modern eatery?

There were several refrigerators, and a massive stove that would have warmed the heart of any chef. Modern stone workbenches and ceiling-to-floor shelf units were stocked with crockery and the latest cooking gadgets.

Alec sat at the large polished-stone table holding the morning newspaper. His cup of black coffee smelled good. He looked up as I came in. 'Morning.' He smiled.

'Morning to you too.'

'Slept well?'

'Very well thanks, although I don't remember my head hitting the pillow, let alone how I got there.'

'You were almost asleep when I carried you up.'

'You carried me?' So, it hadn't been a dream.

'You look really cute when you're asleep,' he said, his smile mischievous.

'Um … thank you for the map,' I said, trying not to react to his comment.

'You're welcome. I thought you might need it.'

'It'd be fun to explore.'

'I approve of your outfit.' He looked me up and down.

I glanced down at my shorts and realised how short they were. Self-consciously I tugged down at the hem.

'What's to eat?' I asked in an effort to change the subject but regretted it almost immediately. His smile broadened, and he gazed at me as if I were on the menu. Hmm, I must remember not to mention the word food and myself in the same sentence.

He waved his arm at the expanse of kitchen. 'You name it, Luc's got it.'

Alec rose, rummaged through the cupboard directly behind him and pulled out several different cereal boxes, two French sticks and strawberry jam and laid them on the table. Opening another cupboard, he took out a bowl, sandwich plate and coffee mug. Finally, he strode to one of the refrigerators, extracted butter, a carton of milk and a glass container of fresh fruit and added them to the rest, after which he sat down and picked up his mug of coffee.

I shook my head. 'You know your way around. Who eats all this?'

'The household staff, and Luc often has Brethren guests who bring their donsangs with them.'

'Household staff? I haven't seen anyone.'

'They catered last night and cleaned up early this morning, so Luc gave them the day off.'

I nodded.

'It's on the stove,' he said. He must have noticed me inhaling the delicious scent of his coffee.

'Do they know what he is?' I asked as I poured myself a mug full.

'Oh yes,' he said nonchalantly. 'He pays very well, and some of them like to donate blood to visiting guests.'

'Hummmph, learn something every day!' I closed my eyes and sipped the delicious brew. He chuckled. I opened my eyes to see him grinning at me.

'Did I say something funny?'

'Laura, you amaze me. Less than a few days ago, you knew nothing of our existence, and now, you're almost blasé about it.'

'I don't know about blasé, but as of last night, I'm accepting. Are you hungry?' I asked, although I didn't really know why. Maybe just curiosity, as I remembered him telling me he could go for a couple of days without feeding.

'I ate last night. But, if you're offering?' The way he looked at me, with that half-smile, made my toes curl, and images of his mouth on my throat sent a delicious ripple through me. I quickly squashed it as his smile grew, and he held out his hand.

I walked toward him wondering how this was going to work. As I placed my hand in his, he pulled me onto his lap. I gasped—it was not what I expected. Alec wrapped one hand firmly around my waist and the other around my right wrist and gently drew it to his mouth. I felt a quick sting as his fangs pierced my skin. At least this time I knew what to expect.

He seemed human as I gazed at his bent head, yet here he was drinking my blood. It was surreal.

Not knowing exactly what to do with my other hand—hold onto the back of the chair, drape it around his wide shoulders (was that too intimate?)—I let it hover indecisively above his head till I gave into the urge and stroked his thick black hair. It was like touching a raven's feathers—soft and silky.

When he stopped feeding, he licked the wound and kissed the inside of my wrist. 'Thank you,' he said almost drunkenly and looked into my eyes.

That other urge, the one I was warned about and experienced the previous night, surfaced. I had no will to fight. He leaned toward me, his lips so close. I lifted my chin …. To my great relief, Luc and Aunt Judy entered the kitchen.

Their appearance snapped me back to my senses. Ours was only supposed to be a platonic relationship, for our mutual benefits. How could I face Matt if I allowed myself to develop feelings for Alec? I leapt off his lap as if shot in the backside, and I ran.

CHAPTER 15
HISTORY LESSON

LAURA

Now what? I was still hungry, and there was no way I could go back to that kitchen while Alec was there. Would it be this bad every time he fed from me? I had a sinking feeling it would. I tried thinking of Matt, but my thoughts kept returning to Alec—and he wasn't even drinking my blood.

I had a major problem.

Desperate to shake off my confused feelings, I wandered through the downstairs hall and came upon another set of stone steps leading up to a half-landing from which streamed a beam of coloured watery light. Curious, I followed them up and came face-to-face with the image of an ancient Roman soldier.

I sat on the topmost step and leaned my back against the wall for a better look.

Within the confines of an exquisite lead-lined window, the soldier—whom I recognised from last night's ceremony as Marcus Antonius—stood at attention. One hand rested on a large rectangular shield at his feet, the other held a spear. The shield carried the image of a sword flanked by two coiled serpents, whose glowing red eyes were shaped like teardrops.

My breath caught in my chest. It was the same image as on my ring.

Hovering on either side of Marcus were eight smaller figures in Roman military uniform. I looked closer and recognised the faces of Alec's friends—Terens, Sam, Cal, Jake and four others I didn't know.

A soft thud sounded behind me. I turned to see Luc coming up the stairs.

'You forgot these.' He handed me half a breadstick and a fresh mug of coffee.

I blinked and refocused as I gratefully took the food, the window temporarily forgotten. Luc sat on the step next to me, leaned his back against the stone balustrade and watched me eat the breadstick. I thought I heard him murmur, ma petite, ma fille, once or twice.

'Yes, that's him—Marcus Antonius Pulcher.' He pointed at the window. 'Your ancestor, my Laura.'

I stared at the image with renewed interest, barely registering the way he called me "my" Laura.

'What you see on the shield—the two serpents—represent his children, twins: a boy Lucius Antonius and a girl, Antonia.'

I was taken aback. Kids could be difficult sometimes, but it was a bit harsh to show them as snakes. Either he was a mind reader or my face betrayed my thoughts, for he gave a faint smile. 'The serpent was not regarded as evil among the ancients. It was seen as a symbol of immortality, for it shed its wrinkled old skin and grew a healthy new one.'

'Oh.' What woman on the planet wouldn't want to do that?

'You are directly descended from Antonia. I was hoping I'd get the chance to tell you the story while you were here.'

'Please do.'

Luc smiled and turning back to the window, recounted Marcus's story. I felt myself drawn back all those centuries, like a silent witness to a long ago scene as he described Marcus's ride into the village, the failed attempt to rescue Roman captives, the massacre of the villagers and the witch's curse turning him and his men into vampires. But his last words haunted me.

"What has been done cannot be undone. But this one thing I can grant. As one of my children escaped your sword, while hunting out in the woods, so will I spare one of yours. Your wife will give birth to twins: Children of Light and Dark. The boy shall be as you, a drinker of blood when he comes of age, but the girl will not. She will walk in the light. Long life will be granted her and her descendants. They will be known as Children of Light, and their blood shall sustain the Child of Darkness. And you, Roman, shall live all through the long ages ahead till one born of your house—a Child of Light and Dark—willingly bears a child to one of Prythin blood; a descendant of my house. For the child shall bear the mingled blood of Roman and Prythin—one race, one blood. Only then the curse shall be lifted."

'Those were her very words. To Marcus that would have been the ultimate humiliation: one of his house, of Roman patrician blood, marrying a painted savage.'

I turned from staring at the window to Luc as the realisation hit. Could it possibly refer to me? The curse presupposed Marcus's descendant to be a woman. And it certainly didn't refer to my aunt otherwise I wouldn't have inherited the cursed gene.

Luc had mentioned a Child of Light and Darkness, whatever that meant. My parents were two ordinary humans—John and Eilene Dantonville—so it couldn't possibly refer to them, nor to me, and as I was an only child, which meant it would have to be someone in the next generation—my child or grandchild—unless, of course, I never bore a child.

That idea left me feeling hollow; I wanted to marry and have kids, although the thought of one of my children being vampire food filled me with revulsion. Then another thought occurred to me—would Alec be their guardian? I suddenly saw myself fifty years from now, standing on a sandstone platform handing over my white silk cloak to my child, much as Aunt Judy did with me. Would she—if it were a girl—experience the same attraction toward him as I? Would he kiss her at the Ritual as he did me?

My stomach bunched into a tight knot.

'Laura, are you all right?' Concern crossed Luc's face.

'Yes, I'm fine, just thinking over everything you've told me.' And it was beginning to sicken me. I didn't want to think about it, let alone discuss it. 'The spirit disappeared after that?'

'No, she added that when the time came he and his men would be given a choice—to remain as they are, or become human again.'

'Why? Surely they'd choose humanity, wouldn't they? Wouldn't you?'

'Yes indeed, my Laura. Unfortunately, it's not that simple. Marcus and his men—and any whom they transformed—would age immediately, as all the years of their lives catch up with them. They'd be dead within minutes. That was her idea of freedom.'

The sorceress certainly had her revenge. Whatever decision they made condemned them in some way. Alec had told me Luc had changed him. But who had changed Luc?

'Can I ask who transformed you?'

He hesitated before answering. 'Marcus's son; one of the twins, Lucius Antonius Pulcher.'

I gasped. 'That means—'

'Alec and I will be given the choice.'

And what a choice! The horrible image of Alec and Luc as wizened old men, ageing, decaying and dying within a matter of minutes, raced through my mind. It was like something out of a horror film, and I realised I didn't want that to happen. Not to Luc—for my aunt's sake. And not to Alec. I liked him, more than I should.

'Then I hope it won't happen for a long time yet,' I said. Only then I realised the implications for us both.

He smiled. 'I understand what you mean, and I'm flattered. But, we shall see.'

'Did Marcus have the rings made in the same image as on his shield?' I asked, wanting to change the subject.

'He did. Before her apparition vanished the witch made one final demand—to take from her ashes the golden medallion she wore. It had the figure of a serpent on it—the symbol of Melusine, the Pict goddess of retribution and vengeance. It contained two unusual red stones for eyes. Marcus was to create two identical rings with the same image, split the stones and place two in each ring, as you can see.'

He lifted my hand and turned it to the light. The serpent's eyes gleamed dully. 'The stones, she said, were actually two drops of her blood and imbued with power. They would glow on the finger of an Antonii—a descendant of the family of Marcus Antonius—and burn that of an impostor.'

I recalled the way the rings glowed when Alec and I first met. He was an Antonii, it seemed, by virtue of his transformation by Luc, who was in turn changed by Lucius, son of Marcus Antonius. In a roundabout way, it made sense.

'They were to be passed on through the generations till the Destined Ones appeared, and only when their child is born in the exact same place where it all began, will the curse be ended. The rings themselves will hum in confirmation.'

I looked at the thing sitting so innocuously on my hand and shook my head. After my initial introduction to the ring on my birthday, I'd have thought nothing more could surprise me. I was wrong. First slithering, then glowing, now humming. What next, magic beans?

'Tell me about the twins,' I asked, to rid my mind of yet another disturbing thought.

'The girl, Antonia, lived for a hundred-and-forty-nine years. She passed on the curse to her firstborn—a boy called Paulus.'

'And Lucius? What happened to him?'

'He's still around.'

'Wasn't he at the Ritual?'

'Oh, he was there, but he likes to keep a low profile. You'll get to know him soon; I promise.'

Strange how I was getting used to the idea of being around people who were centuries, even millennia, old. Only four days ago, I'd been happily ignorant of this parallel world. How far I had come.

'Marcus's men must have taken it very badly, knowing there was no reprieve for them,' I said.

He nodded and pointed to two of the four faces I hadn't recognised. 'Appius and Pudens took their own lives. Walked out into the sunlight one morning, while the rest of them slept. The others … well.' He shrugged. 'They adjusted and left Britain for Gaul, as France was then called. Antonius had a villa there, and his wife, Gallia, had recently given birth to the twins. They remained there for the next sixteen-hundred years, till Claude D'Antonville, the thirtieth Ingenii—and your great, great grandfather—indulged his desire for adventure and gold by going to America and then here—'

'—where he met my great, great grandmother, fell in love and never went back to France,' I finished. 'I know that story. It's our family history. Dad told me when I was little how our name was anglicised and the apostrophe dropped.'

'Exactly. And we've been here ever since.'

'So how did the Ritual develop?'

'It was created in direct response to other vampire attacks on Antonia when she turned fifty.'

'You mean there were others like you?'

'Only a few, and they homed in on her like radar. Lucius wasn't there. He was in Britain. He'd run away as soon as the change came over him so as not to fulfil the sorceress's prediction by feeding from his sister. He was fifteen. Yet, thirty-five years later, when they both reached their fiftieth year—'

'Oh!' The significance of that made me shiver.

He nodded once. 'Yes, her blood matured and seemed to call to him, even over that distance. He couldn't stay away. Meanwhile, her husband had divorced her for not being able to bear children. Marcus and Gallia knew nothing about the delayed conception she and her eventual offspring would experience. The sorceress hadn't mentioned anything about that. And in those days, for a woman not to be able to have children it was, well … a disgrace.'

He stood and leant against the balustrade, arms folded across his chest. 'It happened quite accidentally. Lucius fought off two vampires who'd attacked Antonia. Jake and Terens came to help and they succeeded in killing them—beheading. Next to the sun, it's the surest way to despatch a blood drinker, as long as the head is kept well away from the body, otherwise it simply reattaches itself.'

The things I was learning! I was starting to worry my eyes would permanently remain the size of dinner plates. This was the kind of stuff a person read about in fantasy books, taking comfort from the fact it was far from realty. Yet, here I was, utterly absorbed in a story that was just as real as the man relating it.

'But Lucius had been badly wounded,' he continued. 'Unless he fed, he wouldn't last till the morning to regenerate in the day sleep. Acting on instinct, Antonia sliced open her wrist and pressed it to her brother's mouth. The moment he tasted her blood, strength and power flowed through him. Her blood was unlike anything he'd ever tasted. He found he didn't need to sleep as often and could even walk into the daylight without burning. His strength increased, as had all his other faculties. Antonia's blood was the key.'

'Did Marcus feed from her too?' Sheer curiosity prompted me to ask, even as the thought of it repulsed me.

'No. He never did, and, apart from Lucius, he forbade anyone else to, as the consequences would have been dreadful. Every vampire in Europe would have fought to possess her. And some tried. So Marcus appointed Lucius her guardian, and his own men – Justinus, Sempronius, Terentius, Calixtus, Martius and Galen—were placed under his command.'

I guessed those were the Latin names of the men I knew as Jake, Sam, Terens and Cal. The other two I hadn't heard before. 'What happened to those last two?' I pointed to their images in the window.

Luc's gaze strayed up there and moved from one face to the next. 'They died. Killed by vampire-hunters as they slept. The other vampires they encountered were wild, uncontrolled, killing indiscriminately, giving humans a reason to hunt us, and so had to be stopped.' The passion in his voice made me suspect he may have experienced such a thing sometime in his long life. I hadn't asked him just how old he was.

'It was one of the reasons for the establishment of the Principate—to rein them in and protect Antonia at the same time. That's how it started. Lucius became their leader, and since he was stronger, no one dared challenge him. Those few who tried were quickly dispatched. Then he and Marcus established the Brethren Laws, by which all blood drinkers must abide.'

'And that's worldwide?'

'Yes. Leaders were appointed from among them and made responsible for other vampires in their regions. They're the prefects; those still living are in the Eldership. Zhao and Kwame. You met them at the Ritual.'

'I remember them.' I thought back to last night. Apart from the woman, Maris, who looked like she needed reining in, the others appeared solemn, even wise. Somehow I couldn't picture them as wild and uncontrolled. But then, what did I know?

He let out a deep breath. 'Well, to finish a long story, Lucius noticed that whatever matured in Antonia's blood at age fifty began to wane as she reached her centenary. But her son, Paulus inherited it. His eyes, like hers, like those of all our kind, were lavender. And like her, he aged slowly and his blood matured at fifty. It gave off the same strong, sweet scent as his mother's. If there wasn't a changeover of Ingenii, Lucius could lose his position as princeps as he wouldn't be strong enough to fend off challengers. And it's for that reason,' he said, as he sat back down next to me, 'the Ritual was established as a sort of … coming-of-age rite, and to introduce the new Bloodgifted—as they came to be known—to the vampire community. On that very first occasion, nobody challenged, and everything went seemingly well for the next several centuries, until one arose and challenged Lucius for the right to be princeps. His name was Jaroslav, one of the prefects from Eastern Europe. They fought. Jaroslav bit off Lucius's finger and took the ring.' He indicated his own finger, on which sat a serpent ring identical to mine, except its eyes were green rather than red.

Luc continued. 'He placed it on his finger, but the eyes of the serpents turned black, and the metal began to burn. The ring rejected him. Rather than lose his finger, Jaroslav ripped it off. Unfortunately, Marcus didn't behead him, as he should have. He later became one of the ringleaders behind the Second Rebellion. Lucius was forced to dispatch him after that.'

It doesn't pay to play nice.

'Lucius retrieved the ring and placed it on his own— regenerated—finger. The serpent's eyes on both rings glowed bright red and so became a feature of the ceremony. It's been repeated from then on, every fifty years.'

'And that's how the Legacy began.' Although I said it aloud, it was more to myself. 'When exactly was that?'

'In the middle of the tenth century.'

Yep, I was definitely going to need glasses to hide my perpetually wide-eyed look. Luc must have been used to goggle-eyed Ingenii, for he kept on talking.

'Lucius fed from her descendants for the next nine-hundred years. Apart from one daughter, all the Bloodgifted were males.'

'Who was the daughter?'

'Judith.'

'And now me.'

He nodded then stood and took my hands in his. It was strange, but I felt comfortable with him doing that. It felt almost normal, unlike Alec whose touch made my body tingle.

'Laura, now is the time for you to know all.' He pulled me to my feet.

What else was there?

'My study.' He motioned to a closed door on the landing I hadn't noticed before. 'I tend to spend more time in this room than anywhere else in the house.'

He opened the door to reveal a masculine domain dominated by a massive table carved from malachite with a throne-like leather chair. Against the wall, near the entrance, stood a dark green, well-used Chesterfield on which my aunt sat. She rose as we entered.

'Come in, dear.' She beckoned me forward.

I heard the door close as I crossed the rich burgundy carpet that matched the leather inlay on the desk. Bookcases filled with leather-bound volumes lined the walls, interspersed here and there with silver-framed photographs. Luc, after following me in, stood beside Aunt Judy and took her hand. They looked anxious.

'Please, take a look, my Laura.' Luc swept his hand through the air.

I took a closer look at his personal gallery. Then I heard him softly call Alec.

I did a double take. The photos were all of me. There I was as a baby, maybe less than a year old, my little, chubby arms outstretched to a laughing fair-haired man as I took my first steps. I had a similar photo in my album at home, but only Aunt Judy was in it. Another one showed me, around two years old, being thrown high in the air by the same man. I had golden Shirley Temple curls, and my baby-self laughed down at him. The fair-haired man was Lucien Lebrettan and he looked the same then as now.

Still another photo showed me on my first birthday with Aunt Judy and Luc on either side of me helping me blow out my candle. My gaze travelled from frame to frame until I was dizzy. There was my first day at school, my high school sporting achievements and, in pride of place, my university graduation.

Luc appeared less often as I grew older. In photos of my teenage years, he was in the background and I had to peer closely to see him. It was either Mum and Dad or Aunt Judy who stood next to me.

I looked around and found more framed photos perched on shelves and on piles of stacked books. Every available space was taken up with various stages of my life.

A strange, hollow feeling opened up in my stomach as I tried to understand what I was seeing.

Luc had called me "ma petite, ma fille", which I knew, from my high school French meant "my little girl, my daughter". He'd also called me *my* Laura. I'd wondered at the familiarity I felt toward him, and why my Aunt Judy appeared at all my birthdays. And finally, it explained the gift I received every birthday. My parents never revealed its giver.

My throat went dry.

Alec had entered but seemed reluctant to remain; he stood in the doorway, his hand resting on the door handle.

'Please stay. This concerns you as well,' Luc said.

'This is a private family matter. I shouldn't be here.' He looked at me, his face unreadable.

'I'd appreciate it if you stayed.'

Dad walked past Alec into the room. His face was pale as his eyes connected with mine, and I saw deep sadness.

'Dad, what's going on?'

'There's no way to say it, baby girl, but it's time you knew the truth.' He pulled up a footstool near one of the bookshelves, sat on it and lowered his head. My dad only assumed such a posture when he was reluctant to involve himself in some task.

'You have your mother's colouring,' Luc said, and he looked at my aunt.

'But your father's looks and temper,' Aunt Judy said, and she looked at Luc before turning back to me. 'We're your parents, dear.'

CHAPTER 16
FAMILY MATTERS

LAURA

'This is a joke, right?'

'No, ma petite, it is not. We would never joke about such a thing.'

I felt the blood drain from my face as I stood, staring at both of them. Nobody moved. The tick-tock of the clock on the wall behind the desk was the only sound that broke the heavy silence. I looked at my dad. He raised his head and gave me a slow nod.

At that, my mind went utterly blank. Then slowly, their words sunk in; and it was like pieces of a puzzle coming together. I'd heard that, at the moment of death, your whole life supposedly flashes before your eyes. Well, I wasn't dying, but it was happening to me just the same.

I struggled to find my voice, and when I did, it came out in a hoarse whisper. 'If that's so, why did you give me away?'

'Laura,' my mother said. 'We loved you so very much. You were our baby, and we wanted to keep you with us forever. But we knew you were special and in possible danger. We had no choice.' Her lip started to quiver.

Luc squeezed her hand and took over. 'Because you're part vampire from my side and part Ingenii from your mother. You're unique, ma petite, neither completely human, nor completely vampire. For all we know, your blood could be even more potent than all previous Bloodgifted. I'm sure you've noticed you haven't aged since your mid-twenties. That can only mean your ageing process is closer to that of a vampire than a human—one year in every five hundred.'

I think my brain shut down. Everyone was watching me, concern etched on their faces, perhaps wondering how I was going to take all this. I just stood there, like a deer caught in headlights—unable to move, unable to say anything. First being told my parents weren't who I thought they were, and now that I would age one year in every five hundred! I didn't know which was the bigger shocker.

'Come sit down, my Laura.' Luc manoeuvred me to the Chesterfield, and Judy sat next to me, her gaze never leaving my face. He went to his desk, poured several glasses of brandy and handed one to me.

This was becoming a habit. I'd drunk more of the stuff in the last twelve hours than I had in my entire life.

'Drink it, ma petite.'

The fiery liquid slid down my throat.

Luc continued, 'We feared if the Brethren community found out about you, they would attempt a kidnapping.'

Judy nodded. 'You see, dear, Eilene and I were pregnant at the same time; and we even gave birth on the same day. Sadly though, her baby girl died of SIDS when she was three months old. So, your father and I made the heartbreaking decision to place you with them, hoping everyone would believe you to be hers.'

'Your aunt and uncle agreed to help us and adopted you. It also eased some of their pain,' my father said. 'And the Brethren community never found out what we'd done. We allowed them to believe you were the one who had died. Only our closest friends were entrusted with the secret.'

'By placing you with John and Eilene, we believed you would be safe, and we could watch over your progress without endangering your life.' Tears streamed down Judy's cheeks. I had never seen her cry before, and that alone moved me, although I was too much in shock to feel anything.

I looked at my dad. His face was white. He didn't contradict anything they said. He only nodded.

It was all so incredible, yet it was also a relief. Somehow I had always known. Whether it was some kind of sixth sense or perhaps a memory buried so deep it was like a dream, I'll never know. So, John and Eilene were not my real parents. Not that they had ever treated me anything but lovingly. If anything, they had indulged me too much.

'Laura,' my dad said. 'Eilene and I were overjoyed to have you. The doctors told her she couldn't have any more children after … we lost our own child.' His voice trailed to a whisper. 'Judy bringing you to us was a Godsend. We've loved you as our own. So much so, I didn't want this blasted day to come. You're our baby girl and always will be.'

My dad's words broke the dam. I spoke through tears. 'Is that why you were so … reluctant for me to … leave home? You were afraid … I'd be taken?'

'That's exactly why.'

I closed my eyes and lowered my head into my hands. I only looked up when someone gripped my upper arms. It was Judy.

'Oh, my dear Laura. It was torturous seeing you day after day in the arms of someone else, hearing you call them "mama" when it should have been me.…' She put her arms around me. I rested my head on her shoulder.

'I don't know what to say.'

'We've watched over you your whole life, ma petite.' Luc came to my side and stroked the back of my head. 'When you moved into your unit, I had it watched night and day to make sure you were safe.'

I looked at him, incredulous. I was watched? My emotions were in turmoil. Yet how could I be angry, when it was all done for my safety? Would I have done the same thing for my child? Perhaps. I would sacrifice anything to safeguard my child. But to give it up? Could I?

'I wanted to tell you on Friday night, when you and Matthew were there,' Judy said. 'If not for your father, I would have cracked. It wasn't the right time, my dear, dear Laura.'

'I felt there was something, but I just didn't understand … I mean, that's why I wanted to leave. I sensed there was something between you, but.…'

'We couldn't mention anything then, ma petite.'

Dad shifted on his footstool and looked up at me. His lined face was anguished, and he looked older. My heart ached for him, especially since he had to deal with this on his own. My mum ... no, no ... my Aunt Eilene—how would I get used to that?—was a wonderful mother, and I truly loved her, but she had never been good with stressful or emotionally taxing situations. I understood why she stayed at home. This would have been too much for her.

Luc poured me another shot of brandy. I gulped it down as I tried to pull my thoughts together and sort out the whirlwind of emotions churning within me that moment. Pain? Anger? Resentment? But the only thing that came out of my mouth was, 'Why didn't you tell me sooner?'

'It would have been too dangerous, ma petite. The Brethren community closely watches the princeps,' Luc said. 'We had to keep you hidden till you came of age. We couldn't take the risk—you're too precious. And it has proved to be the right decision.'

'Can you see why we had to part with you, even though we tried to remain as close as possible?' Judy gently brushed the hair from my forehead.

I nodded, but it was probably more of an automatic response than agreement.

'Perhaps if I hadn't fallen so much in love with your mother....'

My parents exchanged a loving glance, and Judy placed her hand over his.

'Luc was my father's guardian,' she said. 'We met, quite accidentally, when I had to drive your grandfather here for a *meeting* – as he called it. I had to wait to drive him home again. I thought I'd take a walk in the garden, and that's where we met and fell in love. But I was married. Until I got divorced from my first husband, William, Luc and I had to meet in secret.'

'For several years, actually,' he said. 'Then as it came closer to the time for your mother's coming of age, I began to worry, in case the Brethren detected we were lovers.'

'Will and I divorced a year before that, so, in essence, I was single.'

I knew she'd been married before and divorced, but it had all happened long before I was born. Dad had mentioned it once or twice and I got the impression he hadn't liked his brother-in-law.

'So you see, ma petite, if Judy had a child, which was inevitable after her fiftieth, guess who they'd think was the father? And they'd be right,' Luc said.

'When I did fall pregnant with you, dear, it was the happiest day of my life.' She beamed and ran the back of her hand softly down the side of my face.

'Scariest of mine.' Luc gave me a broad smile that belied his words. I somehow doubted much would scare him at all.

'Luc worried if he became my guardian, he'd endanger both me and you,' Judy said.

'So I turned to the one person I believed would make a perfect guardian and perhaps, an even better princeps then me. Alec.'

I looked to where he stood. He hadn't moved the entire time, but now he took a sharp breath.

'He needed a lot of persuasion. Alec didn't like the idea of being my lover's guardian. Blood feeding is very intimate.'

His gaze darted between Alec and myself. He had to have noticed the interchange between us in the kitchen this morning. How much of what I felt for Alec stemmed from the blood feeding and how much from a natural attraction? But this was not the time to be thinking of that.

I tried to imagine myself in their place. Who was I to judge? Their decision to hide me as a baby had been heart-wrenching for them both. I could still see it on Judy's face. Not knowing my true background had probably saved my life as well. I now understood what Alec had meant at our first meeting, and why it was decided I should be kept in blissful ignorance.

Yes, it had saved my life, but at what cost?

I looked at Judy, the woman I had known as my aunt, and saw another side to her. All these years she'd had to keep silent and stand in the background as another woman raised me. How it must have torn her heart. That explained why she kept so close and never missed my birthday or any other important event in my life.

They'd sacrificed their own joy for my safety. And the answer came to me – I would do the same for my child.

I took another deep breath and looked at Alec. He never wanted to be princeps, according to my father. Had barely touched her, according to my mother. Never taken advantage of her even though as princeps he had every right. This knowledge, coupled with what I had learned of him from Terens last night, made him grow in my estimation. I couldn't help but admire and respect him.

My gaze shifted to Luc, my vampire father. He smiled and leaned forward to kiss me on the forehead. 'Laura, ma petite, so much has been asked of you in these last three days, and now, on top of everything, you learn the truth of your parentage. You have had to accept much and done it willingly and graciously. I'm proud of you.'

He opened his arms, and I went into them. He was my father. He hugged me tightly and held on as if he'd never let go.

'I've wanted to do this for a very long time,' he said.

Judy leaned her head on my shoulder and placed her arms around the two of us. I looked down to my dad, sitting patiently despite his long legs on that silly little stool. He smiled up at us, not bothering to hide the tears sliding down his face.

I raised my head from Luc's shoulder. 'If you think I'm going to be calling you Uncle John from now on,' I told him, 'forget it.'

'No way, baby. I'm your dad and always will be.'

Turning to Luc and Judy, I said, 'I don't think I can call you "Mum" and "Dad", and "Mother" and "Father" will take some getting used to.'

They laughed. I'm sure out of sheer relief. ' "Luc" will do, ma petite, but if you can manage to call me "Papa", I would be overjoyed.' He beamed, and his eyes welled with red tears.

'I know it will be difficult for you to call me mother, so Judy will be fine.'

'You've always been more than an aunt in so many ways. It makes sense now and explains why I came to you whenever Mum was stressing out.'

'I could never tell you.' Fresh tears ran down her cheeks.

'You're home now, finally home.' Luc hugged me tighter.

I looked at Alec. As our eyes met, he smiled, and my heart leapt.

CHAPTER 17
INTO THE GARDEN

LAURA

There was an hour left before Matt was due to pick me up. His shift didn't end till 8 p.m., so I had time to kill—so to speak. Luc and Judy were giving me some breathing space to digest the momentous revelations about my birth. Even as shocked as I felt, somehow it made sense. I would never stop loving my adoptive parents, John and Eilene. I could not have been loved any more than if I had been their natural daughter. But now I knew, and any stranger could easily detect the physical resemblance between my birth father and myself—the same oval-shaped face, high cheekbones, slightly full lower lip. Why hadn't I seen it? Perhaps I did, but my mind had been unwilling to accept it. Pity I didn't inherit his fair hair, though. My mother gave me her rich copper locks and creamy complexion. Ah well.

I left Luc's study and made my way downstairs and to the other end of the house. There was something I wanted to do, alone. Following Judy's direction, I walked through the French doors in the downstairs dining room and went in search of the garden where my parents had met and fallen in love.

As I stepped outside, the heady scent of gardenias filled the air, and the sky had begun to change from a deep-azure-blue to a dusky apricot. The cicadas were warming up to their nocturnal hum, promising a warm night and hot day tomorrow. A slightly overgrown sandstone path, its edges softened by velvet-eyed pansies and peeping violas, meandered for several yards before opening to reveal a lush lawn dotted with young beech trees at one end.

At the other end towered a majestic Morton Bay Fig tree, whose discarded and decaying fruit littered the ground around its massive trunk. At its base, leaned an ivy-green wrought-iron garden seat with scrolled arms and delicate leaf tracery.

This was the place.

I wandered over and sat on the leaf-strewn bench trying to imagine Luc and Judy in this spot fifty years ago. Had much changed?

I closed my eyes and listened to the sounds of the encroaching night: birds noisily arguing over a disputed nest, the soft croaking of green tree frogs, the breeze whispering through the lofty branches of the fig tree above and stirring my hair, wafting strands lightly across my face.

A cool hand gently swept the stray locks from my cheek and I jumped. Alec sat on the bench next to me, one arm bent on his lap, the other casually curling the loose ends of my hair in his fingers. It was enough to give me a cardiac arrest.

'What are you doing here?'

'Checking if you're okay. That was quite an ordeal.'

'Oh.' I was about to tell him to go. This was my time, and I resented the intrusion. 'How did you know where to find me?'

'Look at your ring. The serpent's eyes glow when we're near one another.'

I glanced down. A strong, warm glow suffused my hand. Why hadn't I noticed it? 'Did it react this way with my mother?'

'No. It was very faint, but enough to convince the Elders. It only flared brightly when your father was by her side. On her visits, I passed the ring to Luc and left the apartment.'

And now mine flared whenever Alec was near. I didn't want to pursue the implications of that at the moment. 'So, you rarely fed from her.'

'I had my own … sources.' He grinned.

I bet he did. I could visualize women trampling over each other in their stilettos to offer him their throats.

'So, how are you?' he asked with real concern, my hair twined around his finger.

'Fine, oddly enough. It slots everything into place for me, and I can't hate them for what they did. Does that make sense?'

'Laura, that was the hardest thing anyone could face. By rights you should be angry, even knowing their actions stemmed out of their love for you.'

'That's the very reason I can't be.' I shook my head. 'In their position I probably would've done exactly the same. You know they sent me a gift every birthday? I never knew who it was from.'

'That sounds like them.' He smiled warmly.

I sighed and bowed my head. 'I would never want to be faced with a terrible decision like that—to give away my baby.'

Alec dropped my hair and lifted my chin to meet his gaze. 'That'll never happen,' he said with such passion that I was puzzled.

He would make a good father. Kind, caring and patient ... I mentally shook my head to clear it of the images those words evoked. Why was I even thinking that way? I certainly had no intention of finding out. Desperate to get my thoughts on another track, I decided to bring up the subject of his kiss. Had that been part of the Ritual or not?

I angled my chin out of his grasp—he had held it for too long—and sat back a little farther. It felt safer. The closer he came, the more he disturbed my peace of mind.

'Alec, can I ask you something?'

'Anything.'

'During last night's ceremony, you kissed me.'

He leaned closer and slid his arm along the back of the seat behind me.

'Was that part of the ceremony or not?' I tried to focus on his eyes, aware of the arm creeping closer to my shoulder, but I refused to budge.

He paused before replying. 'No. I took advantage of the close proximity of your lovely mouth.' His gaze went directly there.

At least he was honest. I thought back to the murmuring I had heard amongst the assembled guests, and even among the Elders.

Alec Munro had added his own personal touch to the Ritual. 'So, it had nothing to do with the bloodlust.'

He shrugged. 'Perhaps a minor part.'

'Then why?'

'You know, we can spend all day discussing the reasons why a man kisses a woman.' His other hand traced the line of my jaw.

I moved away. 'Don't do that.'

'Why not?'

I slid back farther, breaking my resolve to stand my ground. 'It's too intimate.'

He inched forward, closing the gap. 'Why are you nervous?'

'Who said I'm nervous? Besides, I'm not used to being in this position.' I attempted to widen the distance between us. Unfortunately, I had run out of seat.

'What position is that?' he said in a low voice, and his eyes strayed back to my mouth.

The wrought-iron arm of the garden seat dug into my back. There was nowhere left to go. 'In a relationship with one man and....'

'And?' He pressed his other hand against my back and slid me across the bench, drawing me to him. The movement was so sudden, I thought he must have oiled the seat.

'... Seduced by another.' I gasped.

'Is that what I'm doing?' He bent his head to nuzzle the side of my neck.

'You very well know it is!' I barely managed to say, while guiltily enjoying the delicious sensations of his mouth on my throat. His lips were soft and cool and oh, it felt so good.

'Is that a problem?'

He had to be kidding. But still I didn't pull away. 'Being seduced by you? Yes!'

With my hands against his chest, I battled the urges to either push him away or wrap my arms around his neck. Stalemate.

His mouth slowly slid along my jaw. 'Do you love him?'

His question jolted me. 'You asked me that before, and I said it was private.'

He raised his head and looked into my eyes while his hand stroked my cheek. 'If you can't answer, then something's amiss.'

Rather than disagree, I found myself questioning my own feelings toward Matt. A sense of unease stole over me.

Alec didn't wait for my response. His hand moved from my cheek to the back of my neck, stroking and caressing while his arm tightened at my waist. All the while his eyes never left mine and I knew I was in danger. Not in any physical sense, but he was an incredibly attractive man, and I felt flattered by his advances—too flattered. Then, as his eyes travelled down to my mouth and his head bent toward me, he said, 'I'm going to kiss you. Any objections?'

The sensible part of me—my head—wanted to push him off and rush back into the house, but that other part—my heart—said the opposite. For better or worse, I listened to my heart and hoped I wouldn't regret it.

'Yes,' I lied. But there was no conviction behind it. My eyes closed as his mouth bridged the gap between us.

His lips were warm yet firm, demanding, insisting on my response. The tip of his tongue tantalizingly traced the outline of my lips before parting them and sliding in. It was like nothing I'd ever experienced. Total possession. Instead of fighting it, I pressed myself to him. Just as I started to return his kiss, he stopped and my eyes shot open.

Alec looked down at me with half-lidded eyes. 'This is only the beginning.'

He lowered his head and began to work his way slowly and sensually across my face, tenderly kissing my forehead, each eye, the tip of my nose, my cheeks, lingering torturously at the corners of my mouth before skimming over the surface of my lips on his way to my chin. Then he returned to hover teasingly above my mouth while his breath mingled with mine.

It was deliciously agonising, and I wanted to grab his head and force his lips back to mine. He took my hands and raised them up and around his neck, before slipping one arm around my waist and another behind my knees to lift me onto his lap, after which he gently lowered my body so that I leant against his hard shoulder. Then his mouth was back on mine, and my response staggered me.

It was only a kiss, yet my breath came in gasps, and my poor heart beat so strongly I thought it would burst. His presence was overwhelming: his scent, strong and masculine, the slight abrasiveness of his skin as it brushed against mine, the sound of his breathing, and the strength of his arms tight around me. His shoulders were broad enough to envelope me totally.

Was he just as affected? I felt his heart beat strongly once or twice against my breast, his breathing, just as ragged as my own. My earlier decision to keep our relationship strictly platonic now seemed to belong to the realm of fantasy. How on earth was I going to cope with this if we were to meet several times a week?

Now I understood why Judy had Luc nearby. Could I do the same with Matt? If not, I was in trouble for I sensed my growing feelings for him couldn't be blamed entirely on our blood bond. Yet, I was too afraid to admit to anything more. Maybe ... just maybe it was only an infatuation?

The depth of his kiss increased as he crushed me to him and delved into my mouth like he was staking a claim. His hand moved from my back to the curve of my breast and his thumb teased my nipple in slow rhythmic circles, sending waves of electricity pulsing through me. And heaven help me, I didn't want him to stop.

His hand moved slowly over my fluttering stomach, my hip, and even further, sliding beneath the hem of my shorts to stroke my inner thigh.

I gasped and grabbed his wrist.

'No, Alec. Please.' Only Matt ever touched me there.

'If you're worried about anyone seeing us, don't. The men won't rise for another half hour. Luc and Judith are in the house, and there's no one else around. We're quite alone.'

'It's not that....'

'Then what is it?'

In a desperate effort to regain some control, I uncoiled his arms and stood. To my embarrassment, my body trembled, and this time I had no bite to blame it on. 'Why are you doing this?' I asked.

'I want you, Laura.'

His blatant honesty stunned me. 'What if I don't want you back?'

He raised one eyebrow, and a slow, sardonic smile crept across his face. 'Don't tell me you didn't enjoy that. I know otherwise. Your body sent out a very distinct message.'

Traitorous body! 'Well, my mind is giving me another message entirely, and I'm listening to it.'

The smile disappeared and he rose. I had to angle my head to look up at him. 'You're the one who let me go that far. I was wondering when you'd tell me to stop.'

'That's not fair! You came onto me so quickly; I was overwhelmed.'

'You're a grown woman, Laura. You knew exactly what I was doing.'

I hated to admit he was right—I did let him go too far. Angry, I bit my lip and glared back. 'Don't ever touch me again.'

'That's going to be a bit hard, darling seeing as we'll be in close proximity for the next fifty years.'

I baulked at the way he facetiously called me "darling." I clenched my fists. 'From now on, Matt's going to be with me every time you feed from me. So when that rotten bloodlust hits, he'll be there to satisfy it. Not you.'

Judy's voice from the other end of the garden startled us both. 'Laura! Matt's here. He's in the reception room with Luc.'

Crap! Crap! Crap! I turned away from Alec, berating myself for listening to my stupid heart. It was lust, silly woman. Pure lust. Or was it? I wiped away tears of anger with the back of my hand.

'Laura? What's wrong, dear?' Judy asked as I met her halfway.

'Nothing. I'm … just tired, that's all. I'd better go to Matt.' I kept walking, my heart pounding in my ears like an amplified drum.

'Dear,' she said a little breathlessly as she caught up to me. 'Before you go in, you must know that your father and I had a chat with him.'

I stopped. 'What did you tell him?'

I must have looked panicky, for she patted my shoulder. 'It's all right. We thought you might find it difficult to tell him about … everything, you know.'

She was right. Where would I even begin? 'How did he take it?'

'He's very quiet, dear.'

I groaned. Leaving her, I re-traced my steps using the same path that led from the dining room, through the wood-panelled hall to the front reception room.

Luc waited outside. 'Would you like me to go in with you, ma petite?'

I was grateful for his offer, but I needed to see Matt alone. 'No, I think it's best I speak to him alone.'

He nodded and gave me a hug. I tried not to remember what had happened with Alec as I opened the door, walked in and closed it firmly behind me.

CHAPTER 18
MESS UP

ALEC

Damn! I seriously miscalculated Laura's attachment to Sommers, and now it appeared as if I only succeeded in driving her further into his arms. But her sweet little body didn't lie, despite her protests. And if little Miss Ingenii hoped I was going to tolerate her boyfriend being present while I fed from her, then she was in for a surprise.

I paced the scented garden, reliving every word and expression of that last hour. She had been so responsive, I even dared to run my hand down her soft, smooth skin, and it was an effort to stop. In fact, if she hadn't.... Damn, but I wanted her. That had been no lie, and it had nothing to do with Luc's infernal ultimatum, either.

'Alec?' Judith came into the garden and gave me an intent look. 'What happened? Laura was upset.'

I wondered how much she knew of Luc's Machiavellian plans. 'Misunderstanding on my part, that's all.'

'I see. Is everything all right between you?'

'Yes, yes, it's fine,' I lied, before letting out a tense breath. 'Luc spoken to the boyfriend yet?'

'We both did. Luc's still with him.'

'What did you tell him?'

'Laura's bloodline, possible lifespan and the fact she'll outlive him by centuries.'

That would have been interesting. 'How did he take it?'

'Hard to tell.' She frowned and bit her lip the way Laura did. I tried not to smile. 'Any chance he might be scared off?'

'That's what we're hoping. Pity he hasn't any Pictish blood. I quite like him.'

For some reason her remark bothered me. 'Did you mention the danger she could be in?'

'I left that to Luc.' She appeared as if she was about to say something but then shook her head and went into the house, leaving me to my thoughts and the clicking of night crickets.

The sun had long set and I sensed the rising of the others. Two were already in the kitchen pouring small bags of blood into glasses. Snacks. I decided to join them, to keep my mind off Laura.

'So, what's been happening?' Cal asked when I walked in. He'd just placed some blood in a shaker and was in the process of creating his own cocktail with some of Luc's fine Irish whisky and ice cubes.

Jake shook his head and laughed. 'There's no accounting for taste.'

Cal ignored him and gulped his concoction, wiping his mouth with the back of his sleeve, like a child who has just finished a chocolate milkshake.

I sat on the lower steps that led up to the hallway. 'Laura's human is here to take her home.'

'You mean the one's who's been coming and going from her place? The cop?'

'That's the one.'

'Seen him a few times when I was on guard. Possessive type. Tried not to listen in, but you know.' Cal shrugged.

His remark interested me. 'Possessive? In what way?'

He gazed at me over the rim of the shaker as he swallowed the last drop. 'Likes to know where she is, what she's up to. That kind of thing.'

From the expression on Cal's face, I'd say he didn't like Matt Sommers. I recalled my meeting with the man the other day and knew Cal's comment to be true. Laura would have a hard time breaking up with him—when the time came—if our observations were correct.

'Does he know about … us?' Jake queried.

'He knows.'

He and Cal exchanged a quick look. I wasn't in the mood to explain as I tuned in to what was happening above stairs. Laura had just left the house with Judith, which meant Luc was alone with Sommers. I wanted to be there.

CHAPTER 19
SAFE AND FAMILIAR

LAURA

Luc's reception room opened directly from the wood-panelled hallway, and was composed of warm browns and tan tones giving it a cosy and welcoming feel. Three large bay windows allowed the last of the fading light to flood the room and bounce off the stuccoed ceiling. A hefty circular, glass and metal table, with a small bronze bust of Voltaire placed at its centre, sat amidst various-sized leather and fabric armchairs. Soft beige carpet covered the floor, except for the area near the marble fireplace, where jade and cream Victorian flagstones decorated the hearth.

Matt stood by one of the bay windows, looking out. He turned as I entered. He'd just finished a long shift and looked tired, but the circles under his eyes reflected more than that. The look on his face made my heart sink. There was sadness I'd never seen before. We looked at each other for a long moment. Then Matt opened his arms and I rushed to him.

He leaned down and kissed me. Even that felt sad. There was no teasing in it, like last time, and I wanted to cry. Matt must have sensed that, for his hand moved to the back of my head and he pressed me closer, parting my lips, his tongue entwining with mine. I clung to him, willing myself to tremble at his touch – but nothing came.

He lifted his head to look at me, then bent down to kiss me again – deeper and longer this time.

My body remained calm—as always.

Matt was familiar, and it felt good to be in his arms again. I tried to put Alec, and what had occurred between us less than a few minutes ago, from my mind. But, things *had* changed; I couldn't deny it. My own wretched blood-inheritance was the cause, and there was not a thing I could do about it.

I buried my head in his chest and he stroked my hair.

'So,' he said after a while, 'you're Dracula's daughter.'

'Oh, Matt, don't.' I looked up at him. 'Luc's my biological father and Judy's not really my aunt. She's my mother.'

He sighed. 'They told me everything, including your possible lifespan. How do you feel about that?'

'What can I do? I have to accept it.' I shrugged. 'S'pose now I can extend that bucket list!'

Matt's gaze roamed my face as his hand gently traced the curves of my jaw and chin. I had the distinct impression he was memorising my face. Then, as his hand slid to my neck, his brow furrowed.

'I don't recall seeing these two freckles before.'

My heart stopped—Alec's bite. Matt suddenly pushed me away, holding me at arms length, his eyes glacial. 'He bit you. The bastard!'

'Matt! It was part of the ceremony. He had to—'

'Brand you as his possession.' His voice became as cold as his eyes.

'Please understand.' I gripped his arms. 'If he hadn't, they would all come after me. It's for my protection. And he was very gentle. It didn't hurt,' I lied and prayed I wouldn't hiccup.

Matt was breathing hard. 'I want to kill him.'

My stomach clenched as I visualised Matt and Alec literally at each other's throats. I couldn't let that happen. 'You know what I am, Matt. I need him. Compared to the many others I saw last night, I couldn't have a better guardian. Could you protect me against them?'

His shoulders sagged. 'No,' he admitted. 'It's not easy for me to accept something I've always believed to be a myth. And it's right here on my own patch and involving the one person in the world I care the most about.'

'I'm so sorry.'

There was a long silence between us as Matt grappled with the news. A muscle ticked in the side of his jaw. 'So, what were they like, these – vampires?' he said in a resigned tone.

'Beautiful and very powerful.' I remembered Douglas's strength as he squeezed my hand.

Matt drew me into his arms. 'Oh babe, why did it have to be you?'

Coldness crept over me, and I couldn't answer.

Matt lifted my chin to meet his gaze. A determined look was etched on his face. 'Laura, I know how different we are.' That was an understatement. 'But we can make this work. Your parents have. Judith is human, and Lebrettan is ... you know, yet nothing has stopped them being together, even if for only a little while. They understand that every day is precious, and they're making the most of it, before Judith dies. Tell me we've got the same chance.'

For a moment I was stunned. 'Is this a proposal?'

'I suppose it is.'

It was so unexpected. I was unsure what to say. Could I do it? Could I risk the future and create another generation of cursed Dantonvilles, or Sommers' if I married him? As I mulled this over, the spectre of my parents' sacrifice appeared in my mind's eye and I saw history repeating itself, only this time it would be my child.

'Oh Matt.' I pulled out of his embrace. 'What about children?'

'They told me about that. If you and I have any kids, they'll inherit that blasted gene.' He shook his head. 'They think I should do the noble thing and break up with you.'

My stomach went for a dive. How dare they!

'They're right, you know. I should....' He paused, and I vigorously shook my head. 'But I can't do that, Laura.' He gripped my shoulders. 'We can work around this. I can have a ... vasectomy.'

I stared at him, unbelieving. Matt was willing to do that for me and he made it sound as if it was such a simple thing. It was crazy!

'No! No way—on the vasectomy thing. I'm not letting you do that. Forget it.' I threw my hands in the air. It was all too much and I desperately needed to get away. 'I can't discuss this now ... I, need some time to think a whole lot of things through for both of us. Can we just go home?'

'I don't want to lose you, Laura.'

He kissed me before taking my hand. Together we left the front room.

Luc and Judy were talking, heads locked together, at the other end of the hallway. They must have been waiting there the whole time.

'Laura, do you mind if I have another brief word with Matthew before he takes you home?' Luc asked.

What was he up to? I looked to Matt.

'It's okay. Wait for me at the car, babe.'

My mother linked her arm through mine. 'Let's wait outside, dear. It's a lovely evening.'

I couldn't begin to guess what else they wanted Matt to know, but I had reached overload. Judy and I left and stood by Matt's car.

I ground my back teeth together. 'How could you have told Matt to break up with me?'

'Laura dear, we don't want you to suffer what we went through. If you marry him and have children, you know the consequences.'

'But the choice should be mine.'

She nodded. 'You'll make the right decision, dear. I'm sure.'

'Mother, if you think....' I stopped when she smiled.

'Oh, Laura, do you know how long I've waited for you to call me that?' She threw her arms around my neck and anything further I wanted to say just seemed pointless. I gave up and hugged her back.

'Can I ask you something?' I ventured.

'Of course, dear.'

'It's a bit personal.'

'I'm your mother; you can ask me anything.'

I took a deep breath. 'Did you ever, um, tremble after being bitten by Luc or even when he wasn't biting you, when he, for instance … kissed you?'

'Always!' She laughed. A look of understanding crossed her face. 'Ah, that explains what I saw between you and Alec in the garden. Did he try to kiss you?'

'Uh huh, and the awful thing is, I kissed him back and my body shook.'

'Why is kissing Alec so awful?' Her voice was almost a whisper.

'Well, because of … Matt.'

'Does the same thing happen when he kisses you?'

I shook my head.

'Interesting.'

Just then Matt walked out, and she whispered, 'Like mother, like daughter. Remember, dear.'

If that were true, then I would have to keep my distance from Alec Munro. Although how, as he'd be feeding from me for the next half-century, was anyone's guess.

CHAPTER 20
DEPARTURE

ALEC

I raced up the kitchen steps and through the house, pausing just outside the closed reception-room door as I glimpsed Laura leaning against the car, deep in conversation with Judith. Out of respect, I didn't eavesdrop. The expression on her face gave nothing away.

I knocked on the door before walking in. Sommers gave me a curt nod as I entered.

Luc turned from the window, where he must have been watching his wife and daughter. 'Matthew, there is a possibility Laura could be in danger.'

Sommers's head swivelled toward him. 'In what way?'

'There are some among our kind who covet Alec's position. My daughter's bloodline is unique. It enables my kind to daywalk, and there are those who are envious enough to attempt to take her for themselves.'

'Does she know?'

'Yes. I explained it to her last night,' I said. 'We believed she'd be safe after the Ritual. Now we're not so sure, so we're being cautious. We have two men posted outside her flat for tonight, and until I can arrange a female of our own kind to stay with her inside, you'll have to do that.'

He gave me a little smile. 'I've already stayed there on several occasions. She won't be particularly surprised if I suggest it tonight.'

That son of a bitch! It was an effort to keep my clenched my fists by my side.

'But this time it'll be different,' Luc said. 'Under no circumstances are you to sleep with her. You've been told the consequences should Laura conceive a child. Contraception does not work on the Bloodgifted, and condoms are unreliable. You must not take that risk.' Luc's eyes lightened, and he bared his fangs. 'Should I smell you on her in an intimate way, I will kill you.'

Sommers blanched, and the fear that emanated from him turned to terror when the door behind me opened and Jake and Cal entered. They said nothing, but stood, still as sentries, on either side of the door. Sommers must have felt trapped, for he reached for his gun.

'There's no need for that.' I took it before he could loosen it from the holster. 'Calm down. You've nothing to fear from us. We have a common aim, and that's to protect Laura.'

'You're all monsters!' Fear radiated from him, and coupled with anger and aggression, it placed him in danger. In a room full of vampires, he gave off the scent of prey—with the promise of a hunt and a feed.

Jake's and Cal's nostrils flared. They took a step forward and I warned them back with a snarl.

'Alec, get him out of here!' Luc said.

I dragged Sommers from the room, down the entrance hallway and out of the house. Once outside, he began to recover and shook himself free. Beads of sweat stood out on his forehead.

'If not for her, I'd come back and burn this place down with all of you in it.'

'That's the second time you've threatened me, Sommers. It's a nasty habit with you.'

He looked at me with abject hatred, his breath coming in gasps.

'Calm down, Sommers and I'll let you have your gun back. I don't want you accidently shooting someone.'

'Bastard!'

He glanced toward his car, composed himself and held out his hand. I placed the gun in it.

'Take her home,' I told him. 'We'll follow at a distance.'

CHAPTER 21
DECISIONS

LAURA

As Matt wove through the city traffic, my emotions were in a whirl. Alec's face kept surfacing in my mind, and try as I might, I couldn't dislodge it. What was wrong with me? What perversion was in me that responded to his kisses and, even now, wanted more. Matt had been pale as the proverbial ghost when he'd left the house. And now, he kept glancing in the rear-vision mirror.

'Is something the matter?'

'What?'

'You keep looking in the mirror.'

'Just habit.'

'Okay.' He never did that before. What *did* Luc say to him?

After that, Matt remained strangely silent. When we pulled up outside my apartment, he cut the engine and turned to face me. Even in the car's dim light, I could see the vein in his temple pulsing. I chewed my lower lip.

'Laura ... we need to talk.'

Funny, the effect of those five little words. One moment all's fine with the world and the next, it's crumbling around your ears.

From the hollow note in Matt's voice, I knew it was going to be the latter. He'd had time to think and maybe reassess what he'd said earlier. Was this going to be his break-up speech? I took a deep breath and readied myself for the inevitable, although nothing would alleviate the pain of it. I nodded so he wouldn't hear the catch in my throat as tears already threatened.

'I never told you, but the day we met, I kept trying to spot a ring on your hand; I was sure some lucky guy already had you. When I answered a question from one of the kids in your class, I looked at you. The smile you gave me turned my insides, well … you know.'

He leaned over and smoothed the hair off my face. 'Then you brushed your hair back off your forehead, and I checked out your finger. No ring. I thanked my lucky stars. When you asked me to stay for morning tea, my throat dried up. Where I got the courage to ask you out that night, I still don't know, and when you accepted, I thought I was the luckiest man alive. I went back to the station in a delirium, useless for the rest of the day. All I could think of was you.'

I blinked. It wasn't what I'd expected. 'You were so patient with the kids; I liked you straight off, and nothing has changed for me.'

'It has for me.'

No words could have hurt more. A punch in the stomach would have been kinder. I swallowed. 'You're breaking up with me?'

Matt frowned. 'What put that idea into your head?'

I blinked. What was going on? 'But you said … you don't feel the same….'

He took me by the shoulders. 'Laura, I love you. And tonight Lebrettan did everything possible to scare the shit out of me and make me leave you. But all it did was confirm my feelings for you, and I'm determined to get you as far from them as possible.'

'They're my family, Matt. And besides, where could we go where they wouldn't find us? Be realistic! It just isn't possible unless we live six months in Alaska and six months in Antarctica in the midnight sun, perhaps?'

'Maybe we could—'

'Matt stop, please!' I pulled out of his grip and turned to open the door.

'Let's talk about this inside.'

I agreed—we needed to discuss this further. I had no intention of leaving, but I eventually wanted kids, and with Matt, that would be impossible without continuing the family curse. The thought of our child being vampire food filled me with horror, and I would do anything to prevent it. But Matt knew that.

I was preoccupied with these thoughts when I inserted the key into the lock. At that moment the Serpent Ring glared up at me – with black eyes. Too late I recognised the danger sign, and as the lock clicked open, I nearly fell when the door was wrenched open from the inside. Something grabbed me, and I screamed.

A blow struck the side of my head, hard enough for me to see lights and send me sprawling onto the hard wooden floor.

CHAPTER 22
WHEN THINGS GO WRONG

ALEC

I stood at the window and watched the dust billow up from Sommers's car as it headed for the front gate. For some reason, I had an uneasy feeling, although I didn't sense the presence of any of the Brethren, apart from present company. The serpent ring glowed a comforting red, so there was no hint of danger nearby—and Laura was well guarded—yet my scalp prickled.

Just in case the house was being watched, I'd decided to leave two minutes later.

'So *you* drive to Laura's block of flats, park *your* car somewhere out of sight and watch and wait? Is that the great plan?' Jake asked.

'Simple and stupid.' Cal was comfortably settled in a deep-blue velvet lounge chair, his long legs stretched out in front of him.

'Do you have a better idea?' I could always rely on Cal to give me a direct and undiluted opinion.

'Alec,' Jake said, 'that's exactly what they'll be expecting you to do.'

'You're not going anywhere without one of us, and that's not negotiable,' Cal said. 'But on the other hand, we could all be worrying for nothing. It hasn't happened in four-hundred years, nor was an attempt made on Judith. Why Laura, and why now?'

As one voice we answered. 'Maris!'

'Bloody woman,' he growled.

I turned back to the window. Laura and Sommers were temporarily on their own, at least till they got to Laura's flat. What if they were attacked on route? Could he handle a vampire attack? Even with a gun, he was one weak mortal, against the supernatural strength of our kind. His gun would be useless against them. He couldn't defend her against one let alone two vampires. What had I been thinking, leaving her alone with him?

'Alec, what's wrong?' Luc asked.

'We should have stayed close. Sommers can't possibly protect her from a Brethren attack. All they need to do is waylay them on route and take her.'

'What, in traffic? People everywhere?' Cal asked.

'No, near her flat. The streets there are quiet and dark. Less people around.'

'Aren't Sam and Terens on guard duty tonight?'

'Has anyone heard from them?' I asked.

Jake and Cal looked at each other and shook their heads. 'I thought they checked in with you, Luc,' Jake said.

Luc swore. 'Alec, get going. I'll get the swords from the gym and catch up.'

I ran out the front door and into my car.

'No you don't, mate,' Jake called after me. 'Not without us.' He and Cal shot into the back seat just as I opened up full throttle and my tyres screeched over the gravel.

'You really think they'll try something?' Cal asked.

I glanced at my ring. The serpent's eyes were slowly turning black. 'She's in danger.'

'How do you know?' Jake asked.

'The Ring. Look!' I lifted my hand.

'Shit!' Cal exclaimed. From the rear-view mirror, I saw him dig his mobile out of his pocket, press a button and listen a while before giving up. He tried again with another number. I knew he was trying to reach Sam or Terens. 'Damn! Nothing.'

A niggling image from the ceremony on Monday night now made sense.

'Her scent,' I said. 'That's why Douglas danced with her—to get her scent! Didn't make sense at the time, so I ignored it.' I slapped my forehead. 'I let her dance with him, even placed her hand in his; gave them what they wanted, so they could follow her scent to where she lives and lie in wait.'

I berated myself while negotiating the sharp turns down New South Head Road.

'Oh, hell.' Jake slammed the back of my seat. 'Look, if it's any consolation, none of us caught that either. They were masking well.'

'No, you had your suspicions last night, and you were right, Jake. I damn well should have done something about it. Letting her go alone with Sommers was irresponsible.'

'Hey, you think he would have let you do otherwise? She's his girl, Alec, and *he* wants to protect her.'

Whether he's capable or not, I felt like saying, but I let it go. It had been my stupid mistake in the first place.

For a Tuesday night, the traffic was ridiculously heavy. On top of that, we seemed to catch every red light between Vaucluse and Balmain. We needed to get there before them, but at this rate it wasn't looking good. I glanced in the rear-view mirror to see Luc's champagne-coloured BMW close behind. Jean was with him. I could hear him talking on the mobile to Marcus Antonius, informing him of events.

I drove through the city, down George Street and up the Western Distributor, hoping we wouldn't come across a police patrol car, but there was no way to avoid the red-light cameras located at just about every intersection. We sped over the Anzac Bridge and zigzagged through the traffic to get to Victoria Road, which for once, ran smoothly at peak hour. I turned right into Darling Street, and dodged a few startled pedestrians.

Sommers's car was parked in front of her building. It was empty. I tore out of my car and raced to Laura's flat just as the BMW skidded to a halt behind me. The others were right on my heels. I could sense humans all around me in the building, but no blood drinkers. A faint heartbeat came from Laura's flat, but it wasn't hers. The door was ajar. Sommers's body lay face down on the floor. His gun lay nearby, not fired—I couldn't smell gunpowder, only blood. Much of it was smeared along the doorframe and along the floor.

I crouched by the prostrate form. A deep laceration on the right side of his head bled profusely. He must have been slammed into the doorframe—I could smell his blood, not Laura's. She wasn't here, and for a moment I was torn between following her scent and doing my duty as a doctor. Whoever had taken Laura wouldn't harm her—her blood was too precious. Refusing to dwell on the repercussions of losing her, I concentrated on the man's injuries while Luc and Jean ran through the flat looking for clues as to who took her.

'Rebels got her,' Jean said vehemently, and his eyes began to change.

'Mmmmm, he smells good,' Cal said in a hypnotic way, and his fangs slid out.

'No.' I gave him a warning look. He returned it with a challenging stare before recovering, his fangs retracting.

'Sorry. Better if I go and scout outside.' He disappeared into the night.

I bent back down to Sommers while the others fanned out through the unit trying to detect traces of a recognisable scent, one that could be followed back to its source.

'Luc, throw me that towel, will you?' He was leaning out the kitchen window, scanning and sniffing the air, a towel draped over the chair beside him.

He threw it. I caught it, pressed it around Sommers's head to stem the blood flow, and took out my mobile phone. After calling for an ambulance, I checked for other injuries. His shoulder had been dislocated, so I popped it back into place. He would wake up very sore. There was the real possibility he could have a fractured skull as well as a serious contusion. Only a CT scan would determine whether he had any underlying brain injury. The sooner he got to hospital the better.

I turned his body around and placed him in the recovery position. Whoever took Laura would have regarded a human like Sommers as dispensable. The only thing that saved him was that they must have sensed us coming and hadn't had time to feed. And there was another scent on him, one I'd been taught to recognise and avoid—white oak. I searched his pockets and pulled out a small box. It contained six bullets—not lead, but white oak.

Son of a bitch! They weren't in his possession Saturday morning. Sometime between then and now, he must have made the decision to kill us. Why else would he be carrying it?

Sommers stirred, regaining consciousness. 'Laur-a,' he groaned and attempted to sit up. I pushed him back down.

'Lay still. You've been seriously injured. I've called the ambulance.'

He did as asked and closed his eyes. 'They– took her. I– couldn't stop them.'

'I know. There was nothing you could have done.'

His pulse was steady, his eyes closed. My medical oath was the only thing that stopped me from taking his life. How easy it would be, and Laura would believe he'd been killed trying to protect her. End of the Sommers problem. Instead, I made a snap decision.

'Open your eyes, Sommers. Look at me.' Slowly he did so, and I projected my will into his. 'When you wake again, you will have no memory of Laura Dantonville, nor Lucien Lebrettan, nor Alec Munro. Those names and faces will be strange to you, as will the knowledge of vampires in this city. You will have no memory of any events before July this year.' Satisfied my mesmerisation was successful, I told him to sleep.

His eyes closed, and he lost consciousness. Every now and then, I checked by pressing down hard on his fingernail, but he didn't respond to the painful stimulus. I pulled out his mobile phone and erased all correspondence with and images of Laura then wiped my fingerprints clean with my handkerchief before placing it back in his pocket.

I kept the deadly bullets.

Cal returned, a sword in each hand. 'Found these in the bushes.'

They belonged to Sam and Terens. Dried blood was smeared on both, but it wasn't theirs, so we had the scent of Laura's kidnappers.

'From the smell of the blood, I'd say they were taken just before sunrise,' he said.

'How many could you sense outside?'

'At least eight. Our guys put up a hell of a fight judging by these.' He raised the swords.

'They came here right after the Ritual,' Luc said. 'The other three must have come just after sunset and laid in wait.'

'We'll get her back, Luc.' Jake squeezed Luc's shoulder.

When the paramedics arrived, I gave them a quick briefing, passed them my card and watched them carry Sommers out.

I handed Luc the white-oak bullets, and his eyes widened. 'Fils de salope!'

'Said the same thing myself.'

'Why didn't you kill him?'

Jake and Cal both swore when they saw what Luc held.

'And make him a hero in Laura's eyes?' I shook my head. 'Not likely. I mesmerised him instead—wiped away all trace of us and Laura from his memory.'

He pursed his lips. 'I hope you did the right thing.'

I hoped so, too. Now it was time to go hunting.

CHAPTER 23
TAKEN

LAURA

I woke with a pain on the right side of my face. That's right, something had hit me as I opened my apartment door. A tremor of fear rippled through me as I opened my eyes and realised I was bound. Someone had manacled me by the wrists to a metal pole suspended from the ceiling. I tried moving, but my legs had been tied and secured with a short rope around my waist so I couldn't extend my legs.

I writhed around trying to find someone. A scream welled up in my throat when I heard a familiar voice.

'Finally you're awake. Took you long enough.' Douglas, the surfer boy who had danced with me at the Ritual, crouched low, his face directly against mine. A sneer marred his features.

Another voice intruded—female, cold and hard. I didn't recognise it, but somehow I knew exactly who it was and turned my head in its direction.

'Perhaps if you hadn't struck her so hard, she would have been with us much sooner.'

'You told me to bring her, no matter how, and I did.'

'I want her wide-awake before we send Alec our little message. Don't we Laura?' She crouched down, and I was face to face with the vampire-in-red. Maris.

I tried to remain calm even though her comment sent a shiver through me. I swallowed back the scream and stared back defiant, hoping she couldn't sense my fear. I wondered why both of them wore long black cloaks with the hoods thrown back.

'I wonder how different her blood tastes to all the others.' Douglas said. 'It's got to be a hundred times better.' He licked his lips, giving me a glimpse of fangs.

Remain calm. Don't let them smell your fear.

'Give it to me.'

Douglas placed my mobile phone into Maris's outstretched hand. She stood, took a step back and aimed. 'Smile,' she said, but not to me. Was she holding someone else captive? My eyes had begun to adjust to the near dark, and I was able to make out shapes and faces.

'Laura, pet?' A weak voice said somewhere to my left.

I knew that voice too. Terens. Ignoring my throbbing head, I turned and tried to focus. They had him in some sort of metal cage, on his knees, hands bound behind his back. A long, sharp piece of wood attached to the metal bars—a stake—loomed only inches from his chest.

I gasped. His pale skin was blackened and horribly blistered. Almost all his thick, auburn hair had been burned off. If not for the diamond stud in his ear, I wouldn't have recognised him. He'd been deliberately exposed to the summer sun, but not long enough to kill him. It must have been agonising.

Maris and Douglas were monsters.

'What have they done to you?'

'You've been hurt and strung up like a chicken, and you're worried about me?' He croaked and barked out a pathetic sort of laugh. 'They've got Sam.'

I turned my head. Sam, burnt almost beyond recognition, was caged and tied. A low moan escaped his lips.

My breath caught in my throat as I tried to control my fear.

Maris laughed, and I looked up as she threw my phone to Douglas. She bent towards me, slithering her cold fingers across my exposed abdomen. 'Your blood is too sacred to be spilt, but that doesn't mean I can't have my fun with you.'

I recoiled from her icy touch—that only made her smile. I began to envisage all the ways a person could be tortured and was convinced she was well acquainted with them. Without warning, she whipped me across the stomach with a riding crop. I hadn't seen her holding it.

A sharp, searing pain flared across my body with the same intensity as a bluebottle sting. I screamed and doubled over, but my manacled hands prevented any further movement.

Douglas laughed.

Tears stung my eyes, and as the pain spread and intensified, she whipped me again, this time with more force. I screamed again and dry retched as my body reacted to the pain.

'Stop it, you demented bitch!' Terens yelled.

I gasped and struggled for air as the dry retching continued. How much I could endure? I knew she wouldn't kill me—yet—but what other pain was she going to inflict on me. Was this only the beginning?

'Enough for now. Smile for the camera, sweetie,' she cooed then roughly grabbed my hair and pulled my head so far back I thought my neck would snap. Having done that, she struck me hard across the side of the head.

CHAPTER 24
A HUNTING WE WILL GO

ALEC

There was one scent I recognised—Douglas. The others were unknown, but not for long. Luc showed me Laura's bag. She must have dropped it when they took her. Nothing was missing except her mobile phone. Why?

'There were three of them here—for one defenceless girl,' he said angrily.

'I know one of them. Any idea who the others are?' I asked.

'No, but let's go find out.' His fang-toothed smile promised pain.

'The scents all merge.' Jean had just come back from scouring the immediate area. 'They left together, and it seems they all had turns carrying her—making sure they leave an unmistakable trail.'

'They want us to follow,' Jake said.

My mobile rang. I retrieved it from my back pocket. Laura's number shone from the screen. That's why they took her phone. I'd given her my card on our first meeting, and she must have added it to her contacts. I alerted the others before answering then put it on loudspeaker.

'Alec, darling.' It was Maris's silky voice. 'I thought you might enjoy seeing this.'

An image rolled across the screen. It showed Terens and Sam on their knees in a cage, hands tied behind them, sharpened stakes a hair's breadth from their bare chests. They must have been exposed to the sun; both looked blistered and too weak to raise their heads. Then the image swung to Laura. Luc breathed in sharply. She was seated on the ground, legs tied together and folded at her side. Her hands were manacled and drawn up above her head.

Maris appeared next to her. I tensed as Maris ran her fingers along Laura's exposed midriff before producing a whip and striking her.

Laura screamed, and her body convulsed.

We watched helplessly as Maris struck her again, and her screams filled the quiet street. Luc roared, and the vampire was free. There would be no holding him back this night. Maris would die at his hand. I recognised Douglas's laughter in the background.

He was mine.

'Smile for the camera, sweetie,' Maris struck Laura so violently across the head, she lost consciousness.

We didn't see any more as my hand crushed the phone into carbon and silicon dust. I loosened the beast, and from the collective snarls around me, so had the others.

Back in the cars, we sped after the scent. It led to a disused theatre in Rozelle. The men were blocking, so no one inside would sense our presence. I had no need to do the same—the serpent ring did that for me.

As we stood outside, planning our next move, Laura's voice whispered to my mind. Thank providence. She must have regained consciousness and remembered the telepathic powers of the ring.

I'm outside. Hold on, I told her.

Wary lest any of the Brethren overhear us, I mouthed: 'Luc, she's okay for now.'

He looked at me then at my hand.

I nodded. 'Twenty-two.'

'We can take 'em,' Cal mouthed.

'We need something subtle. If we attack, they could kill Laura just to spite us.' Luc stroked his chin.

'I've got an idea but, there's no time to discuss it. You've got to trust me.'

'Give us a hint, at least,' Cal mouthed back.

I shook my head. 'Stay here and cover the exits. I'll go in alone, get some idea what they're up to and make it look like I'm going along with them.'

Jake frowned and shook his head vigorously. 'As if they'll—'

'Jake, Maris is in there. All I need is a few minutes with her.' When no one made a move, I mouthed, 'It's the only way. They can't sense my presence while I've got the ring. It'll shield me, not all of you. I can get in among them before they know I'm there, find out their plans then confront her.'

The others exchanged looks.

'Give me ten minutes. If I don't call you by then....'

'You realise how risky that is? They'll kill you,' Cal said.

I shook my head. 'Not straight away.'

They didn't like it, but we had no other options. 'We can't stand here arguing. Trust me on this one, and whatever you hear me say in there ... don't react. Don't barge in until I give the word. Just cover the exits and wait. I have a feeling they'll come charging out.'

'All right. Ten minutes, no more.' Luc gave me the nod, and, from the expression on his face, he was ready to remove a few heads.

'There's a flaw in this somewhere, but I'm in. At least I'll get to see that venomous bitch suffer,' Cal said.

He wasn't alone in that.

'Maris belongs to me,' Luc added.

No one argued with that.

I took a deep breath and walked in.

CHAPTER 25
MARIS

LAURA

Argh, awake again. How long I'd been unconscious I have no idea. My skin stung like it had been badly sunburnt and radiated heat. I glanced at my abdomen to see two large, red swelling welts. Maris had left her mark. My arms ached and I'd lost feeling in my hands, still raised above my head.

What had happened to Matt? Was he lying hurt, or even worse? A dreadful fear clutched at my heart at the thought that Matt could be lying hurt on account of me, perhaps still in my apartment. The neighbours would find him, surely, and ring the police.

'Laura, can you hear me?' A voice called softly. 'It's me, Terens. I'm here, pet. How are you?'

'Everything hurts.'

Terens strained at his manacles. 'I'll tear that bitch apart. Not one of them'll leave this place with their heads attached. I promise you.' His voice sounded stronger than last time I was awake.

I just wanted to close my eyes and go back to sleep, escape the cramps that wracked my body. Trying to manoeuvre my legs to the other side was pointless, so I relaxed and flexed my fingers in the tight manacles to restore circulation. Terens swore loudly and rattled his cage.

'Where are we?' I asked.

'An abandoned theatre. See the dark curtain in front of you? We're on the stage.'

I could make out the dark walls, floor and heavy roped curtain. Why a theatre? If I trusted the old adage about bad feelings then I had a distinctly foul one.

'Why did they take you?'

'Capturing as many of us as possible to reduce Alec's chances of fighting back, I reckon.'

'Then it's not just Maris and Douglas?'

'If only! Nah, there's more. No way those two could have done this on their own. It took eight of them to grab Sam and me. Looks like we've another rebellion on our hands.'

'So how many?'

'I sense twenty-two behind that curtain.' His brow furrowed. 'One of them feels vaguely familiar.'

'There's no way Alec can take them all on, even if he is stronger and faster.'

He shook his head. 'He won't be on his own. That's what they're counting on. They're hoping to eliminate all of us tonight—Luc, Cal, Jean and Jake. They've already got two of us.'

'And now me.'

Terens nodded. 'We're the bait, pet.'

I was the lure to bring him here, but when I recalled the way we parted, the angry words … I had a feeling he'd come only because he was obligated to, as my guardian. I glanced up at my manacled hands. The ring had a faint glow. That could only mean one thing—Alec was on his way and walking into a trap.

Then I remembered what he had said to me last Friday night, about the rings' telepathic powers in times of danger. And regardless how angry I'd been with him earlier, I couldn't bear to see him killed. Closing my eyes, I mentally called him. *Alec, if you can hear me, it's a trap. There's twenty-two of them.*

I'm outside. Hold on.

My eyes snapped open. It had worked. There's no way it could have been my imagination—I didn't have one that good.

'Alec?' I whispered. There was no answer.

Sam stirred in the other cage and let out a deep groan.

'They kept Sam out for longer.' Anger tinged Terens's voice. 'That sow's arse wanted to hurt him. He's her sire.'

Well, that explained the warning look he sent her at the start of the Ritual. He probably knew her better than anyone else. 'Is that why she hates him so much?'

'More complicated than that. She begged him to change her, and he spent the next century training her. Then she started killing and getting out of control. He threatened to have her executed. She stopped ... for a while. At the end of her servitude, he set her free and walked away.'

Had Alec done that to her? Although Terens hadn't said it aloud, it hung there all the same. It appeared Maris wasn't the type to let her man go easily.

Terens leaned forward as far as his bonds allowed, and looked past me to Sam. 'Wake up, Sam. Come on, my brother, you can do this. Don't let her win.'

Sam stirred, briefly opening his eyes before his head dropped again.

'Will he recover?' I asked.

'We can heal at night, just takes a bit longer. It's the day sleep that works magic on our kind. I only hope he can hang on for another six hours. If not, I'll wreak such vengeance they'll speak of it among my kind for eternity.'

No idle boast, the pain in his voice rang out clearly. He tipped his head back and roared till the ground beneath me shook. The sound reverberated around the walls, the ceiling and through my body like a shock wave. I stared at him open mouthed. Even in his injured state, Terens's power was frightening. What was it like when he was whole?

He finally stopped. 'Sorry, pet. Couldn't hold it back.'

Panic welled in me, and it had nothing to do with Terens's outburst. There was no way I could slip my hands through the tight iron holding my wrists. The more I tried, the deeper the metal cut into my skin and I risked bleeding as a result. I gave up, never having felt more helpless in my life.

'They're going to kill him, aren't they?' I may have been angry with Alec, but the thought of him being killed sickened me. I didn't want to lose him. His kisses had affected me far more than I wanted to admit.

A hideous laugh echoed through the room. I raised my head. Maris strolled up and stood before me, hands behind her back. I trembled. What she was hiding there—the riding crop? Was she going to amuse herself by flogging me again?

Determined not to scream this time, I clenched my jaw. There was no way I was going to give her that satisfaction again.

She didn't bother to crouch to my level and I didn't want to look up at her, so I stared at her knees. Stupid cloak. She bent down; her face only inches from mine. I turned my head away, but she grabbed my chin and forced me to look at her.

I tensed and closed my eyes.

'Look at me.'

What could she do, rip my eyelids off? Actually, she could. I opened my eyes and caught her icy gaze. Her stare was enough to make any snake envious.

She whispered. 'I have no intention of killing him.'

'Then why…?'

'He was my lover and will be again. All he needs is a little persuasion. You are my leverage. As long as you're in my hands, he'll do whatever I ask.'

'So, I'm your hostage am I?'

'No, sweetie. You're the power source and once I and my Brethren take a few sips from your little vein' —she tapped my wrist with a long, red-painted fingernail— 'our strength will be equal to his.'

I'm sure my eyes widened at the thought of being sucked by more than twenty vampires. I'd never survive it. 'How many?'

'Don't worry. You're no use to us dead. It's the Principate we want to end, not the Ingenii. That needs to go on otherwise we'll never be able to daywalk. I need you alive. Then, maybe in a year or two, I'll find a nice human to breed you with to produce the next generation of Ingenii.'

If she hadn't been holding my jaw, it would have dropped. Yet her smiling, manic face told me it was obvious she believed every word. Mental! As if Alec would go along with that. She didn't know him at all. *Delusional*, didn't begin to cover it.

I kicked down my fear. 'You can't think Alec would agree to that?'

'How long have you known him, four, five days? I've known him nearly a century, and there are things about him that would surprise you.'

I had only met Alec a few days ago. Maris was right on that score, but Luc had transformed him into a vampire, and surely he would not have made him my guardian if there were anything questionable about him? Luc was my father, and he'd never … No! Maris was wrong. She had to be.

'You're delusional.' I had to believe that.

She laughed. 'Oh, you are so naïve. Well, keep thinking that, sweetie. There's nothing like misplaced hope.'

I glanced up at my ring. It glowed strongly, and my heart leapt. Alec was somewhere close. I managed to twist the ring so the serpent faced my palm then curled my fingers into a fist.

'I always knew you weren't right in the head,' Terens said from his cage. 'As if the other Elders will go along with that.'

'Doesn't matter. By the time they hear of it, it'll be too late.' She released my chin. I dropped my head.

Maris straightened and walked to Terens's cage. She ran a pointed scarlet nail down the length of his chest as her eyes raked his body. 'Pity.' She sighed. 'I once considered taking you as a lover.'

'I'd sooner bed a cockroach.'

Ooh, that had to be an ego bruiser. I tried not to imagine the anatomical impossibility.

She recoiled and hissed at him. 'Then I hope you'll enjoy their company when we dump your bodies in the morning sun.'

She snapped her fingers. I tensed. The curtain drew back, and spotlights flicked on. I blinked at the sudden brightness as we were illuminated to the waiting crowd. It was difficult to distinguish anything in the darkened space before me. But as my eyes adjusted, I made out movement. Several rows were occupied, and surprise, surprise, the occupants were robed in black; hoods draped low over their faces, making any individual recognition impossible.

Cowards. Some among them must have spoken, maybe even danced, with me at the Ritual on Monday night. Yet now, they had gathered for one purpose—murder. As one, they rose and clapped. Some called out; others jeered and laughed.

'Don't you realise this will cause a civil war!' Terens yelled.

'At least we'll be free!' someone called back.

'To kill?'

'To be ourselves,' another voice said.

The Serpent Ring burned into my palm. Alec! He was near. Yet none of them gave any indication they could sense him.

'Maris,' one of the vampires called out. 'It's time.'

His voice sounded familiar, yet I couldn't place it. As he rose and made his way to the stage, some of the others around him did the same. Maris turned to face him, her hands clenched into fists at her side. I could only surmise she had something to hide. Could it be she had no intention of sharing my blood, or perhaps intended to take more than the others so she'd have the advantage?

As the unknown vampire neared, his hood slipped to reveal a face I knew—Russell!

I was stunned. 'Russell, you're Alec's friend. How could you?' I had actually liked him.

He looked at me with mock sympathy. 'I'm so sorry Laura, but you know how it is.'

'No, I don't know how.'

'You have to understand that you have something we need, and Alec is keeping it all to himself. Share and share alike is what I say.' He stooped low until his face loomed close to mine. An angry scowl darkened his features. 'Why should he be the only one able to walk in the daylight? Do you think we enjoy cowering in the darkness?'

Murmurs of approval echoed around the theatre.

His face resumed its usual bored expression. 'I have nothing against him, really. I like him, and I like you, but....' He shrugged. 'This is purely business. Don't take it personally.'

The bit about the daylight I could understand, perhaps even sympathise, but that last comment was the most lunatic thing I'd ever heard. From my right, I heard a derisive snort. Sam had regained consciousness.

'And how do you suggest she do that, *friend?*' he asked.

I glanced at him amazed his injuries had already begun to heal, even without the day rest. The charred and blistered flesh was slowly being replaced by smooth, pale skin. His fangs showed and his eyes gleamed with menace.

Turning to Terens, on my left, I observed the same thing. It appeared this unholy gathering—in their obsession to take my blood—had forgotten about their captives.

'Sam, I'm glad you're with us again. It would've been a shame had you missed anything. Maris has promised quite a show.' Russell smiled so sweetly, fangs protruding that I shuddered. 'Isn't that so?' He said to her.

'Of course,' she replied. 'Originally I planned to capture you both a few days earlier, starve you then throw in a couple of those street brats I've been feeding on, so we'd all enjoy the spectacle. But' —she shrugged— 'it wasn't to be. Pity, Douglas so enjoyed procuring them for me.'

I gasped. So she was the murderer Matt was hunting.

'You sick bitch!' Sam snarled. 'I should've terminated you long ago.'

'You didn't, and now you're the one in the cage.' She laughed.

Maris turned her back on him. 'I believe our guest of honour needs a little encouragement to join us. We can't perform our ceremony without his presence.'

I had a pretty good idea who this "guest of honour" might be.

'May I suggest you use your two incentives?' Russell looked at the cages on either side of me.

Maris snapped her fingers again. Two hooded figures appeared from one side of the stage. They positioned themselves directly behind Sam and Terens, put their hands through the bars, and placed them firmly on their prisoner's backs.

An awful chill ran through me. I guessed that at a given signal, they were to be thrust onto the sharpened stakes. Both prisoners braced their legs against the cage.

'I do regret this, boys. We've had some good times, but I can't say I'll miss your pretty faces, although, perhaps the ladies will.' Russell grinned. 'I've heard you two have quite a reputation.'

'Jealous?' Terens retaliated.

Russell's eyes narrowed. He glared then collected himself. 'Sorry, but the fish aren't biting today, which is just as well, as you both seem to have passed your use-by date.'

Sam snorted. 'That's lame, even for you, Russell. But I wouldn't be too sure.' He had recovered fully; the vampire in him was loose and straining at the metal bars of the cage.

'It's titanium, especially built to hold one of our kind. Don't strain yourselves, boys,' Russell said with a cold grin while laughter drifted from the stalls. He leapt onto to the stage and joined her.

'Let's begin.' Maris nodded to the two hooded figures.

'No!' I screamed.

CHAPTER 26
CONCEALMENT

ALEC

I rushed through the entrance foyer and up the carpeted stairs to the balcony. From there, I had a clear view of what was happening. Below me, a large group of black-robed Brethren, hoods drawn over their faces, sat silent, as if waiting for the entertainment to begin.

Their cloaks intrigued me. Why the concealment? Yet, on the other hand, why was I surprised? They were too craven for an outright confrontation but brave enough to try to intimidate a helpless woman. So far, no one seemed aware of my presence, so the ring was working. I was about to move when a familiar voice spoke from among the hooded rebels. Russell. What the hell? What was he doing here?

Luc cursed, 'Fils de salope!'

Jake and Cal gave a quick intake of breath. They were listening to everything from outside.

Over several years, Russell had declined our invitations and stopped visiting the house. He'd seemed friendly, if somewhat distant. Would he actually want to kill any of us? Had I been blind to this side of his character, or was this a recent development? Yet titanium cages are not built overnight. How long had he been planning this?

I would probably never know.

One thing was certain, he could dismiss years of friendship without a second thought and Terens and Sam were to be the first casualties. And Douglas? He was nothing but a pawn in Maris's sick games, but he was no innocent. He killed those human children. It explained the DNA the police took from their bodies.

Those two had just signed their own death warrant.

'Luc, you heard?' The rebels were too preoccupied to hear our voices.

'They'll pay,' he replied.

An idea came. 'Leave their bodies here. Burn the place down around them.'

'Police find them—on a mysterious tip off—match their DNA to those on the kids bodies and case closed.'

'Uh huh.'

'I like it.'

Two hooded figures strode up and stood behind Terens and Sam. I stiffened. 'Damn!'

'It's Cal and Jake. I sent them in. No one will detect them while they're blocking.'

I let out a tense breath. 'Luc, I said—'

'That's my daughter they're holding, Alec. We're still waiting on your okay.'

Laura screamed.

'Luc, stay there!' I leapt over the railing and into their midst.

CHAPTER 27
BETRAYAL

LAURA

There's really no need for that,' Alec coolly announced, as he landed on the floor in front of the stage.

Black-clad bodies scattered in all directions. So much for their bravado.

I felt like screaming his name, but as a modern twenty-first century woman I didn't want to appear like the helpless heroine from a Regency novel—even though my current predicament seemed just that. And who was I kidding anyway? I was scared and seeing him was close to heaven.

'You're late,' Maris said.

He gave her a dazzling smile that took my breath away. 'Darling, I always show up at the right time.'

What? I hoped he was being facetious, yet my mouth went dry all the same. He didn't as much as glance at me; his eyes were glued to her.

'Nice of you to join us. At last we can begin,' Russell said, a frosty grin pasted to his face. From my place on the stage, I saw him nod to someone, and four vampires jumped on Alec, brought him to his knees and pinned his arms behind his back. He didn't struggle. Why?

'I'm sorry, Alec, but Russ insists,' Maris said.

'This really isn't necessary,' Alec replied. 'I've come here on my own, following the smelly trail your pet, Douglas, left behind.'

Douglas growled and bared his fangs.

'Tell him to sheath them or I'll rip them out.'

Maris laughed, made a gesture with her hand and Douglas sat back down. She strode to my side, crouched down next to me and grabbed my chin. Her fangs were bared; their tips touched my skin making my nerve endings prickle.

Russell joined her and sniffed at my throat. 'Mmmmm, delicious.'

'Maris, if you want us to be together again,' Alec said dryly, 'all you have to do is ask. There's no need to kidnap and terrorise the girl.'

No! He couldn't be serious. I glanced to either side of me, at Terens and Sam. Terens frowned, and Sam's eyes were narrowed, but they merely watched. Before I could open my mouth to protest, the spotlights that were focused on us, moved. All, except the one trained on me, moved to Alec.

Maris rose and left me, neatly leaping off the stage to stand in front of him. 'Alec, if you're playing with me....'

'Have I ever lied to you?' He smiled at her.

'Not that I found out.'

'Maris.' Russell growled. He followed her, but only as far as the edge of the stage.

In less than a heartbeat, Alec rose and threw his captors off. 'I could have done that sooner, but I wanted to show you I didn't come here to fight but to ask you to be my mate.'

'Shit!' It came from Sam's cage.

Alec took Maris by the waist, and in front of everyone, kissed her.

All I could do was stare and hope this was all a nightmare. Terens had said Alec wasn't interested in Maris, so what was going on? Only a few hours ago, he had kissed me the same way, and stupidly, I had responded. Was this the same man who charmed me last night at the Ritual? Had it all been a lie? I stared at him not wanting to believe what I'd just seen.

'Let me prove it to you.' He took her hand, and they alighted on the stage. 'Go ahead, Maris, take a bite, but just a sip, no more. The taste of First Blood is incomparable.' He finally looked at me, his eyes cold.

I gasped then blurted, 'You're my guardian.... You're meant to protect me. Was it all a lie?' I strained at my manacles. Finally I stopped struggling as I battled to hold back tears.

'I am protecting you. Depends on how you look at it.'

My mind went numb, and my stomach bunched into knots. The fear I'd been trying to control roared through me. How could he betray me like this? It was worse than Russell's, for Alec was my father's man. He had betrayed not only me but Luc and all his men—his supposed friends.

'Alec, this isn't you,' Terens called out. 'What the fuck you playing at?'

'You'll soon find out,' Alec replied.

'You lying piece of trash!' What a fool I'd been! That moment, I hated him and wished with all my heart to be home with Matt, safe and secure, in the warm comfort of his arms. I didn't realise how badly I ached for it until the warm saltiness of my tears landed on my lips. I couldn't bear to look at him, so I closed my eyes, dropped my head and let the tears fall.

'What about the rest of us?' someone called out.

'Maris and Russell first,' Alec said. 'That's all the girl will be able to handle tonight. We don't want to kill her. Tomorrow night, another two can feed.'

Murmurs reached the stage, and then another voice called out, 'As long as you stick to your word.'

His word! I wanted to laugh, but the pain I felt at his deception stopped me. I looked up as I heard him say, 'The wrist only, Maris. Neck's mine, remember? And gently. Russell, you take the other wrist.' He said it so cold-bloodedly; I would never have believed it of him. Was I that bad a judge of men?

'What the shit?' Sam cried out. 'Alec, you can't!'

Alec ignored him, and with his arm around Maris's waist, he led her to me.

'I'll wait for Maris to finish,' Russell said and stood back.

'I'll tell you what it's like, Russ.' Maris licked her lips then crouched over me and slid her fangs along the length of my arm.

I panicked, and no matter how much I hated Alec just then, I turned to him in desperation. 'Don't do this, Alec! Don't let her, please—'

Terens and Sam shouted and swore to kill Alec as soon as they got the chance.

He looked impassively on as Maris bit down hard. I screamed. Her fangs were like two large nails being driven into me. There was no numbing vampire saliva, just agonising pain, and as I struggled, she bit down harder and deeper, seeming to rip my arm apart in her frenzy, sucking my blood with such ferocity I believed she would kill me.

'Bitch!' Alec pulled her off me and yelled out, 'Luc, now!' The door burst open, and with a loud roar, Luc, Jean and Antonius, each with sword in hand, rushed in as Alec tore the metal from my wrists. If he hadn't caught me, I would have slumped to the floor.

'Bastard!' With what remaining strength I had, I slapped his face. 'Get away from me!' I tried pushing him off.

In a blur, Luc was at our side, his chest rising and falling hard as he pinned Alec with a glare. 'I could kill you for this! Why did you risk her life?'

Ignoring him, my protests and the commotion around us, Alec pulled a handkerchief from his pocket and wrapped it around my punctured, bleeding arm. 'I'm sorry I had to put you through that. It was the only way to convince them.'

I looked up at him, totally confused as he ripped the ropes from my legs and cradled me to him. Hooded vampires raced past us and scattered in all directions as Luc's men and the now-freed Sam and Terens went after them.

Nearby, Maris writhed on the ground and screamed. She clawed at her throat, her face contorted in agony. Blood—my blood—dribbled from her mouth. She burst into flames and shrivelled up. The pungent smell of burning flesh filled my nostrils, and I choked. The flames leapt higher and left nothing but a stinking, smouldering, twisted and charred heap. In less than a minute, even that disintegrated into a pile of black ash.

'Mon Dieu! You knew! How?' Luc turned disbelieving eyes onto Alec.

'Not now. We need to get Laura to the hospital. She's lost a lot of blood. That bitch tried to drain her. I thought I could prevent—' He stopped, giving me a regretful look.

I couldn't focus well, and my sight began to dim. 'You could have told me – in my mind.'

'I thought of doing that, but you had to look convinced.'

It had all been an act?! 'You should get an award for that performance. I hated you.' My voice was weak, and my heart was confused all over again.

'You still might.' He picked me up, neatly leapt off the stage and carried me out of the building.

'Did my blood do that to her?'

'Seems that way. How do you feel?'

'Sick. My arm's throbbing.'

Luc appeared beside us. 'We'll take my car. Get in the back with Laura. I'll drive.'

We sped through the dark, near-empty streets. I closed my eyes and buried my face in Alec's shoulder, trying not to admit how wonderful that felt. Even though I was nauseous and my whole arm felt as if on fire, the rest of me glowed knowing that everything he'd said to Maris had been a lie.

'Say the alphabet backwards, Laura. Concentrate; c'mon stay with me.'

I tried. 'Z … y, x … um, w….' I'd reached the letter P when the car stopped. Alec carried me into emergency. I recognised the disinfectant smell I so disliked.

An unknown female voice called. 'Dr Munro?'

'Carol, four units of O negative—the one with my name on it— and I.V. fluid. Hook it up. Now!' he barked.

Who was Carol? Was she the night-duty nurse? Her feet padded off. I heard the chink of curtains being pulled back, felt myself being lowered onto something cold and soft, probably one of those horrid hospital beds with wheels.

'Laura, open your eyes. I need to see them,' Alec said.

'Do I have to?' I hardly had the energy to speak.

'Yes, you do.' I opened them to see a half-smile, which didn't disguise the worried look on his face.

Luc was quickly by my bedside. He took hold of my other hand. 'I parked in your spot,' he said to Alec.

Alec acknowledged that with a quick nod as he untied the handkerchief and examined my wound. The nurse came back carrying a folded white piece of cloth. She removed my blouse and Alec stuck me with yet another sharp, pointy object. As if I hadn't had enough of that tonight. This one had a plastic tube attached to it.

'Laura, I'm inserting an intravenous drip as well as blood. Your haemoglobin count is far too low, honey.' He cupped the side of my face in his hand and gently angled my head toward him. 'Look at me, Laura. Can you understand what I'm saying? Nod if you do.'

I did.

'Good.'

Another nurse rushed in with a plastic bag filled with red fluid. Alec attached it to the tube and hooked it on a pole next to my bed. The rich, scarlet liquid slid down the tube and into my arm.

'I'll give you an injection to ease the pain,' he said.

I groaned, 'Not more sharp and pointy objects.'

He chuckled.

I closed my eyes and felt the wonderful drug snake through my system … felt the world fade … away.

CHAPTER 28
NIGHT WATCH

ALEC

It was after midnight as Luc and I settled into separate chairs on either side of Laura's bed in the emergency ward. It was going to be a long night.

I watched her as she slept. It had been touch and go, and I knew I'd taken an enormous risk. But it had paid off. Maris was dead, yet the bitch had still managed to nearly kill her.

'I should ring Judy.' Luc's hushed voice broke in.

'Mmmm, she needs to know. Tell her Laura's sleeping peacefully. If she can wait till the morning, it'd be better.' I leaned over and stroked Laura's cheek and forehead. Her temperature was up a bit. Only to be expected.

I stood, changed the blood bag and checked the IV line just as Carol did her rounds.

'Shall I bring you some coffee?' she asked.

I smiled a grateful thanks, and she walked out with the emptied bag of blood. Within minutes, she was back with a steaming cup of espresso.

'Carol, remind me to give you a raise.'

'You already have—that's why I'm still here.' She laughed softly.

'You're irreplaceable! Oh, and one more favour. Go to my office, please, and bring me the spare mobile I keep on the desk.'

'Certainly.' She glanced at the bed where Laura slept, smiled at me and left.

Since the previous mobile had met with a rather violent end, and I couldn't be without one, the extra I had been given by the phone company would do till I could arrange for a replacement. When Carol came back, I spent some time redirecting my calls while listening to Laura's steady heartbeat. Soon the anaesthetic would wear off, and she'd be sleeping on her own.

'Judy's on her way,' Luc said.

He had his head bowed over his knees, hands clasped tensely in front of him. Then quite unexpectedly, he began to laugh; his whole body shook with the intensity of it.

'What's gotten into you?' I asked.

It took a while for him to stop. 'Her blood is poison to our kind! If we'd known that when she was born, there would have been no need to hide her. No one would have dared touch her. The heartache I put Judy and myself through, all for nothing. Laura's blood was her protection.' He buried his head in his hands.

'You weren't to know. None of us knew. There's no precedent for what Laura is.'

He lifted his head and looked at me. 'She could have been safe at home with us. The men would have guarded her day and night, as they have these last fifty years.' His voice broke. 'You have any idea how many times I wanted to go to John and Eilene and ask for my daughter back?'

'Luc, listen to me. Even if the Brethren had known about her, known that her blood was fatal to them, you think that would have stopped them? They may have attempted to kill her instead. What if tonight's kidnapping had occurred when she was a child? She wouldn't be alive now. Think about that.'

'I want to believe you're right,' he whispered.

'I'm sure of it. As long as no one knew of her existence, she was safe. Your sacrifice was worth it.'

His eyes bored into mine. 'How long have you known?'

'Since this morning. I'd been running a few tests, and the results were texted to me.'

'You took a hell of a risk with her life.'

'I'm sorry, Luc, but I had to. And I was right.'

He let out a deep breath and sat back. 'Mon dieu! How is it possible? No other Ingenii had poisonous blood.'

'It's the rare combination of Ingenii and vampire, and not just any vampire, but one from the Antonii line—from your father, Marcus. Because you were born a vampire, your blood is unlike any other. And that is just as unprecedented as what Laura is and the reason why her blood didn't kill me during the Ritual. You changed me, therefore, *your* blood runs in my veins, providing me with the immunity I need to remain as her guardian. Maris, on the other hand, was changed by Sam, who is not genetically an Antonii.'

He nodded. 'That's probably why Marcus, you and I can father children, while my men can't. The transformation made them as sterile as the rest of our kind. But the witch's curse ensured we had descendants,' he said bitterly.

'Speaking of which' —I glanced at Laura— 'does she know you're Lucius Antonius, Marcus's son?'

He shook his head. 'She has enough to deal with already. That'll have to wait for another time.'

'Don't delay too long.'

Hurried footsteps came from the reception area. Judith. Luc rose and pulled the curtain aside.

'How is she, Luc?' They embraced before going to Laura's side.

'She's going to be all right, my love.'

Judith took in the number of needles in Laura's arms, the IV fluid, the units of blood, and her face paled. She let her shoulder bag drop to the ground and grasped her daughter's hand. 'Laura, Laura. My dear one,' she whispered, as she sat in Luc's vacated chair.

Luc perched on the edge of the bed, and together they kept vigil.

'I'm curious to know why you avoided seeing her as a child?' Luc unexpectedly asked. 'Jake enjoyed giving her piggy-back rides, Cal made silly faces to entertain her at dinner, and Jean spoke to her in French. She blew raspberries at him.' They both smiled.

I recalled that time. Every week, Eilene would bring Laura to Judith's house. There she would spend the day with her real parents and "uncles". This continued until she reached school age. After that, Luc and the others kept their distance. Only "Auntie" Judith attended her birthday parties. As Laura grew to adulthood, the memory of them faded. They figured it was safer Laura didn't know her true parentage. Luc was extremely careful that none of our kind ever suspected whose child she really was. I tended to avoid those gatherings.

'After all this time, you're asking me now?' I raised my eyes from Laura's face. Their gazes were locked on me. 'You both know how I feel about the Dantonvilles, and I'm not going to apologise, Judith.'

She shook her head. 'It's all right, Alec, I understand. My father was not a good man.'

What an understatement. 'I didn't want to become attached to a little girl who was the granddaughter of my enemy.'

'Oh, Alec, I'm so sorry. We should have known,' Judith said. She reached across the bed and squeezed my hand in a heartfelt gesture. 'But she's my daughter, too, and we're not enemies.'

I smiled. 'No, we're not.'

There was silence again for a while. Laura's breathing was steady. Every now and then, she stirred and murmured something incoherent.

'I'm moving her to one of the private suites,' I said. 'She doesn't need to be in emergency any more.'

I went to the duty desk and arranged for Laura's transfer to a vacant suite. Two of the nursing staff accompanied me. We removed the needles from her arm then wheeled her into the elevator. Once we reached the private room, Luc did his best to persuade Judith to go home and get some sleep. She looked physically and emotionally drained. Her hands shook as she tucked the blankets around Laura. Luc took her elbow to steady her as she stumbled around the bed.

'Judy, Laura won't wake for many hours yet.'

She looked at him, torn between exhaustion and a mother's reluctance to leave her injured child.

'If there is any change at all, I'll ring you straight away. In the morning you'll be refreshed and ready to see her. Please,' he begged.

She sighed. 'All right, at least I know you're here with her.' After a last longing look at Laura, Judith let Luc escort her to her car.

After ensuring Laura was comfortable, I left the room and closed the door behind me. Laura was safe. The danger was over, and I was sure Sam and Terens were taking their revenge. As I leant against the door, I tuned my senses to hear how things were progressing in the theatre. Antonius and Kwome were there, and the executions had begun. I tuned out again, rather than listen to the rebels begging for their lives.

I thought over events of the last two days, and something became glaringly clear. As far as the Brethren had been aware, Judith's only child died in infancy. Now, for the first time in over eighteen-hundred years, there appeared to be no heir. All the rebels had to do was wait. What's fifty years to our kind? They attend the Ritual, expecting to hear the Elders declare there is no successor then, lo and behold, I walk in with Laura. I shouldn't have wondered at the number of shocked and hostile faces. Why hadn't I made the connection at the time?

My pager beeped. I was wanted at reception. I checked my watch—four in the morning. The only people working at this hour were medical personnel, shift workers, drug dealers and the police. I had a feeling it was the latter.

I reached reception. My hunch had been right. Two plain-clothes detectives awaited me. They exuded the air of confidence and cynical expression common to police. I'd noticed the same thing with Matthew Sommers.

The male was the older of the two—a portly man in his mid to late forties, receding hairline. The dark circles under his eyes went with the territory. The woman, maybe in her late twenties, wore a navy-blue pants suit. Her eager expression gave the impression of one just promoted to detective. I guessed she couldn't wait to question me. They both straightened at my approach. It amused me the way the woman bit down on her lower lip and smoothed her brown shoulder-length hair behind her ears.

'I'm Dr Alec Munro. How can I help you?'

'I'm Detective Chief Inspector Delaney, and this is Detective Sergeant Norris.' He gave me a firm handshake.

They flashed their badges. Delaney cleared his throat. 'It's about Detective Inspector Sommers—the assault victim you treated last night, and the young lady, Laura Dantonville. Is there somewhere we can speak privately?'

'My office. Down the corridor.'

I led the way, a confident smile concealing my struggle to concoct a believable story. The absolute truth was out of the question. I hated lying, yet creative invention was an unavoidable part of my life. There was no way I could divulge the existence of my kind and their part in Sommers's injury, and I couldn't see how to leave Laura out of this. The police had found him in her apartment. How could I explain Laura's abduction and my failure to notify them? And how might I explain her not being seen by the paramedics or taken to the same hospital?

Since my transformation, headaches had been non-existent. Now I felt one coming on.

'Please be seated.' I indicated chairs near my desk. They gazed around my office. Delaney's eyes homed in on the framed copies of my various degrees and qualifications. Norris had her incident pad at the ready. I had to be extremely careful what I said.

Delaney began the interrogation. 'You often work this late, or did you have an early start today?'

'This is a research facility as well as a hospital. I often work through the night on experiments.'

'The paramedics said you treated D.I. Sommers at the scene and gave them your card. Is that correct?'

'Yes.'

'Approximately what time was that?'

Damn! I'd almost forgotten the three-hour gap between finding Sommers and Laura's hospitalisation. Carol would have recorded the time on the supply sheet when she fetched the units of blood. If they requested that sheet, the time difference would be difficult to explain. I kept my voice even. 'Sometime after 9.30. It was already dark.'

He nodded. 'Tell us what happened?'

If I couldn't come up with a plausible explanation, I might have to resort to hypnotism. 'I was driving past, testing my new GPS and stopped to check its accuracy, when I heard a scream from the block of units nearby.' I paused for a moment, to give the impression I was recalling events.

'Go on, Dr Munro.' Delaney's eyes never left my face.

'We ran in—'

'We?'

'I had a few friends with me.'

'How many?'

I wondered if I'd blundered in mentioning the men. Too late now. 'Four.'

'We'll get their names later.' He indicated for me to continue.

'We found two injured people—a man with severe head injuries and a young woman with deep lacerations to her left arm. They were both bleeding profusely. I called the ambulance. Treated them immediately. One of my friends—'

'His name?' Delaney interrupted.

'Jake Medsen.'

Norris wrote it down.

'Go on, Doctor Munro.'

'As I was saying, one of my friends looked around … to see if they could spot anyone. Not much more to tell. The ambulance arrived. Gave them instructions and my card.'

Norris fixed me with her cold, pale eyes. 'Dr Munro, why didn't you place Miss Dantonville in the same ambulance?'

I gazed at her and tried to sound convincing. 'Miss Dantonville was bleeding heavily. Pulse extremely weak. I made a professional decision to take her directly to this hospital. It's closer and has a better blood transfusion facility. Probably saved her life.'

So far, I'd told the truth, apart from the GPS device, but I also omitted a great deal.

Norris looked at me with interest. 'The paramedics didn't mention that.'

I shrugged, as if that wasn't my problem.

'We'll check that. Did you see anyone else in or near the building?' she continued.

'No.'

Delaney rubbed his eyes and stifled a yawn. 'Forensic team will be out there later today. See what they can find.'

They'll find our prints all over the place, I was tempted to say.

Delaney stood and extended his hand. 'Thank you Dr Munro. You've been most helpful. Norris will get those names now, if you don't mind.'

I rattled them off, and Norris scribbled away before closing her notebook.

As they headed for the door, Delaney turned toward me. 'Let me say how much I appreciate what you did for Matthew Sommers. The paramedics said you saved his life. He's a friend as well as a colleague, and Laura Dantonville's his girl.'

'Before you go….' I pushed back my chair and strode around to them. 'What do you suppose happened before my friends and I arrived?' I longed to know how close they might be to the truth.

He let out a resigned breath, as if answering my question was unlikely to compromise their investigation. 'We think they interrupted a couple of intruders in Laura's flat. No doubt she saw the aggressors and screamed. That's corroborated by what you said. At that stage, they knocked her out. Matt must have run in and pulled his gun, but someone attacked from the side. At least one of the perps was incredibly strong. Matt's head was rammed into the doorpost like a tennis ball, and he's not a small man. How's Laura?'

'She's going to be fine.'

'Will she be up to answering some questions later today? I need to know what she saw.'

'Unfortunately, there's no knowing how concussion will affect her recall of events.' I knew Laura didn't have concussion, but this diagnosis would help avoid mention of the abduction. I didn't want Laura to lie, just evade the whole truth.

Delaney and Norris nodded. 'Thank you for your help. We'll be in touch.'

After they left, I headed back to Laura's room.

Luc joined me. 'Delicately handled.'

That moment, Laura's voice screamed in my mind. I pushed past Luc and burst through the door.

CHAPTER 29
NOT OVER YET

LAURA

I awoke to find myself out of the Emergency ward and in a hospital room. As fuzzy as my brain felt, the events of the night came back to me, and I checked my arms. No needles. Alec must have pulled them out while I slept. The window in my room showed it was still dark outside. Then I became aware of someone in the room. Not Alec, and not Luc. Something else—a shadow of sorts, but oddly solid. Before I had the chance to cry out or press the buzzer, a large hand slammed over my mouth, while another grabbed my good hand. A head loomed close to mine. Even in the weak light I saw who it was.

Russell.

He wore my serpent ring.

'Hello, Laura,' he whispered.

I struggled to claw his hand off my face, but my injured hand wasn't up to the task.

'Keep still. I'm not going to hurt you like Maris did.'

I shivered.

'I'm meant to be delivering you to someone—like a parcel.' A nasty chuckle came out of him.

Who had sent Russell to kidnap me? Maris and Douglas were dead. So there was someone else. Wonderful! My stomach lurched. I moved my head, not wanting to look at him. But he forced it back until we were face to face.

My eyes darted to the door. Where was Alec?

'Don't expect a rescue this time, my dear. Alec is busy entertaining the police, and Lord Lucien is with Judith. Besides,' — his fanged-smile widened— 'I'm wearing your ring, so they can't sense my presence.'

How had he managed to remove it? I glanced at his hand. My ring was on his finger.

'Amazing what a drop of your blood can do,' he said, as if he'd heard my thoughts. 'The serpent uncoiled from your finger onto mine. Of course, I had to use protection. Just smearing it on my skin wouldn't exactly be conducive to my health.'

That's when I noticed red drops on the celotape. Somehow he'd gotten hold of my blood. That wouldn't have been difficult since some of it dropped onto the ground when Maris ripped into the vein on my wrist.

'Now, I don't have much time. We must move, my dear girl, and not keep someone waiting.'

No! I tried to angle my face toward the door and wondered how long before someone—anyone—noticed an extra vampire in the place. The lower half of my face throbbed from the pressure of his hand on my mouth.

'He wants you for his mate. Tsk, tsk. Pretty desperate, I'd say.'

My brain went numb. Whoever he was, he had to be completely out of his vampiric mind! I closed my eyes and mentally yelled for Alec even though Russell wore my ring.

The door flew open. Alec! His deep lavender eyes shone alien, inhuman, and his razor-sharp fangs slid out.

Rather than fearing him, I thought he was the most wonderful sight I'd ever seen.

In a blindingly fast move, Russell dragged my body into a sitting position, placed himself at my back and held me against his chest as a human shield. One hand gripped my jaw.

Luc burst into the room behind Alec. In the space of seconds they had dropped the human persona and pale reptilian eyes glared at Russell.

'Now gentlemen,' Russell calmly said. 'Come any closer and her head will face backwards.'

Alec's eyes blazed as he looked from Russell to me and back again. He took a step forward, and Russell tensed.

'Alec, stop. He'll do it,' Luc warned.

'It'll be your head on backwards if you dare hurt her,' Alec said.

'What are you doing here?' Luc asked.

'Let's say I'm repaying a debt, and this young lady's the payment.'

'To whom?' Alec stood at the foot of my bed, hands folded over his chest. Slowly, his face returned to human form.

I felt Russell laugh. 'You really don't expect me to reveal that, do you?'

Alec and Luc glanced at each other.

'Let her go and we'll come to some sort of arrangement,' Luc said.

'If I release the girl, I want your guarantee of a safe passage out of here.'

'In return for a name,' Alec said.

Russell didn't reply. From his quickening heartbeat, I guessed he had backed himself into a corner. He couldn't deliver me to whomever had sent him—that one was definitely out—and if he killed me, he might as well commit suicide. Alec and Luc would pounce on him in a second. Russell didn't come across as the suicidal type. On top of that, he had failed whoever sent him to get me, so he was in big trouble from all sides.

Yet, I couldn't just sit here and wait for him to make up his mind as to his next move, or for Luc and Alec to decide how to get me out of this. Surely, there was something I could do. I hated being helpless. Was my blood the only dangerous thing about me? That thought triggered an idea. What if my *other* bodily fluids were just as poisonous – saliva, sweat ... etc? What would happen if I spat on Russell's hand? Would it burn his skin?

I looked at Alec. *Can you hear my thoughts?*

I can hear them, he said in my mind.

I double-blinked. *Even though...?*

We have a connection, whether we're wearing the rings or not.

So, you heard all that?

He gave me a barely perceptible nod. Luc subtly looked at me. A faint smile appeared on his face. I had the feeling he knew we were communicating telepathically.

'Russell, it's over. Give up,' he said.

Russell stiffened, and twisted the ring on his finger. Then I remembered what Luc had said—the ring itself attacks the wrong bearer. Whoever had sent Russell either didn't know or didn't tell him. And it was already happening.

Alec, the ring!

I know. He won't be able to stand it for much longer. Any minute now and he'll have to loosen his grip.

'The ring doesn't recognise you,' Alec said. 'It'll get hotter and start to burn. Eat right through flesh and into bone.' He held up his own ringed finger. 'Mine feels cool.'

Russell was silent, afraid maybe? Yet he maintained his neck-breaking grip on me. I smelt the awful aroma of burnt flesh, and he hissed and squirmed.

Why doesn't he just take it off? I wondered.

He's afraid, Alec replied. *He knows the moment he moves, I'll get him.*

'Well then, it's best if Laura and I left,' Russell said.

'No way!' I gripped the sheets with my feet as he tried to lift me from the bed.

Laura, tell him about your saliva. It might make him flinch.

'Russell, if you try to drag me out of here, I'll lick you. And if you think my blood burns, wait till my saliva hits you. *All* my bodily fluids are like acid. Feel.' I extended my tongue and licked the length of the forefinger he held near my mouth. Russell yelped, jerked his hand away, and I was wrenched out of his grip.

Everything happened at once. Alec grabbed me as Luc seized Russell and threw him to the other side of the room, towards the window. Sunrise was near.

Alec joined Luc and forced Russell face down onto the ground. He snarled and snapped, then screamed as Luc broke off the finger that bore the serpent ring. Luc examined the appendage and the area I had licked. 'Not a mark. It's only your blood, ma petite,' he said, as the golden serpent slid into his palm. 'Hold out your hand.'

I did, and the serpent ring coiled itself around my finger.

It flared brightly before dimming to a deep, dark red. Its companion on Alec's finger flared in response. We looked at each other until I turned away, still feeling Alec's gaze on me.

'You tricked me, dear girl,' Russell called out through pain-gritted teeth.

His voice broke the momentary silence.

'Sorry.' I shrugged. 'You gave me no choice. Nothing personal.' I turned to Luc. 'He knows the ring makes its wearer undetectable—and how to steal it using my blood.'

He and Alec exchanged glances.

Luc crouched low, until his face was barely an inch from Russell's. 'And how did you come to know that?'

Russell struggled, but Alec held him firm. He angled his head to face Luc. 'You don't expect me to answer that, do you?'

Luc rose and lifted the partly-open window blind. Outside it was dark, but faint pink tendrils of light were seeping around the edges of the clouds. 'The choice is yours. Either tell me what I want to know, or face the sun.'

'You're going to kill me anyway.'

'There's a difference between a slow, painful death and the quick death I could offer. Answer my question.'

'A little bat told me,' came the reply.

'Then I'll keep you here, till the sun rises.' Alec growled.

Lightening flashed, followed by a clap of thunder, and then rain pelted down. Russell's laugh was grim. 'Looks like the sun's not interested in coming out to greet me.'

'That doesn't change a thing,' Luc said. 'I'll take your head off, regardless of whether I do it with my bare hands or the sword.'

'Really? In front of our sweet little Ingenii?'

I swallowed and felt myself pale. Would Luc really kill him – in front of me? The very thought made me shiver. In spite of that, something in Russell's mocking tone brought out the devil in me. 'I may be tougher than you think.' I still hoped my angry father wouldn't put me to the test.

'Luc, let's take him back to the house. There'll be more time to question him there,' Alec suggested. 'The morning shift will be doing their rounds soon, and I don't want my staff alerted.'

'Agreed.'

Luc grabbed Russell's other arm and hoisted him up. Russell didn't struggle. He looked straight at me as I sat on the edge of the bed. 'This isn't over yet, dear girl.'

There was a tinkling of glass, the sound of a thud and the bored smirk on Russell's face gave way to surprise then shock. He slumped in Alec and Luc's arms. His body began to crystallise. Turning almost translucent, his skin hardened, and delicate blue veins snaked their way up his neck and over his face. They dropped him. As it hit the ground, Russell's body shattered into a million pieces, his intact clothes crumbling down after him.

'What… what just happened?' I asked, my mouth falling open.

'White-oak bullet, ma petite.' Luc and Alec rushed to the window, leaned out and sniffed the air. 'Damn rain! I can't get a scent,' Luc said.

'That's the second time tonight I've seen white-oak bullets.' Alec left the window and crouched next to what was left of Russell's body.

'Vampire hunters?' Luc suggested. 'Used to be their weapon of choice. But they haven't been around for at least a century.'

'That wouldn't make sense. Why kill Russell when they could have me or you?'

'I'm going out for a quick look.' Luc raced out.

I couldn't stop staring at Russell's remains. How could a physical body just disintegrate like that? It wasn't normal. It wasn't *human*.

'Laura? You all right?' Alec's voice roused me.

'Yeah, fine.'

'I hope you never have to see anything like that again.' He rose, went to the washbasin and tore off a piece of paper towelling, wrapped it around his hand then knelt and thrust it into the sparkling, sandy mound that had once been Russell, as though searching for something.

'So, um … you wouldn't have any timber furniture and stuff in your house, would you?'

'As a matter of fact, I do.' He pulled his hand out and gazed at a few splinters of wood—all that remained of what must have been the bullet. 'My father's old dining suite. It's the only thing I have left from him. But it's made of elm—pretty safe. Only white-oak is poisonous. Once it gets into the bloodstream—well, you saw.' He peered at the tiny, dark fragments. 'It crystallises our cells.'

'It was like something from a sci-fi movie.'

'Once in the bloodstream, it acts fast. Only if we're shot in the arm or leg, is there a chance of survival, and only if it's amputated in time, before the cellulose spreads.'

'Where was Russell shot?'

'In the heart.'

Like snake venom, I remembered Alec saying. 'You said this was the second lot you've seen tonight. Where was the first?'

He looked at me as though deciding something then stood and deposited the paper-towel wrapped bullet fragments on the bedside table. 'Your boyfriend had six of them in his pocket.'

The force of his words hit me like a shock wave, and words stuck in my throat. Matt couldn't have had those things on him; he would've told me. 'No. I can't believe that. It's not possible.'

Alec pressed his lips together. 'Why not? How well do you know him, Laura?'

Maris had asked me that about Alec. What about Matt? 'He would've told me!' I desperately wanted to believe we had no secrets from each other, especially something like this.

Alec laughed. 'You really think so?'

I stared up at him.

'I have no reason to lie, Laura.'

'You've lied before.' Here I was clutching at straws again.

'Only when absolutely necessary.' His brow creased.

I shook my head, unwilling to believe Matt would deceive me. 'I can't....'

His eyes narrowed, and he strode to the bed. I scooted backward until my back pressed against the cold metal rails. Alec leaned in and placed his hands on either side of my head until our faces were barely a breath apart. 'He was planning to kill us—me, your father, our men, all of our kind. And in the process, what if he hit you? You're half vampire, remember? That damned substance would probably kill you as well!'

I stared at him, hating the idea that Matt would do such a thing; yet the more I thought about it, I had to acknowledge that he could —he even suggested it. No, Alec had no reason lie about something like that. What would he have to gain?

We gazed at each other for what seemed like ages, when he suddenly straightened. He went to the window and stared out. I drew my knees up and lowered my head onto them. My head spun. Why did Matt have those bullets, and did he plan to tell me … ever? I lifted my head and looked at Alec's back.

'Is … is Matt okay?'

'How commendable of you. Asking after his welfare when he was planning to murder your family.'

'I have only your word for that.'

He turned and looked at me. 'You really don't want to admit you could be wrong about him, do you?'

'I've got to give him the chance to defend himself.'

Alec huffed. 'Well, that's going to be a bit difficult, since he's unconscious and won't be doing any talking for a while.' My expression must have said it all, for Alec hastened to add, 'Don't panic; he's okay. He'll live.'

I didn't know whether to be relieved or angry, for if Alec was telling the truth, Matt had a lot of explaining to do.

'What did you do with the bullets?' I asked.

Without turning around, he answered. 'Took them. Gave them to your father if you want proof.'

I nodded, not knowing what else to say. My mind was still processing the fact that Matt was intent on destroying my family – albeit the vampire side—in order to save me. There could be no other explanation, and in his eyes it wouldn't be murder, because they weren't human. I could understand his reasoning, but condone it? Never. For one thing he'd make matters worse by destroying my protectors, leaving me vulnerable to creatures like Maris and Russell. Or was he expecting to wipe them all out? It was ludicrous, especially as it wouldn't end the curse and he'd only end up wrecking both our lives.

What hurt most was that he had kept it from me.

The silence stretched out between us like a tight line.

'I … um, didn't get a chance to thank you for, ah, coming after me.'

He finally turned and looked at me. 'You mean *rescuing* you.'

I hated the idea of a rescue; as it went against my twenty-first century sensibilities. 'Yeah, that.'

'You thought I wouldn't?'

'Oh, I knew you would. You need me to maintain your exalted position.'

He huffed again. 'First you call me a liar and now I'm a mercenary. Congratulations, Laura.'

'Okay, okay, I'm sorry. But how do you expect me to react when you accuse my boyfriend of planning murder?'

'White-oak bullets are used for one purpose only. Why else would he have them?'

I sighed. What could I say?

He sat on the edge of my bed. 'What if I had been serious about sharing you with Maris?'

'Terens told me a little about her, and I reckon it wouldn't have lasted.'

'Oh, really? And you've become a great expert?'

'No, but if you'd loved her, you wouldn't have broken up.' As I was thinking of doing with Matt.

His eyes travelled to my mouth and lingered there causing the butterflies in my stomach to take off. Suddenly he stood. 'You're right. We'll pursue this conversation later.'

The door opened, and Luc entered, followed by Jean. 'Nothing! Not a trace. Rain's washed away all traces.'

I barely registered what he said, affected still by Alec's proximity.

'What happened?' Jean glanced around and took in the sandy crystalline mound partly covered by Russell's clothing at the base of the window, and his eyes narrowed.

Luc kicked the sandy heap. 'Russell here, tried to take Laura.'

'That's Russell?'

'What's left of him,' Alec said, passing the paper towel with its deadly contents to Luc. 'Unfortunately, we didn't find out who he was in league with.'

'Probably whoever shot him is my guess; stop him from talking. Meaning they'll try for Laura again.' Luc eyed the bullet fragments then pocketed them.

I couldn't stop the shiver that ran through me and hoped he was wrong.

'They won't succeed,' Alec said. He must have sensed my fear. Of course; he could probably smell it.

Jean moved towards me. 'I came to return this to you.' He produced my mobile phone and passed it to me. 'I took it from Douglas before Marcus's sword removed his head. I also took the

liberty of removing the offending material. I hope you don't mind.'
His French accent was particularly pronounced.

I knew to what he was referring—the sadistic video Maris took of her torturing me. 'Thank you.'

'Alec is very fortunate.' He slid his hand along the length of my cheek and down to my chin. For some reason, his touch made me uncomfortable.

'Jean!' Luc's voice cracked like a whip.

Jean blinked and dropped his hand. 'Please, excuse me.' He turned on his heel and left.

I didn't know what to think. He was Luc's man as well as Alec's friend, and he helped in my rescue. Maybe he was just the intense type. His uncanny resemblance to Philippe, the young man I knew when I was eighteen, unnerved me, and seeing him up close, the similarity was eerie. Could it be...? Yet, everyone called him Jean.

'Laura?'

Alec's voice drew me from my thoughts. 'Yes?'

'I need to check your arm.'

He unpeeled the dressing, and with a gentle prod here and there, tested my reflexes.

'How bad is it?' Luc asked, before sitting next to me. He took hold of my hand.

'No lasting damage, thankfully.'

Luc let out a relieved breath. 'Her mother will be happy. She isn't exactly thrilled with me right now.'

'Why?' I asked.

'Said if she'd been in the room as she'd intended, Russell wouldn't have tried anything.'

'We don't know that for sure,' Alec replied.

'She came here last night?'

'Yes, ma petite. But she was exhausted, needed sleep. I persuaded her to go home and,' —he looked at me sadly— 'promised her you'd be safe.'

'Oh.' I could understand why she would feel that way, yet I could just as easily sympathise with my father. I couldn't begin to imagine how much he must be blaming himself. But Russell had been cunning, and he'd had help.

As Alec cleaned and dressed my stitches, my head slipped back onto the pillow. Overpowering tiredness stole over me. I closed my eyes – only for a second.

CHAPTER 30
JEAN

ALEC

I looked up after dressing and binding Laura's arm. Her breasts rose and fell in a steady rhythm, and her eyelids fluttered.

Luc strode to the window and strategically positioned two chairs to screen off Russell's chalky dust, its crystalline sparkle beginning to fade.

'I'll clean that up later,' I said. Now that we were alone, I could bring up the subject of Jean.

'Anything wrong?' he asked, perching on the edge of Laura's bed. 'You've got that look on your face.'

'I need to ask you something.' We spoke so low, no human—even if in the room—would have heard us.

'What?'

There was no subtle way to put it. 'Is Jean in love with Laura?'

'What makes you think that?'

'Didn't you see the way he looked at her? That touch on her cheek had nothing to do with avuncular affection. It was a lover's caress. He masked his scent, but I still smelled it.'

He rubbed his hand down the side of his face. 'I warned him.'

'I noticed.'

'I've kept him away from her for as long as I could.'

'How long has he felt like that towards her?'

'Over thirty years.'

My eyes widened. How many other secrets was Luc hiding?
'Why didn't you tell me?'

He sighed. 'I was hoping it wouldn't be necessary, especially
since Laura doesn't seem to remember him.'

'They've met?'

'She was eighteen. Like all her friends, she too wanted to travel
after her high school graduation. I didn't like the idea, but....' he
threw his hands in the air, 'what could we do? I finally said yes, and
sent Cal and Jake along to watch over her. Jean was in France at the
time. Jake invited him over, as he hadn't seen Laura since she was
little. He came out of curiosity.' From the expression on his face, it
appeared he blamed himself—probably thinking if only he had been
there.

'What happened?'

'From what Jake told me, when she and her friends were in
Sorrento, they went out for dinner. The stupid local boys pestered
them. Jean intervened, and they struck up a friendship. He
introduced himself by his middle name—Philippe. I got on the first
available flight; but by the time I got there, it had gone beyond the
hand holding stage. Jean was serious, and Laura was returning his
affection.'

Luc had asked me to accompany Cal on that trip instead of Jake,
but I made an excuse. What if I had gone? What if...?

'As I recall, you didn't want to be involved.'

'I had my reasons.'

'I wish I'd known then.' He gave me a lopsided smile before
continuing. 'I ordered him back to France.'

'And a few months later he shows up here.' Things began to fall
into place.

'Judy was worried, as it wasn't what we had planned for her.' He
looked at me meaningfully. 'But she was a child still, and we hoped
she would get over it quickly. She had a place at university, and then
of course there would be her studies, as well as other distractions.
And that's what happened. Laura came home, got caught up in
university life and eventually she forgot all about "Philippe".'

'They didn't keep in touch?'

'No. Eilene kept us informed. Laura had been infatuated but not in love.'

'But Jean was.'

'Yes,' he said then slowly added. 'He refused to go back. Said he had a right to love her … that he had as much Pictish blood in him as you.'

My hands gripped the sides of my chair tight enough to crush the metal arms. If that was true, he could have challenged me at the Ritual. Why didn't he? I rose and faced Luc. 'The issue here is not so much the Pictish blood as his ancestry—the witch's blood, Luc. Does he have that?'

'I'm not sure. The thing is,' he took a deep breath, 'his mother told him his father was the Duke of Atholl.'

I groaned. The Duke's bloodline was without dispute. More than a thousand years ago, his estate lay smack in the midst of the once-powerful Pictish kingdom. But was he descended from the witch? Did Jean have a valid claim?

'I made a deal with him.'

I raised my eyebrows. It appeared Luc's business methods spilled over into his personal life. 'What deal?'

'To wait till Laura came of age, when she could decide for herself.'

I gasped. 'So that's why you asked me to meet her last Friday night.'

He nodded. 'I was worried Jean might show up at the house or even intercept her on the way if she was on her own.' It explained why Judith drove her straight to the front door of the cathedral. 'That's not all,' he continued. 'He was here the night before reminding me of our bargain, determined to speak to her. I had to forestall him somehow, told him Judy was going to reveal everything to Laura on her birthday … give her time to get over the shock … wait till the Ritual.'

'He was okay with that?'

'Not really, but I didn't give him any other option.'

My mind flashed back to Monday night. Like everyone else gathered that night he would have seen the way our rings glowed even before we reached the pavilion. Laura had already made her choice. He knew it was too late. 'That's why he didn't openly challenge me,' I said aloud.

He nodded.

Luc's machinations, which would have made Machiavelli proud, now created another problem—Jean would never trust Luc again, even though they'd known each other for over two-hundred years. It was a dangerous position to be in. Luc didn't need to say that. It was evident on his face. Yet I sensed there was more.

'Why me and not him? Surely a kinsman of yours, especially the son of a duke would have been preferable?'

'Yes, but … I knew his mother, the Duchess d'Orleans.'

My scalp prickled.

'There is the possibility he could be' —he swallowed hard and added almost sheepishly— 'my son. Laura's half-brother.'

I shook my head in disbelief. 'Does he know?'

'No.'

'Do you plan to tell him?'

'It's my word against his mother's. Who do you think he'd believe? How can I tell him he's in love with his half-sister?'

'Oh, Luc!' I slumped into the chair by Laura's bed. 'If he's half-vampire and half-human then….' My mind was trying to keep up.

He uttered an oath in French then stood, moved to the end of the bed and leaned his hands on the metal frame. 'He never changed at puberty, as I did. So I can't be sure. But then, it's the Ingenii gene that makes the difference. And I'm not a carrier, Judy is. Laura's unique. Jean is not—that I know of.'

'Okay. A DNA test will give us the answer. My lab can do it. I need a sample of skin or even a hair. See if you can get it. It'll take a few days, but at least we'll know for sure. You've got to tell him. I need to know if he's got a claim or not.' I ran my hand through my hair. 'Have you considered what this will do to Laura? If she finds out Jean's the man she met in Sorrento and he just might be her half-brother…?'

'Mon Dieu! How can I tell Judy!'

The longer I knew Luc the more I realised his perception of events was very different from my own. 'That's not exactly what I meant. You said that Laura doesn't remember him?'

'No, I don't think so.' He shook his head. 'I watched her at the Ritual. Surely she would have said something if she'd recognised him? Did it look to you as if she knew him?'

'Not then, no. But she did look at him closely, just now, as he returned her mobile, and she watched him until he was out the door. I had to get her attention.'

Luc pursed his lips. 'Let's assume she didn't.'

I hoped he was right. Yet it didn't solve the problem of Jean, and I had a feeling there would be no easy solution. His actions had the hallmarks of a man who refused to acknowledge his lack of hope, and a desperate man always clings to hope. His words from yesterday made chilling sense to me now. *What if something were to happen to you?* Indeed. But I couldn't believe he would ever do me any harm. How excruciating must it have been for him, watching over her every day – without her knowing—then to stand silently by as she dated other men. Waiting. Hoping. Only to be thwarted at the end. His features hadn't revealed any emotion, but I'd smelled his hatred.

'He hates me now.'

'Probably, but not as much as he does me. It's my fault Laura chose you. He feels angry and betrayed. I'm worried about his mental stability, afraid he might do something stupid.'

'Why do you say that?'

'He's withdrawn even further into himself. I don't know when was the last time he fed. You know what can happen to a vampire if he starves himself.'

He looked at me pointedly. I didn't need reminding. Following my transformation, I'd nearly gone insane from hunger after refusing to feed from humans.

'Where is he now?'

'No idea.'

'You've got to find him and get that DNA sample, Luc. It can't wait. And if you're right about his mental condition, he mustn't be allowed to go anywhere near Laura.'

He nodded.

I wondered if the others knew, or perhaps even guessed that Jean had feelings for her. I hoped they didn't. It would be humiliating for him. But, more importantly, Laura must never know. How would she take it, knowing that the young man she had known as a teenager was her father's kinsman, a vampire and possibly her brother? I didn't want to picture it.

Laura tossed restlessly in her sleep. She flailed her free arm and cried out. It was as I feared—a post-traumatic nightmare. I stroked her face in an effort to wake her. 'Laura? Laura, wake up...'

CHAPTER 31
BUSINESS ARRANGEMENT

LAURA

A voice said, 'Laura?' A cool hand touched my cheek. 'Laura, wake up. You've been dreaming.'

Dreaming? I didn't know I'd fallen asleep. It had seemed so real. My eyes struggled to open. 'No dream. Nightmare.' My words were slurred.

He looked at me with concern. 'After trauma, you can get nightmares.'

For how long? The thought raced through my mind. I had dreamt of my best friend, Jenny, as a vampire, and the image was still burned into my eyes. No matter that it was only a dream, a phantom of my imagination. It was disturbing. *It's not real!* I tried shaking it and the accompanying grogginess from my head. Besides that, the inside of my mouth felt like cotton wool.

I turned my head toward the window. A couple of chairs hid Russell's dust from view. The memory of his breath in my face brought up bile. I forced it down. *I must get out of this room.* The urge was so strong; I pushed the sheets off and tried to get out of bed.

A firm hand gently pushed me back. 'No, ma petite. Stay there.' A plastic cup was placed into my hand. 'Here, drink this. It'll make you feel better.'

'I want to get out of here.'

'Drink first,' Luc said. 'And we'll arrange something.' He glanced at Alec. 'She'd be safer at the house. None of the Brethren would dare try anything there.'

'You're probably right.' Alec turned to me. 'I can't guarantee your safety here. It's best if you stay at Luc's for a while, till we catch whoever sent Russell.'

'And....' my father added just as I opened my mouth to ask if I couldn't simply go home to my own flat. 'Your mother and I would love to spend some time with you.'

How could I argue with that? 'Can we go there now?' I pushed the cotton blanket aside and swung my legs over the edge.

'Laura!' Alec protested.

I ignored him and stood, only to have my legs buckle beneath me as if made of jelly. Two pairs of hands caught me and lifted me back onto the bed.

'Not until you've had something to eat,' my father said, the tone of his voice making it clear he would brook no argument. 'I'm already in enough trouble with your mother.' He tucked the blanket around me, his face softening as he added, 'Laura, ma petite, you're the most precious thing in my life, next to Judy. And right now, you need to give your body a chance to recover.'

'Breakfast is on its way,' Alec said as he sat on the edge of my bed, near my feet. Probably to ensure I didn't try crawling to the door.

I gave a resigned sigh and looked down at my bandaged hand. 'How long was I asleep?'

'Little over an hour. Not enough.'

'I had a horrible dream.'

'Want to talk about it?'

I shook my head. Alec had never met Jenny. I'm sure my father knew her though, since he'd been secretly watching over me all my life. But that wasn't all of it. Maris had been in it, too.

Luc's mobile rang. 'Excuse me.' He walked outside, graciously sidestepping one of the hospital staff who walked in carrying a hot tray. It smelled delicious, and my stomach grumbled.

Alec smiled. 'Good sign. Let me arrange for you to eat it in another room.' He took the mobile from his jeans pocket and rang reception. 'Dr Munro here. Do we have another suite available?'

He waited while the receptionist did a search. All the while his eyes never wavered from my face. I must have looked terrible. My hair was loose and tousled and I'm sure my eyes were red and puffy from lack of sleep. I probably resembled an unkempt red setter. I brought the cup to my lips and drank—freshly squeezed orange juice. It was good. The dizziness I'd experienced on waking began to wane.

'Perfect.' He paused. 'No, I won't need a wheelchair.' He tucked the phone back into his pocket. 'There's a room available down the hall, so I'm moving you there now.'

He rose and wrapped the cotton blanket around my waist, scooped me up like I was an invalid and made his way down the corridor. 'Follow us,' he said to the young woman carrying my breakfast.

'I can walk, you know.'

'This is quicker.' To prove it, he strode at such a fast pace that the girl carrying the breakfast tray clunked it back onto the trolley and practically ran after us.

Since there was no arguing with him, I put the bad dream—and everything else that had happened in that room—behind me.

As we reached the end of the hall, Alec turned into an open doorway. The early morning light streamed in and bounced off glass-covered pictures lining pale-apricot walls. Twin beds, separated by a three-drawer cabinet, stood adjacent to a window that overlooked a leafy suburban park. He lowered me onto the nearest bed, removed the cotton blanket in which I'd been cocooned then tucked me into fresh sheets. He took the tray, perched himself on the edge of the bed and watched me eat. Since I was unable to use my right hand, he buttered the toast, sliced the bacon and cut up the baked tomato. He was as attentive as any nurse. The contrast between his vampire-self and the caring physician could not have been greater.

'Now, our unfinished discussion.' He leaned toward me. 'Do you love Sommers? I've asked you three times, and each time you've neatly side stepped it. Why?'

'Why does that matter to you?'

'You're doing it again—evading.'

Was I? Or was I afraid to admit I had my doubts since learning what Matt was planning to do with the white-oak bullets? Not only that, but were I to marry him, we could never have kids—it would only continue the curse, and being an only child, I wanted a house full.

'I don't know!' I finally admitted. 'How can I love him after what you told me? He's not the man I thought he was.' It'd been playing on my mind all this time. He and Alec and Luc would only ever be enemies. How could I marry someone who hated my family enough to want to kill them? 'Besides, I want kids, yet I don't want to pass on this wretched gene.' I gave a derisive laugh. 'I need to end this curse and the only way is to find someone with Pictish blood and have a child with him.'

Alec's eyes flared. 'Would you be willing to do that?'

'Do I have much choice?' Up until last Friday, I believed my future lay with Matt. Now, in the space of four days, all that had changed, and I was faced with the decision of my life—marry for love or end my family curse. It looked more and more like it was going to be the latter.

'In this situation, no you don't, since you're the Child of Light and Darkness the prophecy spoke of. Whether you like it or not, it's your destiny to end this curse.' He paused. 'As it is mine.'

'What do you mean?'

His hand scrunched a section of the sheet on which it rested. 'I'm descended from the witch who uttered the curse. My blood is Pict.'

My stomach felt as if I'd swallowed rocks. 'Why didn't you tell me sooner?'

He huffed. 'You always want to know everything before you're ready to hear it. If I had told you last Friday night that you need to have a child with me in order to end your family curse, I doubt you would have ever wanted to set eyes son me again.'

'Probably not.' Matt would probably have tried to kill him sooner.

'Would you consider it?' His gaze burned into mine, the usual lavender shade of his eyes now a deep, dark purple.

'Have a child with you?'

He nodded.

Could I do this? My parents had placed me in the care of others to ensure my safety, at great cost to themselves. Could I do any less? I tried to imagine myself fifty years from now, having to explain the Coming-of-Age ceremony to my child, and the very thought chilled me. I couldn't let that happen. I wouldn't let that happen.

I gazed back at Alec while weighing up every possibility. We'd known each other less than a week and if I agreed to his suggestion, he would become the father of my child. The enormity of it all struck me—whatever decision I made affected the future. Yet I couldn't deny the attraction I felt toward him, and the image of the two of us making love rose unbidden in my head. A rush of pleasure surged between my thighs, and I tried to mask it by looking out the window.

I felt his hand turn my chin to meet his gaze. 'Laura, this isn't easy for you, I know. Think of it as a business arrangement. We'll come together until you fall pregnant, and when the baby is born, our contract is at an end. After that, you need never see me again.'

It was so clinical, so cold, yet what choice did I have? 'That simple, huh?'

He shook his head. 'Anything but. The baby needs to be born in Scotland, at the site of the Roman massacre. I'll arrange all that, be with you when the time comes.'

He said nothing about feelings. How could two people be so intimate and then go their separate ways? 'Then you'll be gone.'

'You won't need me any more. Once the curse is lifted, there's a chance your blood will revert to human, and its unique properties will disappear. My role as a guardian will be over. You'll be free to marry whoever you want and have as many children as you like.'

I should have welcomed that knowledge, but instead it filled me with emptiness. He wouldn't be there. But I couldn't let my mind— or my heart—dwell on that. As long as I could be assured that my child would never have to undergo the Ritual, I could go through with it—no attachment, no obligation, no emotion.

I took a deep breath. 'All right. I'll do this.'

'Good. It's best we start tonight, while you're ovulating.'

I'm sure I looked startled, not just by his reference to my cycle but his suggestion for us to be together so soon. 'How did—'

'I can smell it on you, Laura. This is the most fertile time for an Ingenii, so we have to take advantage of it.'

We could have been discussing the price of fish.

He dropped his hand, and his head turned toward the door. A few seconds later, a young woman stood there. It was one of the hospital staff. 'Excuse me, Dr Munro, there's a Mr and Mrs Dantonville asking to see their daughter.'

Two dear and familiar faces appeared in the doorway. It was Mum and Dad.

CHAPTER 32
FAMILY TIES

LAURA

Mum and Dad, my human mum and dad, both stood in the doorway, hesitant. I smiled, extended my arms and temporarily put Alec's "business arrangement" out of my mind. Mum practically threw herself over me in a huge hug.

'It's okay, Mum. It's all okay,' I whispered into her ear and patted her shoulder as she heaved with sobs.

Dad came over and kissed the top of my head. 'You're still my baby girl,' he said. He appeared even older than the last time I'd seen him.

'I know, Dad. That'll never change.'

'We got a phone call early this morning,' Mum said. 'We came as soon as we could.' I nodded and glanced up to see Alec quietly leave the room. 'I'm so sorry I didn't come to the Ritual. I just ... couldn't. The thought of seeing you as some creature's blood supply....' Her eyes glistened.

Oh no, please no tears, I silently begged. That's all I needed to set off my own waterworks. I took both her hands in mine. 'Mum, I know and I understand. It's all right. Really.'

'We had to keep the truth from you all these years. 'Your father—' she stopped then corrected herself. 'John and I promised not to reveal anything to you till you came of age. And even then Judy wanted it to come from her.' She looked at me with tear-stained eyes. 'I've loved you as my own child. Never doubt that.'

'I know Mum, and I couldn't have had a happier childhood. This doesn't change anything between us. I love you as my mum and always will. The same goes for you, Dad.'

He squeezed my hand then sat down in one of the two empty chairs by my bedside.

This had to be hell for them.

'Thank you, Laura, love.' She cupped my cheek. 'We've had the privilege of having you in our home all these years, and it's only right that Judy and Luc share that joy now. They suffered to keep you safe.'

'I know, Mum. They told me everything.'

'Lucien's a good man despite … what he is,' Dad said.

I smiled. He couldn't bring himself to say the word "vampire."

'I met Dr Munro only once; the day they brought you to us,' Mum said. 'He came with them and arranged the necessary papers – birth certificate for you and death certificate for my little Katie.' She smiled to cover her sadness. Dad placed a comforting arm around her shoulder. 'Parental names were swapped, of course.' She paused. 'He came across as a very sympathetic man. I never saw him after that – till now.'

I gazed at Dad. His lips were set in a firm line as he stared out the window.

'I was worried sick how you were going to take it,' Mum said.

'Don't be. I really am fine—with everything.' I gave her a reassuring smile.

'Do they know who did it?' Dad's gaze came back to me.

'Yep. They were all caught. They won't be committing any other offences.' I raised my right eyebrow at him meaningfully.

Mum moved off the bed and sat in the other chair while I briefly outlined what had happened Tuesday night.

'Thank God your injuries weren't worse.' She clasped my hand. 'Have you heard how Matt is?'

'He's okay.' I repeated Alec's words. 'The police spoke to Alec earlier this morning while I was still out of it. Said they'd be back later today to interview me.'

'Want us to be with you?' Dad asked. 'You shouldn't be alone.'

'Look, I'm sure I'll be fine, but it's really up to you.'

As I finished saying it, Alec walked in and declared the police were here to speak to me.

'We're staying.' Dad said.

CHAPTER 33
MEMORIES

ALEC

I stepped out of the room to allow Laura some precious time with John and Eilene. Luc waited at the end of the corridor. 'I saw them arrive. Thought it best not to go in,' he said.

'Laura will be too preoccupied to notice you've even gone.'

'That's what I thought. I'm going to the house now ... see how Judy is. Be back in an hour to take Laura home. By then they will have gone.'

'Fine. Then I'll head down to my office.'

I took the fire-escape stairs, as it allowed me to move at my natural speed unnoticed. The other hospital staff rarely used them, preferring the elevator. I walked into my office, sat at the desk and stared vacantly at the pile of papers next to my laptop. Several important articles waited for my attention, yet I couldn't get my mind off Laura—could still smell her conflicting emotions. My mind replayed every word spoken between us, every expression that flitted across her face and the resigned determination when she agreed to my suggestion. I hated the thought of outright seduction and the deceit that accompanies it; better she knew the truth.

Now, I had to choose where we would meet—my apartment in the city, Luc's place or Laura's flat in Rozelle? And then what?

I rubbed my face as I considered the months ahead. There was someone out there who wanted her, who had sent and killed Russell. There could even be another faction who desired to end the Principate, although not the curse itself, as it bestowed power and privilege on whoever possessed the Ingenii. If anyone outside our immediate circle discovered my lineage—a Pict descended from the witch, Eithne—they would kill me in order to prevent our child from ever being conceived. We were both in danger, and seeing John and Eilene after all these years brought back the memory of the day Luc and Judith handed an infant Laura into their care. And it was one I'd rather forget—sunny with a blazing blue sky, as if the weather mocked the sad events taking place.

Luc had asked me to drive so he could sit in the back with his wife and child. It was impossible to forget the haunted look on his face as Judith pleaded with him not to give up their child.

I closed that memory and forced myself back to the present, lifted a few papers and sorted through others—I had a duty as head of this hospital. Sure that Laura was safe, I scanned through the top layer of reports. Several results needed to be published, while others needed re-examining. I went through a great many, using the supernatural speed of my kind, then stood and headed for the shower, discarding my jeans and T-shirt along the way.

The steaming water was refreshing as it washed over me, but I couldn't relax and automatically fingered the gold crucifix around my neck. Images of my mother came to mind. It had been hers once, a very long time ago. I was eleven when she died. Tuberculosis. I'd determined to become a doctor, to find a cure for the wretched disease that had killed her. It was one of the few times in my life when I saw my father cry. It was also the reason he later decided to leave Scotland.

'This is yours now, Alec,' my mother had said, her voice painfully weak. She held out the gold crucifix at her throat. 'You have to undo it. I haven't the strength.'

I leaned over her, fighting back tears as only an eleven-year-old boy could—with anger. 'I don't want it, Ma. It's yours. Give it to me when I'm all grown.'

She reached out and touched my cheek, before letting her hand fall back onto the bed. 'I'm not going to be here to see that,' she whispered as a tear rolled down her sunken cheek.

I shook my head and refused to take it.

'Let me,' my father said, as he gently unclasped the chain from around her neck and placed it around mine. Then he went back to her side, took both her hands in his and kissed them. 'Sleep darling.'

She closed her eyes, and I ran out of the house, my mother's small gold cross bouncing on my bony chest, and my tears mingling with the rain as I cursed all and sundry for taking my mother from me.

The shrill sound of the ringing phone shocked me into the present. I grabbed a towel, wrapped it around me and strode out to answer it. 'Doctor Munro.'

'The police are here to see Miss Dantonville.'

'Okay, tell them I'll be right out.' I cleared my mind from the painful memories and strode from my office.

The same two detectives from this morning waited at the Reception Desk. Detective Chief Inspector Delaney looked even more tired than earlier—the dark circles under his eyes were quite pronounced. The younger detective—the woman, Norris—appeared fresher. She must have managed to get some sleep since our last meeting.

Both smiled, and Delaney extended his hand. 'Thank you for seeing us again, Dr Munro.'

I nodded curtly and returned the handshake.

'Is Miss Dantonville up to speaking to us?' he asked.

'I think so. If you'd like to come with me, her room is on the first floor.'

They followed me into the elevator. 'Nice facility you got here,' Delaney said.

'Thanks.'

'Your, uh, father started this place up. Is that right?'

He'd been doing his research. 'Yes.'

'What year was that?'

I turned to look at him. '1961. Checking up on me, Detective?'

He gave me a ghost of a smile. 'Only part of the job.'

The elevator doors opened, and we strode down the corridor toward Laura's room.

'Must be proud of the work you do here,' he said.

He had been doing his homework. 'Don't know about proud. We're all dedicated to finding a cure for some of the world's worst diseases.'

'How do you stay funded? You're a private hospital. Government support must be pretty meagre.'

He was right there. 'We're lucky enough to have some generous benefactors who are grateful for the work we do.'

He nodded. Like an ever-present shadow, Norris followed, jotting in her little incident book. This was going to be tricky. I sensed Delaney's questioning was more than just interest. He was fishing.

'Would you mind waiting here a moment? I'd like to check if she's awake and up to it,' I asked as my hand curled around the door handle.

Delaney nodded. I walked in and closed the door behind me.

CHAPTER 34
INTERROGATION

LAURA

Alec closed the door and approached John and Eilene. He briefly nodded to Dad and extended his hand to Mum. 'It's a long time since I've had the pleasure,' he said. He looked from one to the other. 'I assume you know all that's happened?'

'We got the story from Judy,' Dad replied. 'It's not in anyone's best interest for the police to connect you personally with Laura.'

'Lying to the police?!' Mum's eyes widened.

'Mum, you don't have to say anything. Only sit quietly. I'll answer their questions and be as truthful as I can without compromising anyone.'

'Eilene, would you prefer to wait in my office?' Alec asked.

She examined each of our faces in turn. 'No. I want to be here for Laura. I didn't have the courage to attend the Ritual, but I'm not going to back out now.'

Dad ran his arm around her shoulders and gave them a squeeze. 'We're both staying,' he said to Alec.

Alec nodded and turned to me. 'I didn't mention anything about your kidnapping. Actually, I had to bend the truth a little. Told them we found you both unconscious and bleeding in your flat. I decided to take you here, as my hospital was closer and has better facilities – which it does—while the ambulance took Sommers elsewhere.'

'Okay.'

A gnawing fear grew in the back of my mind that I may know the two detectives waiting outside. Since Matt and I had been together, we'd attended one or two functions where I'd met several of his friends and work colleagues. His partner, Jonno, knew me well—I taught his kids. The police community was quite tight-knit. If I broke up with Matt, word would soon get around, and it would hit him hard.

Alec opened the door and said, 'Mind if I stay?'

'Yes, that's fine, since this now involves you as well.'

I knew that voice. Then his face appeared in the doorway. 'Dave.' My heart sank. Of all the people! I nearly groaned aloud. Why couldn't it have been someone we didn't know?

Dave Delaney smiled and walked to my side. 'Hey, Laura,' he said then frowned as his eyes travelled over my injuries. He and Matt had been partners before Matt's recent promotion to the city. Dave had been his mentor in many ways, and Matt once mentioned his mind was as sharp as a switchblade—that he made connections others missed.

My stomach clenched.

'How are you?' he asked.

'Sore.' I managed a half-hearted smile.

'Look, I know Jonno should be in charge here, but I specially requested this assignment. We're working together on this one. I want to catch the bastard.'

'We all do. Whoever it is has attacked one of our own,' a low female voice said. It belonged to the other detective—a pretty young woman in navy pants and a black-and-white-polka-dot blouse—who stood behind him.

'Oh, sorry! Laura, this is Detective Sergeant Norris.'

'Barbara.' She gave me a warm smile.

'Nice to meet you,' I replied. Although she kept most of her attention on me, I did notice the way her gaze strayed to Alec, when it wasn't necessary. It rankled me, though I couldn't say why. I looked back to Dave who eyed Eilene and John with interest. 'Dave, I'd like you to meet my parents.'

'Glad to meet you, Mr and Mrs … Dantonville?' He didn't take it for granted that our surnames were the same. People divorced and remarried too frequently these days. I always had to be careful when addressing my pupils' parents. On one occasion, I'd made the mistake of assuming a parent's surname was the same as their child's—much to our mutual embarrassment.

'That's right,' Dad answered.

Dave smiled. 'It's always good to check.' He turned his attention back to me. 'Laura, I know this is painful for you, but I'd like you to try and remember exactly what happened Tuesday night.'

'Well, Matt and I drove up to my block of flats. We got out and went to my door. I unlocked it, opened it and someone grabbed me. I screamed and got hit on the head. That's it.' I shrugged.

'What time was that?'

'Um, after nine, nine-thirty? I'm not that sure.'

'That coincides with the neighbours' statement. They said they heard a scream from your flat around that time. Whoever it was, was waiting for you. If it had been a straight burglary, they would have fled the scene as soon as they heard you coming—out the window. But, they didn't.' He stopped for a moment, his penetrating gaze never leaving my face, as if he were trying to probe my mind. 'Did you see anything?'

'No. It was dark, and besides, I never got the chance.'

'Sure.' He grabbed a spare chair from near the door, brought it next to Dad and sat down facing me. 'Laura, what I don't understand is why they'd slash your arm when you were already unconscious. From what we can tell, Matt pulled out his gun and tried to fire.' I must have reacted when he said that, for he added, 'It was at least a few feet from where he fell.'

Mum's hand found mine and squeezed.

'If it was just an individual, Matt would have easily dealt with him, but his head was shoved into that doorframe with such violence, I can't see one person doing it. There had to have been two or three, at least, and Matt saw them.' He paused. 'Mmmmm, then what were they after?'

I knew exactly what they were after, and I didn't want Dave to go there, so I tried changing the subject. 'How is Matt?'

'They've got him in an induced coma. But at least he's out of emergency.'

I felt the blood drain from my face. Alec told me Matt was unconscious but that he was okay. He didn't mention anything about a coma! I turned my head to where he stood near the window, watching proceedings.

'Laura,' he said. 'It means they're giving his body a chance to recover, and hopefully, once they're sure there's no bleeding on the brain, they'll slowly bring him out of it.'

'Bleeding on the brain,' I repeated, as it slowly sunk in.

'You mean he could have brain damage?' Dad asked.

'There's always that possibility,' Alec replied.

I resisted the urge to cry and swallowed the rising lump in my throat.

'He's strong. He'll get through this.' Dave cracked a small smile.

His words felt like a punch in my stomach, confirmation that the sooner I left him, the safer he would be—and so would my family.

'Anyway, that slash on your arm's bothering me,' he went on.

No one said a word. I'm sure I wasn't the only one wondering where this was headed.

Dave pursed his lips. 'Know what I think?' I nearly stopped breathing. 'We're dealing with the same killer who's responsible for the current spate of murders Matt's been investigating.'

He was right on both counts. Mum's hand squeezed mine so tightly I was sure she'd cut off my circulation. Dad fidgeted, licked his lips once or twice but said nothing.

Dave twisted in his chair to face Alec. 'Doc, I'm willing to have a bet here that there was something unusual about Laura's injury, and you brought her here for immediate treatment and possible tests. Am I right?'

'Yes,' Alec replied.

'You also told me that Laura had lost a lot of blood.'

Alec nodded, and Barbara rifled through her notebook.

'Now, what's bothering me is that there was no trace of Laura's blood at the scene. Matt's, yes. But, Laura's? Not a drop. How could anyone lose so much blood and not leave a trace? Forensics was pretty thorough. So, where did it all go?'

Alec calmly returned Dave's gaze, but his lips were a tight line.

'Do you mind if I take a look at your medical records for last night?' Dave asked.

'Be my guest.' Alec pulled the mobile phone from his pocket and asked for the necessary documentation.

While we waited, Dave took the notebook from Barbara's hands and flicked through a few pages before handing it back to her. It was the longest couple of minutes of my life. No one spoke. There came a knock on the door, and an orderly stepped in, a manila folder in his hand. Alec indicted he hand it to Dave, who perused it thoroughly before passing the loose-leaf copies to his partner. She made more notes in her little pad.

'Four units of blood? That's quite a bit, isn't it?' He looked questioningly at Alec.

'Yes, it is. That's why I brought her here. It's much closer than Balmain. I was worried we could lose her.'

Dave nodded, apparently satisfied. Barbara handed the folder back to Alec.

'Then correct me if I'm wrong.' Dave kept his eyes fixed on Alec. 'But if I were to unwrap Laura's bandage, would I find bite marks or, perhaps, deep puncture wounds?'

I think I may have let out an audible gasp, surprised he had stumbled onto the truth. Suddenly, I had the attention of everyone in the room.

'I'm sorry, Laura, I didn't want to tell you,' —Alec turned to me— 'I was waiting for the right opportunity.' He glared at Dave. 'You may at least have prepared her.'

Alec had brilliantly salvaged the situation, giving Dave the impression I knew nothing about it. I sincerely hoped my shocked expression would be interpreted that way.

'I won't apologise, Laura. I needed to see your reaction—give your memory a jolt, in case your mind was blocking something out,' Dave explained.

'I told you exactly what happened, everything from the moment I walked in till I was knocked out!'

'And that's what I needed to know.'

'You think my daughter is suppressing something?' Dad asked.

'It happens.' Dave shifted his attention back to Alec. 'Tell me, Doc, *did* you see something unusual, and were there traces of saliva on the wound?'

Alec briefly glanced at me before answering Dave. 'Yes to the former, but the results of the saliva test only just arrived on my desk.'

'Are they human?'

'Yes.'

'Same as the others then,' Dave said. 'Appears we're dealing with one or more perps who believe themselves to be … *vampires*. Tell me, have you written your report yet?'

Alec coughed. 'No. I was actually procrastinating. How do you think it would look if I wrote her blood loss was the result of possible human exsanguination?'

Dave snorted. 'Up until a week ago, I probably would've agreed with you. Now I'm open to a more … imaginative explanation. We've had a series of unusual murders lately. Victims completely drained of blood and, what appear to be, puncture marks on the bodies. This information has been deliberately kept from the media, so, I'd appreciate your co-operation, Doctor.'

'I don't think you need worry there,' Alec replied.

If only Dave knew how incredibly close he was—circling the target without hitting the bullseye. I hated having to circumvent the truth like this, yet I knew there was no other way.

Mum relaxed a little, allowing circulation back into my fingers, but I knew she was worried. Once or twice, I felt her tremble. Dad tried his best to keep still, yet every now and then, he shifted uncomfortably.

Alec was the only one out of the four of us who seemed unfazed. 'You think the attack on Laura and this spate of killings are related?'

'Could be. And what I want to know is whether she was a random victim, or deliberately chosen. And now they've added a detective to their tally.' He shook his head as if trying to sort out all the possibilities.

'You think she's still in danger?' Alec asked.

'Well, if they're following their MO, the job wasn't finished. They were interrupted. None of the previous victims survived. Laura did. Unless they're suddenly deviating, I'm guessing they might come after her. I might even consider giving Laura some protection. That way, they might think twice before coming back to finish the job.'

'Protection?' I almost choked and looked—with panicked eyes, I'm sure—at Alec.

'That's not necessary,' Alec began slowly, almost hypnotically, and his eyes turned a much lighter shade of lavender as he locked his gaze on Dave. 'Perhaps it's best for Laura to remain with her aunt in Vaucluse and police protection be given to Detective Inspector Sommers, in hospital?'

'Yes, that's a consideration,' Dave agreed.

'Oh, and if you want, I can let you have that saliva sample, although, it will be almost impossible to find a match.' Alec's eyes resumed their normal appearance.

'Yes. I'll take it to forensics.' Dave blinked a few times. 'Laura, it may be necessary for you to stay with your aunt rather than be on your own, and we'll put a guard around your flat, in case the perps come back. We're expending a lot of manpower on your case. This doesn't just involve Matt and you any more. It's a personal attack on the police, and we can't let them win. I want you out of danger. And once Matt wakes up, hopefully he'll remember, and we'll have more details to go on. Enough to catch whoever's responsible.'

Alec smiled.

Dave slapped his knee and rose. 'Right. I think that's all for now. Thank you for your help, Doc.' Dave extended his hand. He turned to John and Eilene. 'Pleasure meeting you, Mr and Mrs Dantonville.' With Barbara on his heels, he left the room.

Alec strode to the door and closed it.

Mum leaned her head on the back of the chair. 'That was the most nerve-wracking experience of my life.' Her head suddenly shot forward. 'They're not going to come back again, are they? Rethink what was said and want more of an explanation? What on earth would I say to them?' Her frightened gaze went from me to Alec and then to Dad. 'Oh, dear, I'm not going to sleep tonight for worrying!' She sank her head into her hands.

My mum was a gem, but the biggest worry-worm I ever knew. She could stress out a meditating monk. Unless we could reassure her, she'd have to be sedated, and poor Dad would spend the next couple of days calming her down.

'Eilene,' Alec said. 'Everything's going to be fine. They won't come back. I promise. Rest easy.'

She looked up, into his face. 'Really?'

'Really.' He gave her his best smile.

Dad stood and came around to her side. 'I think we both need a strong drink.'

'A bit of brandy won't harm you,' Alec said.

'There's a nice little pub just down the street from here. C'mon Leeny,' Dad said and helped Mum from the chair.

'I'm glad we could be here for you,' she said as she hugged me goodbye.

Dad kissed me on the forehead. 'Goodbye, Baby.' It felt so final, as if he were saying it for the last time.

'I'll come and visit, soon.' I gave him a big squeeze. 'Thanks for being the best dad a girl ever had.'

He squeezed back, and I felt his emotion.

Alec escorted them to the door and we were alone again, my heart still thumping from the police interview. But another type of emotion took hold as I watched Mum and Dad leave. I knew for certain a part of my life went with them—my old life.

CHAPTER 35
BONDING

LAURA

Alec sat on the edge of my bed and gazed at me with a half-smile.

'Laura? You've got that faraway look. What are you thinking?'

'Old parents, new parents. My changing life.'

'It's not over yet.'

'I know.'

Alec's proposition for tonight stood like an invisible wall between us, and my stomach clenched in anticipation. I suddenly felt uncomfortable in his company and when my mobile phone went off, I nearly jumped. I picked it up and checked the screen. It was Jen. After everything that had occurred over the past few days, I'd forgotten about her. 'It's my best friend, Jen.'

'I'll leave you to talk then.'

I waited till he left the room to answer it. 'Hi Jen. It's me.'

'Laura! Are you all right?' she shouted.

'Yes, yes, I'm okay. No need to yell.'

'Where are you?' She lowered her tone, just a fraction.

'A private hospital in Rozelle, but I'm being discharged later today.'

'It's been on the news. That was your flat, wasn't it, they were talking about?'

'Um … yes.'

'What happened?'

'Some burglars, the police think. We must have disturbed them. They were still inside and knocked both of us out.'

'You were lucky you weren't killed,' she said, a tremor in her voice. 'Oh, Laura!'

'I'm okay, honestly, Jen.'

'Does your family know?'

'Oh yeah. As a matter of fact, they just left.'

'So, how are you getting home? Don't dare tell me you're taking a bus or taxi or something. I'll come and pick you up.'

'No, no, it's fine, Jen. Aunt Judy wants me to come and stay with her for a few days. She's on her way now.'

'All right, then. As long as you're not going back to your flat. Otherwise you could always come stay with me.'

'Thanks. You're an angel. But I promised Aunt Judy.'

'Ring me when you get there, so I don't worry, okay?'

I rolled my eyes. 'Yes, Mum!'

'You know what I mean, Laura Dantonville!' She laughed. It was good to hear the anxiety had gone from her voice. 'Have you heard how Matt is?'

I swallowed. 'Yeah. He's still unconscious, but out of danger. They rammed his head pretty hard into the door frame.'

'The shits! I hope they catch the lot and put 'em away for life.'

I wanted to say that's already been done, that they won't be bothering me, or anyone ever again. How I longed to tell her everything, but I couldn't. Not yet.

I heard the clip-clop of Judy's high heels as she came through the door. 'Jen, my aunt's here. Can I ring you back?'

'Fine. Give me her address, and I'll pop over while you're there, if that's okay?'

'I'll check with her. Shouldn't be a problem. I'll text you the address,' I said, as Judy dropped a light kiss on my cheek.

'Talk to you later, then. I'm so glad you're okay, hon. Bye.'

I put the phone back on the bedside table. 'I can't keep this from her for too long,' I said to Judy.

'We'll work it out, dear. How are you feeling?'

'Better, thanks.' I smiled up at her.

'So, ready to come home?'

Home. That was something else I was going to have to get used to. Until now it was a little one-bedroom flat in Balmain, but if my parents had their way, I was sure I'd soon be calling their massive mansion in Vaucluse, aka Vampire Central, home. Still, anywhere was better than here.

I threw back the covers only to realise all I had for clothing was the hospital gown and the shorts I'd been wearing when Alec brought me in. Oh, and the shoes. If I put those on, I made a real fashion statement.

'Don't worry, dear. You're not going out like that. I came prepared.' Judy lifted a small bag she brought with her onto the bed and unzipped it. She must have gone through the closet of my room at Luc's before coming here, for I didn't recognise any of the clothes she pulled out.

'Your father and I went shopping for clothes for you to celebrate your homecoming,' she said. 'We hoped you'd stay for a while. At least for some part of the holidays.'

'Of course I will. We have a lot to catch up on.'

Her smile widened and I found myself looking forward to spending time with them both. There were questions I wanted answers to, particularly from Luc.

As I threw off the drab hospital gown and slipped into a pale-green, knee-length shirtdress, I peppered Judy with questions. 'Mother?' I had to say it. Calling her "Judy" seemed wrong and the affectionate look she gave in return confirmed it. But something had been niggling at me since witnessing my parents closeness.

'Yes, dear?' She sat on the edge of the bed and elegantly crossed one leg over the other.

'Have...' I swallowed and tried again. 'Have you ever considered becoming ... like Luc, a vampire? That way you'd always be together.'

Her eyes widened.

'I mean,' I began quickly. 'You love each other so much and knowing that you will eventually ... um, die—'

'Laura dear,' she held up her hand, 'if only that were possible. We *did* discuss it early in our relationship, but unfortunately the very gene that blesses the Ingenii with youth and longevity prevents our transformation into vampire form. It's been tried.'

I sat next to her, not knowing what to say. Two people I was beginning to love—as my parents—and who undeniably belonged together were doubly doomed to not only carry the cursed gene which drew vampires like bees to blossom flowers, but to stand by and helplessly watch as one of them slowly succumbed to the inevitability of old age and death while the other remained forever young. I wanted to yell at the unfairness of it.

Judy patted my hand. 'I've accepted it, dear. But your father and I have made … arrangements … for when the time comes.'

She spoke calmly, and a small smile hovered at the corners of her mouth, yet I felt that was for my benefit. Beneath the surface, her emotions must have been churning. Mine were.

'Arrangements?' I didn't like the sound of that. Was it some sort of suicide pact or something? How would they do it? Most vampires, apart from Alec and Luc, would simply walk into the sunlight and wait for their own personal Armageddon. A wooden stake through the heart? Would my mother have the mental strength to do that to him? And then what? Take poison or something?

'Laura?' Her voice dragged me away from my morbid thoughts.

'Yeah, I'm here.'

'For a while you weren't.' She sighed. 'There's nothing for you to worry about, so don't dwell on it, dear.'

'You think? After opening a Pandora's box in my mind with that word?'

'Then put the lid back on it. It's nothing drastic or tragic, as I believe you're imagining. Besides, it's still a long way off. I intend being here for at least another fifty or so years. To see my grandchildren.'

I tried smiling but that uneasy feeling didn't leave me, so I decided to be circumspect about it. Since whatever they planned lay in the distant future and I couldn't do anything about it anyway, I took her advice and shelved it—for the present.

CHAPTER 36
THE PLEDGE

ALEC

I left Laura in Judith's care and went back to my office. It gave me the opportunity to look over the blood-supply list. Why hadn't Delaney questioned me about the time? There had been at least a good two-hour delay between the time I brought her here and when she'd received blood. He was too good a detective to miss something like that.

Scanning down the column, the vacant time entry stared up at me. Carol had forgotten to fill it in! In her hurry, she'd left that unrecorded. Everything else was there—date, number of units, blood type and the requesting doctor, but not the time.

The woman deserved a bonus!

I filed it back into the folder. There were emails to reply to and conference dates to confirm.

The phone rang. It was Luc. 'Alec, I've been in contact with the other Elders, and we're thinking of holding the Pledge, but you've got the final say. Is it yea or nay?'

'You've got my yea. No argument on that one. As long as this rogue is at large, Laura's not safe. Only the Pledge will guarantee that.'

'That's what I thought. We could hold the ceremony in the pavilion again, although the ballroom would be better.'

He was right; it'd be perfect. The idea of holding the Pledge in the garden seemed impractical, especially as a public recitation by several hundred vampires could attract unwanted attention.

'This ceremony needs to be conducted away from prying human eyes.'

'My sentiments exactly. Anything on Jean?' I asked, as I rifled through the papers on my desk.

'I've just spoken to him. He's on his way. Reluctantly, I may add. He doesn't trust me.'

'Can you blame him?'

'You know my reasons. I did what was necessary to keep them apart. What if the DNA test proves positive?'

'I'm not accusing you, Luc. In your situation, I may have done the same. I don't know.' Since coming to know Laura, I could understand why.

'No, I believe you would have acted very differently.'

'As long as Laura's with me, I doubt he'll try to make contact.' But what if he was desperate enough to? My mind raced ahead already putting a plan into action to avert that very situation. I was sure Luc was doing the same.

'That's good. Tie her to your side if you have to.'

I couldn't tell if he was serious. 'I don't think that'll be necessary. Besides, she's with Judith right now.'

'She's been waiting a long time to be a mother, mon ami.' I could almost hear his smile.

'That's why I left them together for a while. They've got a lot to talk about. And don't worry' —I had heard his sharp intake of breath— 'it's daylight.'

'Still, whoever our rebel is, they may have minions.'

I extended my senses. Even though I promised not to listen in, I homed in on their voices to check everything was all right. Just as quickly, I withdrew and glanced at my ring. It glowed a healthy scarlet. 'Everything's fine, Luc. They're getting to know each other.'

'I'll take your word for it. Bring her here as soon as she's ready.' He rung off.

I left my desk and headed back to Laura's room.

It was time to take her home.

CHAPTER 37
COMING HOME

LAURA

We sat in my mother's favourite part of the house—her sitting room she called it, situated opposite the dining room at the end of the hall. It was as feminine in decor as Luc's study was masculine; cream walls and beige sisal rugs blended with the plush softness of two linen-covered sofas, whose muted sage greens complemented the lichen-coloured, glass-topped wicker coffee table, the centre of which held a crystal pitcher filled with fresh roses.

A vintage wrought-iron chandelier, entwined with green enamel leaves, hung from the stuccoed ivory ceiling, and various botanical prints vied for attention with framed photos of my mother as a young woman. White wrought-iron bookshelves filled with pot plants and mismatched pieces of English china lined the walls, while expansive French doors opened to reveal another view of the garden.

Judy settled herself in one of the sofas after making sure I was comfortably reclined in one of the armchairs.

Alec had taken the small bag she had brought with her to the hospital and deposited it in my bedroom. Then he joined us.

'Laura, I believe we may have come up with a solution to end your present danger,' Luc said. He sat next to Judy. 'It's the Blood Pledge.'

'What's that?' I asked.

'A sacred oath sworn on the serpent ring, and taken by all the Brethren to protect the Ingenii and Guardian. Any who break it, die.'

'You mean, they're ... executed?'

'Not by any living being. It's the ring that strikes them down. The eyes of the serpents erupt fire and destroy them.'

My gaze automatically drifted down to the ring on my finger. Here was yet another thing I would have to add to the list of other things in this strange new world I had to accept. Magic. Who believed such stuff in the twenty-first century? Yet how could I deny it? The serpent's eyes gave off a subtle glow. It gave a completely new twist to the old saying, if looks could kill.

'Luc....' I started then changed my mind. He said it would please him if I could call him Papa. I thought I would give it a try. Would it feel strange? 'Papa, have you ever seen it happen?'

His face beamed. 'Merci, ma petite.' But his smile faded as he told me about the first two rebellions and how they were dealt with; how one of those who had taken the Pledge broke his oath and fire flared from the serpents' eyes. Since then, there had been peace. 'Many are still alive who remember, but the newly transformed, like those who attacked you, have never seen it happen.'

'Maybe it's time they did,' Alec said. He was leaning against the wall by the French doors. I noticed it gave him a direct view of me.

He and Luc started to discuss the logistics of summoning all the Brethren to swear allegiance to the two of us.

'We'll begin the Summons. Before this year ends I want every last of the Brethren to take the Blood Pledge,' Luc said.

'Prefects only?'

'Best way, since they're responsible for the Brethren in their respective territories. Any breach of the Pledge will be a reflection of their own loyalty, and they will be liable. Much more effective than individual oath taking and' —he emphasised that last word— 'it will be faster. It can also be accomplished in one night.'

'What happens to those who refuse to show?' I asked.

A dangerous gleam appeared in Luc's eyes. 'Stripped of their offices and reacquainted with the sun.'

I swallowed. It was hard getting used to vampire politics. A compassionate democracy it was not. Yet I couldn't deny Luc's harsh judgement, having experienced first hand the cruelty of those who hated the princeps. Still, it was too frightening a thought for me to dwell on now. From their conversation, I assumed the "prefects" were similar to magistrates, who dealt with the vampires in their respective cities or countries. So a pledge taken by them would be binding on all under their rule. And if it could be done in just one night, even better.

'Laura, I know that's not what you're used to, but we have no choice,' Alec said.

'It's okay. I'm beginning to understand.' Deep down I hoped there'd be no dissenters—I didn't want anyone killed on my account. I'd seen too much of that already. At least now I knew they didn't go "whoosh" in the sunlight, as I once laughingly expressed to Judy. They kind of … sizzled.

'How about this coming Sunday night?' Luc asked. His gaze ranged between Alec, Judy and myself.

We all agreed. I certainly didn't have anything planned.

'Good, then that's settled,' Alec said.

The way his gaze locked onto mine resurrected images of the two of us together, linked in the most intimate way, and, once again, I looked away and tried to think of something else.

'Let's start contacting the prefects,' Luc said.

'I can send the necessary emails. Just let me know to whom,' Alec said.

'I'll send you the list.' Luc leaned down and kissed Judy. 'I'll see you later tonight, ma cherie.' Then coming over to me, he said, 'Get some rest, ma petite.' He kissed the top of my head before strolling from the room.

Just as I relaxed, confident everything would be okay, my injured arm began to throb. The painkillers had worn off. I leaned my head back and closed my eyes.

'Laura, are you in pain?' Alec asked.

'Uh huh.'

'Judith, can you please bring some Panadol and a glass of water.'

I heard her padded footsteps cross the rug as she left. Cool fingers against my temples caused me to jump.

'Take it easy,' Alec said. 'Only trying to help. Close your eyes.'

My heart thumped at his touch, and I had to force myself to relax. He rubbed my temples till Judy came back, his fingers soothing against my skin. I had to resist the urge to place my hands over his.

'Take this,' he said.

I opened my eyes, took the glass of water and the two tablets he held out and quickly swallowed them. 'I'm tired.'

'You've had very little sleep, and after everything's that's happened to you, I'm surprised you've been awake this long. That police interview was exhausting enough. Try to get some sleep; the tablets will help.'

He was right. If not for Russell, I would have easily slept several hours more. I curled up on the sofa and tried not to think of the way my life had changed in the last few days.

Alec sat in one of the recliners opposite me. He twirled the serpent ring round his finger as he gazed at me. Neither of us said a word. As the seconds passed, heat rose to my cheeks, and to hide my discomfort, I turned my head into the side of the chair and closed my eyes. Yet, still I felt his gaze on me.

CHAPTER 38
PRECIOUS JEWELS

ALEC

While Laura dozed, I thought of the impossible situation I'd deliberately placed her in. She'd now have no choice but to leave Sommers. Would she want to stay with him after learning of his intent to kill us? Then, of course, there was the matter of the Child. My child, not his—should Laura conceive tonight.

My body reacted in anticipation, and to ease the tightness in my jeans, I stood up and walked to the French doors. Judith was still in the room. I didn't turn back around till I heard her leave, and then my gaze went straight to Laura. She stirred and sighed in her sleep, and her deep-copper-coloured hair spilled over the floral-patterned green cushion, almost like molten bronze. A slight curl made it turn up at the ends, and I remembered the silky feel of it round my fingers from the last time I touched it. I crouched next to her, smoothed some fallen strands away from her face and gently tucked them behind her ear, careful not to wake her. Her lips were slightly parted, and the memory of how they felt against mine came rushing back and my blood began to heat.

Damn! No other woman had ever had this affect on me.

Judith returned, carrying a steaming cup of tea and a book. She said nothing, but her smile when she looked at me spoke volumes.

I grabbed my laptop, sat down and sent emails to the various prefects, but damn if it didn't take all my concentration to stay on task. Judith settled herself on her sofa and started reading – a crime novel, by the cover. Within an hour, she too had dozed off. Both slept peacefully for a few hours.

Luc popped in a little while later. Seeing Judith asleep on the armchair, he made his way to her side, took the book from her hand and placed it on the coffee table. He kissed her cheek before spreading a blanket over her. 'Isn't she beautiful?' he said proudly, his voice barely above a whisper. He straightened and looked at Laura. 'The two precious jewels in my life. My women.'

I closed my laptop. 'How's it coming?'

'Three prefects haven't responded. I'll give them another twenty-four hours.'

'Which three?'

'The Eastern Europeans—Karel, Timur and Milena.'

'Jake mentioned them, although I haven't really had a chance to talk to him about it.' That's all we needed, three of the most powerful and ancient districts causing trouble. Karel had been ruling the Bohemian Brethren for nearly three-hundred years and was usually at loggerheads with the other two. They were continually fighting over territory. Last I heard, Karel and the Hungarian prefect, Timur, were trying to squeeze out Milena, take over and divide her Slovak Prefecture between them. Hence, their absence from the Ritual.

'I sent him over to broker some sort of peace between them and put an end to their petty squabbles.'

'And?' I prompted.

'They were all compliant….'

'But?'

He let out a deep breath. 'Jake felt he wasn't really needed. They'd worked it out by the time he got there. It was almost as if Milena created it in order to get him there.'

'Huh! Interesting. Did he say anything more?' Jake was no fool, and if he felt something strange was going on in Europe, it needed investigating. I made a mental note to speak with those prefects right after the Pledging.

'No. Anyway the problem—whatever it was—is settled, so they've got no excuse not to come.'

I nodded.

He walked to the French doors and looked out. 'Soon as my men rise, I'll station them around the grounds. The area down near the water isn't secure.'

We spent the next hour planning the ceremony, no detail left out. There was too much at stake. Never had it been more personal for Luc. By the time we'd finished, it was late afternoon, Laura still slept, and I didn't want to wake her. She was home; she was safe, and since both her parents were here as well, it gave me the perfect opportunity to step out and visit the lab. There were several experiments needing my attention. I was back at the house by early evening. Laura had slept through lunch and I didn't want her to miss out the next meal. It was time to wake her.

I leaned down and softly stroked her face. 'Laura, wake up.'

CHAPTER 39
HUMAN OR VAMPIRE?

LAURA

Something soft and feathery touched my face. I opened my eyes to see Alec leaning over me. His bent fingers gently brushed my cheek.

'Hello,' he whispered. 'You've been asleep for over seven hours.'

'What time is it?' I said sleepily.

'Just gone six.'

My stomach rumbled. 'I'm hungry.'

'I'm not surprised. You haven't eaten since early this morning. How do you feel?'

I did a mental check then flexed my hand and tried twisting my wrist. It felt more comfortable—less painful than before. 'Better, I think. It doesn't seem to hurt that much any more.'

'Good. I want to take a look at it; change the dressing and check the stitches.'

My stomach rumbled again. He smiled. 'Dinner's on its way up.'

A light snore came from the other end of the room. I turned my head to see Judy asleep in the armchair.

'She fell asleep while reading,' Alec whispered. 'I don't want to wake her.'

'You've been here the whole time?'

'Just some of it.'

I breathed out a contented sigh and sat up. He looked at me and smiled, but I didn't miss the way his eyes moved down to my throat. He'd fed from me yesterday morning, yet I was reluctant to offer him my blood. It was fear of succumbing to him that held me back.

I started at the shrill ring of Alec's phone. He stood and dug it out of his back pocket. 'Alec Munro here. Yeah....' His expression changed, alert. 'Has he said anything, asked for anyone?' His eyes were on me. 'Uh huh ... right ... okay, thanks for letting me know.'

I knew it was something to do with Matt.

Alec shoved the mobile phone back into his jeans pocket, braced his hands on the arms of the recliner and leaned down toward me. My eyes were automatically drawn to his mouth. 'He's awake and out of intensive care,' he said. Every nerve in my body tensed, but I couldn't tell if it was from Alec's closeness or the fact I'd have to confront Matt. 'There doesn't seem to be any brain damage, but they'll be conducting tests tomorrow morning just to be sure. His family's there with him.'

'Okay. I need to see him, speak to him.'

'Tomorrow.'

He stared down at me, and I couldn't pull away. My insides tightened with a strange mix of excitement and fear—fear at the growing depth of my feelings for him and the knowledge that it wasn't going to go away. How on earth was I going to tell Matt of the pact I'd willingly made with Alec? A growing pregnancy wasn't something I'd be able to hide for very long. And no matter the valid reason for it, Matt would never understand.

Alec's gaze slowly slid to my mouth, and as he leaned further toward me, Judy stirred. 'How long have I been asleep? What time is it?'

He froze, and I turned my head away as a hot blush crept up my cheeks. Alec was about to kiss me, of that I had no doubt. And ... I wouldn't have stopped him. My stomach clenched all over again. I couldn't go on like this.

Alec straightened, and without taking his gaze from me said, 'Dinnertime, and I'm about to check Laura's stitches.'

'Is she awake?' Judy asked.

'Have been for some time,' I answered.

She rose and came over, smoothing her hair back into place. 'I need a cup of tea.'

It was just the thing I needed to hear at that moment—trivial and inconsequential. I stretched to ease the tension from my body while Alec went to stand by the French doors.

Luc walked in carrying a tray smelling of roast beef and mashed potatoes. 'The cook just finished it.'

I sat up. How I was going to balance that huge tray on my lap?

'Take this, dear.' Judy plucked a metal fold-up tray from beside my armchair and set it up on my lap.

'But what about you?' I asked.

'This will do nicely.' She picked up a plump cushion from the sofa.

As I ate, I tried to avoid looking at Alec, yet once or twice I snuck a look. Each time he was staring at me. I swallowed and dropped my eyes again. Judy and Luc's voices filled in the void as neither Alec or I spoke. I was too aware of the hours that were left before he and I were supposed to have sex.

The knot in my stomach tightened, and I pushed the rest of my meal away.

A barely audible alarm went off in Alec's watch. 'Time to change your dressing, Laura.' He opened his medic bag and removed a pair of scissors and a small metal tray.

'All yours,' I said, and held out my wrist.

His eyes crinkled at the corners but that soon disappeared as he unpeeled the dressing and removed the gauze. 'Luc, take a look at this,' he said.

'What is it? Something wrong?' I didn't want to look, as blood and anything associated with it always made me cringe. But there was something in Alec's tone that made me want to. I looked down expecting to see a nasty gash with dark stitching and ugly puckered skin, but instead there appeared a near-clean whitish scar with the surgical stitching half hanging out.

Alec glanced at me questioningly. I shrugged. Luc and Judy were at my side in an instant. 'Laura, even for one of the Bloodgifted, this is unusual. Your body has completely healed itself in … one day!'

As we watched, one of the stitches popped out, slid down my arm and onto the blanket. The skin around it was a healthy pink.

Luc's brows were drawn. 'She's more vampire than human,' he whispered.

'I can't be absolutely sure,' Alec replied. 'But the healing process is definitely not human.' He pulled a pair of tweezers from his bag and removed the rest of the stitches. My skin closed over the neat, little pricks, leaving a smooth, unmarked surface.

'Laura, have you ever had a craving for blood, dear?' Judy asked.

'No.' I looked at my father. A vampire. Was there a possibility that one day I could become one? The thought sent a cold shiver through me.

'Have you always healed so quickly?' Alec asked.

'I think so.' I turned to Judy. She probably knew every injury I'd ever had.

'When she was little she healed faster than anyone else, but we didn't make much of it.' She looked at me. 'I lost track when you left home.'

'I've rarely been injured, and if I did get a cut I just shoved a bandaid onto it and forgot it.'

Alec didn't say anything. He just looked thoughtfully at me.

'Well, I suppose there's no need to keep the bandage on anymore, is there?' I asked.

He took it and threw it into the bin. 'You're a puzzle, Laura.'

'Then it's a pity you don't intend being around to solve it.'

His eyes narrowed slightly. 'I thought that's what you preferred?'

'I've changed my mind.'

Without any warning, he took my hand and pulled me from the sofa. 'Excuse us,' he said to Luc and Judy as he dragged me from the room.

'What do you think you're doing?' I tried to break his grip but his hand only clenched mine tighter.

Up the wide marble stairs we went, to the next level, past my bedroom to the next wing of the house and to a door I didn't recognise. He pushed it open. After he ushered me through, I heard the lock click in place.

CHAPTER 40
BARGAIN SEALED

LAURA

A lone tall lamp lit in—what I assumed to be—Alec's room. Bare white walls with recessed shelves filled with books stared back at me. There were no windows. A crystal chandelier, on a long chain, hung from a pale, stuccoed ceiling. In one corner stood a four-drawer cabinet, identical to a smaller version next to a four-poster iron bed. The tall lamp next to it was also metal. Actually, apart from the bed coverings and the needlepoint floor rug, everything was metal.

'Let's discuss this, shall we?'

I spun around to face him, but as I was still out of breath, all I could do was stand there, with my arms clenched by my side, and glare at him. He moved away from the door and came slowly toward me. I took a step back.

'It occurred to me, I don't like the idea of becoming a single mother,' I managed to say between breaths.

'You should have thought of that sooner.' He pulled his T-shirt over his head and dropped it on the floor.

I stared open mouthed at his chiselled body, at the rippling muscles of his torso and the sword-and-serpent tattoo on his left breast. It was identical to the image on the stained-glass window. On impulse, I reached out and touched it.

'All the men have one. It marks us as belonging to Luc's clan.'

'Does he have one, too?'

'Yes.' The look in his eyes intensified. 'Keep touching me, Laura.'

My hands traced the hard planes of his chest, stomach and the delectable trail of dark hair that disappeared below the top of his jeans.

'You told me never to touch you again. You still feel that way?'

'If I did, I wouldn't be agreeing to this. It's only sex, nothing more. A means to an end.'

'Did I promise anything more?'

No, he didn't. This was, as he so succinctly put it, a business arrangement.

He leaned down, as if to kiss me.

I turned my head away. 'No kissing.' I couldn't afford my heart to be engaged any more than it already was. I needed this to be mechanical, detached, void of emotion. If he could be like that, then so could I.

Something flickered in his eyes. 'Sorry, *darling*, but it comes with the whole package.' He drew me to him, and my protest ended the moment his mouth touched mine.

How did he know to part my lips just the right way and delve into my mouth like he owned it, kissing me with an almost fevered energy I couldn't help but return? How wrong I'd been to tell him never to touch me again, nor kiss me, when my whole body came alive when he did—when it ached for him. There was no way I could fight this, and if I lost my heart to him, what then? Could I stand it if he went away?

The thought frightened me. *This is only sex, only sex*, I repeated over and over in my head, but I knew I was fooling myself. It was far too late for that.

Slowly he undid the buttons on my shirtdress, slid it off my shoulders and let it drop to the floor. My bra soon followed, my nipples hardening as his hands caressed my breasts, while his mouth teased and taunted mine, reducing me to a helpless mess.

He scooped me up and laid me in the centre of the bed. Taking my face in his hands, he tenderly kissed my eyelids, my nose, cheeks and chin, before returning to my waiting lips. The serpent rings blazed into life, eclipsing the sad, little light emanating from the bedside lamp. Alec leaned over and switched it off. The room was bathed in a warm red glow as if the rings themselves endorsed what we were about to do.

He lowered his head, and this time his mouth and tongue tickled one breast while his hand cupped the other, his thumb and forefinger circling and teasing my already sensitised nipple.

I closed my eyes and sighed, arching into him as my body purred at his every touch. My hands roamed his back and firm shoulders. As he eased down the length of my body, leaving a burning trail with his lips, any coherent thought disappeared. As his tongue dipped into my navel, his fingers hooked into the top of my panties and slowly drew them down. They joined my dress and his T-shirt on the floor.

I lay there totally exposed as Alec hungrily devoured me with his eyes.

'You're breathtaking,' he said, then rose and removed his jeans. His naked body was the most beautiful thing I'd ever seen, and for what seemed like ages, we simply gazed at each other. In the glow of the unearthly rosy light, I could see his eyes had darkened into a deep purple vortex from which I never wanted to emerge.

He crawled onto the bed, parted my legs and lay between them.

His kisses seared my mouth as his hands touched, stroked and sweetly tortured my most secret place till I was scrunching the sheets and moaning his name.

He lifted his head and looked at me through hooded, almost drunken eyes, his breath as ragged as my own. Then raising himself slightly, Alec hooked his arms beneath my knees, lifted them and spread my legs as wide as they'd go.

My heart hammered in my chest like a construction drill. I could almost hear it. I'm sure Alec could, for his eyes blazed just before our mouths meshed once more and he surged forward into me.

I sighed in sheer relief as his body fit perfectly into mine. There was no discomfort, no hurt, only the sweet friction as he plunged fully into me, moving slowly at first then increasing the rhythm until my body tightened like a coiled spring, building, building, until it broke, and my body shuddered with the strength of my release. Alec continued until another peak washed over me with such intensity I cried out, and only then he tensed and moaned, and spilled deeply within me.

I lay there breathing heavily, unable to think, unable to move, utterly in bliss. Matt had never been able to take me that far.

'Oh, no, I'm not finished with you yet,' Alec said, as he slid down the length of my body again. As he reached the apex of my thighs, he looked up at me, and the hunger in his eyes was clear.

I nodded, grasped the bars of the bedhead behind me and held on for dear life as Alec dipped his head between my legs. His fingers gripped my thighs and held them apart as his tongue slid over my sensitive core. Oh my stars! Oh my stars! My body began to quiver, and when his fangs penetrated the soft skin of my inner thigh, I came so strongly, I nearly ripped the bars from their sockets. The mix of pain and pleasure was exquisite and unlike anything I'd experienced before.

He then cradled me in his arms, utterly sated and content. For a while, only the sound of our breathing filled the darkened room. Eventually I angled my head up to see him looking at me. His eyes caressed my face then swept down to my mouth, before he lowered his head and kissed me again, long and deep, his tongue stroking and enticing mine into total surrender.

Soon he was on top of me again, holding my thighs wide apart and plunging even deeper, his groans and sighs mingling with my own. He lifted my hips for even greater penetration, moving within me in a steady, all consuming rhythm, and as I threw my head back, his mouth locked onto my nipple, drawing it into his mouth, teasing and sucking till my whole body convulsed with the intensity of the coming climax. And when it did come, I screamed and felt tears slide down my face.

Once again, I lay panting, exhausted. Alec kissed my eyelids. 'Go to sleep,' he said softly.

I was sure I heard him say, "my darling," as I closed my eyes and yielded to the darkness.

CHAPTER 41
"CURIOUSER AND CURIOUSER"

LAURA

I'm not sure how long I slept, but the electric clock on the cabinet showed 1.35 a.m. If not for the glow of the serpent rings, it would have been impossible to know whether it was day or night. Several days could have passed while we made love—for that's what it was. It had gone beyond the sex-to-end-the-curse bargain we had made. Alec had kissed me with such passion; I wondered whether he was as detached as the impression he gave.

My body felt sore, but wonderfully exhilarated, and I was still tender where Alec had bitten my upper thigh. I mentally shook my head as I recalled the way I reacted when Lora, the young woman I had met at the Ritual, told me where her vampire boyfriend liked to bite. Now I let Alec do the same. So much for *Buckley's*.

I gazed at his beautiful face as he slept. He looked so young, one arm thrown above his head, the other around me, that it was hard to imagine he'd been alive for nearly a century. His cheeks were no longer pale; they were flushed and healthy, and his lips, which had been colourless just a few hours ago, were stained dark crimson with my blood.

I wanted to kiss them, wake him and make love again. In fact, I wanted to lave my way down the length of his body as he had, so wonderfully, done to me. He brought my body alive, and not only that, but I realised I wanted no other man to touch me but him.

That moment, I gave up the fight and completely surrendered to my heart, which now belonged to the man sleeping beside me.

Oh, did I have a problem.

I needed time to think and work things out, and I couldn't do that with him so close. Alec completely scattered my thoughts.

Careful not to wake him, I moved out from under his arm, got out of bed and searched for my clothes. They lay on the floor where Alec had stripped me, and pleasant butterflies went off in my stomach at the memory. I quickly put them on, tiptoed to the door and slipped out, then made my way down the hall toward my room.

I reached the staircase that separated the two wings and noticed light coming from the next level. As far as I knew, no one usually ventured up there. I guessed that was where the ballroom Luc and Alec had spoken about would be. From my knowledge of Victorian houses, the more ostentatious ones had ornate domed ceilings and long galleries their wealthy owners used to showcase their latest acquisitions.

Something beckoned me onwards, and I ascended the stairs to the very top. Ornate rose-shaped plaster mouldings adorned the ceiling, and the fine-veined marble on the stairs and balustrade stood out in the glare from the overhead lights. Pity it was night, as the darkness hid the glorious colours on the tall, narrow lead-light windows. I would have to see this during the day. It must be beautiful, I mused, but it needed airing. I wrinkled my nose. The closer I got to the top, the mustier the smell. Did the cleaners ever come up here?

On reaching the top, I was confronted by a gilt-framed mirror spanning the width of the wall. My reflection gazed back at me. Well. Now what? I looked down one length of the corridor. It led to the west wing, while another led to the east. It was odd; unless the ballroom was somewhere behind this mirror, it was simply a dead end.

Curiouser and curiouser, I thought, as I crouched down and ran my hand along the base of the mirror.

I remembered reading somewhere that occasionally these old mansions had trick walls. But my fingers detected nothing unusual. What I did find strange was that although this level hadn't been visited in who-knows-how-many years, there was no dust. I slid my finger along the mirror to be sure. It was clean. Maybe the cleaner did know about it.

I stood in front of its wide expanse with hands on hips. Here was a mystery I was dying to solve. As I moved, I noticed a barely perceptible aberration in my reflection. I peered at it more closely, moving a little to the left and then to the right. It was definitely there. Placing my finger where it began, I could feel a hairline join. Bullseye! Now all I needed was to find how to open it. There was no indication anywhere near the mirror. I'd checked that already. If the original owner had wanted to surprise his guests and create the desired effect, the mirror would have had to open as they reached the top – as if by magic.

I scanned the ground for a hidden button or pedal that could be tripped by foot. Nothing. Perhaps it was somewhere on or under the balustrade. Running my fingers under the smooth marble, I felt a small metal lever and pushed it up. Bingo! My reflection widened as the mirror slid apart and flooded the corridor with light.

'Laura, are you up there?' It was Alec.

'Yeah. The ballroom's incredible!' I called down to him.

Slowly the ballroom appeared. I had the impression of light bouncing off more mirrors, crystal and brass chandeliers and parquetry flooring. The scent of oil paints assailed my nostrils just as a hand covered my mouth and another dragged me in.

Jean's face loomed inches from mine. The mirrored doors clicked as they snapped closed behind me.

CHAPTER 42
HIDDEN DOORS

ALEC

I woke to find Laura gone. The fact I had fallen asleep surprised me, as that hadn't happened in a long time.

At first I thought she may have gone to the bathroom, but I had no sense of her there, nor anywhere on this level, although I knew she was in the house. I homed in on Luc and Judith. She wasn't with them, and it was then my scalp prickled.

I jumped out of bed, located my jeans on the floor, slipped them on and headed out the door. Halfway down the corridor, I stopped, closed my eyes and picked up her scent. It led to the staircase and up to the next level, which contained nothing but a mirrored wall as far as Laura would have known. Why would she go up there?

I called to her as I made my way up the staircase. She sounded excited, but something was wrong. It was then I sensed Jean. I ran up the steps in semi-panic, only to see light spill out of the opening, and Laura staring, rapt, as it widened. Too late, I saw him step out, clamp his hand over her mouth and drag her in.

'Laura!' I called as I raced to her side. But the entrance closed just as I reached it.

An almost infinitesimal crack spliced the mirror in two from top to bottom. Even using full strength, I couldn't pry it apart.

Jean! I knew he was in love with her and had been since she was eighteen. But, surely he wouldn't try to rekindle.... My serpent ring flashed. The eyes of the serpent had darkened. Holy mother of....

'Laura!' I yelled and hammered the mirror's surface. It didn't even crack under my relentless assault. Nothing. Not even a fracture, but I could hear what was going on behind it. In fact, I heard every word in my head, as if our minds were linked. The telepathic bond between us had grown stronger. It was then I remembered the secret lever beneath the balustrade.

I spun around, groped with my fingers beneath the cold marble till I located the metal and pushed it upwards. Nothing happened. I did it again, and still the doors remained sealed. Jean must have locked it from within.

I had to reach her.

I sensed a new presence and whirled around to see Luc emerge from a wooden panel in the wall. 'Alec! What are you doing up here?'

'Never mind that. Jean's in there,' —I pointed to the mirror with my thumb— 'and he's dragged Laura in.

Luc's eyes widened. 'Merde!' he swore. 'Have you tried the lever?'

'Of course I did. It's not working. He must have done something to the locking mechanism.'

He stared at the mirror then turned around and bolted back through the panel. 'This way,' he said over his shoulder. 'I've been checking the old servants' passages. Refitting the lights.'

I ran behind him along a musty narrow passage that curved gently to the right, all the while listening to what was happening in there. Laura called him Philippe, and he appeared to be showing her something. My stomach tightened as I sensed her anxiety. Whatever she saw made her uneasy.

'What is she doing up here?' Luc called back to me.

'Exploring.'

Luc groaned. 'Just like her mother.'

The passage ahead split in two directions. Luc veered to the left – following the sound of Laura's voice—sweeping veils of cobwebs out of the way as we darted toward a distant doorway. The closer we got, the more I felt her fear, and Jean's deep hatred of me became clear. He'd loved her first, and in his mind, she belonged to him.

I yanked the door open. 'Shit! That son of a bitch!' The exit had been bricked up.

'I thought you knew the way.'

Luc cursed. 'I haven't been up here for over a hundred years. Got the damn passages confused. This way. Quick.'

As we turned and raced back to the other tunnel, which veered to the right, I tried to keep track of what was going on between Laura and Jean.

Laura! Laura, are you all right? I had to know if he had hurt her.

We reached the end of the tunnel, but another closed doorway loomed ahead. *Laura, answer me!*

When I heard her cry out, I barged past Luc and crashed through the thick wooden door. Jean was going to pay. *Now.*

But what I saw stopped me just inside the door, and my incisors slid out.

CHAPTER 43
PAST LOVES

LAURA

My initial shock at being confronted by Jean turned to anger. I slapped his hand off my face. 'Get your hand off my mouth!' The last time someone did that, I had been terrified and terrorised. I suppressed a shiver.

'I'm sorry. I don't want anyone to disturb me. No one comes to this part of the house anymore, so it's become my secret place.' He reached behind me and pulled down a hook on the wall. 'What are you doing here, anyway?' He spoke lightly but there was a strange edge to his voice.

It was incredible the way he reminded me of Philippe. Even his voice was similar—from what I remembered, but it was so long ago. I twisted out of his hold and moved away from him. 'Wandered up here to take a look. Alec and Papa mentioned the ballroom as the perfect place to hold the Pledge.'

'So you know Luc's your father? When?'

'After the Ritual, they told me everything.'

'Ah.' He cocked his head to one side, the way Alec did sometimes.

A nervous tingle ran through me. I recalled the strange way Jean had stared at me at the time, and his lingering touch on my face in the hospital.

'You kept the locket I gave you in Sorrento.'

I froze. How did he know? Philippe had bought me a silver heart-shaped locket and asked me to wear it always. I promised I would, but I'd been only eighteen. I'd kept it all these years as a memento, and it hung on my dresser mirror alongside my other pieces of jewellery. Had he been in my bedroom? My stomach plummeted as the realisation hit me. He had been in my flat, in my room, with the others the night I was taken. Jean … No. The anxious face gazing at me now was not Jean. It was Philippe. *Philippe!*

I had no doubt. Here was the young man I'd met in Italy when I was eighteen. He was handsome, and I'd had the biggest crush. Compared to the boys I had known in high school, his was the first manly kiss I had experienced. It was the most wonderful holiday of my life, and I hadn't wanted it to end. We parted suddenly. I thought I would die, but I didn't. I grew up, and he eventually receded to the memories-you-treasure part of my mind.

'Philippe?' I stared at him in disbelief.

'You do remember.'

'Yes, but … you had blue eyes then.' Had he become a vampire after we'd met?

'I wore contacts.'

'Why? So I wouldn't be curious, you having the same eye colour as me?'

'Something like that.'

He smiled and became the handsome young man I'd known all those decades ago. But seeing him again didn't resurrect those same powerful emotions. I was no longer the adolescent girl he had met and kissed in Sorrento.

'Do you want to see what I do up here?' he asked, just as I was about to bombard him with a million questions.

'What?'

'Let me show you.'

He took my hand and led me to the other end of the ballroom, to a small raised area with a wooden railing all around. Presumably, this was where the orchestra had played in the days of grand parties. Candles flickered in ornamental brass holders attached to wall sockets, illuminating—what appeared to be—a number of pictures and drawings. In the centre of the stage sat an easel covered with a dark blue cloth. The floor around was littered with sketches, boxes of artist's charcoal and pencils of various thicknesses. A fold-up stool leaned against the wall.

'Go ahead, have a look,' he said.

I stepped into his makeshift studio and picked up one of the discarded drawings. It was a sketch portrait of me, my hair loose and draped over one shoulder. He had captured my image perfectly. Philippe had talent. I dropped it and scanned the floor. All the others were the same—different scenes, some coloured, some black and white, but they all portrayed one face: mine.

I sucked in a breath.

He stood behind me. 'No one bothers me up here and I spend most of my time drawing.'

Pinned to the wall, between the candles, were hundreds of photographs of me, all taken at various times and on different nights—out shopping, evening school functions, going to the theatre with friends, entering and leaving my unit … and many more. The shock gave way to fear. How long had he secretly watched me?

'Do you like them?' I looked at him, unsure what to say. His eyes were bright with excitement. 'Look. My latest one.'

He whipped the dark blue cloth from the easel to reveal a coloured drawing of me. But unlike the others, this one was more than a portrait. It showed my upper body, hair flowing down over my breasts, my head turned slightly to the side, lips parted, gazing longingly up at someone outside the picture. My left hand appeared to be poised ready to sweep the hair away from my neck. It was beautiful, but disturbing.

'Who am I looking at?' I asked, my heart rate increasing.

He lifted the picture and exposed another beneath. I gasped. It was a sequel to the one before, but Philippe had drawn himself into it. It showed him standing behind me, my hair gathered in his hands, exposing the curve of my breasts. My head was angled back, onto his shoulder, eyes closed, lips slightly parted, his mouth at my throat.

My stomach plummeted. I needed to get away from him, now.

'Tell me what you think of them, Laura?'

What could I possibly say? That they were beautiful and frightening at the same time?

'They're beautiful.' I didn't want him to detect the tremor in my voice, so I willed myself to be calm.

His smile widened. 'I wanted you the first time I set eyes on you.' He stepped toward me and touched my hair. 'Jake and the others were guarding you in Italy. Luc never knew I was there. By the time he found out, it was too late to interfere—we'd already met, and he couldn't let himself be seen by you.'

I backed away from him. 'Then why now, after all these years? And why not at the Ritual? I saw you there.'

His shoulders rose and fell, and his breath came fast as if grappling with some deep emotion. He gripped my upper arms. 'How desperately I wanted to, but I was forbidden to come anywhere near you. It was made very clear that I was not meant for you. So I took my chance at Sorrento before they could stop me.' His voice softened. 'I wanted to make love to you. But I daren't. You were so innocent. Then Luc showed up and ordered me to leave. I was forbidden from even leaving you a note ... to explain. I knew I couldn't live apart from you, so I left my home in France to settle here – to be near you. If I couldn't touch you, at least I could watch you from a distance. These thirty-two years have been torture.'

My breath caught in my throat. 'Is that why you disappeared so suddenly? I cried myself to sleep that night because you hadn't shown.' I had thought he'd got bored with me. I was only eighteen, after all, and naïve to the extreme. 'I didn't know.'

The anguish on his face was heartbreaking. 'How could you have known? They wanted to keep you well hidden and ignorant till you came of age.'

'There was a reason for that, so don't accuse them of wrongdoing. It saved my life. You know that Philippe.'

He smiled again. 'It's been a long time since anyone has called me that.'

'Then where does "Jean" come from?'

'That's my name—Jean-Philippe Louis Auguste Reynard,' he said proudly. 'But, I prefer Philippe.'

His eyes travelled to my mouth, and he leaned down toward me. 'Don't.'

'Why not? I've been waiting a long time. Now here you are, as if sent by fate.'

'But, it's different now. I don't feel that way toward you anymore.'

'Can't you even try?'

I shook my head. 'I'm so sorry; I can't.'

Silence. He leaned toward me and sniffed, and his expression changed. It hardened. '*He's* bedded you! All these years, waiting, watching—all for nothing!' He growled. 'I defied Luc, left France for you. Would have done anything for you. Dared anything. I didn't do all that and wait for you to come of age only to see you choose *him*.'

'It's not what you think—'

'I waited for you!' He shook me.

I winced as his fingers dug into my shoulders, and my heartbeat raced. 'Let go, Philippe. Stop!'

'Don't you see? Luc planned for you to be with *him*. All because of his Pictish blood. Luc chose him when you were a child. It was all planned.'

'That's not true!' I tried to wriggle free, but his grip tightened.

'I don't lie, Laura. Ask him yourself. Luc won't be able to deny it. *He* went to meet you the night of your birthday because Luc ordered him. I heard it all. He didn't want to go, had no interest in meeting you, but Luc promised to end his servitude if he did this for him, otherwise he'd increase it indefinitely and he'd be indentured to Luc for life.' He sneered.

I stared at him, unwilling to believe that could possibly be true. 'What do you mean?'

'When we're transformed, we serve our sires for a century. Munro has five years left, and if he doesn't do Luc's bidding, that could be increased for another century, even more. That's why he's doing this.'

I felt dizzy, nauseous. I needed to sit and only just managed to stay on my feet. If Philippe wasn't lying, then my falling for Alec was the stupidest thing I could have ever done, especially if it meant I was nothing more to him except a ticket out of servitude. It would explain his eagerness to end the curse, and if "bedding" me – as Philippe put it – achieved that, then Alec had succeeded.

No wonder he'd been so keen to point out I'd be free to marry whomever I wanted afterwards—Alec Munro had no intention of remaining my guardian, or, perhaps, even princeps. After I gave birth, he'd be free.

Horribly, it all made sense, but the worse thing—my own father was behind it all. Was that also for my benefit?

But then, Alec made you no promises, my inner voice yelled at me. I had gone along with his proposition knowing full well he didn't love me. It was a business arrangement, and I'd consented, so I had no right to be angry with him. I was the one who made it more than it actually was by falling for him. My head had been right all along. It was my heart that was diseased. Why did I listen to it?

Yet it didn't ease the pain, and I swallowed the rising lump in my throat.

Laura? Laura, are you all right? Alec's voice boomed in my head. I blocked my ears and refused to answer. *Laura, answer me.*

Go to hell, Alec Munro!

I was sure I heard him swear, but I couldn't care less; all I wanted was to spit in his face, and do the same to Philippe for telling me.

'You must really hate Alec. You can't even say his name.'

'I hate anyone who tries to take you from me. I love you. I never stopped loving you.'

Philippe crushed me to him and kissed me, his mouth fierce, as if making up for those lost years. All his pent up feelings came out in one explosive contact. He crushed my shoulders and bruised my mouth. It was impossible to scream as his tongue forced its way past my teeth and down my throat. My struggles only enraged him further. He pressed my mouth harder, until our teeth clashed. I struck out and he grabbed my wrists.

Finally he raised his head. 'You once loved me. I remember, and so do you. I'm not giving you up that easily, especially not to that son of a blacksmith. He's not worthy of you.' His eyes blazed; his face contorted with rage.

'And you are?'

It was pointless struggling against him. Philippe's strength was far greater than any human's, and I would only end up hurting myself. He imprisoned both my hands behind my back in one of his while he grabbed a fistful of my hair with his other, his nails raking my scalp.

'Yes. I have every right to claim you.'

'Claim me? What era do you think we're living in, the middle ages?' I spat. 'This is the twenty-first century, in case you've

forgotten. Women are no longer taken by the toughest thug around.'
I kneed him in the crotch.

He looked at me, stunned, and his grip temporarily relaxed. I
tried to take advantage and break free. And failed. *He must have balls of
steel.*

'Don't try that again. You're mine, Laura, and I will take you
from him by any means necessary. Return my kiss and remember the
way it used to be between us.'

He was pathetic. I looked at him incredulously. 'You think
treating me like this will rekindle a past romance? That's not going to
happen.'

His pupils elongated into vertical reptilian slits as the rest of his
irises paled. I baulked, but there was no way I was going to give in.

'Kiss me!'

'You have paintings of me—kiss them.' I drew my lips into a
tight line.

His handsome features changed, revealing the monster within –
fangs slid out, lips pulled back in a snarl.

A paralysing chill ran through me, but I fought against it and
tried to twist my head to the side, but he dragged my face back to his.

'Open. Your. Mouth,' he slowly enunciated, his voice low and
cold.

I sucked in my lower lip and bit down hard while trying to
control my fear.

'Have it your way then; but if I hurt you, you only have yourself
to blame.' He squeezed my hands until the pain became unbearable
and I cried out. He swooped, and his mouth was on mine, crushing,
invading.

I tried to scream as his fangs sliced through my bottom lip,
filling my mouth with blood. His tongue licked and sucked as tears of
pain streamed down my cheeks.

There was a loud crash, the sound of wood splintering, and, in
an instant, I was pried free to collapse into Luc's arms as Alec tackled
Philippe to the floor.

CHAPTER 44
DECLARATION

LAURA

Luc carried me off the stage. 'Laura, ma petite. I have you now. You're safe.' He held me tightly.

Blood dribbled down my chin and onto my dress. Some slid down my throat making me gag. I glanced up into Luc's alarmed face. He sat me on the floor and pressed a handkerchief to my mouth.

'Is it true what Philippe said? How could you do something like that?' I managed to say, even though my lip throbbed and I wanted to throw up. On top of that, I began to shudder uncontrollably.

'Laura, ma petite, I didn't want you to suffer the way your mother and I did. Please, believe me when I say I was only thinking of you.'

I wanted to say more, but growls and snarls filled the room as a barefoot and shirtless Alec engaged in a deadly struggle with Philippe—barred fangs, pale reptilian eyes. I looked on as they battled—two deadly predators circling each other—until Alec took advantage of an opening, grabbed Philippe, flung him onto the floor, wrenched his head back then violently twisted it until it snapped.

All went still, and I was sure Alec had killed him.

'He's not dead, just rendered helpless,' my father said. 'His body will recover within the next fifteen, twenty minutes.'

Alec stood. The serpent tattoo on his muscled chest almost glowed as he strode toward us, and as he looked at me, his eyes resumed their normal shade of deep lavender. He was beautiful, and I was in love with him, but he cared not a jolt for me.

My body still shook and tears burned my eyes.

'You can't play with people's lives like this.' I extricated myself from Luc's arms and stumbled as I tried to stand. Other hands grabbed me, but I threw them off. 'Don't touch me!' I screamed and ran to the door.

'Laura.' Alec blocked my way. I tried to push past him, but he locked me in a strong embrace.

'Let go!' I screamed, and I kicked his shins.

Alec grunted, but his grip didn't lessen. 'You can kick me all you want, but I'm not releasing you till we talk this out.'

I squirmed and struggled, but he held me tighter. Tears of frustration welled until I broke down, sobbing into his chest, hating myself for being so weak and hating him for making me feel this way. Yet, I managed a few words. 'There's nothing to talk out. You did what Luc told you. End of story.'

Alec lifted my chin, even as I tried to evade his hand. His eyes lightened as he looked at my lip. He removed the handkerchief and examined my mouth. A deep snarl rumbled in his chest as he saw the damage. His hands shook with barely controlled rage. 'I swear I'll kill him for this!'

He bent his head, as if to kiss me, and I tried to turn away. 'Don't fight me, Laura. I only want to lick your lip to speed up the healing process. Vampire saliva does that.'

I closed my eyes and tried to pretend it was Matt's tongue that gently laved my lower lip, first from one side and then from the other. As long as I kept telling myself that, I could remain calm. But, it wasn't Matt's arms I wanted around me, nor his lips touching mine. Within seconds, the sting lessened, and the painful throbbing ceased.

'Thank you,' I grudgingly said.

'Laura, my darling, look at me.'

'Don't call me that! You don't mean it.' I hiccupped and looked down at his bare feet.

'Why does that suddenly matter to you?'

'Please, just let me go.'

'Not yet.'

I looked up, and, through tear-stained eyes, gave him my coldest glare. 'Job well done, Dr Munro. Now you're free to go and do whatever it is you do. If I'm as fertile as you say, then I'm probably already pregnant and you don't need to hang around anymore.'

Alec lifted an eyebrow. 'Oh, but I very much do. I like to see a job through properly. It might take a few more times till I'm absolutely sure.'

'You bastard.' He had the effrontery to smile! 'Go to hell!' I stomped down as hard as I could on his foot.

He didn't even wince. Instead, he caught my wrists and held them in front of me. 'Before you decide to become any more violent, let me tell you why you're wrong.'

I tried to wriggle free. 'Huh!'

'Yes, wrong!'

'Let me go.' Just as I raised my leg to knee him, he twisted me around so my back was against his chest. Damn!

'Not till you tell me why you're so upset. I know Jean's not the only reason you're crying.'

I shook my head. No way was I going to tell him how I felt.

'In that case, I'll say it.'

I went absolutely still. Was he about to humiliate me? How could he do such a thing?

He turned me around to face him. 'I love you.'

I gazed at him—dumbfounded—my body still sobbing and hiccupping. 'You can't be. You want to leave me once the baby's born.'

'I only said that because I thought you were in love with Sommers.'

The proverbial penny dropped. 'Is that why you kept asking me if I loved him?'

'I didn't want to hurt you. Yet I didn't want you going back to Sommers, so I made that crazy bargain hoping ... I don't know' —he ran his hand through his hair— 'that somehow you'd realise I was anything but indifferent. Tell me I was right, Laura. Do you love him?'

This time I had no hesitation answering. 'No. But, I thought—'

'Do you love me?'

'Yes.' The word leapt from my lips – I'd never been surer of anything in my life.

'That's all I want to hear.' Alec leaned down and kissed me tenderly, mindful of my sore lip.

He loves me! My heart danced, and my breathlessness had nothing to do with recent events. I hugged his neck and pressed myself to him, revelling in the feel of his arms around me.

'Seeing you with Jean-Philippe nearly sent me insane. I wanted to kill him. Still do.' I didn't doubt it. His voice was filled with deadly menace.

'Philippe said—'

'I know, and he heard right, but that was last week. A lot has happened since then.' He looked past me, presumably to Luc then back to me. 'As for Luc's hold over me, I'll just go to the Elders, and they'll overturn it. After all, I'm princeps.' For an instant, he cracked a smile then his expression sobered. 'I love you, Laura. Now and for all eternity, my heart belongs to you. And if anyone tries to take you from me, I swear, I'll kill them.'

I gasped at the depth of passion in his voice.

'Marry me?'

I felt as if the ground shifted; if Alec hadn't been holding me.... A loud guffaw came from the small stage. Luc sat there grinning at us. 'I was right!' He clapped his hands together. 'You do love her. And if I hadn't given you that little push, you would've done nothing about it.' He looked at me. 'I had no intention of keeping Alec in servitude, ma petite, but I had to do something drastic for him to act. He's been in love with you for years but too blind to see it.'

'You scheming old fox,' Alec said. He didn't appear to be angry at all. On the contrary, he was smiling. 'Are you sure you didn't inspire Machiavelli?'

'Who do you think wrote, *The Prince*?' He winked at us.

Alec's thumb gently rubbed the tip of my nose. 'You haven't answered my question.'

All I could do was nod.

'Is that a yes, my darling?'

I nodded again.

'Say the words, Laura. I want to hear them.'

His eyes were filled with such love as they gazed back down at me that my words came tumbling out. 'Yes, yes—'

His mouth effectively prevented me from saying more. I melted into his embrace and returned his kiss with a hunger that matched his.

'Ahem!' We reluctantly stopped kissing. 'Now that that's sorted out, we have another problem that needs dealing with.'

I'd completely forgotten about Philippe, or Jean-Philippe, or whatever he called himself. It occurred to me, he had tasted my blood and was still alive. He hadn't burnt up. Why? Not that I had wanted it to happen; the thought of him dying the same way as Maris, sickened me. I didn't want him to die at all – just get over me and find someone else to be his muse for the next thousand years.

I shuddered.

'He'll never touch you again,' Alec said with unmistakeable menace.

'Mon Dieu! Look at this.' My father was examining Jean-Philippe's work, peering at the photos, then he crouched down to rifle through the myriad drawings scattered on the floor and swore again. What would he do when he saw his latest one? As his gaze moved up to the easel, I stiffened. Luc stood. His eyes widened then quickly narrowed into pale slits. A deep snarl echoed around the room.

'What is it?' Alec asked.

Luc turned the drawing around for him to see.

Alec gasped. 'Son of a bitch!'

'He's more unstable than I thought,' Luc said.

'You think? Look at those photos.' Alec jerked his head toward the stage. 'He's been stalking her for years.'

Luc growled and ripped the drawing into several pieces. 'I'll take him down to my study and get Cal to watch him. We'll decide what to do later. And all this' —he waved at Jean-Philippe's work— 'burn it. I want this room prepared for the Pledging ceremony on Sunday. Leave nothing.'

It seemed savage to destroy a man's lifetime work. Some of the drawings were beautiful. If Jean-Philippe hovered near the edge of instability, such an action would surely push him over the brink. Yet, I could understand why he gave such an order—they were the product of a deranged mind, and like Luc, I never wanted to see them again; never again be reminded of what he had tried to do to me.

He bent and picked up Jean-Philippe's limp form, slung him over his shoulder and re-entered the same door from which he and Alec had emerged.

'Are you okay? And I don't mean physically.' Alec brushed a few strands of hair off my face. I probably looked a mess. 'No one should ever have to experience something like that.' His eyes lightened.

'I'm okay, though a little shaky.' I shuddered. 'It's the photos and drawings that freak me out the most. What will Luc do to him?'

'Don't know, but he certainly can't stay here anymore, nor can he be allowed to wander free. We'll have to work something out. Now, where else did he hurt you, darling?'

'Um … shoulders.'

Alec undid the buttons of my dress and slid it off my shoulders. He went into physician mode, professionally examining my shoulders and upper arms for bruising.

'Sorry, I kicked you and stomped on your foot.'

He gave me a dazzling smile. 'It told me all I needed to know.'

I winced when he pressed a particularly tender spot – where Jean-Philippe's fingers had dug deep, leaving red inflamed marks.

Alec's expression darkened. 'You were supposed to be safe here.' He covered me up and re-buttoned my dress. 'I never expected this.'

'Neither did I. Not from someone I….' With his vampire hearing, Alec had probably overheard everything, so there was no need to explain my past relationship with Jean-Philippe.

'You don't need to explain.' His hand brushed my cheek.

'How did you get in?'

'There are a couple of former servants' passages that lead through the house and end up in the kitchen. One of them comes out behind the raised platform. Just there.' He pointed. 'Usually used by an orchestra so they can leave discreetly when they're done performing.'

'You couldn't get that mirrored door open?'

'No. I think Jean tampered with the mechanism. Locked it from inside so the hidden lever wouldn't work. I was about to try that old passage when Luc came stumbling out of the wall.' He turned to look at the wall behind us—where the entrance should be with the mirror on the other side. 'So, what did he do to it?' Alec said.

He went to the brass hook located about five-and-a-half feet from the floor and raised it. The wood-panelled wall in front of us noiselessly divided, revealing the corridor and marble staircase. He pulled the hook downwards and it shut again. I heard a slight click as he twisted the hook to the right and then to the left.

'That's how he's done it. He's even kept it oiled.' Alec tucked me into his side. 'Feeling better?'

'Yeah.' I shuddered as I ran my tongue over Philippe's cruel bite on the inside of my mouth and looked at the reddish marks ringing my wrists. As soon as I lost one set of bruises, I gained another. I sighed.

Alec gently cupped my face, his thumb stroking my cheek. 'If he ever comes near you again, I won't just knock him unconscious.' There was dark certainty in his voice.

'Can I ask you something?'

'You know you can ask me anything.'

'Why didn't my blood kill him?'

Alec brows drew together, and he rubbed the back of his neck.

'What is it?'

'I'm not sure I fully understand, myself.'

'He said he had every right to claim me.' I grimaced. 'What did he mean by that?'

Alec licked his lips and looked thoughtfully at me. It was obvious he didn't want to answer the question. He knew something and didn't want to tell me.

'Alec?'

'Honey, it's your father who needs to tell you, not me.'

The last time Alec called me "honey", I was in hospital and he was worried. An evil blonde vampire who fancied him had nearly sucked the life out of me. This time the roles were reversed, and I was the one being pursued by another blonde vampire. But unlike Maris, my blood seemed to agree with Jean-Philippe. As far as my knowledge of the curse went, only someone descended from the Pictish witch would be unaffected—someone like Alec. Could that possibly mean…? My mouth went dry at the implication, and Jean-Philippe's words made sense. He'd shown no hesitation in biting me—confident he wouldn't suffer the same fate as the other two.

'Jean-Philippe has the witch's blood, doesn't he?'

'Possibly.'

'How long have you known?'

'Since the hospital … I didn't like the way he touched you … how he looked at you.' A smile curved his lips. 'I was already in love with you then, I just didn't know it.'

'I tried so hard not to fall for you.'

'Glad you failed, otherwise I'd be forced to dispatch any male who'd dare come near you.' He sobered. 'I spoke to Luc. Asked him what he knew, and it appears Jean-Philippe's father was the Duke of Atholl, a noble of Pictish blood. But whether he's descended from the witch … I don't know.'

'That's why he came onto me in Sorrento. It was only because he wanted to be princeps.'

Anger surged through me, and my hands balled into fists. I wanted to hit something—preferably Jean-Philippe—and not just for payback. It was the thought of him romancing me all those years ago so he could be top dog in the vampire world. It was simply my wounded pride, I had to admit, but knowing he'd never loved me and that it was just his way of achieving his own ends was an affront to my dignity.

Alec placed his hands on my shoulders. 'Laura, I believe he genuinely fell for you. How could he not, darling?' He added when I glared at him. 'I'm not defending him, especially after what he did to you, but I don't think he even thought about it. You became his obsession.'

'The night of my birthday, why did Luc send you to meet me instead of Jean-Philippe?'

Alec's gaze roamed my face. 'Right,' he said and took me by the hand as we started down the staircase.

'Where are we going?'

'You want answers, Laura, and your father's the only one who can provide them.'

As we headed for Luc's study, I glanced down at my blood stained dress. Jean-Philippe would be in the room. Would he go for me again? My hands began shook.

'I can't insist you go in there—not after what just happened. We can talk to Luc on the mobile. It's up to you.'

We were on the landing outside his study. I really didn't want to see Jean-Philippe again, but there was no avoiding it. There were questions that needed answering, and clearly Alec didn't want to be the one supplying them. I could ask Luc to come out, but why should

I? I did nothing wrong. Let Jean-Philippe see what he did to me, and let him suffer a guilty conscience—if he had one. I certainly wasn't going to hide.

Alec waited patiently while I went through my inner debate. 'I'm not going to let him make me afraid.'

He nodded. 'The moment you feel uncomfortable, we're out of there. All right?'

'All right.'

Alec squeezed my hand and knocked.

'Come in,' Luc called.

CHAPTER 45
NO MORE SECRETS

LAURA

I took a deep breath as we entered Luc's study. I glimpsed Philippe—Jean-Philippe, now that I knew his full name—seated on the Chesterfield. He was conscious, and his head shot up the instant we walked in. I couldn't bear to look at him, so I deliberately kept my head averted, but I could feel the heat of his eyes on me.

Luc came over to us, glanced at Alec and nodded toward his head. 'Fax.'

Alec released my hand and went over to the desk.

'How are you, ma petite?' Luc's eyes alighted on my swollen lower lip.

'Okay, I suppose.' I tried smiling back, only it hurt my lip, and I winced.

'I'm so sorry, my Laura. It's my fault. If I had only acted sooner.'

There were footsteps behind me then Judy's voice. 'Luc? Well, seems everyone's here....' She stopped as she took in my face and bloodstained dress. 'Laura dear, what happened?'

From the corner of my eye, I caught movement as Jean-Philippe bowed his head over his knees, hands clasped in front of him. He didn't make a sound – no groans, no pleas, no apology, nothing.

I hope he feels rotten. A tinge of satisfaction warmed me when I glimpsed a line of blood from his mouth to his chin. Luc must have hit him, for that broken lip hadn't come from Alec. If that wasn't humiliation enough, I was sure there was more to come – some form of harsh punishment for what he did. If Luc and Alec hadn't found the entrance into that ballroom…. How far would he have gone?

'Um….' I remembered Judy's question when Alec returned to my side. He held a sheet of paper and gave Luc a nod.

Luc briefly raised his eyes to the heavens as he turned to Judy. 'I need a private word, ma cherie.' He ushered her to a corner.

I turned to Alec. 'What is it?'

'Luc's telling her now.' He placed his hand on the small of my back and pulled me close against his bare chest. 'Darling, this is going to be hard on you, and no matter how much I would want this to be otherwise' —he waved the paper in the air— 'you need to know the truth.'

'About what?'

Alec hesitated. 'Jean-Philippe's father.'

Now I was really confused. I looked at my parents. Whatever Luc was telling Judy caused her eyes to widen, and she placed her hand on his cheek. He turned his head, placed his own hand over hers and kissed her palm.

As he spoke, I watched, fascinated, as her expression darkened. She left his side, marched over to Jean-Philippe and struck him hard across the face, the crack reverberating throughout the room.

Jean-Philippe looked up at her—stunned for a moment—then rose to his full height. His eyes changed.

'Jean!' Luc cried and flew to Judy's side.

Alec pushed me behind him. I felt his entire body tense. I peeked out from behind his arm.

Judy glared at Jean-Philippe, fists clenched by her side. 'You mongrel! How could you do such a thing? Only a beast treats a woman like that! She's so much smaller and weaker than you. Mongrel! I want to see you punished for this.'

Luc managed to drag her away, but she shook off him off and came to me. White with fury, her face softened on seeing me. She tucked my hair behind my ears, closely examined my mouth then hugged me to her. Alec dropped his arm but not his guard. His watched Jean-Philippe. While I returned Judy's hug, a low, deep growl emanated from Alec.

Jean-Philippe spoke. 'Bear witness, Lord Lucien Lebrettan, as an Elder of our kind, I challenge Alexander Munro for the right to claim Ingenii Laura.'

Judy and I looked at him open mouthed. 'No! No way. You will not be princeps over me. I refuse.'

Alec stood in front of us, arms folded over his chest. 'You had your chance at the Ritual.'

He and Jean-Philippe glared at one another. Any moment and the fangs would appear.

'You're excluded from the office of princeps because you are Laura's brother,' Luc stated.

Brother?

He moved toward Jean-Philippe till they stood only a step apart. 'You are my son, Jean,' he said. 'I would have told you sooner, but I wasn't sure. Forgive me.'

The shock on Jean-Philippe's face was as great as my own must have been, and he shook his head in disbelief. 'Father? *You're* my father? No, no … that's not possible! My mother … on her deathbed … she said … my father was the Duke of Atholl.'

I had the same trouble believing it, but I knew Luc wasn't lying. There was no disguising the anguish on his face. My stomach clenched as images of Jean-Philippe, both past and present—touching, holding, and kissing me—raced unbidden through my mind. I wanted to retch.

Jean-Philippe's face changed from shock to anger. 'How long have you known?' he snarled.

'The last few minutes.' Luc pointed to the paper in Alec's hand. 'DNA results. Just faxed through. I took a lock of your hair and sent it to Alec, together with a cheek swab from me. The test came back positive. There's no doubt, Jean, I'm your father.'

Jean-Philippe gazed at Luc for what seemed like an age, while I stared at him. He was my brother, yet there was no physical resemblance between us. I was the image of my father, so he must take after his mother—whoever she had been.

He doubled over, and an anguished cry rent the air. It was the sound of a soul in torment. Strangely, I had to resist the urge to go to him, offer comfort, as one being to another, so agonising was the deep sob torn from him.

Luc gazed at his son with a pained stare, his hands clenched into fists by his side. The rest of us stood there, stunned.

Jean-Philippe raised his head, and his blood-rimmed gaze swept the room. Deep hatred burned in the pale-lavender depths of his eyes. 'Why did she tell me it was the Scotsman, the Duke of Atholl? Why?'

'Sit down, Jean.' Luc's tone brooked no argument.

Jean-Philippe complied, his angry gaze fixed on Luc.

Luc poured five glasses of the brandy from the bottle on his desk. He gulped one, emptying his glass before he poured another and handed a full glass to each of us. 'Drink it,' he commanded Jean-Philippe.

Judy and I downed ours as well. Alec held his and watched his former friend.

'To answer your question, your mother wasn't sure.' Luc paused. 'She was a sad and lonely woman. Her husband treated her with contempt, womanising and gambling away his fortune. I was visiting with her father, the Duke d'Orleans. He knew what I was – as did she. We liked each other. I needed to feed, and she needed comfort. It was a mutual agreement. I left the next day when the Duke of Atholl's carriage arrived.'

'It seems my mother had a lot of comforting that week,' Jean-Philippe said, his voice acid.

Luc ignored the disparaging remark, poured himself another shot of brandy and continued. 'We didn't see each other again after that night. Later I learned she'd had a child, exactly nine months after we were together. I knew the Scottish duke had also become her lover during that time. Whether she was with anyone else, I couldn't say. I didn't get close enough to catch a scent. So you see, I was never sure you were mine.'

'Then why didn't you check? You could have come back to see her, make sure.'

'I did, Jean. I did. I risked my life to slip into your room when you were a child, even though I was being hunted – as our kind were during the Revolution. In those years, I had to keep my distance to protect you and Adelaide.'

'Is that why she told me the Duke was my father?'

'Try to understand your mother's position. She was separated from her husband, took a lover—or two—and had an illegitimate child. As if that wasn't bad enough for her reputation, do you think she would reveal that one of those lovers was a vampire, a creature of the night, a blood-sucking fiend the local villagers would have come after with pitchforks and wooden stakes?'

He had a point. Jean-Philippe bowed his head and twirled the empty brandy glass in his hands.

'In spite of that,' Luc continued, 'I came back when you were fourteen, to see whether you'd changed at puberty, as I had. I watched and waited for many years, but you didn't change, Jean. You. Didn't. Change!'

I felt like an intruder in a private conversation, yet fascinated all the same. Judy, Alec and I may as well have been invisible.

'Next time I saw you…' Luc shrugged helplessly. 'You'd become one of us.'

'Lucinda changed me. Found me wounded and dying on the battlefield.' His words tumbled out in a hoarse whisper.

Luc's eyes closed, and he gave a barely detectable nod. 'I know her.'

'My mother lied to me,' he murmured.

'To protect you.'

Jean-Philippe's head snapped up. He glared at Luc then slowly turned his head in my direction. 'My sister. And I wanted to….'

So, he *was* going to do it. He'd been desperate enough to try to take me by force, and there was no way I could have stopped him. The thought sickened me. If Alec and Luc hadn't arrived when they did…. I covered my eyes with my hand.

Judy hugged me close. 'It didn't happen, dear. It didn't happen.'

'It nearly did. I'll never get it out of my head.'

'Judy's right, darling. We came in time, and it didn't happen.'

Judy let go as I twisted out of her embrace into Alec's. I was aware of Jean-Philippe's gaze. Was he trying to see me with new eyes – as his sister? Could we put this horrible incident behind us?

I dared to glance at him, and what I saw had my insides crawling. There was no hint of remorse in his eyes. Instead, they narrowed into pale, lavender slits on seeing me in Alec's arms. I realised then, he would never regard me as his sister. Alec was right. What Jean-Philippe felt for me was not love, but obsession—an unnatural and frightening desire to possess something forbidden.

He turned to Luc and snarled. 'This is your fault. If you had only warned me ... told me sooner.'

'I can only ask for your forgiveness.'

The room was deathly quiet as Jean-Philippe shook his head. 'Whatever friendship I felt for you is over. Fini! A partir d'aujourd'hui, nous sommes adversaires, mon pere!'

I sucked in a shocked breath. Even with my limited high-school French, I knew what that meant. He and my father were now enemies.

Jean-Philippe pinned Alec and myself with his gaze. 'I withdraw my challenge but, my dear *sister.*' He sneered. 'This isn't over between us!'

Dreadful certainty filled his voice, and I felt the blood drain from my cheeks as icy coldness settled in the pit of my stomach. I turned my face into the sheltering warmth of Alec's chest. As his arms tightened protectively around me, I heard glass shattering in the fireplace, receding footsteps, then the opening and slamming of a door. After that, silence, except for my rapid breathing.

Alec handed the paper to Luc as he walked me over to the settee. Luc placed another glass of brandy in my hand. 'Drink, ma petite. All of it.'

It was Luc's cure all. He looked stricken, as if he blamed himself for everything. Alec sat next to me and kept his arm around my shoulders. Judy sat on my other side and took hold of my other hand.

'He won't be allowed back in this house,' she said.

'What's going to happen to him?' My initial anger and shock had begun to pass with the understanding Jean-Philippe would have to live with the knowledge of what he did to me for the rest of his life. Could he live with that and know his desire would not, and could never be, satisfied? Those long-held, cherished memories of my youth, and the young man who'd once been part of it, were destroyed. What pity I may have felt for him had been dashed by his brutal treatment of me. I could only think of him with loathing.

His parting words haunted me.

'He'll be punished. As Ingenii, you have the power to order his death.' Luc crouched on the floor in front of me. There was pain in his voice.

'No. I could never do that. Could you?'

He shook his head. 'I'll confer with the other Elders. They'll decide what to do with him. I can't be involved since he's my son.'

'Any other secrets we need to know about while we're at it, Luc?' Alec asked.

Luc let out a pent up breath. 'That's enough for any man.' He rose and took our empty glasses and to his desk. 'I'll send Cal and Sam after him, ask Marcus to hold him till a decision is made.'

He moved to the door, opened it and quietly spoke Cal's name. In minutes, his smiling face appeared. 'What's up?'

'Get Jake and go after Jean. Take him to Marcus's and hold him there.'

'Jean?' Cal looked stunned. 'Why?'

'He tried to force himself on Laura,' Alec answered.

'What?' Cal's eyes widened as he scanned my face—my tear-stained cheeks, torn and swollen lip, and bloodied dress. 'Shit. Dark horse, isn't he.'

Luc helped himself to another shot of brandy from the near-empty bottle. 'Approach him carefully. He's … disturbed.'

Cal nodded. 'I'll get Jake.' He sped from the room.

I had no idea how late it was, but exhaustion hit me. Alec must have sensed it. He squeezed my shoulder. 'You need to get some sleep. I'll give you something to help.'

The door opened and Terens and Sam strode in. They looked at me. 'You okay, pet? Cal told us,' Terens said. I nodded. Terens turned to Luc. 'He and Jake have gone after Jean's scent. What's this about?'

Luc explained and again the whole thing replayed in my mind. Both men had difficulty believing it if the shake of Sam's head was anything to go by.

'Your son!' Terens exclaimed.

Luc handed him the slip of paper. Terens and Sam quickly perused it then looked at Alec for confirmation.

'Holy shit, what a mess. She can't stay here, Luc,' Sam said. 'Jean knows every corner of this house. And if he decides to come back here, he knows where every surveillance camera is and how to avoid it.'

My stomach lurched. I wanted to vomit. 'He'll come back?'

'From what Cal told me, I think he will.'

'Get him to take the Pledge,' Alec said.

Luc opened another bottle of whisky and poured himself a full glass. 'Perhaps I can ask the Elders to banish him; send him back to France. I could persuade him.'

'He didn't listen to you thirty years ago; what makes you think he's going to do so now? He's not going to let this go. You heard what he said.' Alec's voice rose.

'He's right,' Terens said. 'And Jean's even more dangerous now that he can't ever have her. I noticed the way he kept staring at her during the Ritual.' He looked straight at me.

I nodded, remembering the way Jean-Philippe had stared at me that night.

'He must take the Pledge,' Luc conceded, 'and swear never to come near Laura again.'

'And till then,' —Alec turned to me— 'I'm taking you to my apartment, darling. I'm not risking leaving you here—not until Jake and Cal find him. Go pack some things. We'll leave as soon as you're ready.'

Judy helped me throw a few things into an overnight bag, and we were in the hallway within minutes. Alec—who must have dashed back to his room to throw on a T-shirt and shoes—took my bag and headed out the door. I kissed my parents goodbye. Within seconds our car was through the front gates and speeding through the dark and empty streets.

CHAPTER 46
BLOODLINES

ALEC

Laura looked tense as I drove to my apartment in Pitt Street. Her hands were clasped tightly in her lap, her face pale. I didn't have to smell it to know she was scared. I placed my hand over hers and squeezed. 'The men will find him, darling, and bring him to Marcus. I promise.'

She turned to look at me. 'What if they don't and he comes to your place instead?'

'I'm stronger and faster.'

'I hope so. The thought of him touching me makes me sick.'

'He'll have to kill me first.'

'I don't want you to die. I love you.' Her eyes glistened and she angrily swiped the tears away.

'I love you, too, so listen to me. We're meant to be together. I don't believe for a second it's going to end tonight. We have eternity, remember?'

She smiled, squeezed my hand then gazed out the passenger window.

What else could I say? I'd waited my whole life for her and now, when there was everything to live for, would Jean's obsession with his half-sister jeopardise that? I wasn't going to let it happen.

Before we left the house, Luc had made arrangements to have Jean sent back to France—forcibly. But he blamed himself for this incident. 'It's not all his fault,' he had said as he slumped in his chair and spun it to face the window.

'You can't possibly—'

'It's Lucinda's fault. She transformed him while still a juvenile. There was nothing wrong with Jean while he was human.' He looked at me through the reflection in the dark window. 'She was punished with imprisonment and I took Jean into our household ... to watch him ... see if he showed signs of instability.'

'Why didn't I know about this?' I'd been leaning against one of his bookshelves, and this made me straighten and move to his desk.

'It wasn't relevant then.' He shrugged and spun the chair around to face me. 'Jean appeared fine; no signs of instability, so,' he waved his hand before letting it drop onto the desk, 'when he came of age I let him go.'

'And he remained in Paris until he met Laura.'

He nodded.

Juveniles were forbidden from transforming anyone. Since their blood was still undergoing the process from human to vampire, such transformations often led to mental instability in the changeling. The usual punishment for both sire and juvenile was death. 'You intervened, didn't you? Saved them both from the death penalty.'

'I made a mistake, and now my daughter is in danger because of it.' He rubbed his face.

'Is Lucinda still imprisoned?'

'No. She's since been released. And before you ask, no, I have no idea where she is.'

I paced the room trying to work out what our options were should Lucinda show up. Sires and dames do anything to protect their changelings. And right now, Jean wasn't only facing banishment, but the death penalty. 'Sam's right, this is a mess.'

Luc stood. 'There's something else you need to know ... Lucinda may herself have been changed by a juvenile. She's unstable. Couldn't tell us who her sire was so we don't know for sure.'

I laughed. 'This is just getting better isn't it? Well, now's not the time to deal with that problem. I need to get Laura out of here.' I left him and sprinted to my room where I threw on a clean T-shirt and jeans before meeting Laura in the hallway for the drive to my apartment.

CHAPTER 47

LAURA

'Here we are,' Alec said, as we turned into a modern apartment complex.

A private elevator whisked us straight up to his penthouse suite. The doors opened to reveal ceiling-to-floor tinted windows with a glorious, unhindered view of Sydney Harbour.

'It's incredible.' My tiredness disappeared.

'Glad you like it.' We stepped out of the elevator and into the main living area.

Alec's apartment was modern and spacious, with pearl-grey tiled floors, chrome, steel and black furniture. A black leather lounge suite faced the harbour view. Nearby, an onyx and jet alabaster chess set sat atop a low glass stool. Metal stairs led up to an open loft containing a king size bed. The view of the harbour would be unparalleled from up there.

'Take a look around.'

Two walls were fitted with criss-cross shelving and layered with books, journals, CDs and a range of DVDs, a few watercolour landscapes, but no photographs. Odd, that he didn't have any of that type of memorabilia, unlike Luc, who surrounded himself with pictures of my mother and myself. Perhaps he didn't have a family or didn't want to be reminded.

'This is such a bachelor pad,' I said.

'How so?'

'No soft touches.' I waved my hand around. 'All modern eclectic, a bichrome colour scheme, metal—very male.'

'You could change that,' he said quietly behind me.

Did that mean he wanted us to live here after we were married? Perhaps that's why he brought me here now. I shelved that thought for the time being. As I went to stand by the massive window, I spotted the Australian Colonial timber dining table and chairs, all alone, at the far end of the room. I recalled him mentioning it had belonged to his father.

I gazed out at the city lights and shivered.

Alec stood behind me, wrapped his arms around my waist and pulled me back against him. 'Cold? I can turn the air conditioning down.'

I relaxed against him. 'No, it's not that. Just … Jean-Philippe's out there.'

'We'll get him, Laura. I promise.'

His warm body and the heat of his words enveloped me in a comforting cocoon. I consigned my fears to the back of my mind to let myself enjoy the present.

Alec swept my hair aside and nuzzled my neck.

'Mmmmm, that's nice,' I cooed. 'A little higher.'

He chuckled and kissed the hollowed spot behind my ear. 'I've never brought any other woman up here—except Judy of course, and she was with Luc.'

'Never?'

'Never.'

'Then I'm privileged.'

'Sorry to contradict, but I'm the privileged one.' He angled my head to meet his lips. 'How's the lip?'

'Fine. Almost completely healed.' Although the swelling had nearly disappeared, the puncture marks caused by Jean-Philippe's bite were still sensitive.

'Good.' He gently kissed me.

Sunrise wasn't due for another couple of hours, and the waning moon glinted on the calm harbour waters.

'It's magic. Do you stand here often and watch?'

'Sometimes. Normally I stay at work, or I'm at Luc's. There's no one to come home too.'

'Were you lonely?'

'Never really thought about it till recently. I suppose I was. I hated coming home to an empty apartment, so I stayed at the lab, always looking for more work to keep me occupied. You?'

'I was surrounded by people all day—kids, other teaching staff, parents. So when I came home, it was a welcome relief. Yet other times I felt it—before Matt came along—when I just wanted the feel of someone's arms around me, and there was no one there.'

'Any man would be privileged to have you by his side. Yet I'm glad. I hate the thought of any other man touching you.'

Alec's compliment touched me deeply. 'I gave in to Matt, and now I wish I hadn't. I wish I'd waited for you.'

His embrace tightened and he kissed the top of my head. 'You weren't to know, darling, and you waited long enough as it was.'

I didn't want to tell him that Matt never satisfied me. I didn't want to discuss Matt at all. It was him I was interested in. 'Alec, was your father a blacksmith?'

He huffed. 'I heard Jean's disparaging remark. Arrogant bastard. My father was the village smithy in Dunkeld. That's where the Munros are from. I helped him as a boy and well into my teens, till we emigrated here. Later, I got a scholarship to study medicine at Sydney University. Helped at the forge during term breaks.' I spun around to look at him. He smiled and his voice took on an almost reverential tone. 'He managed to set up a business here and later expanded to include motor vehicle repairs. Very enterprising, he was. Wanted me to be a doctor; said saving lives was more important than shoeing horses or fixing busted radiators.' The smile widened. 'He was a kind man, but not one to be taken advantage of.'

'Like father, like son. I would've liked to have known him.'

'He would have loved you as a daughter-in-law. Brave, clever women earned his respect. Didn't agree with the suffragettes but he admired their courage and tenacity.'

Sometimes I forgot how old Alec was. Yet, every now and then, a word of his or gesture reminded me of his antiquity. He really was from another time.

'I'm from a humble background, Laura. But I'm not ashamed of it.'

'And why should you be? My dad—uncle, I suppose—is a builder. It's who you are as a person that matters. Besides, who cares about such things anymore? I'd want to be with you even if you were nothing more than a' —I searched for a lowly enough profession— 'garbo.' Garbage collector. He gave me one of his dazzling smiles. 'And for your information, don't you know that doctors are practically royalty in this day and age?'

He laughed and leaned down and kissed me. My knees gave way and I put all my weight on him. 'Laura, when was the last time you ate? I seem to be propping you up here.'

'Um, round sixish.' I'm sure my unsteadiness had little to do with hunger.

He fished the mobile out of his back pocket and pressed a few buttons. 'What kind of pizza do you like?'

'Pizza? Aren't they closed at this hour?'

'No, this lot are open twenty-four-seven.'

'How do you know?'

'My staff at the hospital. They always order pizza from this place during all-night sessions when we're waiting for results.'

'Oh, okay. Supreme, meat lovers. Whatever. No anchovies.'

'Yeah, I'd like to order one large supreme, no anchovies,' he said to whoever was on the other end of the line. 'Coke?' he looked down at me. I shook my head. Never did like the stuff. 'No thanks, no coke,' he said. 'No, that's all thanks. Address is, the Penthouse, Pitt Street Towers.'

He rung off and tossed the mobile onto the sofa. 'Got thirty minutes before your dinner arrives. What would you like to do?'

That was a loaded question. 'What do you have in mind?'

A devilish glint lit up his eyes. 'Where do I begin?' Suddenly he stiffened. His smile vanished and he looked at me in alarm.

'What is it?'

He grabbed my hand and pulled me toward the elevator. 'Need to get you out of here. Luc just told me Jean's on his way and he's crazy—he nearly killed Jake. They couldn't hold him.'

My stomach bunched into a tight knot. 'Oh Lord.'

A shadow appeared outside, on the window, even though we were twenty-five storeys up. Glass exploded into the room as a figure crashed through the window, shards peppering our feet. The intruder rose from its crouching position. Jean-Philippe stood before us. His eyes didn't resemble anything human. They were reptilian—pale, cold and frightening. He locked his gaze on me and grinned, revealing cruel fangs, before beckoning me with his finger.

Alec threw me behind himself. His hands clenched into fists as his arms anchored me in place. 'Get out, Jean!'

Jean's grin turned into a snarl. 'She's mine!' He lunged toward me.

I screamed.

Alec hit him, sending Jean-Philippe sailing across the room.

'Laura, get in the lift!' Alec cried as Jean-Philippe recovered and went for him, sending the two of them crashing into the dining chairs. Wood splintered and flew in all directions.

I ran and pressed the elevator button. A loud grunt sounded. I turned. Jean-Philippe had plunged a long piece of splintered wood into Alec's chest.

I screamed as Alec collapsed.

Oh God! Oh God! He can't have. My mind blanked. I stood frozen, not knowing what to do. Alec was still alive, blinking in confusion as he stared at the stake planted deeply in his chest.

'No!' I screamed and raced to his side.

Blood smeared my hands as I tried to pull the thing from his body, but it was firmly wedged between his ribs. Jean-Philippe's arms caught me around the waist, and I kicked and screamed as he tried to haul me away from Alec.

'Your turn now. We have unfinished business, little sis.' He clamped his hand over my mouth. 'If Russell hadn't botched the job, none of this would be necessary right now.'

He tucked me under his arm and headed for the loft. My stomach lurched while my mind grappled with what he had just said. Images of that awful night Russell snuck into my hospital room flashed through my mind. Anger and fear swept through me. I bit into his hand on my mouth till I tasted blood and scratched his other.

'Aahhh! Little cat,' he growled out through gritted teeth and dropped me.

I broke from him and dove under the dining table, amid pieces of broken chairs and split timbers. I hefted a particularly sharp and nasty looking fragment as Jean-Philippe came after me. My hands shook, but I didn't dare let go. Alec was only a few feet from me – eyes closed, grimacing as he attempted to pull the stake from his body.

Thank God it wasn't made of white oak, but what other damage could it do? He could still die of blood loss.

I choked back a sob and resisted the urge to run to him. If Jean-Philippe knew Alec was still alive, he'd go back and finish the job. I had to keep him as far from Alec as possible. Luc would be here soon too, I told myself. I held on to that lifeline.

'There's no use fighting me, little girl.' Jean-Philippe sneered and poked his head under the table, trying to grab me.

'You bastard. You sick, sick bastard!' I wacked him on the side of the head with the chair leg so hard, the wood splintered and fell apart.

He snarled, got to his feet and upended it, sending the heavy table crashing into a wall lined with books, pictures and other objects. Debris scattered to the floor. He stood glaring down at me. My knees were tucked under my chin, and my heart pounded as I looked back at him.

He grinned, exposing fangs, and extended a hand down toward me. 'Come to me, Laura.'

I shook my head and slid backwards while my hand searched for another weapon. '*You* put Russell up to it.'

'You think that fool would've been able to get into your room on his own? I was the one who told him about the serpent ring. Alec very conveniently revealed how it worked, the night of your abduction. He used it to get into the disused theatre without being detected.' He was boasting about it, smiling, proud of his cleverness.

I remembered my terror and pain, and adrenaline coursed through me. I grabbed another long piece of wood and swiped the back of his knees. He lost balance and stumbled backwards.

'Merde,' he swore.

I got up and ran for the closest door. It appeared to lead outside—a rooftop garden perhaps? It would draw him away from Alec. As I reached for the handle, he tackled my legs. I went down, the wood flew from my grasp and skidded across the floor. His powerful hands grabbed my waist, spun me around and ripped open the top half of my dress. Buttons bounced on the tiles, and his eyes burned as he stared at my body.

I aimed a fist at his face, intending to ram his nose through to the back of his skull, but my action was too humanly slow. He growled, grabbed my wrists and pinned my arms above my head. 'Stop struggling! I did it for you—for us. Russell knew how I felt about you, noticed it that night, and we came to an arrangement: I spare his life, and he helps me get you.'

My legs were still free. I raised them and kicked into his chest as hard as I could. It dislodged him for an instant, enough time for me to try for another run, but he grabbed my ankle, and I fell onto the tiles, face first. The fall winded me, and I struggled to breathe.

He was on top of me in a blink, pulling up my dress and slipping his hand down the front of my panties. 'I don't want to take you like this, Laura, but I will if I have to,' he panted in my ear.

'Bastard! I hate you!' I screamed and kicked at him while reaching out for the alabaster chess pieces on a nearby table. I grabbed two of the larger ones, twisted around and thrust their pointy ends into his ears. He roared in pain and reared up in an attempt to pull them out. That was all the time I needed to scramble out from under him.

I got to my feet, but Jean-Philippe caught my hair and pulled me toward him. I screamed and reached behind me to scratch the back of his hands, adding to the ones I gave him previously.

He let go of my hair, grabbed me by the neck and threw me down. As my forehead grazed the tiles, he grabbed my shoulders and spun me around to face him.

'Thought you could get away from me?' he growled, pinning me under him again, imprisoning my hands above my head with one hand as I kicked at every soft part of him. Still, it was impossible to prevent him from wedging his knee between my legs and forcing them apart. My stomach tightened. 'I'm going to have you and watch your face while I'm doing it.' He grinned. His other hand slowly undid the rest of the buttons on my dress.

I gasped and tried to wriggle my hips out from under him, but he dug his knee deeper between my legs and pressed down.

'Stop struggling! It's really up to you whether this will be a pleasant experience or not.'

'You sick son of a bitch.'

He struck me hard across the face. My head snapped to the side and tears welled up in my eyes. 'See what you made me do. If you had only come with me when I'd asked. As it is....' he shrugged, and his fingers undid the front clasp of my bra. 'It was such a simple plan.' He stroked my breast as he pushed my bra aside. I tried to shrink back in revulsion.

'Exquisite!'

'Don't you touch me you sick bastard.'

He laughed. 'Too late. Now, as I was saying, Russell was supposed to have taken you out of there and down to my car.' He ran his hand back and forth slowly over my breasts as he spoke. Bile rose in my throat, and I had to force it down. 'Instead, he stayed too long and got trapped, the idiot.' A look of disgust crossed Jean-Philippe's face. 'I waited outside, listening, then Alec shows up, and then my dear *Pere*! I should have known better than to rely on that fool, Russell.'

I couldn't bear to listen to any more. He was clearly deranged, and I turned my head away, praying that someone, anyone, would get here.

He clutched my chin and forced me to look at him. 'No more waiting. I'm going to fuck you now, after which I'm going to kill you. It's the only way I can be free of you.'

It wasn't just his vulgarity, but the chilling way he said it that terrified me. Alec's life was slowly ebbing away just a few feet from me—and I was in the hands of a monster. A deep resolve took hold, and my terror gave way to anger. It welled up in me like a giant wave, and I struggled even more. 'No! I won't let you.'

Jean-Philippe laughed. Quicker than a snake, he lowered his head till his mouth was on mine, his tongue forcing its way past my teeth. I squirmed and kicked, and then bit down hard on his tongue. He growled and pulled out of my mouth. Strength I never knew I possessed surged through me. I strained against his powerful grip and managed to free my hands long enough to push him off.

There was a loud roar, the shattering of more glass, and Luc was pulling me free. I saw Alec rise and grab Jean-Philippe from behind and ram the bloodied piece of wood that had been embedded in his own chest deep into Jean-Philippe's back, until the tip protruded out the other side. Jean-Philippe's eyes widened, his shoulders bunched back, and his body convulsed as the deadly splinter did its job. Ashen faced and with blood pouring from the gaping wound, he collapsed and writhed on the ground as his hands clawed at the protruding stake.

I pulled out of Luc's embrace, re-hooked my bra clasp, and went to Alec, who had collapsed next to Jean-Philippe. Jake, Terens and Cal were at his side. They'd torn off his shirt in an attempt to staunch the blood flow.

'Alec! Alec! C'mon my brother, hang in there,' Jake urged. I heard the panic in his voice.

'Shit!' Terens uttered when he saw Alec's wound. He glanced back at Jean-Philippe's still form. 'He planned Laura's kidnapping – with Russell.' The expression on his face, and Cal's, was one of disbelief and anger.

'Alec.' I knelt by him. He was pallid, and his breath came in gasps. I took his hand and held it to my cheek.

'Laura.' Jake got my attention. 'He needs your blood, now.'

'Quickly ma petite, or he won't survive,' Luc said.

I lovingly touched Alec's face, bit back tears—this was not the time—gathered my hair to one side and leaned down. Cal and Jake lifted his upper body and angled his head till his mouth was against my throat.

'Alec, don't die. Please, please don't die. I don't want to be without you.' His beautiful face had gone deathly white. Tears stung behind my eyes, then I felt his fangs slide out, the quick sting and he was sucking—weak at first, then stronger. 'Oh yes,' I heard myself say, and my body relaxed into him. I closed my eyes as he drank, could feel his strength returning.

He gripped the back of my neck and pulled me closer as his other arm encircled my waist. I felt myself utterly possessed, and my body hummed with another sort of pleasure—that my blood was for him alone, his life giver and sustainer. As he drank, I felt no dizziness, no weakness, only an intense peace I didn't want to end. It was the effect of the vampire's bite.

My vampire.

Too soon it was over. He finished and licked the puncture marks he'd made, kissed my neck and gazed at me.

The adrenaline gone, I slumped against him and my body began to shake. Soon the shock of what had just occurred would follow. But for now, we were both alive. Neither of us spoke as Alec cradled me in his arms.

'Ma petite.' Luc was on his haunches next to us, his face sorrowful. 'What can I say? I'm so sorry. I've watched over you your whole life. Yet now, when I thought you were finally safe….' He bowed his head.

'Papa, you did everything possible.'

He opened his mouth to say something but closed it again. 'We'll talk later.' His gaze drifted to the still figure of Jean-Philippe. 'I'll go see my son now.'

Alec and I watched as he went to Jean-Philippe, who lay face down on the pearl-grey tiles, the jagged piece of wood sticking out of his back.

Terens squeezed Alec's shoulder. 'You gave me one hell of a scare. And, Laura, pet, I'm so sorry we didn't get here sooner.'

'You came in time.' I wouldn't let myself dwell on anything else.

He nodded and joined Luc.

'Good to see you alive, my brother,' Cal said. He turned to me and placed a hand on my shoulder. 'Laura, angel, are you all right?'

'I suppose.'

He patted my shoulder, and then, with a deep sigh he rose and went to Luc, who knelt by his dead son.

I shivered at what Jean-Philippe had nearly done to me and it would be a long time before I would be able to say his name again without shuddering.

'Take him back to my estate,' Luc said.

He stood as Jake and Cal carefully wrapped Jean-Philippe's body in the rug on which it lay. Hoisting it carefully over his shoulder, he rose and strode over to the elevator. The other three followed. The doors to the elevator shut behind them.

Alec and I were alone again, with a broken window and a wrecked penthouse.

'He nearly killed you,' I said in a hoarse whisper.

'Nearly, sweetheart. That piece of wood came so close my heart. I'm lucky to be alive.'

'I tried to pull it out.' I ran my arms around his neck.

'Seeing the terror on your face was enough to give me the strength to rip the thing out.'

I pulled out of his embrace and ran my trembling hands over his smooth, muscled chest. The gaping wound had sealed. There wasn't even a scar. Not much blood either. His T-shirt must have absorbed most of it.

I placed my lips over his heart and kissed the spot where the stake had been. My eyes caught the glint of light on the gold crucifix round his neck. I lightly touched it. 'I prayed.'

'It was answered.' Alec kissed me then folded me securely in his arms. 'I was helpless, and you had to fight him on your own.' Anger tinged his voice. 'I heard every word. The rage I felt and then the fear at what he was doing to you....' His teeth gritted, and his breaths came faster. I placed my hand soothingly on his chest. Alec's jaw clenched as he looked at my ripped clothes. 'No one undresses you but me.' He pulled closed the torn remnants of my dress.

I nestled back into his embrace. It was the best place in the world, even though we were sitting on the floor surrounded by the remains of his ruined apartment.

'You'll need a new dining suite.'

Alec's body shook with laughter. 'As if I care. You're all that matters to me. I'd happily have the whole damn place wrecked if it meant having you safe in my arms—where you belong.'

He knew just the right thing to say. I closed my eyes and allowed myself to drift on a cloud of bliss as every one of my senses savoured him – his scent, the strength of his arms around me, his soft breathing, the feel of his skin beneath my cheek, the delicious taste of his kiss.

The intercom buzzed. Alec frowned. I didn't want him to let go. 'No, don't answer it.'

It buzzed again, and I clung to him. 'It's all right.' He kissed my forehead, scooped me up and walked to answer it. 'Yes?'

'Anyone order pizza?'

CHAPTER 48
AFTERMATH

LAURA

I woke up in Alec's bed. We were in the loft, and he lay next to me, wearing only his jeans. My head rested on his bare chest and my hand on the rippling mass of muscles that was his stomach. His arm cradled my shoulder while the other drew circles on the back of my hand.

Strong daylight stole into the room from the living area. 'Is it morning already?' I asked.

'Afternoon.'

'I slept that long?' I didn't know what time I finally fell asleep, but sometime soon after I ate. 'Thank you for not leaving me alone.'

'As if I would. You screamed and thrashed about in your sleep. At one point you wept.'

I sat up aware I was still in my torn clothes from last night. 'The whole time?'

'No. Intermittently.' He brushed the hair off my shoulder. 'You were traumatized. I would've been surprised if you didn't have nightmares. It's why I didn't leave you, even for a second.' His gaze swept over my face and neck, and his expression darkened.

'You didn't sleep at all?'

He shook his head. 'Don't really need it. Your blood.'

'How long?'

He raised a questioning eyebrow.

'The nightmares, Alec. How long will I have them?'

He sat up and took my hands in his. He glanced down at the bruises on my wrists and frowned. 'Don't know. Everyone's different. Your mind's trying to cope with what you experienced. It's going to take time, darling, but I'm going to do my utmost to help replace the frightening memories with joyful ones.'

'You have my permission to do that.' I smiled.

He leaned in and tenderly kissed my forehead, the hollow of my throat, then my neck and jaw. 'Does it hurt?'

'What?'

'You're face and neck are bruised, and there's a nasty graze on your forehead.'

I remembered the way Jean-Philippe grabbed me, and I instinctively ran my fingers over my face. It didn't really feel sore, just a little tender. 'No, it doesn't hurt.' I wanted to erase that memory forever.

Alec pulled me back into his arms. I felt a tremor run through him. I wasn't the only one affected by last night's events. We'd fought for our lives, and Alec had been forced to kill a friend, someone he'd known as a brother for longer than I'd been alive. Neither of us had come through unscathed. It would haunt him for a long time.

I reached up and cupped his cheek. 'How are you? You saved my life and lost a friend.'

He took a deep breath. 'He stopped being my friend the day he saw me as a rival. It seems kissing you during the Ritual earned me a few enemies. But I don't regret it, not for one moment.' He looked lovingly at me, dipped his head and kissed me lightly, mindful of my injured mouth. He lay down taking me with him.

'Alec?'

'Mmmmm?'

'How was he able to overpower you? Doesn't my blood make you stronger?'

'I've been thinking of that. The only thing I can come up with is that a combination of your blood—when he bit you—and adrenaline created a dangerous combination. I was surprised myself.'

Alec ran his fingers soothingly through my hair. I thought over the events of the last twenty-four hours. Then the realisation hit. 'You nearly died. Alec. You nearly died!' I raised my head and looked down at him.

'But I didn't. I'm here, with you.'

'Philippe was going to kill us both, and he nearly did.'

'He didn't,' he said quietly.

My breathing sped, up and before I knew it, hot tears spilled down my cheeks.

'That's what I've been waiting for,' Alec said and wrapped me securely in the strength of his arms.

I sobbed till my body shook. He held me tightly against his chest, cooed soothingly and stroked my hair till my tears had run their course. 'Want to talk?' he softly asked.

I shook my head. 'What's there to say?'

'How you feel.'

I tipped my head up to look at him. 'Better, now that it's out. He was my half-brother. He was supposed to protect me, look after me. Not what he was planning to do.'

'He's paid for it.' He drew me to him, wiped away my tears and kissed me tenderly.

My lip had healed completely and I didn't want him to stop. I ran my arms around his neck and pressed myself to him. He stiffened and lifted his head.

'What's wrong? Why are you stopping?' I asked.

'I forgot—your lip, darling. I don't want to hurt you.'

'It's fine. Don't hold back. I need you to kiss me right now.'

He nodded and gently drew me down, rolling me beneath him. 'You don't ever have to ask,' he whispered against my mouth, and the passion and depth of his kisses did indeed begin to wash away the frightening images of the night before.

How could I possibly love anyone else? Were I to be brutally honest with myself I'd have to admit that I'd never really been *in love* with Matt. There was affection and a certain type of love that develops over time with someone you've grown very fond of, but I'd never experienced the depth of passion that Alec aroused in me.

Thoughts of him consumed me, while being in his arms melted me to my core. It was like comparing an old, familiar dressing gown that didn't quite fit, though one got used to over time, to a ravishing designer gown that slid over your body like a second skin.

'It's your touch I long for. It's you, Alec. Only you.'

'My Laura,' he whispered. He bent his head and kissed me slowly, deeply and lovingly until I was lost in him.

This is right. I thought. *This is how it should be.* Utter contentment blanketed my being and suffused my every pore until I felt myself drawn into him. I knew now what it meant to be part of a whole.

Always, darling, and forever I'll love you. I heard his deep, rich timbre in my head. I'd forgotten we could hear each other's thoughts, and not only in times of danger, it seemed. It was strangely comforting. I'd never have to pretend with him, but on the other hand, it'd be hard keeping a secret. I snuggled into his embrace, filling my senses with his scent.

He slipped open my dress, unclipped the front clasp of my bra and cupped my breast. I arched into him, impatient to feel his touch—his touch and not another's. My nipples hardened immediately. His fingers explored; his kiss deepened, and my body quivered. Soon the dress and my underwear were on the floor with his jeans and T-shirt and he was sinking into me, moving with a rhythm I loved and matched. Our bodies melded, as if made only for one another, and when I came, I cried out his name. Alec's own release followed, and he collapsed on top of me then rolled to the side and cradled me with him.

We lay cocooned in our own blissful bubble, and I knew no other man could possibly compare to him. Luc had been right. He chose Alec for me because he knew no one else would understand me as well, nor make me as happy. I looked into his beautiful lavender eyes, and stroked the raven-black hair off his forehead and fell in love with him all over again. I realised then that not even eternity would be long enough to love him and learn everything about him. And there was something in particular I wanted to know.

'Alec?'

'Mmmm?'

'Were you, um … married before?'

'Long time ago.'

'Did you love her—your wife?' I asked.

'I liked Eleanor, and in some way I did love her.' His fingers danced around my back. 'Very different from the way I feel about you. I've never been in love before. It's a new experience for me.'

'Is it?' I couldn't help the broad smile that stole across my face, flattered beyond reason that I was the first woman Alec had fallen in love with.

He chuckled. 'Yes, you'll be happy to know, Miss Dantonville.'

'I know this will probably sound awful, so please don't take it wrongly, but if your wife and baby hadn't died, you wouldn't have gone to war, been shot by my grandfather, changed by Luc and' —I took a deep breath— 'we wouldn't be together, like this, right now.'

'In those few words, you've summed up my life, *my* reason for existence. It's you. Any pain I've suffered, the mistakes I've made, the path laid out for me have all led here, to you.'

I released the breath I'd been holding. 'I believe in destiny. Things just don't happen randomly. There's a reason behind it all. What does the Bible say about all things working for good? And meeting you last Friday was very good.'

He kissed me again. 'I'm yours for eternity.'

'Eternity,' I repeated, the words burning into my brain, so much so it felt we'd made some form of sacred and unbreakable bond.

Then we made love again.

Long afterwards, as I lay contentedly in his arms, he said, 'I phoned the hospital earlier. Sommers is recovering. You still want to see him?'

'I need to say goodbye. He nearly died trying to protect me. I owe him that, in spite of his lousy intentions.' Saying goodbye wasn't going to be easy.

'I'm coming with you.'

After one last kiss, we both got out of bed. Alec pulled out his phone while I showered and changed. He must have rung for takeaway, as there was a full English breakfast—although it was lunchtime—of scrambled eggs, two mini sausages, baked beans, and a hash brown, waiting for me. His espresso machine provided the coffee. It was delicious, and I ate it all. There was a grim task ahead and I needed my strength.

CHAPTER 49
GOODBYE

LAURA

Alec drove me to RPA. He parked in the section reserved for medical staff. I didn't get out of the car straight away. Summoning the courage to walk into the hospital was harder than I thought it would be.

Alec took my hand. 'Hey, I'm here. You're not alone.'

'I'm the one who has to tell him.' Even though I was tempted to send him a break-up text message. But that would have been cowardly.

'Shall we go in then?'

'Yeah.'

He knew which ward Matt was in, which room, which bed. Fourth floor, room near the nurse's desk. My stomach churned more the closer we got. He held my hand and squeezed reassuringly.

We stopped just outside Matt's room. The double doors stood wide open, and voices drifted out. I recognized some of them—Matt's mum, Evelyn, and one of his sisters.

'I'm coming in with you,' Alec said.

'No! You can't.' I let go of Alec's hand. Last thing I wanted was curious or questioning looks. Taking a steadying breath, I entered.

There were three unoccupied beds in the room. A blue curtain had been partially drawn around the bed Matt occupied—the side facing the corridor. At the foot of the bed, a dark-haired young woman holding a clipboard looked up as I stepped into view. She came to me but glanced over my shoulder. 'Dr Munro?' she enquired.

'Yes,' he replied.

Somehow I just knew Alec wouldn't stay outside. I didn't know whether to be angry or relieved.

She turned to me. 'Miss Laura Dantonville?'

I nodded.

'I'm Dr Claudia Cardacci.' She extended her hand to us in turn. Her large brown eyes examined Alec. 'I spoke to you on the phone the other day. Can I please have a word?' She indicated for us to move away from the door, to a quiet corner near the end of the corridor. Several chairs and a coffee table had been set up for visitors.

'Is something the matter?' I asked.

'Maybe you'd like to sit down?'

Whenever anyone said those words, it never meant anything good. And I was restless enough as it was—nervous energy made me fidgety. I wanted this morning to be over. 'No, I'd rather stand, thanks.'

'All right,' she started cautiously. 'Our recent tests reveal he may have suffered slight brain damage.'

My stomach plummeted. Alec's hand snaked around my waist.

'It's called an RML–'

'Retrograde Memory Loss,' Alec finished for her.

She nodded.

'What does that mean? Some kind of amnesia?' I looked from her to Alec and back again.

'In a way,' she continued, 'although it doesn't impact all memory, only a part. His injury caused a small blood clot to form on the brain, which we've removed, but it's resulted in his inability to recall some events. We don't fully understand yet how it works, but it seems he doesn't remember the last six months.'

This was a clanger.

Dr Cardacci lightly touched my arm. 'Mrs Sommers told me you and Matthew have been together for about four months?'

I nodded.

'I'm sorry, but he'll have no memory of your relationship. You'll be a stranger to him.' She looked at me sympathetically. 'I thought you should know before you walked in there.'

My mind went numb, and I had no idea how to react.

'I'll get you a glass of water, ' Dr Cardacci said before going to the small sink and filling a polystyrene cup with tap water.

Alec sat me down and placed the cup into my hand. 'Laura, drink this, honey.' He was crouched on the ground in front of me, anxious, his hands over mine.

'Look, I'm fine. It's just the shock.'

'You went white,' Alec said.

'I really am so sorry. I tried to tell you as best as I could,' Doctor Cardacci said.

'Thanks for telling us. She'll be all right,' he assured her, but his eyes didn't waver from my face, and his hands remained over mine.

Dr Cardacci's glance darted between Alec and myself, and a knowing look appeared in her eyes.

Just then, I didn't care. Matt had amnesia. Amnesia! The word swirled round in my brain, trying to sink in. *He wouldn't know me!* And in that surreal moment, I realised the man I'd feared to hurt wouldn't know me from a bar of soap. I should've been relieved, yet I felt sadness. Matt and I had known and loved each other for nearly four months, and now unexpectedly, suddenly, it was over. Finished. I was having difficulty processing it.

'Will his memory ever return?'

'Probably not,' Alec replied. 'In rare cases it does, in others....' He shook his head and shrugged.

If Matt's memory never returned, I reasoned, he wouldn't miss what he couldn't remember and he wouldn't suffer the pain of our breakup. And with that understanding, I finally allowed myself to feel a sense of relief, although I had good reason to leave him.

Alec sat next to me and put his arm around my shoulders. I leant into him, past caring who saw.

'I'd better get back,' Dr Cardacci said, and she walked back to Matt's room.

'Can't hurt him now,' I said.

'Laura, he doesn't deserve such consideration. He didn't exactly confide in you when he got those white-oak bullets, did he?'

No, he didn't. Matt had been ready to kill those I loved, without a word to me.

I bit my lip, wondering what to do next. Should I still go in? Would seeing me somehow jog his memory, so I could ask him about those bullets, give him the benefit of the doubt? Maybe they were for a police training exercise? Highly unlikely, my common sense said. Or should I return the way I came, not go in, and leave him in blissful ignorance? But then, Dave would have mentioned me. After all, he was found unconscious in my apartment. And his mum knew me. She'd mention something.

I released a deep breath as I weighed up my options.

'Still want to go in there?'

'I don't know what to do, and how did she know we were coming?' I gulped down the rest of the water.

'I phoned ahead, to see if there was any news on the test results. But they were still conducting them.' He paused. 'You have a choice. One is to walk into that elevator and not look back. The second is to go in there, face him and have closure. Decision's yours.'

I sighed. 'Flight or fight, huh?'

Alec nodded.

I glanced at the door, heard laughter coming from within and made up my mind. 'Second option, I think. If I don't show it'll look suss. Matt may not know me, but his friends and family are bound to ask.'

I gingerly rose from the chair and steeled myself to face Matt. Alec stood next to me, his arm still supportively around my shoulders.

'Okay?' he whispered.

'I suppose.'

We started for the door. Alec released me just as we walked in, but he remained close by my side. The blue curtain had been drawn back. Matt's mum, Evelyn, saw us first. She smiled and got up from Matt's side.

'Laura, I'm sorry we didn't come to see you. We were told you were hurt. You still look so pale.' She gave me a hug.

'No, don't be. Matt needed you.'

It was then I turned my attention to him. Strips of gauze and tape bound his head, but he was smiling—at Dr Cardacci. The dimple in his right cheek danced as he spoke to her.

'Matt, look who's here. It's Laura,' Evelyn happily announced. 'And…?' she stopped when she spied Alec.

'This is Dr Munro. He treated Matt at the scene,' Dr Cardacci said.

A huge smile spread across Evelyn's face. She went to him and took hold of his hand. 'Thank you for saving my son's life.' Her voice broke, and she tried blinking away tears.

'No need to thank me, Mrs Sommers.'

A weepy smile curled her lips. Her daughter, Clare, moved up behind her. 'Our whole family thanks you.'

'Me too, Doc,' Matt said, as he extended a hand to Alec, who gripped it in return.

'Maybe Mum and I'll go for a coffee, so you can talk,' Clare suggested.

'Good idea,' Evelyn said. 'Laura, you stay and talk with Matt and jog his memory.' She looked hopefully at me, eyes glistening. Before I could reply, she had ushered me to his side.

Clare touched my arm. 'Good luck,' she mouthed, and together they left.

Matt regarded me blankly. There was no sign of recognition, no welcoming warmth in those icy-blue depths. I was torn between giving him a hug or standing motionless by his bedside to wait. I decided on the latter.

'Hi Laura. I've been told you're my girl.' His expression belied his words. There was no smile, no dimple. He scrutinised me, head to toe like I was a suspect in a police line-up. This wasn't the Matt Sommers I had known for several months. The man lying in that hospital bed was a stranger.

'You really don't remember?'

'Just said so. Pity. I couldn't help Dave. You talk to him yet?'

'Yes.'

'It happened in your flat, I'm told,' he said in a way that demanded a response. Why couldn't he stop being the detective, just for once?

'Uh huh. You drove me home after a family event. I was knocked out the second the door opened.'

'You didn't see anything at all?'

'I've already gone through all this with Dave. I didn't come here to be interrogated but to see how you were.'

Alec touched my arm.

'Yeah, as you can see,' —he waved absently to his bandaged head— 'not all okay, but getting there. They want to keep me here for a few days. I don't mind.' He smiled up at Dr Cardacci then looked back to me. 'How badly were you hurt?' he asked, almost as an afterthought as he glanced at my bandaged arm. Alec had insisted I keep up the pretence as long as we were coming here.

'Not as bad as you. I'm okay.'

'They told me you lost a lot of blood, so it was bad. Could be the same guy who's been—'

'Matt stop it, please. I don't want to talk about it.'

I looked away from him and focused on the Get Well cards sitting on the table by his bed. 'Nice collection of cards.'

He cracked a smile. 'Yeah. Sometimes you've got to get yourself half killed to find out who your friends are.'

There was an awkward silence after that. Neither of us knew what to say. Alec hadn't said a word since greeting Matt, and Dr Cardacci stood silently watching the three of us. The old cliché, slicing the atmosphere with a knife, was never more apt.

'Did I give you that ring?' Matt said, his voice as blank as his stare.

I followed the path of his eyes down to my hand. 'No. It's a family heirloom. Got it on my birthday, last Friday. You were there.'

'Sorry, don't remember. Didn't think it'd be something I'd give you.'

'How long do they want to keep you here?' I asked in an attempt to change the subject.

'Few days, not sure.'

It was enough chit-chat. I wanted to get this done and mentally framed my breakup speech. I turned to Alec. 'Could you please give us a few minutes alone?'

'Are you sure?'

I nodded.

'Okay, I'll be just outside.' His fingers briefly touched mine before he turned and walked out.

I glanced at Dr Cardacci. She shifted uncomfortably from foot to foot. 'I'll come back later,' she said and made a move to leave.

'No, I'd like you to stay,' Matt said and grabbed her hand.

I noticed she didn't pull away, but looked at me half apologetically, half—what? She held his hand and looked down at him, almost ... protectively.

Well, well. She's attracted to him. And the way he looked at her completed the picture for me. I should have felt jealous. Only a few days ago he looked at me like that. Now....

I clasped my hands behind my back, afraid he'd see how much they shook. 'Matt, I ... I need to speak to you, privately.'

'She stays.'

I looked at her. She blanched. This was a side to him I'd never seen before—inconsiderate and callous. Had he been hiding it these last four months?

I took a deep breath and thought of Alec waiting for me out in the corridor. 'Matt ... Alec, err, Dr Munro and I met a few days ago. We ... um....' My hands began to sweat. This had to be one of the hardest things I'd ever had to do. Matt's gaze bored into mine, his mouth a tight line. Perhaps if I didn't look at him, I could do this. The word *coward* seemed appropriate. *Do this!* I mentally yelled at myself. 'I'm so, so sorry, Matt, but I can't be ... with you anymore. Something's happened to me, and I can't pretend that's it's going to go away.' I took a deep breath and blurted, 'I'm in love with someone else.' There, I'd said it.

'So you've come to say goodbye,' he said flatly.

'I'm so sorry. It just happened.'

'He must've made quite an impression in those few days. It's Munro, isn't it?'

'What? How could...?'

'I may have lost my memory, but not my sight. It's obvious from the way you oggle each other and ... he touched your hand.' His expression betrayed no emotion.

I bit my bottom lip. What could I possibly say?

He shrugged. 'You know, it's just as well I have no memory of our time together or this would probably hurt like hell. As it is, I really don't care.'

I don't know why, but that comment stung, and for a moment I was speechless. 'Well, since you don't remember me....'

'Obviously our short time together wasn't memorable enough.'

Dr Cardacci gasped. I was stunned. This was not the Matt I knew. It was as if he was being deliberately cruel—pushing me away from him. Or, maybe, this was the real Matt Sommers.

Okay, I probably deserved that, an accusing voice in my head said. *After all,* it continued, *you're the one leaving him for another man, after he nearly died trying to save your life.* Until another voice in my head said, *He was planning to kill your family, and the man you love. Say goodbye and walk out.*

I felt Alec's presence before I saw him. He came back in and grasped my hand. 'I can understand your anger, Sommers. But don't take it out on Laura. If you want to level blame where it's due, then here I am.'

Matt tried to sit up. The action only made him grimace. Dr Cardacci persuaded him to lie back.

'Please, Matt....' I began to say.

'Don't,' he said. 'Do what you came here for and … go!'

I swallowed hard. 'Goodbye Matt. I wish you only happiness.'

I turned and walked out of his life.

CHAPTER 50
ETERNITY

LAURA

'How are you?' Alec asked, as we waited at the end of the corridor for the elevator.

'Sad, but relieved.'

Just like that, Matt and I were no longer a couple and the sting of his parting words played in my mind. I blocked them out as I rested my head in the hollow of Alec's neck, enjoying his scent and mulling over the last week. My whole life had changed, so had my world. But now, at least, I was free to love the man who truly claimed my heart. With that came a sense of acceptance and peace.

Neither of us spoke for a while, until Alec lifted my face. 'Goodbyes are always painful.'

I laughed bitterly. 'I didn't realise how nasty he could be.'

'Forget about him.'

'He has every right to be angry, though.' I thought of his mother and sister downstairs in the cafeteria. So full of hope my presence would restore his memory. Full of expectation our relationship wouldn't be affected by this. How on earth were they going to react when they discovered otherwise?

I dropped my head onto Alec's chest and sighed.

'He'll survive, Laura. They all will. You've done nothing wrong. You don't belong with him, in his world, but the one you were born into and destined to share with me. This is where you belong, my darling' —his arms tightened around me— 'and the promising millennia that stretches before us.'

I was struck by the intensity of his words and tilted my head to look at his face. The depth of love written there caused my heart to leap. I knew with absolute certainty that no man could ever love me the way Alec would; a love that eternity would not, could not, erase.

All thoughts of Matt faded as I reached up and wrapped my arms around his neck.

'Laura,' he whispered, his voice a caress as he bent his head and kissed me.

I thanked whatever providence had mercifully provided my escape route. The blow Matt had received only resulted in wiping me from his memory, as well as the last few months. I was sure pretty Doctor Cardacci would aid his complete recovery, very nicely. I'd said goodbye to him and the old me. This new, part-vampire me had a thousand years to look forward to with the man I loved. There was only one question that needed answering. 'Alec, do you like bagpipes?'

'Playing or listening?'

'Either.'

'Mmmmm, both. I have my own set. Why?'

'Would you like to come to the Edinburgh Military Tattoo with me and Jen?'

He blinked before letting out a peal of laughter.

I heaved a sigh of contentment and snuggled further into his arms.

EPILOGUE

Three days later, Detective Inspector Matthew Sommers was allowed to go home. He left the hospital that morning. His sister, Clare, and her husband had picked him up and dropped him off in front of his flat. There was no need for them to come up, he told them. He'd be okay. He needed to be alone to work some things out. One included that woman—his alleged ex-girlfriend—Laura Dantonville.

Why had she bothered to see him if only to say they were breaking up?

A package lay on the ground outside his door. He picked it up. What had he ordered? Damned retro whatever-they-called-it. It was going to make life a misery for the next few days or weeks or however long his memory would be out. But he'd be damned if he wouldn't try and recall something, anything. The doctors had tried some mental exercises on him, but so far, nothing had worked.

He dumped the package on the table and went to make himself a cup of coffee. He'd been given three weeks off to recover, but he didn't want it. Work is what he needed to keep *her* face out of his mind.

Something niggled at him, something he couldn't put his finger on. He swore in frustration and briefly closed his eyes to try and summon a memory or an image or even a feeling of the last few months. Nothing. It was as if that time hadn't existed. Back at the hospital, he'd rifled through his phone messages and notes, and then his photo gallery. There wasn't a single picture of her, not one, yet he was told they'd been together for four months. Had someone tampered with his phone? What the hell for? There was nothing on it worth erasing.

Sommers shook his head, took his mug of coffee into the living room and sprawled into a settee. The package on the table stared at him. He took a few sips of his coffee and stared back before he got up and tore it open. Inside was a small, sealed cardboard box. Within that were six wooden bullets.

What the hell had he ordered?

There was a receipt attached. He quickly scanned it to find that this order was the completion of a previous one—twelve white-oak bullets in all. Had there been an earlier one? He left his coffee on the table and went in search of the other cartridges he'd supposedly bought. But he found nothing. So, where were they? At his desk at work? Would he really have brought a box of those to the station? Not damn likely.

He sat at his computer and looked up any reference to white-oak bullets, and what he found made him shake his head. It seems they were the only effective substance used against vampires. It killed them by crystallising their blood.

Huh, nice. He downed the rest of his coffee. People actually believe this shit? He didn't know whether to laugh and throw the damned things away or keep reading. Well, he had three weeks off. Why not? It's not like he had anything else to do.

Another website stated that vampires had the ability to mesmerise their victims and wipe out their memories. Those who were bitten didn't remember it to tell.

That made him sit up and take notice. He felt his neck. Nope, no bite marks. Yeah, sucked in. He laughed at his own joke. Then something caught his eye, and the laughter abruptly ended. Vampires were distinguished by the unusual lavender colour of their eyes, so many had taken to wearing contact lenses.

What the hell? He read and reread that line. Then he thought back. Both his ex-girlfriend and that doctor had lavender-coloured eyes. But his brain had been too addled by painkillers at the time, so he couldn't be sure.

Ah, it's ridiculous! he thought. But then, for some odd reason, he'd ordered those damn bullets.

He decided to Google their names, anyway, just to be sure. He'd been told she was a primary school teacher. Her photo should feature on the school website, and his should appear on the hospital staff list. Dave mentioned the hospital he ran.

Their faces appeared. He magnified the images for a better view. Strange but beautiful lavender eyes smiled back at him.

He sat back in his chair, picked up one of the bullets and twirled it around his fingers as he considered what a session with the hypnotherapist at the hospital would reveal. It took less than a minute for him to ring Dr Cardacci and leave a message on her answering machine.

He stared at his keys where he'd dropped them on the table. Among them was one he didn't recognise. Could it be hers? His ex? Only one way to find out. Might even jog his damn memory. It'd be easy enough to get her address—he had a mate in Traffic.

Forty minutes later, he sat in his car outside her block of units. Nothing looked familiar. He fiddled with the key and wrestled with the ethics of what he was about to do.

What the hell.

He strode to her door and slotted the key into her apartment door.

It fit.

END OF BOOK ONE

If you enjoyed reading this book, Id love you to write share it with others, RECOMMEND it to friends, family, and reading groups or clubs, or online forums. You can also REVIEW this book at the site where you purchased it. That is the best gift, you as a reader, can give an author. And if you happen to do that, email me at, timamarialacoba@bigpond.com and I'll send you a personal message of thanks.

Bloodpledge, Book 2 in The Dantonville Legacy, is available at Amazon.

Connect with the author on her website
http://timamarialacoba.com
Facebook – http://www.facebook.com/TimaMariaLacoba
Twitter – http://Twitter.com/TimaMariaLacoba

Here's an exclusive sneak peak of Chapter 1.

CHAPTER 1 – BLOODPLEDGE
NECESSARY SECRETS

LAURA

Abandoned. That's how my apartment appeared to me after I'd been away a week. The police had been. They had even hired a cleaner to wash my ex-boyfriend Matt's bloodstains from the doorframe and wooden floor after the forensics people had finished.

As I sorted through the mail, Alec casually checked out the framed photos I kept on the dining room buffet. Looking at him, I had to remind myself that he wasn't human. Up until a week ago, the only supernatural creatures I believed in were angels.

He picked up the one of Matt and myself and looked at it for a long while. It was hard to know what he was thinking. His face betrayed nothing.

'Who's this?' he asked, as he held up another one. It was a silver-framed photo of Jenny and me taken at the Randwick races one Melbourne Cup Day. She had won a pre-cup sweep at work and asked me along.

We went out and bought hats and dresses especially for the occasion. Neither of us won anything on the horses, but it had been a great day out.

'That's Jenny.'

'The one who phoned you in hospital the other day?'

'Uh huh. My best friend.' Jenny and I had known each other for years; we taught at the same primary school and had become close friends, almost like sisters. I hated not being able to tell her about Alec and the vampire side of the family.

I noticed the way he smiled as he looked at it. I'd worn a black, knee-length, figure-hugging pinafore I'd teamed with a jade silk scarf and matching peep-toe shoes.

His eyes lit up with a devilish glint. 'I need to think of some excuse for you to wear that dress for me.'

I laughed and shook my head as I turned and walked into my bedroom and rummaged through my wardrobe, choosing what to take for the few days with my biological parents. Even though the walk-in closet in my bedroom at my father's house was brim-full of the latest designer wear especially selected for me, I still felt I needed some of my old, familiar stuff. To me, it was proof I hadn't really changed; I was still Laura Dantonville, primary school teacher, albeit daughter of Lucien (Luc) Lebrettan, millionaire real-estate magnate, vampire and Alec's sire.

As I began to throw a few things onto the bed, I noticed something odd. On my dressing table, next to another framed photo of me and Matt, lay the key to my unit. It was the spare I'd given him when our relationship had become serious. I'd posted my copy of his apartment key back to him three days ago.

A cold shiver rippled through me. He'd been in my apartment. Without my permission!

'Laura, everything all right?' Alec's voice came from the living room.

'Um …yes.' I wasn't sure whether to tell Alec about this or not. I glanced around. Nothing else in my room seemed different or out of place. Yet, there it was, the unmistakable evidence of my ex-boyfriend's presence.

Pushing the memories of our four months together aside, I unclipped the back of the frame, took the photo out, and laid it face down on the dressing table. Later, when I'd have time, I'd place it in my album. Matt had once been a part of my life, even if only for a short while.

'You're very quiet. Anything wrong?' I spun around at the sound of Alec's voice directly behind me. His gaze went from my face, to my hand, then to the key, and I knew I couldn't keep it from him.

There was a loud knocking on my front door. 'Miss Dantonville? Are you in there?'

I groaned. That slightly croaky but belligerent voice belonged to one of my neighbours, Mrs Henderson, head of the Body Corporate. She knew all that went on, and what she didn't know, she made sure to find out. In other words, she was the local busybody. And unless I opened the door, there was a good chance she'd walk around the side of the building and press her face up against the windows to see if I was in. Matt and I once hid from her—behind the settee—pretending we weren't home. 'Checking up to see if everything's all right,' she would say.

'It's Mrs Henderson, from upstairs. I have to let her in, or she'll come noseying around the windows.'

'You know there's a solution for that.' Alec's eyes lightened in mischief.

'No! Don't you dare!' I knew he could mesmerise people, and I saw him use it once.

He chuckled.

I palmed the key and hurried to the door. 'Hello, Mrs Henderson. What can I do for you?'

She was in the process of rapping her walking cane on my front door again and stopped mid-action. Her wide frame filled the doorway, blocking any escape.

'Are you all right, love?' She said breathlessly. 'Such a to-do earlier in the week, what with all the police and ambulance and reporters here asking so many questions. We heard you and your young man were hurt … taken to hospital …' Her triple chins wobbled in excitement making her look like an oversized ram. 'Dreadful business, being attacked like that in your own home. Are any of us safe…?' Her eyes landed on Alec and she stopped abruptly.

Her jaw dropped mid-speech and her hands smoothed down her tent-like dress. Before I had a chance to say anything, nosey Mrs Henderson barged past me into the living room, and made straight for Alec.

If I didn't know what a big, bad vampire he was, I'd swear he backed up a step as she sailed toward him like a battleship on a mission.

Her cat, Salieri, on the other hand, took one look at Alec, screeched, and arched it back. Its fur stood on end like porcupine quills as it hissed and ran off.

Mrs Henderson briefly turned to me and said, 'Strange, that he'd react like that. Did the same, the night the police were here. I hope he's not getting distemper.'

That was the night I was kidnapped and Matt was seriously injured trying to protect me. It appeared Salieri could sense the undead.

She promptly resumed her advance on Alec. 'And who might you be?' she asked, in a honey-sweet voice.

'Um … this is Dr Munro,' I said. Alec was a doctor, and head of Munro Research Labs, a research hospital that specialised in treating blood diseases. I'd been taken there the night I was attacked. Maris, a former lover of Alec's, had tried to kill me by taking as much of my blood as she could, but in the process it had destroyed her. I'd been shocked to discover, my blood was poisonous to all vampires, except those transformed by Lucius—Marcus Antonius's son—such as Luc and Alec.

'Well, well, a doctor. And how is your nice young policeman chap? He was here this morning, you know,' Mrs Henderson said without taking her eyes off Alec. 'Saw him from my window.' I felt myself pale. Next to me Alec stiffened. Mrs Henderson continued on her merry rant. 'Oh, but you have the same eye colour! How unusual … a brother or cousin then? I had the telly on that night you see, and didn't hear anything—' she turned to face me '—till all these flashing lights woke me early next morning. And then a couple of nice policemen spoke to me—' back to Alec '—are you a GP? You know I have this mild discomfort, right here—' she placed her hand poignantly on her ample bosom.

If I wasn't so tense I may have giggled.

'Mrs Henderson,' Alec interrupted, 'I'm sure it's only mild indigestion. May I suggest some antacid.' His eyes lightened. 'But, just to be sure, I think it best if you go back to your flat and lie down for the rest of the day.'

'Yes, lie down,' she repeated slowly, her eyes glued to Alec's.

He placed his arm around her shoulders and led her to the door. 'That's right. A cup of tea and a lie down.'

I remembered something. 'Alec wait! I need to give her my phone number. The flat's going to be empty for a few days.'

'Good point.'

'Mrs Henderson, listen carefully.' He stared into her glazed eyes and repeated my mobile number. 'Ring Miss Dantonville only if necessary. Now, go and have a lie down.'

She nodded dumbly and he closed the door behind her.

'All right, this time I agree with the mesmerisation.'

'It has its merits.' He leaned back against the door, arms folded across his chest. 'So, Sommers was here! They must have discharged him this morning.'

'And he came straight here.' I sighed, held out my hand and opened my palm. 'It's my spare key. Matt had it. He left it on my dresser.'

Alec's brow creased. 'I noticed his scent when we arrived. I thought it must be the remnants of his blood on the doorframe. Damn!' He looked thoughtfully at me. 'Why come here? He could've sent it. And why your bedroom instead of the kitchen table?'

I shook my head. 'Don't know, but nothing else was touched,' I said, when I saw the questioning look in his eyes.

'Mmmm ….' His lips drew together in a tight, disapproving line and he glanced at the window. 'There's no time for that now. We should get back, so you can have a rest before tonight's Pledging ceremony.'

The Pledging. It was scheduled for midnight, when all the prefects from around the world would swear their loyalty to Alec and myself. It was binding on all the Brethren in their respective countries, and the penalty for breaking the oath was death. And, since the ceremony could take several hours, a nap beforehand would ensure I stayed awake and alert.

I placed the spare key back on my key ring. 'If Matt's got amnesia, how come he knows where I live?'

'Detective Delaney. He probably told him.'

Detective Chief Inspector, Dave Delaney, was in charge of the investigation into the break-in at my flat and the assault on Matt and myself. He interviewed Alec, and then later me, at the hospital. To Matt he was both mentor and friend.

'Of course.'

It didn't alleviate my uncomfortable realisation that Matt had been here without my knowledge. Had he hoped to regain some of his lost memory by coming somewhere he thought would be familiar? But, why did he have to do it behind my back? Yet, the fact he left the key behind, was proof our relationship was truly over.

After locking the door securely, Alec and I headed out to his car for the drive back to my father's old-Victorian gothic mansion in Vaucluse. Mrs Henderson wasn't anywhere in sight.

She must be lying down after her cup of tea, I thought. Salieri hissed at Alec as we strode past, then ran and hid in a nearby bush.

I took a long, last look at my unit as we drove away. Who knows when I'd be back here. Luc and Judy were keen to have me stay with them, and as long as rogue elements among the Brethren wanted to seize me for their own purposes, it was safer to remain with them.

As we drove through the wrought-iron gates of Luc's palatial, residence in Fitzgerald Street, the LEDs that lined the gravel driveway lit our way to the front entrance. The house itself was dark. Apart from the porch light, and the tiny twinkling bulbs on the Christmas wreath on the front door, everything was in darkness, except for a glow emanating from the top storey where the ballroom was located.

As we stepped into the hall, nobody seemed to be around. He flicked a switch and the place burst into light, illuminating the stencilled griffins and unicorns that ran the length of the plastered walls and the stuccoed ceiling with its molded roses picked out in bold Victorian colours of red, blue and gold.

Luc's house was a relic of a grander era, when riches found on the goldfields of Swan Hill and Bathurst were poured into the lavish houses of the nouveau riche. It was one of the few stately homes that the National Trust hadn't been able to acquire. And Luc aimed to keep it that way.

Thankfully, he had it modernised where required.

Well, this is home, for now, I thought, and inwardly sighed as Alec and I strolled hand-in-hand to the kitchen at the other end of the house, feeling less and less the independent twenty-first century woman I once believed myself to be.

GLOSSARY OF CHARACTERS AND NAMES

Alec Munro – Vampire, Princeps and together with Lucien Lebrettan, leader of the 'Brethren', a community of vampires living in Sydney. Originally a doctor, he had enlisted in the AIF soon after the death of his wife and child. He was later transformed by Lucien while serving in an army medical field hospital in northern France in 1918. He owns and manages a private hospital in Sydney dedicated to blood disease research.

Antonia Pulchra – Daughter of Marcus Antonius Pulcher, twin sister to Lucius. Antonia was the first to carry the Ingenii mutation. She lived for 218 years and was the mother of Paulus, the next Ingenii.

Appius – Vampire, former Roman soldier, and part of the First Cohort of Frisians cavalry unit, stationed at Vindobala (Rudchester). Unable to bear life any longer as a blood drinker, he took his own life by walking out into the sun, soon after his transformation into vampire form by the Pictish witch, Eithne.

Bloodgifted – Term given to certain members of the Dantonville family who carry the cursed gene, giving them unnatural long life and youthfulness. Their blood alone provides vampires with superior strength and senses and the ability to daywalk. The Bloodgifted – Ingenii – are much coveted by the Brethren community and were the epicentre of two previous rebellions; the first taking place in the tenth century, resulting in the deaths of tow of Luc's men – Galen and Martius – and the other in the seventeenth century.

Cal (Calixtus) – Vampire, former Roman soldier, First Frisian Cavalry Regiment, stationed at Vindobala (Rudchester), on Hadrian's Wall, northern Britain. Part of Marcus Antonius Pulcher's cohort, he was cursed (along with his comrades) by a Pictish witch into vampire form. Cal is also a widower, having lost his wife in childbirth. Currently he is bodyguard to the Ingenii, friend to Alec Munro and he owns an Armagnac distillery in France.

Dave Delaney – Human, Detective Chief Inspector, friend and mentor of Matthew Sommers, in charge of the investigation into his assault.

Elders – Group of the world's oldest vampires, who set the rules by which all blood drinkers must abide, in order to keep their presence hidden from the human world. They have power over life and death in the Brethren community. They also officiate at every Coming-of-Age ceremony and induct the princeps. They are among the oldest living creatures on Earth.

Eilene Dantonville – Human, wife of John Dantonville. Her first child, a baby named Katie, died of SIDS at aged three months. She and John accepted the infant Laura in place of their deceased daughter, in order to help out Lucien and Judith. She loved Laura as her own child.

Eithne – Pictish witch and high priestess of the Caledonian goddess, Melusine. She cursed Marcus Antonius Pulcher and his men for killing her people in the mid 3rd century, effectively turning him and his men into vampires. She used kidnapped Roman captives as human sacrifices in bloody religious rites.

Galen – Former Roman soldier in the First Frisian Cohort Cavalry Regiment stationed at Vindobala (Rudchester). Along with his comrades, he was cursed into vampire form by the Pictish witch, Eithne. Until his death—at the hands of vampire hunters in the First Rebellion—he was one of the bodyguards to the Ingenii.

Ingenii – Latin term meaning 'Bloodgifted'.

Jake (Caius Justinius) – Vampire, former Roman soldier and physician attached to the First Frisian Cavalry Regiment, stationed at Vindobala (Rudchester) on Hadrian's Wall, northern Britain. Along with his comrades, he was cursed by a Pictish witch into becoming a vampire. He is close friend of Alec Munro, and loves sports cars and racing horses. Currently he is bodyguard to the Ingenii.

Jean-Philippe Louis Auguste de Reynard – Vampire, and 18th century French nobleman who once fought for Napoleon. He was Lucien's illegitimate son and Laura's half-brother. His mother was the Duchess D'Orleans. He was also a well-known portrait artist who first met Laura in Italy where he fell in love with her unaware he was her half-brother. Jean introduced himself to her by his second name, Philippe. Lucien broke up the relationship. Their romance is the subject of the short story, **Laura's Locket.**

Jenny Callen – Human, Laura's best friend and work colleague in a primary school in Balmain. She's had several failed relationships and is currently single.

John Dantonville – Human, Laura's foster-father and maternal uncle. He is Judith's youngest brother and Eilene Dantonville's husband. He and Eilene adopted Laura as a favour to Lucien and Judith, but came to love her as their own. His pet name for her is, 'Baby'.

Judith Dantonville Lebrettan – Human, thirty-third Ingenii. Pressured into marrying her first husband, William Allerdyce, by her father, Owen Dantonville to clear gambling debts. Only meant to be a business arrangement, he raped her on their wedding night. Judith met Lucien some time after and they became lovers. Later she divorced William and secretly married Luc after giving birth to their child, Laura.

Kari (Karelia Anakeinen) – Born in Finland in the late eighteenth-century, Kari's family moved to France when her father was offered the position of chief stonemason on the D'Antonville estate in the Rhone Valley. She had been transformed by Jake, when the rest of her family died in an epidemic which swept the region. Kari is Judith Dantonville's best friend, and unofficial bodyguard to the current *Ingenii*, Laura Dantonville. She is also secretly in love with Jake.

Karl – Czech prefect, Count Karel von Czernin; vampire and Principate spy who befriended Count Timur Széchenyi, the Hungarian prefect, and infiltrated the Rebels ranks to learn of their plans and report back to Luc. His easy-going nature hides a sharp mind and decisive nature. He's friends with Alec Munro, and secretly in love with Baroness Milena Flaks.

Kwome – One of the Elders, and originally king of the ancient kingdom of Benin. He was transformed by his teacher and mentor.

Laura Dantonville – Part human/part vampire, thirty-fourth and current serving Ingenii, and Lucien and Judith's biological daughter. She is a primary school teacher and former girlfriend of Detective Inspector Matthew Sommers, before meeting Alec Munro. Laura was raised by John and Eilene Dantonville, who she believed to be her parents. She was also Jean-Philippe's half-sister.

Lucien Lebrettan – Vampire who underwent transformation at puberty. Known as 'Luc' to his friends, Lucius Antonius Pulcher was born in the mid 3rd century AD to, the son of Marcus Antonius and Gallia. He was the first princeps, and Alec Munro's sire and friend, and Laura Dantonville's father. He secretly married her mother, Judith, a week after Laura was born. Lucien Lebrettan is the Gallic version of his Roman name, and means 'Lucius the Briton.'

Marcus Antonius Pulcher – Vampire, former Roman legionary cavalry commander – Praefectus Equituum – stationed in Vindobala (Rudchester) in Britain in the mid 3rd century AD. It was his actions, which led to him, and his men, to be cursed by the witch Eithne. Marcus Antonius is the father of the twins, Lucius and Antonia, and husband to Gallia. He departed from Britain after his transformation into a vampire, and went into hiding in his villa in Gaul (France).

Martius – Vampire, former Roman soldier in the First Frisian Cohort cavalry unit stationed at Vindobala (Rudchester). Along with his comrades, he was cursed into vampire form by the Pictish witch, Eithne. Before his death, Martius was one of the bodyguards to the Ingenii. He was killed by vampire hunters during the First Rebellion.

Matthew Sommers – Human, Police Detective Inspector. He was Laura's boyfriend and rival with Alec Munro for Laura's affections. He was attacked and nearly killed by rogue vampires while trying to protect her. Laura broke off their relationship at the end of Book 1 when she learnt he was planning to kill the vampire side of her family in a misguided attempt to protect her.

Melander – Human, former Roman soldier of the First Frisian Cohort Cavalry Regiment stationed at Vindobala (Rudchester). Sent back as guard to Nepos who had been wounded in a surprise Pict attack. Killed by Calixtus during the early stages of his transformation.

Milena – Baroness Milena Flaks, vampire, the Slovakian prefect and supporter of the Principate. Her concerns over Count Timur's ambitions – and threat to her territory – has led her to approach Jake into becoming her consort, and thus her protector. Like other aristocrats of her generation (eighteenth-century) she believes in the superiority of her noble blood, although Brethren law discourages class discrimination. Her old-world attitude leads to clashes with more-recently transformed Brethren.

Nepos – Human, Roman soldier of the First Frisian Cohort Cavalry Regiment stationed at Vindobala (Rudchester). He was seriously wounded in a surprise attack by Pictish raiders and sent back to the fort by his commander, Marcus Antonius Pulcher. While recovering from his wounds, he was killed by Terens during the early stages of his transformation.

Princeps – Latin term for First Citizen and the origin of the English word for Prince.

Principate – The Brethren political system established by Marcus Antonius Pulcher and his son, Lucius (Lucien) to control the Brethren and protect humans. It's composed of the Elders – Kwome and Zhao – as well as Marcus, Luc and Alec. As a result of the death of Maris Quesnel, there is a vacancy in the Eldership for a female representative.

Pudens – Vampire, former Roman soldier in the First Frisian Cohort Cavalry Regiment stationed at Vindobala (Rudchester). Along with his comrades, he was cursed into vampire form by the Pictish witch,

Eithne. Unable to endure life as a blood drinker, he took his own life by walking out into the sun.

Rasputin – Vampire and former confidant of the last Russian royal family, the Romanovs. He was transformed in 1917 by Hungarian noble, Count Timur Széchenyi, the Brethren Hungarian prefect. Many blame him for the demise of the monarchy in Russia, and his sinister influence over the Russian royal family. He has the ability to mesmerise humans as well as vampires, and uses that to further his master's ambitions to overthrow the Principate.

Sam (Sempronius) – Vampire, former Roman soldier in the First Frisian Cavalry Regiment, stationed at Vindobala (Rudchester) in northern Britain. Along with his comrades, he was cursed by the Pictish witch, Eithne, into vampire form. He is also the former lover and sire of Maris Quesnel. Sam is a Techno wiz and responsible for security in the Lebrettan household. Currently, when not hacking into Rebel phones and computers, he is one of the bodyguards to the *Ingenii*.

Serpent Ring – Ancient artefact created by Marcus Antonius Pulcher on the instructions of the Pictish witch, Eithne. It's in the form of a golden serpent with blazing red eyes – symbol of Melusine, Caledonian goddess of vengeance. It renders the wearer invisible to vampire senses as well as burning the fingers of imposters, and shooting fire from the serpents' eyes, destroying those who physically threaten either Princeps or Ingenii. In times of danger, the eyes turn black. Every fifty years the ring is passed down to the next Ingenii.

Terens (Sextus Terentius) – Vampire, former Tribune attached to the First Frisian Cavalry Regiment, stationed at Vindobala (Rudchester), northern Britain. Along with the rest of the cohort, he was cursed by the Pictish witch, Eithne, into vampire form. Although he has a reputation as a ladies man, Terens is also a deadly swordsman and is known to have fought off eight armed Rebels in the last Rebellion. He's always wanted to try skydiving. Currently, he is one of the bodyguards to the Ingenii.

Timur – Count Timur Széchenyi, Hungarian prefect, and leader of the rebellion to overthrow the Principate and kidnap the Ingenii to breed her with a human and produce the next generation of Ingenii. He used his family crest – a snarling wolf's head – to create the outlawed wolf's-head ring, which contains a deadly white-oak spike. It's believed he is the centre of the illegal blood-slave racket, which traffics in selling under-age humans to the Brethren. Timur is also Rasputin's sire.

His castle is located outside Budapest.

Zhao – One of the Elders. Ancient Chinese warlord turned philosopher. His sire is unknown.

A NOTE FROM THE AUTHOR

A former ancient historian and archaeologist, I accidently smashed a 3,000 Egyptian vase while on my first dig! My supervisor made me glue it back together again. It took a week. From there I went on to specialise in late Roman-British archaeology, and the military forts along Hadrian's Wall, because buildings don't smash as easily. Now I've combined my love of history with another passion—story-telling—to create a dark tale of Roman soldiers who've waited nearly two thousand years to be released from an ancient curse.

I have always been a storyteller, but it wasn't until five years ago that I seriously ventured into writing. The result was *BloodGifted*. In 2011 it was shortlisted in the Atlas Award and eventually came fourth place. In 2012 it was listed among the top ten in the Choclit Search for an Aussie Star Competition. In 2013, I was offered a publishing contract but declined in favour of going indie, preferring the idea of being in charge of my own creation.

Laura's Locket (prequel), *BloodGifted*, *BloodPledge*, *BloodVault* and *BloodWish* are the five books that comprise *The Dantonville Legacy* series. I also intend to satisfy my fans requests by writing individual books on the other characters in the series. So Terens, Cal, Jake and Sam will each have their own story.

Currently, I live on the Central Coast, an hour's drive north of Sydney in Australia. My little house is surrounded by bushland, possums and seed-dropping Rosellas on one side, and waterways on the other.

Between bouts of writing, I can be found in the kitchen baking yet another chocolate recipe. This activity is responsible for forming more gothic, urban fantasy stories in my mind for future books

CONTACT INFO

Tima Maria Lacoba
Visit me at my website:
http://timamarialacoba.com

If you enjoyed reading this book, I'd love you to share it with others, RECOMMEND it to friends, family, and reading groups or clubs, or online forums. You can also REVIEW this book at the site where you purchased it. That is the best gift, you as a reader, can give an author. And if you happen to do that, email me at, timamarialacoba@bigpond.com and I'll send you a personal message of thanks.

BOOK 2, BLOODPLEDGE, IS OUT NOW.

Bloodpledge

Tima Maria Lacoba

http://www.timamarialacoba.blogspot.com.au/p/home.html
https://www.facebook.com/timamarialacoba

Paradox Book
Cover Designs